Lehigh County

A Bicentennial Look Back at an American Community

Written by Frank Whelan

Foreword by Don Cunningham

Published by County of Lehigh
17 South Seventh Street
Allentown, Pennsylvania 18101
www.lehighcounty.org

ISBN: 978-0-976283-17-1
Library of Congress Control Number: 2012932192

The publisher thanks The Morning Call, the Lehigh County Historical Society,
the Moravian Archives, the Allentown Art Museum,
and numerous historical societies, organizations,
and individuals throughout Lehigh County
for their generous contributions of
images used in this book.

Cover images:
Front and back: Main Street, Macungie
Back insets: Lehigh Valley Railroad station, Allentown; Coca-Cola Park; Central Park

Printed in Pennsylvania
by The Kutztown Publishing Co., Inc.

CONTENTS

Donald T. Cunningham, Jr.
Lehigh County Executive
March 2012

Dedicated to all the past and future residents of Lehigh County.

FOREWORD BY DON CUNNINGHAM

LEHIGH COUNTY: A BICENTENNIAL LOOK BACK AT AN AMERICAN COMMUNITY

One of my earliest childhood memories is walking the streets of Bethlehem with my grandfather. As we walked, he would point to buildings and houses and hillsides, telling me their history. Some of it was significant – "there are hundreds of Revolutionary War soldiers buried on this hillside in unmarked graves" – and some was of importance to only those from the neighborhood or, maybe, only to him – "that's the house where the Hillaires lived during the Depression, they had seven kids. They used to throw rocks at birds from that attic window."

It was all fascinating to me. Fascinating that he knew so much about everything and fascinating that different people used to live in those houses and those buildings; the people of faded black and white photographs or paragraphs in news articles or history books.

We would walk the streets of West Bethlehem, the Lehigh County section, once its own borough, separate and distinct from the boroughs of Bethlehem and South Bethlehem. My grandfather would tell of the day when those grand avenues were once lined with farms and apple orchards. They were made of dirt, not macadam. There were no cars, only horses. He could remember when there were outhouses in the alleys and trolley tracks to take you from west Bethlehem to downtown Allentown.

It was 1918 when Charles Schwab, the powerful chairman of the even more powerful Bethlehem Steel Corporation, led the drive to consolidate the three boroughs of Bethlehem into one Third Class City. It was a wise and progressive move that also created an oddity that exists nowhere else in Pennsylvania: a city that lies in two counties. I learned of that when I was about ten while trying to keep pace with my grandfather. Thirty years later when campaigning for Lehigh County Executive, I found out that my grandfather hadn't taken enough people on those walks. The most frequent question I was asked: "How can you run for Lehigh County Executive when you live in Bethlehem?" If I had the time, I told the story of Charles Schwab, the 1918 consolidation, and the making of one city in two counties. Often I only had enough time to shrug and say, "because it's in Lehigh County." Every time I was asked, I thought of my grandfather. I wished he was still around, as I do today.

But, as we quickly learn in life, the only constant is change. Time marches on. People come and go and the events and people of today are only as remembered as we work to make them. My grandfather loved history of all kinds, right down to the neighborhood variety, the kind where he would tell you who once lived in that house on the corner that still has the hitching post where they used to tie up the horses. For the most part, he was an oral historian, in the Irish tradition of his grandparents who came here after the famine. It's a race of people who have figured out that it's easier—and more fun—to take walks and tip beers while telling stories instead of bothering to write it all down.

With this book, we have forced ourselves to stop and to write it all down, or at least as much of it as we could fit in here. We did it because 2012 is the year of Lehigh County's Bicentennial. We also did it because too many of us don't know why Bethlehem is in Lehigh County; or that there was once a trolley train linking our two cities; or that the first unit of civil war union soldiers to respond to President Abraham Lincoln's call to defend the nation's capital from the confederate rebellion came from Allentown and throughout Lehigh County; or that hundreds of Revolutionary War soldiers were taken from the battlefields of Germantown and Brandywine to the Moravian hospitals in Bethlehem where they perished and are now interred on a Lehigh County hillside at the banks of the Monocacy Creek, with only a small marker recognizing the remains of those who died to give birth to this nation. This book is about our grandparents and for our children.

It's not often we are compelled to stop and reflect on how we got here. A Bicentennial seems as good a time as any to do so. We don't get many of those milestones in our lifetimes.

Two hundred years is not really that long ago. But, wow, a lot has changed!

When Lehigh County was founded, America was but thirty-six years old, and that's if you mark the birth of America when independence was declared. It took another seven years to win that independence on the battlefields. By the time Lehigh County was signed into existence on March 6, 1812, America was on the verge of declaring war on Great Britain again in what would become known as the War of 1812, which would last until 1814. Our young nation's future was far from stable. Despite that, the independent-minded residents of the western end of what was then Northampton County were determined to create their own county. Most of them were farmers and most of them were of German descent, referred to as Pennsylvania Dutch. It was a long way from the farms of Fogelsville and Macungie to the county seat of Easton along the Delaware River. A lot of time was wasted traveling on horseback to file deeds and wills and to do other necessary business.

While it didn't take armed conflict to secede from Northampton County and create a new county, the effort was driven by the same spirit of independence that gave rise to America. The new county would be named Lehigh, after the river that runs through it.

Instead of bearing arms, petitions were taken to the Commonwealth of Pennsylvania. Many residents wanted their own county with its own county seat in the growing city of Allentown. Their request was granted, and in 1812, the voters of Lehigh County selected their first county government as Americans were making James Madison the first U.S. president to be re-elected during wartime.

Two hundred years later, in an age of superhighways, the Internet, and instant global communications, the primary condition that created the impetus for a new county—the burden of geographic distance—has been transcended. Today, from time to time, the issue of consolidating the counties of Lehigh and Northampton is discussed. Many who discuss it probably don't realize that it is one of those Back to the Future plans that would bring the history full circle. And, while the concept has some merit, I would guess that this time it may take armed conflict to put together what was once peacefully divided. Therefore, most of the progressive movements of today aim to share services and to consolidate functions of the counties, looking for appropriate ways to save money and to be more efficient.

This is but one example of how a knowledge of our history, a knowledge of how we got here, is helpful to us in plotting a course for our future. The people who founded and built this county were real people, with their own hopes and dreams and their own plans. They lived on those streets of our county, plowed those farm fields and worked in those factories, many of which are no longer here. They may be mysterious faces in black and white photos but their actions and decisions and the events that took place in their lives have created the Lehigh County we inherit today. Some were our relatives. And, the values and traditions of those generations are alive in us today, whether they are of our direct bloodline or not. While our landscape may look different, the work ethic, the pride in our communities and our country, and our shared purpose of place is the same whether we came here from lands far away or from generation upon generation of Lehigh County stock.

This book is a chance to reflect, a chance to see that our county is but a microcosm of America from the age of agriculture to the industrial revolution to the explosion of technology that propels this age of information. In each phase of our 200 years, Lehigh County has helped to make America great, whether it's been our people, our factories, our farms, our churches or schools. So, it's on the occasion of our Bicentennial that the Lehigh County Bicentennial Committee, a group of Lehigh County residents, some in government, some in the private sector, but all interested in celebrating and telling the story of our special little place in America, commissioned this book: Lehigh County: A Bicentennial Look Back at an American Community.

On these pages, the reader will see how the people who called this county home during their snapshots of time, during their lifetimes, reacted to the events of their day, forged a living and struggled to build a future for themselves and their children and grandchildren. And in that living, they wrote the pages of what would become our history and built the foundations upon which the next generations would add or subtract. You will see how this agrarian community settled by Pennsylvania-German farmers and William Penn-era colonials became an engine of America's industrial revolution by utilizing the rich nearby fields of iron ore and limestone, by capitalizing on the river and building the transportation corridors of canal, railroad and, ultimately, highway and fiber optics—while taking advantage of the plentiful and hard-working labor fueled by a steady stream of emigration. Along the way, they developed the cities, and boroughs, and townships, and neighborhoods. They gave them all unique names, some named after themselves like Laurys Station and Allentown, and some paying tribute to the land's original Indian inhabitants like Catasauqua and Hokendauqua.

We are fortunate to have so many people in our county that take pride in our history, from those grandfathers who walk their kids around and pass down the history of their neighborhoods to the school teachers that focus on local history in our elementary schools. Every corner of the county has its own historical societies, ethnic organizations, churches, synagogues, and temples that capture the history of smaller communities and groups. On a larger scale, we have the Lehigh County Historical Society housed at the Lehigh Valley Heritage Center and Museum, a beautiful facility in downtown Allentown that is testament to the importance of history to the people of our county. This book wouldn't be possible without the support of the Historical Society and its amazing leadership in Director Joe Garrera, a passionate lover of history, and the talented Assistant Director and Curator Jill Youngken.

This book's principal author, Frank Whelan, is a true local treasure. We are blessed to have Frank, who has made himself into the Lehigh Valley's foremost historian through decades of research and writing for local newspapers, organizations, and historical societies. Frank spent nearly two years working on this project, researching, writing and searching for photos and illustrations. His has been a labor of love and all of us today and future generations are the beneficiaries of Frank's scholarship and knowledge.

Frank had a great Editorial Committee to work with to fact check and edit all his writing and to help with information gathering. Ann Bartholomew, who has the patience of Job, has served as the project editor, pouring over all of the words and photos that went into this book to ensure the best possible presentation. She worked closely with Dina Hall, a very talented graphic designer, who has made history become attractive and jump off the page with her eye for art and talented layout and design. We are also grateful to Dina for creating the striking Lehigh County Bicentennial logo. In addition, Dan McCarthy, one of the best writers and editors I've ever known, who has spent more than thirty years working in newspapers and coordinating communications and public information for PPL, a Fortune 500 company and a bedrock of employment and corporate support right in the heart of Allentown and Lehigh County, worked on the Editorial Committee and wrote the corporate sponsor profiles at the back of the book. We are grateful to all of those sponsors, entities who play a lead role in our community, creating jobs and opportunity, which have supported this book and the Bicentennial. Dan's masterful writing tells the story of those companies and institutions in a readable and interesting way.

Finally, to my staff in Lehigh County government, I want to thank them for driving this project to conclusion, particularly Frank Kane, my chief of staff, who has chaired the Editorial Committee, working with writers, designers and me to make sure everything stayed on track and doing it all in his own easy-going, relaxed way. But the real leader of this book and all the projects around the Bicentennial year celebration has been Cindy Feinberg, Lehigh County's Director of Community and Economic Development. Without Cindy's hard work, tenacity, and drive, this book—and the Bicentennial projects—would never have occurred. From lining up sponsors to setting up chairs at events, to pushing me to finishing this Foreword, no task has been too large or small. Cindy has been at the core of all aspects of this book and beyond. I am forever grateful to Cindy for her service to the residents of the county. Current and future generations are all beneficiaries of her deep commitment to this county and its people.

For me, this all started with those walks with my grandfather. He instilled in me an appreciation for all that has come before us, for the sacrifices and the foresight of the people who lived in our neighborhoods and laid down the pathways for us to follow. They were just ordinary people like us, ordinary people who did extraordinary things. They should not be forgotten, nor should the institutions they built and the communities they crafted from the wilderness. We honor them by working hard every day to make our community a better place. But, we also honor them by stopping once in awhile to reflect upon what they did and how we got to where we are today. Today, I take my children on walks over the same ground that my grandfather took me, but sometimes we have to stop and write it down for them, for us, and for the generations yet to come. That's what this book is about. I hope you enjoy reading it as much as we enjoyed compiling this fascinating—and continuing—story.

Don Cunningham
Lehigh County Executive
Chairman of the Lehigh County Bicentennial Committee
Allentown, Pennsylvania
March 2012

What the Heck's a Lehigh?

At first glance county names in Pennsylvania seem simple. The state has a Washington and a Jefferson county, the usual suspects in the long-dead-president category. Centre, even if spelled like it should be located outside of London, is right where it is supposed to be in the center of the state. Head east and York, Lancaster, Berks, Bucks, and Northampton breathe the spirit of homesick Englishmen, even if they were largely settled by Germans and the descendants of Germans.

But what the heck's a Lehigh?

True, it is a river, along with being a college, a county, and, in the form of Lehigh Valley, a geographical expression. Every other business seems to try to fit the word "Lehigh" into its name. But where did this word come from? To know, we have to start at the beginning. In the Lehigh Valley, that means the Native Americans, the Lenni Lenape or the Delaware tribe.

It all began when Moravian missionaries tried to find out what the Lenape called the river that ran into the Delaware. As the Native Americans had no written language, all the missionaries could do was write down what they thought they heard the Lenape saying. The result, according to Wesley Dunn, director of education at the Museum of Indian Culture, was Lehanweking. This word was later corrupted a number of ways, most commonly as Lechauweki. No matter; the spelling Lehanweking/Lechauweki was later translated into English as "where there are forks."

Even here, as the professors say, sources differ. Did it mean where the Lehigh "forks" into the Delaware? Or did it mean where a series of trails or streams forked off the Lehigh in different directions? One school of thought believes Lehanweking/Lechauweki actually means both. But either one is still a far word from Lehigh, and here is where the real fun starts.

According to most sources it was the Pennsylvania Germans who took the name and shortened it to Lecha. From here it was simply transformed into Lehigh. Yet, going back to the original sources, a lot more history is involved than that. In the words of the late Casey Stangel (a baseball manager before your time, boys and girls), "you could look it up."

On March 31, 1701, the Governor's Council of the colony of Pennsylvania, Governor William Penn presiding, was meeting in Philadelphia. The minutes show that one of the chief items on the agenda was keeping a rather ambitious fur trader of Swedish descent, John Hans Steelman (the Swedish government had established a colony called New Sweden in the future Delaware/Pennsylvania border region as early as the 1640s), from trading with the Lenape without a license. License fees were a source of revenue for his colony and Penn was particularly sensitive on this point. The minutes state Steelman wanted to establish his trading site "at Lechay or ye forks of Delaware."

It did not end there. On April 12, 1701, Penn, apparently at the end of his supply of friendly persuasion, expressed his frustration in a letter to Steelman. He wrote that he had "stopt thy goods intended for Lechay, till … thou come hither thyself and give further Satisfaction that thou hast yet done to thy friend, W.P." The record suggests the fur trader never did this.

These two documents are generally considered the first written examples of the word that became Lehigh. "Ye forks of Delaware" was the future site of Easton, which would not be established until 1752 by Penn's son Thomas.

Now the plot thickens. The year 1701 was about forty years before the first Moravian missionaries arrived in Pennsylvania. Yet something like the root word of Lehigh was already being bandied about by the governing class of Pennsylvania. Was it actually Steelman, or some other fur trader, maybe a Holland Dutchman from New Netherland, now New York, who turned the Lechauweki of the Lenape into Lechay? At this distance of time it is impossible to know.

This puts us on the banks of the "Lechay" or "Lecha." But how to get from there to Lehigh?

That brings in the English. For a long time, almost up to the outbreak of the American Revolution, they were referring to the river on their maps as the "western branch of ye Delaware." Apparently by the 1760s that had begun to change. In a letter, James Allen, third son of Allentown founder William Allen and owner of Trout Hall, writes phonetically of the "Lehi" river.

Perhaps our current word came about this way: There is an old English word, "leigh." Pronounced "lee," it is said to have Saxon roots and mean "meadow" or "clearing in the woods." Many very ancient towns in England include Leigh in their names. Maybe, hearing Lachay or Lecha, the English heard echoes of an ancient and familiar word. As the masters of Penn's Woods, they adopted it as Lehigh. And that is probably as far as we are ever going to get in knowing what the heck a Lehigh is.

Engraving of islands in the lower Lehigh River Valley, from a painting by Gustavus Grunewald.
(Lehigh County Historical Society)

THE CREATION OF LEHIGH COUNTY MARCH 6, 1812

It was Friday, March 6, 1812, and the Pennsylvania General Assembly was in a state of bedlam.

Working feverishly, legislators were struggling to complete their unfinished business by the end of the month before they would have to move from Lancaster, the state's capital since 1799, to the new capital city of Harrisburg. Among the bills passed by the Assembly that would be signed that day by Governor Simon Snyder was one to create a new county out of the western townships of Northampton County. A subject of political wrangling since the 1770s was finally to be resolved.

The General Assembly's sessions took place in a handsome two-story late-Georgian-style brick structure with a clock tower topped by a weather vane. Built in 1784, the building also doubled as the Lancaster County Courthouse. The House of Representatives met on the first floor, the Senate on the second. The senators had insisted on having a private stairway built for them so they could come and go without having to mingle with the "rabble," as they called the representatives who occupied the "lower" house.

The chambers were heated, more or less, by two Franklin stoves. It was a common joke among Pennsylvanians of the day that Ben Franklin's contraption was so complicated that he was the only one that could get it to work properly. Alas for the legislators, the good Dr. Franklin had been dead since 1790.

The building's chief drawback was its location at the busy intersection of King and Queen streets. Sometimes the bang of Conestoga wagons, passing in a nearly steady stream over the cobblestones, and the loud profanity-laced oaths of the teamsters made it almost impossible for the legislators to hear either each other or the gavel of the Speaker demanding order.

Most of the members, eighty-four Democratic Republicans and eleven Federalists in the House and twenty-six Democratic Republicans and five Federalists in the Senate, preferred to discuss legislative business at Colonel Matthias Slough's White Swan Tavern just off the courthouse square. The genial innkeeper, a former Federalist legislator and local

Revolutionary War figure, had entertained President George Washington at the inn in 1791.

Governor Snyder, a Democratic Republican and the first Pennsylvania German to be elected to that office, was among those who frequented the White Swan. In 1814 Snyder, twice a widower, married Mary Slough Scott, innkeeper Slough's daughter and herself a widow. Links like these to both political parties made the White Swan a safely neutral space for bi-partisan horse trading. Over a steaming bowl of flip—a popular mixture of hot beer, rum, sugar, and fresh eggs—or a tumbler of Pennsylvania rye whiskey much of the real work of the legislature, including that which led to Lehigh County, was probably done.

There were many reasons why Lehigh County took so long to create. Until the Revolution it had been blocked by members of the Penn family who held extensive property in the county seat of Easton. The events of 1776 swept them out of power, but the state's largely English-speaking political élite, centered in Philadelphia, had little interest in expanding the political influence of the Pennsylvania Germans by granting them a new county. This may explain why Lehigh County's creation attracted almost no attention in the élitist-dominated Federalist press of Lancaster.

Except for Congressional debates over the possibility of a war with Great Britain, nothing preoccupied the politicians and the "chattering class" who wrote about them more than the impending move to Harrisburg. In truth, the legislators had no one to blame for the chaos but themselves. The move, in the works since 1809, had been planned to take

place in October 1812, but on February 7 the lawmakers suddenly passed a supplement to the law requiring that all officers of the state be moved to Harrisburg by April. On March 10, another supplement was passed ordering all the state's records and its tiny bureaucracy (quill pens, ledger books, tax forms, ink-stained clerks and all) be moved by June. Suddenly it seemed everyone was on the road between Harrisburg and Lancaster. Even the Slough family, seeking a site for a tavern, headed west to the new seat of government on the Susquehanna.

Harrisburg's accommodations were few. Although the state government's requirements were limited compared with twenty-first century standards, the move still taxed its slender resources. Did the legislators who started it all—and ended up meeting at the Dauphin County Courthouse for the next ten years while the capitol building was being built—ever wonder what the rush to get to Harrisburg had been about?

The creation of Lehigh County may not have attracted much attention in the Lancaster press, but it was big news in the pages of the only newspaper in the Lehigh Valley region. *Der Unabhaengiger Republikaner*, or *The Independent Republican*, a four-page German-language weekly printed in the borough of Northampton (as Allentown was then known) had been founded in 1810. As with most newspapers of the day it unabashedly represented the views of a political party. In this case it was the local voice of the Democratic Republican Party, the distant ancestor of the current Democratic Party.

Under the headline "Division of Northampton County!" the *Republikaner* claimed on February 28 that the legislation, whose title translated into German was given as "An Act to Take Specific Parts of Northampton County to Form a New County," had been "passed on the 22nd of this month with a considerable majority of the entire committee in the House of Representatives"—but it gave no vote total. The newspaper's staff should not be

Deshler's Fort, Erected in 1760.

blamed too harshly for not publishing one. Surviving official accounts of the legislative action creating Lehigh County don't record a tally either.

To a reader in the twenty-first century the debates about Lehigh County as recorded in House and Senate journals seem fragmented and disorganized. This may be unfairly imposing modern values on the early nineteenth century, a time when many people lived by the seasons rather than the clock. They were willing to tolerate more ambiguity in their lives and records than their descendants.

Old Northampton County, founded in 1752, was huge. It stretched from the New York border to the Bucks County line. Eventually eleven counties, Sullivan, Susquehanna, Wayne, Pike, Wyoming, Lackawanna, Luzerne, Carbon, Monroe, Northampton, and Lehigh, and parts of four other counties, Bradford, Columbia, Lycoming, and Schuylkill, would be carved out of it.

The first reference to the creation of Lehigh County in the legislative process of 1812 appeared in the Senate's journal under the date of January 3. Senator James Wilson of Northampton County presented to the Senate that day nine petitions signed by 972 inhabitants of the townships of Lynn, Heidelberg, Lowhill, Weisenberg, Macungie, Upper Milford, South Whitehall, North Whitehall, Northampton Borough [Allentown], Salisbury, Upper Saucon, and part of Hanover. Because of "the hardships and inconveniences of having to travel a great distance to the seat of justice and for many other reasons," the petitioners requested "that a law be passed for removing the seat of justice to a central situation, or for a division of the county."

After being read twice, the issue was referred to a committee chaired by Wilson. His colleagues were senators Watson, Ralston, Gross, and Gemmil. Their task was to consider the petitions and report back to the full Senate. The next reference in the Senate's journal is on January 8, when Senator Wilson presented petitions signed by 898 citizens of western Northampton County asking for the creation of a new county. Unlike the first petition, which included the request that if a new county could not be formed perhaps the county seat could be moved, the second made reference only to the establishment of a new county. This was the real issue.

No further reference to the issue appears in the upper house's journal until March. Apparently the Senate committee appointed in January produced a bill that was agreed on by that body, as it was passed on to the House sometime in early February. This was probably what the House's journal later called Senate Bill No. 203 titled "An Act erecting part of Northampton into a separate County."

Debate over the creation of Lehigh County seems to have begun in earnest in the House on February 20, 1812. On that day, according to the House journal, Rep. Jacob Weygandt of Northampton County presented forty "remonstrances" from "sundry inhabitants of the county of Northampton against the division of said county." He was followed by Northampton County Rep. Jacob Newhard, who came forward with five petitions supporting the creation of Lehigh County.

Weygandt, apparently deciding if you can't beat them join them, responded with three petitions from East Penn and Lausanne townships in Northampton County, "praying" that they might be included in the new county. In 1808, East Penn and Lausanne townships, mountainous rural districts of Northampton County, had been carved out of Penn Township. Perhaps, like the petitioners in the western townships of Northampton County, they too had become tired of having to travel long distances over bad roads to Easton every time they needed to record a deed, file a will, or settle a lawsuit.

The House journal makes no reference to the vote that the *Republikaner* claimed had taken place on February 22 and won a considerable majority of the entire committee in the House in support of the new county. In fact, there is no reference to a House committee at all.

The issue is not mentioned in the legislature's journals again until February 24, when Senate Bill 203 was read a second time to the House. At that time Weygandt and a Rep. Winter formally requested an amendment to the bill to include Lausanne and East Penn townships. The House rejected his proposal on a vote of 47 to 33. Weygandt and Winter made another attempt that day to amend the bill. Now they were asking the legislators to strike out the section that set the new county's northern border at the Lehigh Water Gap, which would open the possibility of Lausanne and East Penn being added to Lehigh County at a later date. This also was rejected by the House, by an even larger margin of 61 to 19. The petitioners of Lausanne and East Penn were fated to continue making those long

Craig's Hotel at Lehigh Gap in Carbon County just north of Slatington. An ancient Indian trail, the Nescopeck Path, went through this gap long before European settlement. Rufus Grider, 1853. (Moravian Archives)

journeys to Easton until 1843, when they were incorporated into the newly created Carbon County.

On February 25, 1812, at a third reading, the House voted to approve the Lehigh County bill. The House journal, without giving a vote total, merely notes it was passed and ordered the clerk to return it to the Senate requesting their "concurrence" to the House's actions. The Senate, according to the House's journal, returned the bill the next day, February 26, with their agreement.

Why the tally of the third vote never made it on the public record remains a puzzle. Perhaps that document was lost in the confusion of the move to Harrisburg, or maybe it was a voice vote that was drowned out by those noisy Conestoga wagons passing over the cobblestone street at the front door of the legislative chamber. If that document did somehow find its way to Harrisburg it may well have been destroyed in the fire that swept the capitol's archives on February 2, 1897. It is nowhere to be found in the highly detailed, information-packed *Anniversary History of Lehigh County*, published for the county's 100th anniversary in 1912.

There is also nothing in the surviving public record about the role Governor Snyder might have played behind the scenes for the creation of Lehigh County. It is, however, hard to imagine that having a "Dutchman" in the governor's chair as head of the legislature's majority party didn't help in resolving an issue that had been an extremely important one to Pennsylvania Germans for many years.

With all of Lehigh County's many fathers celebrating its creation, at least one of its mothers surely was pleased. Ann Penn Allen Greenleaf of Allentown, the oldest child of Trout Hall's builder James Allen and granddaughter of city founder William Allen, had long been working behind the scenes with the legislators of the region for this day. She shared her home at the southeast corner of Fifth and Hamilton streets with her husband, James Greenleaf, a former diplomat and speculator in Washington D.C. property, and their daughters, Margaret Tilghman Greenleaf and Mary Livingston Greenleaf. It was the largest

in the borough. The creation of Lehigh County didn't just raise the value of the Greenleafs' property in Allentown, which would be chosen as the county seat that June. It also paid tribute to her attachment to the resting place of her younger sister, Margaret "Betsy" Allen, who had died in childbirth in Trout Hall in 1799 and was buried at St. Paul's Lutheran Church at Eighth and Walnut streets, and where she had spent many summer days as a child.

Mrs. Greenleaf's strong attachment to Lehigh County is clear in an 1817 letter she wrote to her brother-in-law William Tilghman, Chief Justice of the Pennsylvania Supreme Court, trustee of her estate and the husband of her late sister Betsy whose child she was then helping to raise. She told Tilghman she had no interest in moving to Washington D.C. where her husband, deep in land deals and litigation, was urging they relocate: "Mr. Greenleaf does not suspect this … but I long for retirement, particularly the retirement of Allentown." Eventually, in the 1830s, they would separate though not divorce, Greenleaf living in Washington, his wife dividing her time between homes in Philadelphia and Allentown.

When it finally came, Governor Snyder's formal message to the General Assembly of March 6, 1812, was simple and direct:

> I have this day approved and signed the following acts of the general assembly
> and directed the secretary to return them to the houses, in which they respectively
> originated …

As the third bill Snyder signed that day, Lehigh County's founding document was sandwiched in the docket between an authorization to increase the number of constables in Lancaster and Easton (apparently there was a crime problem), and approval of the establishment of a committee by the Court of Common Pleas of York County to sell the estate of the late Abraham Cook, "a lunatic."

Along with Snyder's signature on the document were those of two others: Rep. John Tod of Bedford County, the Speaker of the House, and that of Sen. Presley Carr Lane of Fayette County, Speaker of the Senate.

Lane was said to be a distant relative of Thomas Jefferson through the founder's sister, Martha Jefferson, and her husband Dabney Carr. In 1812, the former president and author of the Declaration of Independence was in retirement at Monticello. "I have given up newspapers for Tacitus and Thucydides; Euclid and Newton and find myself much the happier," he wrote in January of that year to his fellow founding father John Adams.

If Jefferson had retreated from current events to the ancient classics and higher mathematics, folks in western Northampton County had not. They were waiting anxiously for the official word of Lehigh County's creation. It came in the March 6, 1812, issue of the *Republikaner.* Since it took several days to travel between Allentown and Lancaster the signing must have been expected and perhaps the newspaper had access to a copy of the act before it was signed.

The "article" was simply a reprint in German, without comment, of the county's enabling act. Everything from the building of a county courthouse to regulating service in the local militia units was covered. The opening paragraph defined the history-making event best:

An ACT erecting part of Northampton into a separate County

BE it enacted by the senate and house of representatives of the commonwealth of Pennsylvania, in general assembly met, and it is hereby enacted by the authority of the same, That all that part of Northampton county, lying and being within the limits of the following townships, to wit, the townships of Lynn, Heidelberg, Lowhill, Weissenburg, Macungie, Upper Milford, South Whitehall, North Whitehall, Northampton, Salisbury, Upper Saucon and part of Hanover within the following bounds, to wit, beginning at the Bethlehem line, where it joins the river Lehigh, thence along the said line until it intersects the road leading from Bethlehem to the water gap, thence along said road to Allen township, westwardly, to the Lehigh, shall be, and the same are hereby, according to their present lines, declared to be erected into a county, henceforth to be called Lehigh.

A dream of their fathers and grandfathers had at last been realized. Lehigh County, named for its river, was born.

COUNTY COURT-HOUSE, ALLENTOWN, PA.

Lehigh County Courthouse, completed 1816.

CHAPTER ONE

LEHIGH COUNTY IN 1812

In 1812 the new Lehigh County was little changed from the day thirty-one years before, when the British surrender to Washington at Yorktown brought the American Revolution to a close.

Statistically, it was 28 miles long and 15 miles wide. Its total area was 389 square miles, or 248,960 acres. Extracted out of the 1810 federal census of Northampton County, its population was 15,561. The 1820 federal census, Lehigh County's first as a separate county, would show an increase to 18,895.

Pennsylvania's population in 1810 was 1,049,458. Philadelphia County, roughly fifty miles to the south of Lehigh County, had a population of 111,210, making it the second-largest urban area in America after New York City.

The county was typical of the state in that most of its people lived in small crossroads communities and on farms. "In 1810," writes historian Sanford W. Higginbotham, "only Philadelphia, Lancaster, Pittsburgh, Reading and York claimed more that 2,500 inhabitants, though Carlisle had nearly reached that level."

Easton, Northampton County's county seat, had 1,657 inhabitants in 1810; by 1820 that number had increased to 2,370. Bethlehem, still largely a closed Moravian community, had, according to the 1800 federal census, 543 inhabitants. This figure had remained relatively stable since before the Revolution and would remain so into the 1820s.

Allentown, still officially named Northampton, was the most populous town in Lehigh County and the only organized borough. In 1810 it had a population of 710. This was up from 573 in 1800 and 486 in 1790. By 1820 the borough's population would increase to 1,132. Part of that substantial growth was due to its drawing power after being adopted as the county seat in June of 1812. The establishment of a courthouse attracted lawyers. The first was Connecticut Yankee Henry King who "hung out his shingle" in 1815. Later elected to several political offices, he died rich and well respected in Allentown in 1860.

The 1800 census recorded a small number of black people in the future Lehigh County. There were twenty-one African Americans, almost all of them females, in what was to be-

come Lehigh County. Only one was a slave, a house servant who belonged to Rev. Jacob Van Buskirk of Macungie, then known as Millerstown.

Under the state's Gradual Abolition of Slavery Act of 1780, the "peculiar institution" was slowly being phased out in Pennsylvania rather than ended immediately. By its terms all those who were slaves in 1780, when the bill passed, would remain so until their death. Their children were given the status of indentured servants until the age of twenty-eight, when they became free. Any children born to them were born free. Under this law, slavery was not totally abolished in Pennsylvania until 1847, when the last elderly slave died fourteen years before the Civil War.

The original inhabitants of Lehigh County were the Lenape or Delaware tribe of Native Americans. Their roaming territory stretched from Cape Henlopen, Delaware, to Kingston, New York. Lehigh County was primarily a hunting, fishing and jasper-quarrying area for the tribe.

By 1812 the Lenape were gone from the region in any organized way, although some may have lived on the margins of white society. Most had left in the eighteenth century after being removed following a number of dishonest land deals by colonial officials. The ill will bred by these led to much violence on the Northampton County frontier during the

The Lenape: Lehigh County's Original People

Long before there was a Lehigh County there was a Lehigh River. Living on its banks was a group of people, Native Americans, known as the Lenni Lenape, the "Original People." Later the Europeans would give them the name Delawares after Lord De la Warr, an early English colonial governor.

Some anthropologists claim the Lenape came to the region in 1700 BC, but arrowheads and other relics that date to 10,000 BC belonging to the so-called Paleo-Indians, presumed to be ancestors of the Lenape, have been found in Berks County.

A semi-nomadic people, over time the Lenape created a general roaming territory that stretched roughly from today's Cape Henlopen in Delaware to the lower Hudson River community of Kingston, New York.

Lehigh County was roughly in the center of the Lenape territory. The Allentown plateau was a vast grassland dotted with scrub oak, which was regularly burned off to encourage small game. The Lenape hunted grouse and other game birds there. Interestingly, it was grouse hunting that also brought wealthy Philadelphians like William Allen to the Lehigh Valley.

The Lenape were divided into three groups or clans, the Minsi, the northern Unami, and the southern Unami. The Minsi occupied the country at the headwaters of the Delaware River. The northern Unami occupied the west bank of the Delaware from the Lehigh Valley southward. The southern Unami were generally found in what is now Wilmington, Delaware. Clan membership was through the mother's family.

Originally the Lenape survived by hunting, fishing and gathering. Later they began to grow corn. Soon it became their chief crop. As it required planting and tending it changed the Lenape way of life. No longer would they have to follow the migratory paths of animals in order to survive. Growing it enabled the Lenape to adopt a less-nomadic culture and settle in small villages. "It gave them time to stop and think, to attend council meetings and so to develop political forms," writes historian Paul A.W. Wallace in his book *Indians of Pennsylvania*.

Another resource of which the Lenape took advantage was the vast supply of jasper located in southern Lehigh County. It was found in pockets on South Mountain; in Lehigh County the largest number of pits have been found in the Macungie area. *Preservation Pennsylvania* magazine calls the Vera Cruz jasper quarries "one of the most significant archeological sites in eastern Pennsylvania." It was used primarily in tool and weapons making, and was flaked into shapes at campsites near the quarries. The jasper was of such superior quality that it was traded among Native Americans up and down the east coast.

The Lenape lived in a spirit-filled world. They believed that all things—men, animals, trees and rocks—had souls. From the Great Spirit or creator who ruled in the twelfth or highest heaven, through the eleven demigods that ruled in the lesser heavens, to the spirit forces on Earth, all were recognized as playing a role. In one of the Lenape creation myths the earth was re-born on the moss-covered back of the turtle.

Calling themselves the Original People, the Lenape occupied a special place among the Algonquian-speaking tribes that predominated in northeastern North America. They were considered the "grandfathers" from which all other Algonquian peoples originated.

The Troxell–Steckel house in Egypt was built in 1756 and retains the characteristics of an early Pennsylvania-German farmhouse. The Lehigh County Historical Society opens it for tours weekends during the summer season.

French and Indian War of the 1750s. But that was long-ago history by the time of Lehigh County's founding.

Immigration and Settlement

Lehigh County's most populous township in 1810 was Whitehall, with 2,551 residents. It was divided that year into North and South Whitehall. The 1820 census shows a population of 1,807 for North Whitehall and 1,623 for South Whitehall. The current Whitehall Township was not formed until 1867. Number two on the list was Macungie Township, with a population of 2,420 in 1810. It would be divided into Upper and Lower Macungie townships in 1832.

The population was overwhelmingly Pennsylvania German, descendants of German-speaking immigrants who came to the region in the mid to late eighteenth century. The roots of the majority of them were in the Rhineland, Alsace (a German-speaking region on the border with France), and Switzerland. Except for African Americans, they were the largest immigrant ethnic group in the United States whose ancestors did not come from the British Isles.

There had been a fair number of Scots-Irish, people of Scottish Protestant descent who had settled in Northern Ireland in the seventeenth century, but they had largely moved out of Lehigh County by 1812.

Why was Lehigh County seemingly a magnet for the German immigrants? It began with Pennsylvania founder William Penn who, as a pious young Quaker, had toured the German states. When he founded Pennsylvania he encouraged sects like the Mennonites, who were persecuted in German states, to settle here, where he had established a policy of religious tolerance. The word then spread to so-called "church" Germans, those of the Lutheran and Reformed faiths.

In the eighteenth century the Rhineland Palatinate region, which many of those who immigrated to Lehigh County came from, was a cockpit of conflict. The armies of French King Louis XIV used it as a major invasion route. Other armies attempting to drive out the French did the same, burning farms and destroying crops in the process. A series of droughts and severe winters at that time added to the woes of the people. The population was also subjected to high taxes and meddlesome policies imposed by their landlords, nobles who aspired on a small scale to the lavish lifestyle enjoyed by the French monarchs at Versailles.

The promise of land and the chance to own farms of their own, something that was virtually impossible for the vast majority in the German states, was what attracted them the most. This was something they could use to live on, and could pass on to their children.

"The immigrant letters and return visitors told tales to those who stayed behind of a land where three or four families might own as much land as belonged to an entire village at home," writes historian Aaron Spencer Fogleman in his 1996 book, *Hopeful Journeys: German Immigration Settlement and Political Culture in Colonial America 1717–1775*. "Though usually forbidden by the authorities, emigration from the southwest [German states] and Switzerland had become an uncomfortable fact of life by the middle third of the eighteenth century." Their rulers "could not stop hundreds of thousands from leaving the realm."

It was not easy to reach this seeming paradise. Even though many letter writers told of the importance of money in the New World, few had any. Most rulers demanded a large fee before they would allow their subjects to leave. By the time the fee and the ship's passage had been paid, few had any money left to buy land. They would travel to port cities like Rotterdam, where they boarded sailing ships bound for England and then North America. A voyage of three months was common; one of six months was not unusual.

Fogleman notes that most traveled in large groups with family, friends, and fellow inhabitants of their town or region. Water, food and other essentials often ran out. In

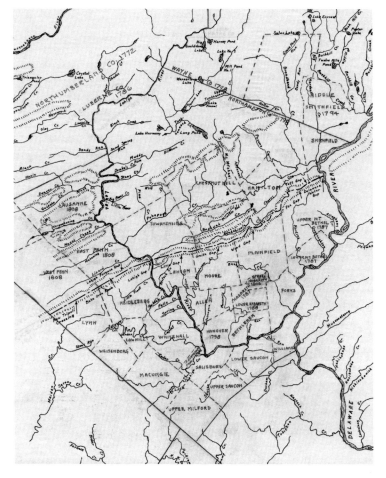

Map dated 1809 showing Lehigh County as part of Northampton County.
(Lehigh County Historical Society)

some cases immigrants were reduced to eating the rats that inhabited the ship. Many died, children and the elderly being the most vulnerable.

When the immigrants arrived in Philadelphia many discovered that the promise of free land was untrue. By 1734, when land in the future Lehigh County officially opened for settlement, Penn's heirs had sold it to land speculators like William Allen, future founder of Allentown, who expected to make a profit by either selling or renting it. The reaction of many newcomers was simply to "squat" on the property they wanted, start clearing the land, and begin farming. As early as 1727, colonial official James Logan commented on this phenomenon:

> When they were sought out and challenged for their right of occupancy, they allege that it was published in Europe that we wanted and solicited for colonists and had a super abundance of land, and therefore they had come without means to pay.

After a few years, admitted Logan, many German immigrants managed to buy the land they occupied. According to James J. Hauser's 1902 *History of Lehigh County*, on the eve of the American Revolution taxes on the average farm in the western townships of Northampton County were 80 cents to $1.50. Laborers were paid on average between 8 and 12 cents a day. Rents on houses averaged between $4 and $8 a year. This normally included several acres of land and a woodlot.

With very few people available to police the vast areas of land involved and to collect the rents, enforcement of rent agreements was virtually impossible.

Both William Allen and his son James, owners of vast acres of western Northampton County, complained bitterly about the failure of tenants to pay their rents in a timely way. James Allen noted in his diary on October 17, 1777— at the height of the Revolution

— that some tenants came forward with several years' worth of rent paid in virtually worthless Continental currency instead of shillings. "I dare not object, tho' I am as much robbed of 5/6ths of my property, as if it was taken out of my [cash] Drawer," he wrote.

The oldest surviving Pennsylvania German homestead in Lehigh County is that of Peter Troxell, along the Jordan Creek in what is now South Whitehall Township. Troxell, a native of Switzerland, came to America in 1733 at the age of 42. The two-story stone Troxell home was built with a large hearth. When the hearth was removed in the nineteenth century the date 1744 was discovered carved in the mantelpiece, giving the year of its construction.

At least as early as 1761 the Troxell building was also used as a tavern. How long it served the joint roles of home and inn is unknown. An unusually large and sturdy barn was built on the property in 1806 by Peter Troxell, Jr. The farm remained in the Troxell family until the 1850s and today is owned by the Bronstein family, founders of the former Trojan Powder Company on whose property the farm was located. It is maintained as a well-preserved private house museum.

Most of the early settlers followed "The King's High Road" from Philadelphia into the Lehigh Valley. Surveyed and opened in August, 1735, this was the first public road in what is now Lehigh County. The route was described this way in the 1912 *History of Lehigh County*:

> It began in Macousin (Macungie) township, a short distance northwest of Breinigsville, on land of Peter Trexler; running through the borough of Macungie [which did not exist at that time] and Upper Milford … crossing the land of Derrick Jausen (Shimersville), Christian Crall (Zionsville), John Meyer, Dewalt Mechlin, Henry Geber (Hosensack), Peter Walber, Ulrich Rieszer, and Alexander Diefenderfer, crossing the county-line between Bucks and Philadelphia counties (now Montgomery county) through Geryville into Gussenhopen (Goshenhoppen), to North Wales where it joined the road leading from Goshenhoppen to Philadelphia. It was reported that this road was laid out 52 feet wide.

This route was the one most traveled by local farmers taking their produce to Philadelphia. They would return with manufactured goods and cloth for their wives and families. In the 1970s Charles Jarrett, a long-time resident of Lower Macungie, told authors Craig and Ann Bartholomew for their *History of Lower Macungie Township* that his ancestors traveled the route together with other farmers for reasons of safety.

A road from the Moravian settlement in Emmaus to Bethlehem was proposed in 1753, but not approved. Until 1760, when it was laid out along what today is Emaus Avenue, travelers continued to use an old Indian trail along South Mountain.

The Walking Purchase of 1737

Thomas Penn, son of William Penn and Proprietor of the colony of Pennsylvania, with his brothers John and Richard, has gone down in history as not always the most pleasant of men.

Benjamin Franklin, who encountered him in England while serving as an agent for the colony, noted the imperious Penn treated him on a visit to his estate at Stoke Park like "a low born Jockey." About 150 years later, Charles Rhoads Roberts in the *Anniversary History of Lehigh County* refers to Penn as the "cheating, land grabbing offspring of an honorable father."

Thomas Penn might have argued in his defense that he had watched his father defrauded and forced into debtor's prison, and eventually his grave, by those he trusted. That is what being fair and honorable had gotten him.

Young Penn had grown up trying to help his mother, Penn's second wife Hannah Callowhill, hold the family together and restore some of the family fortune his father had lost on account of debts and lawsuits over Pennsylvania. He was not going to let what happened to his father happen to him. Penn had inherited Pennsylvania, and he was going to make some money from it and live the life of a landed English gentlemen.

It is understandable that the Lenni Lenape Indians, whose land he was selling out from under them, would remain less than sympathetic. To this day they call what he did to them a fraud.

The chief cause of Thomas Penn's reputation is the so-called Walking Purchase of 1737. Penn produced a treaty that he claimed had been negotiated many years before, in the 1680s, between his father and the Native American Lenape or Delaware tribe that occupied the land. The sons of William Penn said it allowed them to acquire all the land a man could walk in a day and a half.

The Lenape did not protest even though all the chiefs who had signed their marks to the document were long dead. They trusted the sons of their friend William Penn and assumed it would be a peaceful stroll with stops to hunt and fish.

For his part, Thomas Penn planned a foot race. He selected three of the fastest walkers that he could find for the race: Edward Marshall, James Yeates, and Solomon Jennings. They trained for months while settlers helped clear their route of brush and trees before the walk.

The long-awaited event was held on September 19, 1737. The starting point was at Wrightstown in Bucks County and headed northwest to follow the Lehigh River.

Jennings became exhausted and dropped out before he reached the Lehigh River. Yeates and Marshall raced on. Eventually Yeates collapsed from exhaustion and suffered a seizure that left him blind. He died three days later. Marshall was the winner. He collapsed while grasping a sapling near Tobyhanna Creek, not far from what today is Jim Thorpe, Carbon County, having covered roughly 65 miles. Marshall received a 500-acre farm near Stroudsburg for his services.

Later colonial surveyors, instead of drawing a boundary line directly east to the Delaware, made the line run northeasterly at an angle from the sapling that Marshall had grasped to the mouth of the Lackawaxen River in what is now Pike County. In total it gave the Penns 1,200,000 acres of land.

Disgusted, the angry Lenape protested. "If this practice must hold why then we are no more Brothers and Friends but much more like Open Enemies," a chief said. At first they refused to leave the Walking Purchase land.

Thomas Penn had an ace up his sleeve. Working through acting governor James Logan, a long-time agent of his father, he got the powerful Iroquois nation that had once defeated the Lenape in battle and had been allies of the English for many years to take his side. Calling the Lenape "women," the Iroquois commanded their fellow Native Americans to go "instantly." Faced with the choice of engaging in a fight with the fierce and powerful Iroquois or relocating, they reluctantly packed up and moved beyond the Blue Mountains.

Despite their quick response to the Iroquois demand, the loss of their ancestral hunting lands was not something the Lenape took lightly. They were not about to simply "get over" the Walking Purchase.

To Thomas Penn, living on the manicured grounds of his Buckinghamshire estate Stoke Park, surrounded by one of the best collections of rare books in England, and separated from the Pennsylvania wilderness by three thousand miles of Atlantic Ocean, the wrath of the Lenape, while annoying, had no personal impact. Edward Marshall, winner of the Walking Purchase was not as fortunate. Ten years after the walk, in 1747, Native American warriors attacked his farm, the prize he had received for his part in the "walk," killing one of his sons. After living in New Jersey for several years Marshall returned to Pennsylvania.

The Native Americans had a long memory. In 1756, nineteen years after the Walking Purchase, during the French and Indian War, either by chance or plan, Marshall's frontier cabin was again attacked, this time by a war party of sixteen Lenape warriors. His wife was killed and scalped. He lived on, dying an old man in 1789.

Thomas Penn died in England in 1775 on the eve of the American Revolution. He did not live to see a Pennsylvania that his family no longer controlled.

Of the three walkers, only Solomon Jennings had a close and prominent connection to future Lehigh County. He had secured a warrant the year before the walk for a 200-acre farm in future Salisbury Township, at the great curve of the Lehigh River. He was a commissioner of Northampton County in 1755, and was known as a strong man. As a reward for his role in the walk, he was forgiven payment of his annual quit rent to Penn's heirs. His son John became a quartermaster in the Continental Army during the Revolution, and served several terms as sheriff.

During the Revolutionary War, a number of wounded soldiers were brought to the farm, where some died and were buried. In 1764 Solomon Jennings' heirs sold the farm to Jacob Geisinger. It remained in the Geisinger family until the end of the nineteenth century. In 1917 the City of Allentown purchased it to use for a sewage treatment plant, which was never built there. During World War I it was used as the city farm, producing food during a period of severe rationing. In 1920 the city sold it to the Lehigh Valley Railroad for a large freight yard, which was never developed.

The 1950 issue of the Lehigh County Historical Society's *Proceedings* notes a number of Indian trails that became roads:

> The Old Warrior's Path came through the Lehigh Gap on the east side of the river and crossed the river at a ford somewhere north of the present river bridges at Slatington. On the east side of the Lehigh River there was one branch of the trail which ran through what are now Bath, Nazareth and Easton and another branch which ran southwardly and crossed the Lehigh River at what is now Central Park [today Westminster Village Nursing Home]. …

> On the west side of the Lehigh River, the Old Warrior's Trail branched again—one branch running westwardly along the Blue Ridge and another branch turning south and running through what are now Balliettsville, Ironton, Meyersville, Wennersville, Dorneyville, west side of Emmaus, Vera Cruz and then turning south. The Vera Cruz jasper mines were located on this path or trail. …

> In all cases these so-called roads were nothing more than trails for some years after they were laid out and before they were improved to the point where they could be called roads even in those days. …

Ways of Life

As it had been since the arrival of Europeans in the mid-eighteenth century, farming was the chief occupation in the Lehigh County of 1812. Even those who were not directly connected to it depended on the success of the farmer for their livelihood. Merchants and tradesman could not thrive unless the farmer brought in a good crop, and, although they were self-sufficient in many ways, Pennsylvania-German farmers depended on merchants for sugar, tea, coffee, and other luxury goods, and on millers, coopers, blacksmiths, wagon makers, and harness makers for essential supplies and services.

What was it like to be a Pennsylvania German farmer? In 1950 historian David G. Williams, writing in the Lehigh County Historical Society's *Proceedings*, made it sound anything but pleasant. "The life of a Pennsylvania farmer was one of unceasing toil—with few recreations to break the monotony," he writes. "He was up before sunrise and to bed soon after sunset. This was his routine day after day, year after year." Others agree. The Bartholomews' history uses much the same words to describe the early Pennsylvania-German farmer's lot.

Farm equipment was crude, mostly hand tools made of wood. Shovels, hoes, and rakes were common. Plows were heavy and cumbersome. "It took two men or a man and a boy, using two or three horses or four to six oxen, an entire day to plow one or two acres," writes Williams.

Invariably, mixed farming was practiced. Farm families grew a variety of grains and raised chickens, hogs, sheep, milch cows, and cattle. Oxen and horses provided power and transportation. Flax could be seen growing throughout the area into the nineteenth century, and women and girls spent extraordinary numbers of hours preparing textiles and clothing.

Most people today would not want to live the way Pennsylvania-German farmers had to live. But it would be wrong to judge their lives by modern standards. German immigrants created a vibrant folk culture that met their needs within their tradition. Their farms were the envy of many. The neatness and order of their well-cultivated fields, their skillfully built barns, and their large sturdy homes were much commented on by travelers.

Christmas and, after the Revolution, the Fourth of July were holidays. Harvest season was an opportunity for families to share the labor at each others' farms, the work often accompanied with games designed to bring young people of marriage age together.

In the winter there was time for dances, weddings, and other events. Gathering at the tavern, the men discussed politics and caught up with the news. The church provided an outlet for both men and women. Sunday-school classes were part of all-day church meetings for many.

Work and leisure were combined rather than separated, as they would become with the arrival of industry. The rhythms of life were defined by the crops and the seasons. Wheat was the cash crop. Farmers' wives would make bread out of the rye and barley their husbands grew for the family. The farmer would take the wheat to Philadelphia to sell. Tenant farmers used the money they received to pay the rent. Farm owners used it for house and barn improvements, to purchase seed and livestock, or, if times were really good, to buy more land.

Families with eight or nine children were the norm. Mortality was high, not just among the poor: Of the nine children born to William Allen and his wife Margaret Hamilton, among the richest families in the colony, only six survived to adulthood.

Most Pennsylvania Germans saw themselves as Americans of German heritage, and during the Revolution the majority were active and ardent supporters of the cause of independence. But they saw no reason why being good Americans would require them to give up important aspects of their culture like the use of their traditional German dialect. Pennsylvania Dutch, as it came to be called, was far more commonly heard and understood in Lehigh County's streets and homes in 1812 than was English.

On July 8, 1776, when the Declaration of Independence was read for the first time in Lehigh County in front of the German Reformed Church—now Zion's Reformed UCC Church in Allentown—it was read in German and in English. Courts in Philadelphia, where

federal grand juries would meet and federal cases were tried, were required to have translators for German speakers; many members of the state legislature spoke German more fluently than English; schools were largely taught in German, particularly in rural Lehigh County, into the early twentieth century.

Some educated German visitors commented unfavorably on the local dialect. Still, it is hard to imagine how much different it could possibly have been from the way German peasants spoke in the Rhineland.

Not all of the early settlers of Lehigh County lived on isolated farms. Among the earliest communities was Emmaus, a successful venture of the Moravian Church's missionary outreach to nearby Pennsylvania Germans, most of whom professed Lutheran or Reformed beliefs.

Emmaus was located in an area known as Maguntsche, taken from the Lenape word meaning "feeding place of the bears." It is the root of the current word Macungie. Its rich soil attracted many immigrants. One was Lutheran Jacob Ehrenhardt, a farmer and blacksmith from Marstadt near Worms. His "next door neighbor" was Sebastian Knauss, a native of the Rhenish Palatinate who was raised in the Reformed Church.

Frustrated that they could not find an educated minister of either faith to settle near them, in the fall of 1742 Ehrenhardt and Knauss visited Bethlehem with their wives. Just

established in 1741, Bethlehem's orderly religious community, under the leadership of the pious German nobleman Count von Zinzendorf, impressed them. Eventually Zinzendorf even preached in the Ehrenhardt home. Both families were pleased to accept the opportunity of joining the Moravians and donated land for church use. Ehrenhardt gave land for a small log church built in 1742 and a school built in 1746. He and his wife later gave fifty-five acres to the Moravian Church authorities in Bethlehem, who controlled the village. Knauss and his wife gave forty-five acres.

In 1747, the Gemeinlein in Maguntsche (little congregation in Macungie) was organized by the Moravian Church in Bethlehem. It had thirty-four founding members. When Salisbury Township was formed in 1753, it became knows as the Salisbury congregation. On April 3, 1761, Moravian Bishop Augustus Spangenberg gave it the name Emmaus, after the Biblical town where Christ is said to have appeared to two of his followers following his resurrection. It was to remain a closed Moravian village until the 1830s and did not become fully secular until 1859.

One curious fact about Emmaus over the years is the spelling and pronunciation of its name. Originally, Emmaus was written with a double "m" and pronounced E-may-us, with an emphasis on all three syllables. But it was also spelled "Emaus," after the German fashion with a dash over the single m to indicate a double consonant.

Typical internal mechanism of an early overshot mill. The bevel gear in the foreground turned one set of grinding stones. (Lower Macungie Township Historical Society)

As use of the High German fell out of favor the dash over the "m" was lost. "A-mouse" or "Ee-moss" became the accepted way of pronouncing the town's name among the folks who lived there. To this day this has not completely changed. A remnant of that alternate spelling remains to this day in Emaus Avenue.

"Happily the citizens of the Borough took legal action in 1938 and the second m was once more restored to its rightful place," wrote Muhlenberg College historian Preston Barba in 1959 in his book *They Came to Emmaus.* "Today the name is written Emmaus, but the pronunciation—that is another matter!"

The Founding Family

Allentown, which would become Lehigh County's largest community and the county seat, was founded in 1762. Its founder was Philadelphia merchant William Allen, the second-largest landowner in the colony after the Penn family, and its wealthiest citizen.

Over six feet tall with blond hair and blue eyes, Allen, physically as well as fiscally, towered over contemporaries, who called him "The Great Giant." His temper was legendary. On hearing Allen unload a stream of colorful oaths at a political opponent in the colonial Assembly one observer noted they were delivered so loudly "that on a clear morning they could be heard as far as ye Jersey Shore."

Not shy about displaying his wealth, Allen's most visible status symbol was a London-made coach drawn by four horses, with a driver or "whip" trained in England. Philadelphian Timothy Matlock recalled the coach, the only one like it in Philadelphia, "carrying its owner in a state unequaled down Germantown Road" from Allen's country home at Mt. Airy to his counting house on Water Street.

Allen's fortune was based on trading ventures in Europe, the West Indies, and South America. Flour produced from Pennsylvania-grown wheat was his major commodity. He inherited the business from his father after his return from studying at Cambridge University in England in 1725 and greatly expanded it. Allen's cargo sometimes included slaves, but there was very little demand for them in Pennsylvania except as domestic help. Land speculation and the manufacturing of iron in furnaces in New Jersey added to his wealth. One of Allen's iron ventures, the Union Forge in High Bridge, New Jersey, founded in 1742, was taken over by his manager Robert Taylor during the Revolution. It became part of the Taylor-Wharton Steel and Iron Company in 1912 and when closed in 1972 was the longest-running privately held ironworks in the United States.

Allen held major governmental posts including serving as a legislator in the colonial Assembly, as mayor of Philadelphia, and Chief Justice for the colony's Supreme Court from 1750 to 1774. He was also a patron of the arts, most notably sending a young Benjamin West, the first internationally known American artist, to study in Italy, and aiding Charles Willson Peale.

His interest in the lands of the Lehigh Valley began early. On May 18, 1732, Thomas Penn conveyed 5,000 acres of wilderness land of the future Lehigh County, then part of Bucks County, to Joseph Turner, partner in the firm of Allen & Turner of Philadelphia. On September 10, 1735, Turner assigned the property to his business partner, William Allen. The tract was first surveyed on November 23, 1736. A list of eighteenth-century land warrants and patents in the Lehigh County Historical Society's *Proceedings* for 1950 show two warrants were issued to William Allen, one on February 24, 1737, for 765 acres, and another on February 28, 1739, for 200 acres.

A warrant was an official order of the colonial deputy surveyor to initiate a survey of a piece of land described in it. On August 8, 1739, Allen was granted a patent, which gave him "full, clear release and title" on both properties. It was here that Allentown began.

The land had been a popular hunting ground with the Native-American Lenape tribe, who regularly burned it off to make it easier to hunt small game. Sometime in 1739 or 1740 Allen built a two-story cabin on that property for hunting, fishing, and entertaining. Frequent visitors included several mayors of Philadelphia (a post Allen once held), James Hamilton, an acting colonial governor who was his brother-in-law, and John Penn, the governor of the colony and Penn heir who was his son-in-law.

The cabin was located on what is now Jordan Street, behind Central Catholic High School. Allen named it Trout Hall, after a fictional English inn mentioned in *The Compleat Angler*, a popular seventeenth-century tale about the joys of fishing. Its author was Izaak Walton, still considered the "godfather" of the sport.

"My fishing place," as Allen sometimes called it, was first shown on a map in 1753 by David Schultz, a surveyor laying out the King's Highway between Easton and Reading. On his map Schultz called it "William Allen's house," placing it "north of the road and west of Jordan Creek." According to Charles Rhoads Roberts' *Anniversary History of Lehigh County*, "it was the first building erected on the tracts which are now included in the areas of Allentown." There is little known of it. Roberts records that the foundations of the first Trout Hall were visible as late as 1845, when they were removed to widen Jordan Street.

Lynford Lardner, a wealthy Philadelphian, relation by marriage of the Penn family and friend of Allen, was also attracted to the future Lehigh County. An avid hunter and fisherman, on August 8, 1745, Lardner acquired a land warrant and built a hunting lodge that he called Grouse Hall. It was a large one-story structure roughly where Crest Plaza Shopping Center is today.

Roberts, who saw the remains of Grouse Hall in 1909 and wrote about it that year in the Lehigh County Historical Society's *Proceedings*, called it a "shooting box"—a term still used in England and Scotland for a simple building where well-to-do sportsmen retire to smoke a pipe, "share a glass," and tell tales of their sporting exploits while the servants prepared that day's game for dinner. Roberts observed that Grouse Hall had a hearth large enough to roast an entire deer. Part of the 195 acres of Lardner's estate became "Springwood," General Harry C. Trexler's country property which is today Trexler Memorial Park.

Some theorize that because Grouse Hall was white, local residents or land agents called the township "Whitehall" after Lardner's shooting box, or that it was named after Whitehall in England. Others suggest the name may be derived from a place name in Switzerland that had been home to early settlers in the area.

After 1750 Allen began withdrawing from some of Allen & Turner's more risky overseas ventures and aggressively buying even more land. Economic historian Augustine Nigro, in his 2001 online article "William Allen and the Search for Economic Security," notes that with land "Allen found a safer business arena when he turned his gaze away from the Old World and looked West to the heart of the New World. By abandoning mercantile trade and entering land speculation, Allen consolidated his business ventures from a global to a much more controllable, regional focus." Allen's commercial success, Nigro writes, was "not an end in itself but a means to an end, gentlemanly retirement," as landed gentry.

In a letter to Thomas Penn, Proprietor of Pennsylvania and son of William Penn, which appears excerpted and undated in Matthew Henry's 1860 *History of the Lehigh Valley*, James Logan told of Allen's methods for acquiring the best new land for the lowest price.

Allen, writes Logan, reached "private agreements … with surveyors who traversed the wild lands of Northampton County" offering them "douceurs" (a French word literally translated as "sweet things," i.e. gifts or bribes), if they would tell him where the best land was so he could buy it before the price went up. "As persons desirous of purchasing good tracts would purchase from him in preference to all others," Logan wrote, Allen "became the wealthiest of the land speculators."

Only after the French and Indian War ended in 1760 with a British victory did Allen feel the region was stable enough to support a town. He assumed the Lehigh River would become a trade route and his town a trading center. Allen had a plat map drawn up, a survey that divided the property into lots for a town he called Northampton. The exact date is unknown, but it was probably sometime early in 1762. Almost from its founding local people found it impossible not to bless the little town with its founder's name.

Although officially named Northampton until 1838, it was popularly known as Allentown far earlier. The earliest known recorded reference was on October 23, 1764. The Moravian diary keeper in Emmaus noted a local woman was returning from Bethlehem with her husband when her services as a midwife were suddenly required to help bring into the world a new resident of "Mr. Allen's little town."

Allen's plat map covered the section of the future city from what is today Fourth to Tenth streets, between Union and Liberty streets. There were 756 neatly drawn building lots, almost all of them 60 feet in width and 230 feet in depth. All the sidewalks were 60 feet wide except on Hamilton and Seventh, where they were 80 feet wide. Seventh Street, the main north-south road, was called Allen Street on the map, and Hamilton was the main east-west highway as it is today.

Like a proud housing developer today, Allen named the streets for his six surviving children. Fifth Street was Margaret; Sixth was William; and Eighth was James. Ninth was named for daughter Ann; Linden was Andrew; and Walnut was John. Those family names were largely replaced in the early to mid-nineteenth century by tree names.

Allen also included his business associates and friends. Hamilton Street was named for James Hamilton, Allen's brother-in-law, a wealthy land owner and twice colonial governor of Pennsylvania, 1748 to 1754 and again 1759 to 1763. His father, Andrew Hamilton, had been an attorney and is best known for successfully defending John Peter Zenger, a New York printer, in a libel case that safeguarded freedom of the press.

Chew Street was named for Benjamin Chew, an attorney and former Chief Justice of the Pennsylvania Supreme Court. As a young man he had studied law with Andrew Hamilton. Chew's second wife, Elizabeth Oswald, was the niece and heir to William Allen's business partner, Joseph Turner. This added to his family's considerable fortune. When the troubles with England broke out Chew spoke out forcefully against King and Parliament. But as a pacifist he opposed the violence of the American Revolution. Some accused him of being lukewarm to the cause of independence, and he fled with his family to a home in rural Delaware. They returned to Philadelphia in 1783 after the peace treaty between Britain and America was signed. A lifelong friend of George Washington, Chew later provided pro-bono aid in writing both the U.S. Constitution and later the amendments known as the Bill of Rights.

Gordon Street honors Major General Patrick Gordon, a professional soldier from Aberdeen, Scotland. After a successful military career with the British Army in Europe, Gordon served as Pennsylvania's acting governor from 1726 to 1736, and was widely recognized as efficient and fair-minded. In the early part of his governorship Gordon helped break up a gang of fur traders who were illegally selling rum to Native Americans and cheating them out of their furs in what is now Exeter Township, Berks County.

Before leaving the area, Gordon appointed three men to keep the peace. One of them was Mordecai Lincoln, a farmer and blacksmith. With him was his brother Abraham, the first in the Lincoln family to have that name. Mordecai Lincoln's great-great grandson, Abraham Lincoln, was the sixteenth president of the United States.

Gordon is buried beside his wife Isabella in Philadelphia's Christ Church Cemetery. Their sole surviving child, a daughter born while they were in America, was named Philadelphia Gordon.

Turner Street recognizes Allen's business partner, Joseph Turner. Their firm, Allen & Turner, was among the most successful in the colonies. Turner, who went to sea at age 14, had worked for Allen's father as captain of the firm's chief trading vessel, the brig Lively. He wore a pirate-like black eye patch and was known for his "salty" language. Turner had large land investments in what is now Lehigh County.

Exactly when the future Allentown went from the inked lines and names on the surveyor's map to stone-and-mortar reality is unknown. Evidence suggests it was sometime in the spring of 1762.

That March the Northampton County Court received a petition to build a road from Jacob Collier's mill in Whitehall Township to "a new town to be erected on Part of a Tract of Land Belonging to the Honorable William Allen." This "to be erected" suggests that building had not yet begun.

The petitioners asked their "worships" to be "pleased to appoint six proper persons who are in no ways interested in the said Road," to oversee its construction. Apparently there was concern about conflicts of interest even then.

On June 22, 1762, the six "proper persons," William Craig, Stophel Waggoner, John Tool, Paul Balliet, Thomas Hunsicker, and George Rex, reported the road "to the new town called Northampton," which ran on what is now Seventh Street south to the Little Lehigh Creek.

On June 28, 1762, Allen's agent James Burd wrote to his employer of Northampton Town's progress:

I had a letter the other day from Mr. Klotz [his assistant] and he informs me that my house goes very well and that there is ten more houses building in Northampton.

According to a local census done at the end of 1765, there were 29 houses in Allentown, and 35 lots had been sold. The inhabitants had 15 horses and 31 cows. By 1768 the number of houses had increased to 36. Among the residents was Mordecai Martin, the first known Jewish resident of what became Lehigh County. But it would not be until the 1880s, over 100 years later, that Jewish worship services were regularly held in the city.

In 1767 "John Ritter, J.G. Enex and others" petitioned Governor John Penn, William Allen's son-in-law, for the right to build a Catholic church in Allentown "whereby they may have the peaceable and quiet enjoyment of their religion." The nearest church was at Goshenhoppen, Berks County. Petitioner "John Ritter" was probably Father John Baptist de Ritter, its priest.

Penn rejected the petition. Pennsylvania was open to all religions, but the issue was more about state than church. Catholic France, England's long-time rival for the control of America, was the enemy. Native Americans, allied to the French, were blamed on the Pennsylvania frontier for the violence of the time. Ninety years would pass before Allentown's Immaculate Conception, the first Catholic Church in Lehigh County, was opened in 1857.

Among the houses already in place in 1763 was that of David Deshler, the owner of a saw mill and grist mill on the Little Lehigh Creek at what is now Seventh and Union streets. It is believed to be the first mill built in Allentown. Deshler was among the most affluent members of the community. Allentown's 1762 tax list, its first, shows he paid nine pounds in taxes, more than any of the twelve other taxpayers in the community. During the Revolution he would play a significant role as a leader of the local militia and a commissary of supplies for the army. He was later a delegate to the Pennsylvania Convention that ratified the U.S. Constitution, and helped win support for it among Pennsylvania Germans.

Another house was that of Peter Rhoads, later a judge and prominent official. Built near what became the northeast corner of Seventh and Linden streets, it was a two-story stone structure that was to remain relatively intact until 1917, when two large picture windows were placed in the front to convert it to an automobile showroom. The building was being used by a dry cleaner in 1967 when it was torn down to expand a parking lot.

The growth of Northampton/Allentown slowed in October, 1763. Responding to a theft of their trade goods at a local tavern near Bethlehem over the previous summer, several Native Americans staged a raid on it and some surrounding farms. This led to fighting between them and the local militia that left some fifteen settlers, including women and children, dead.

Fearful that this raid was the start of a general uprising, refugees poured into Northampton town. Rev. Jacob Joseph Roth, a Lutheran clergyman, in an October 10 letter to acting governor Hamilton, noted that on October 8 "as I was preaching, the people came in Such Numbers, that I was obliged to quit my Sarmon [sermon]."

A quick check of the resources of the community with James Burd disclosed to Roth

George Taylor house, Catasauqua

that "the inhabitants had neither Gons [guns] Powder nor Lead to Defend themselves." He added that a company for mutual defense had been formed with George Wolf and Abraham Rinker selected as officers. In his own letter to Hamilton on October 17, Burd stated that "in the Town of Northampton ... there was only 4 guns, three of which unfit for use & the enemy within 4 miles of the place."

Hamilton acted quickly and ordered the raising of an 800-man defense force. This proved to be unnecessary. The Indians had made their point. They retreated into the wilderness of the Wyoming Valley, never to be seen again. But fears lingered and Northampton/Allentown's population growth slowed to a trickle.

The church where Roth had been preaching was St. Paul's, a log structure at the northwest corner of Church and Walnut streets. It was then a union church and the Lutherans shared the space with a German Reformed congregation, now Zion's Reformed UCC. In 1773 the Reformed congregation moved to a stone sanctuary on Hamilton Street. St. Paul's congregation remained at the log church until the 1790s when, thanks to a donation of land by a member of the Allen family, they built their own church at Eighth and Walnut streets.

The south to north pattern of settlement in what became Lehigh County can be followed in the establishment of townships. It began in 1734 with Milford Township, at a time when present-day Lehigh and Northampton counties were still part of Bucks County. In 1737 this township was split into Upper Milford (in future Lehigh County) and Lower Milford in Bucks County. Lehigh County's Lower Milford Township dates from the division of Upper Milford in 1853. The original Macungie Township was founded in 1742, as was the original Saucon Township. Upper Saucon and Lower Saucon were created in 1743.

The original Heidelberg Township came along nine years later in 1752. It was followed by Lynn, Weisenberg, Whitehall, Salisbury, and Lowhill, which were all founded in 1753. These were townships as they stood until well after the American Revolution.

The 1760s were notable in the future Lehigh County for the building of two large homes by two prominent men: George Taylor and James Allen.

Taylor, an iron maker, had risen from the rank of indentured servant to owning Bucks County's Durham Iron Furnace. In 1767 Taylor purchased a property of 331 acres for 700 pounds from William Allen, who was acting with power of attorney as agent for the property's owner, John Patterson of London. Its official title was the Manor of Chawton; it was in what is now Catasauqua. On it Taylor had erected a Georgian-style mansion. He lived there for a number of years before returning to Durham in 1774 to supervise the iron works, then gearing up for the American Revolution.

Some local historians claim that the Manor at Chawton was primarily a summer home for Taylor. Others state it was his full-time residence. Taylor sold the Catasauqua property in March 1776, shortly before going to the Second Continental Congress, where he would sign the Declaration of Independence. One of its subsequent owners was one of Lehigh County's most prominent citizens, wealthy miller and businessman David Deshler. Today, after passing through a series of owners, Taylor's Catasauqua home, a National Historic Landmark since 1971, is run as a house museum by the borough of Catasauqua.

On January 5, 1767, William Allen gave his third son, James, 3,338 acres and 114 perches of Lehigh County land for a wedding present. In 1770 young Allen established there a country home he named Trout Hall, after his father's fishing cabin. A stone three-story manor house set in a 764-acre private estate, Trout Hall was designed as a summer mansion. The remainder of the land was rented to tenant farmers for eventual purchase.

It took the American Revolution to bring out the long-simmering tensions between the Allens and their Pennsylvania German tenants. At the start, William Allen and his family supported the cause of seeking justice against King and Parliament. As early as the Stamp Act Crisis of 1765, the Allens were pushing against the actions of the British government. The act, passed by Parliament, required that all paper items, from legal documents to playing cards, bear a stamp showing that a tax on it had been paid. With the Allen family's extensive legal and financial transactions such a tax would soon become costly.

On October 9, 1765, Deborah Franklin wrote to her husband Benjamin, then in London acting as an agent for Pennsylvania, that riots against the Stamp Act, whose passage he had supported, were breaking out in Philadelphia. Looking out her window she could see a familiar figure leading them. "Jemmy [Jimmy] Allen is out in the street spirit'en up the mob."

In 1774 meetings were held at William Allen's home to plan how to address Britain's actions. John Adams was among those present. But the Allens could not bring themselves to make the final break with Britain to which, as judges and attorneys, they had sworn an oath of loyalty. They also feared that independence might call into question their legal rights to the vast amounts of land they owned.

In their feelings the Allen family was far from alone. John Adams estimated only one-third of colonists supported the cause for independence. The rest either declared their support for England or wanted to avoid taking sides. While many Americans after 1783 resigned

themselves to the American victory, an estimated 80,000 to 100,000 fled to England, Canada, or other places to live under the British flag.

Fearing personal harm because of their opposition to independence, Andrew Allen, James's older brother and the colony's attorney general, and his sisters fled to the protection of the British Army in New York in late 1776. At the close of the Revolution they became expatriates in England.

Young William resigned his commission in the Continental Army and formed a regiment of Tories, the Pennsylvania Loyalists, to fight beside the British. Much to his disgust they were not allowed to fight in Pennsylvania but ordered to Florida to fight Spain, America's ally. Here large numbers died from disease. At war's end Allen would join his brother and sisters in England, dying there in 1833.

James Allen, on first hearing about his brother forming a Loyalist regiment, admitted in his diary it was probably true, yet "I cannot conceive how my father would consent to it, as he looked with abhorrence on the thought: nor that my brother should engage in it against his will."

William Allen, Sr., adopted a neutral stance. He retreated to his country estate at Mt. Airy. His son James did the same and occupied Trout Hall with his family. He was determined, he wrote in his diary, to be "a calm spectator" of the conflict. But for most of the fiercely pro-independence Pennsylvania Germans who lived in western Northampton County, James Allen's stand was tantamount to being in league with the British. In their eyes, after July 4, 1776, anyone who did not support independence was a Tory.

As early as May 27, 1776, a group of 900 local Pennsylvania-German militiamen headed by John Siegfried, a tavern keeper and ferry boat operator from Whitehall Township, gathered at the farm of Lorenz Guth to declare their support for independence. Siegfried was later to lead many of these same men in battle.

"It is quite obvious that at the outset of hostilities most Americans were matter-of-factly loyal to the Crown, wanted to be left alone, and certainly did not want to get chewed up in a rough-and-tumble fight," writes historian D.W. Meinig. "It is the special agony of civil wars that such indifference cannot be allowed by the contending forces."

It was into this maelstrom that James Allen and his family descended when they arrived at Trout Hall on June 16, 1776.

Volunteers from the 6th Pennsylvania Regiment, a living history organization, honor soldiers buried in west Bethlehem. November 2011. Every November the DAR and SAR hold a ceremony for Revolutionary War veterans at the Tomb of the Unknown Soldier, where over 500 soldiers were buried in 1776 and 1777. The tomb is on First Avenue in west Bethlehem, high above the Monocacy Creek. In 1776, sick and wounded soldiers were moved from the general hospital of the army at Morristown, NJ, to Bethlehem and other locations in the interior of Pennsylvania. In 1777, wounded soldiers from the battles of Princeton, Brandywine, and Germantown were sent to Bethlehem. Army doctors, assisted by the Moravians, cared for the soldiers in the Bethlehem hospital. Many of the deaths in 1776 and early 1777 were due to the effects of exposure to the weather during the trip to Bethlehem in horse-drawn wagons. Most of the soldiers wounded at Brandywine and Germantown died from "putrid fever," which swept through the overcrowded hospital. These deaths far outnumbered deaths from battle wounds. (Ed Redding)

Allen's diary gives a fascinating account of his life there from 1776 to 1778. It includes raids on his property and in one case an attack on his wife and daughter's carriage by the militia. As the women screamed, soldiers ran bayonets through the carriage's side; only the intervention of Col. David Deshler, the most influential leader of the patriot cause locally, prevented far worse things from happening. Allen wrote of one militia officer, a Colonel Boehm, who "assured me, that the soldiers were ripe for doing some violence to my house which he had with difficulty prevented."

When the British occupied Philadelphia from September of 1777 to August of 1778, the future Lehigh County was thrust into a strategic role in the conflict. The Continental Congress was forced to flee to York, which became the temporary capital of the United

States. The Reading Road, the King's Highway between Reading and Easton, became part of a chain of roads that linked the region to New York and New England.

The Moravian diary keepers at Bethlehem, who kept extensive records, noted that among the leaders of the Revolution who passed through the region on the road were John Adams and his cousin Samuel Adams, John Hancock, George Washington, and Martha Washington—called Lady Washington in the diary. She had traveled the King's Highway in a coach with an escort of officers after a visit to her husband.

The Reading Road passed James Allen's front door. He noted in his diary that it had become "the most travelled in America." In November of 1777 John Adams, seeking refuge from a snowstorm, stopped briefly at Trout Hall. Allen noted in his diary that Adams told him attempts to reconcile with Britain were fruitless and foolish and that the issue of independence was "unalterably settled."

Other "guests" of James Allen were less popular with local patriots. In November, 1776, a group of British officers, POWS captured in a failed invasion of Canada and passing through the Lehigh Valley on their way to New York to be exchanged for American officers captured at the battle of Long Island that summer, were, in Allen's words, "entertained" at Trout Hall. Circumstantial evidence suggests that among them may have been Major John André, who was later hanged as a spy in 1780 for his role in the treason of Benedict Arnold.

The most significant local event of the Revolution locally was when Philadelphia's State House bell was hidden with other bells from the city in Allentown during the British occupation of 1777–1778. Congress, fearing the bells would be melted down into bullets by the British, ordered them moved.

The bells arrived in September 1777 in wagons of Pennsylvania German farmers who often sold produce in the city. They were placed under the floor of the German Reformed Church, today Zion's Reformed UCC, then serving as a military hospital for American soldiers wounded at the battle of Germantown. The bells were not removed until the end of the British occupation in the summer of 1778.

In 1812 the story of the bells' journey was largely preserved in the strong oral tradition of the Frederick Leaser and John Jacob Mickley families who had taken part in moving them. Its first known appearance in writing was not until the 1820s in a speech by Allentown attorney Robert Wright, Sr. Many years later, when the State House bell became an American icon as the Liberty Bell, it provided a significant link for Lehigh County citizens in their ancestors' role in the struggle for independence.

James Allen was never to live to see the end of the war. He died in Philadelphia, probably of tuberculosis, on September 19, 1778, while planning to take his family to France and sit out the war there. He was 37. Both he and his father William, who died in 1780 at age 79, lie

in unknown and apparently unmarked graves. Almost all of their property was confiscated by the state of Pennsylvania because they were Loyalists. Some was restored to the family after the Revolution.

Although it was almost thirty years since its end, there were still many men and women in the Lehigh County of 1812 who had personal memories of the American Revolution and bore on their body wounds, and in some cases shrapnel, from that struggle.

Fries's Rebellion

The only major national event to disturb the general rural tranquility of the region after the Revolution and before the creation of Lehigh County was the anti-tax revolt known as the Fries Rebellion or the Hot Water War of 1799.

It began in the late 1790s when Revolutionary France and England were at war. To meet the threat of a possible war on the new United States, American policy makers decided to increase the size of the U.S. Navy. The administration of John Adams asked for and Congress passed a new tax to pay for building ships.

When the government tax men arrived to assess property, they were met with deep suspicion and hostility. "The assessors exceeded their directive and counted the windows in houses," writes Macungie historian Dale Eck. "Counting of windows was not part of the assessment, but it raised suspicion that it was being done for the purpose of some future taxation."

The Pennsylvania-German farmers and small merchants of the Lehigh Valley were distrustful. Historian Paul Douglas Newman, in his 2004 book *Fries's Rebellion: The Enduring Struggle for the American Revolution*, notes this was the first time the federal government had decided to impose a direct tax on the population.

Some historians suggest that the language barrier played a role in the failure of the local folks to understand the tax. Newman believes that the Pennsylvania Germans were perfectly aware of what was going on but were justified in taking action to preserve their fundamental liberties. He sees it as an example of the political struggle that led to the emerging "popular" Democratic-Republican party in reaction to the "aristocratic" Federalists. Interestingly, before this issue arose many local voters, because of their total devotion to Revolutionary hero George Washington, supported the Federalists.

It was John Fries, a tavern keeper and auctioneer from Charlestown, now Quakertown, Bucks County, who led a loosely organized group of local men against the federal tax assessors. Millerstown/Macungie was the focal point of the tax revolt locally. Millerstown, founded in 1776, was the second-largest community in the future Lehigh County. Established by Peter Miller on 150 acres along the north-south King's High Road from Philadelphia, it was designated as a location where militia training took place after the Pennsylvania Militia was organized in 1777.

David Schaeffer was the leader of the rebellion in Millerstown. One of the most famous figures of the rebellion was Schaeffer's wife. When the assessors arrived at her door she got out of a bed where she had recently given birth to a child and poured boiling hot water and the contents of chamber pots down on them. This inspired other women to do the same and gave the revolt its distinctive nickname, the Hot Water War.

Not everyone in Macungie opposed the tax. Rev Jacob van Buskirk, the first Lutheran minister born, educated and ordained in America, was pastor of Zion Lehigh Church, the owner of a tannery, and a Federalist. At the height of the rebellion he was sitting at home with his family, a wife and ten children, when a bullet came whizzing through his window. No one was hurt.

After hearing that nineteen tax resisters were being held at Bethlehem's Sun Inn by the federal marshal, Fries and about 140 men, many of them members of the Millerstown Militia, marched to free them. After successful and peaceful negotiations with the marshal, the resisters were released. Fries and his men then dispersed and returned to their homes.

Most historians believe that Fries and his followers felt they had made their point and at no time did they think they had committed a disloyal act. But ultra-conservative Federalist politicians, a faction of the party led by Adams's rival Alexander Hamilton, thought the president had caved in to sedition. They accused Fries and his farmers of being in league with Revolutionary France.

In response, Adams called out the state militia units of Philadelphia, Bucks, Montgomery, Chester, and Lancaster counties, over 600 infantry and 320 cavalry, to put down the now non-existent rebellion and bring Fries and others to justice. Fries was apprehended when his little dog, Whiskey, led the soldiers by his barking to his master's hiding place.

The others were also rounded up and taken to Philadelphia.

When one tax rebel asked a Federalist magistrate what his fate would be he received this icy reply, "In a fortnight [two weeks] the Circuit Court will meet and you will be tried, and in a fortnight after, will be in hell, sir."

The prosecutor was Samuel Sitgreaves of Easton, a Federalist, Northampton County's Congressman, and a backer of Hamilton. He was also an expert on the field of treason and impeachment.

There were two Fries treason trials. The first was declared a mistrial. The second led to convictions for Fries and the other tax rebels. "It is the judgment of the law that you be hanged by the neck until dead," Federalist Judge

Samuel Chase solemnly intoned, "and may God have mercy on your souls."

President Adams decided they were misguided innocents and pardoned them all. The pardon came too late for David Schaeffer, who died in jail of yellow fever along with fellow Macungie resident and tax rebel Michael Schmoyer. Schaeffer's wife, the icon of the Hot Water War, is believed to be the same person who was photographed as an old woman in 1855, when she was known as Grandy or Granny Miller.

In the election of 1800 the Democratic Republicans swept the Federalists out of power in both the White House and Congress. They were never to hold national office again. Sitgreaves, at least in part for his role as prosecutor in the Fries trial, was defeated.

The War of 1812

With the end of the Fries Rebellion, western Northampton County returned to its quiet role as breadbasket of the United States. That peace was shattered by the outbreak of war with Great Britain in 1812.

Although no battles were fought here, the War of 1812 had a larger significance for Lehigh County. This was the first national conflict in which local militia members acted as a

part of a military force under the banner of the new county. On May 12, 1812, when war clouds were gathering, Governor Simon Snyder called for militia troops. By July 1, 1812, 462 volunteers from Lehigh County were enrolled.

The exact number of Lehigh County men who served in the War of 1812 is unknown. But it is estimated by Roberts in the 1912 *Anniversary History of Lehigh County* to have been between 600 and 800. Most were assigned to Fort Snyder, fortifications at Marcus Hook on the Delaware River roughly eighteen miles south of Philadelphia.

The closest the war came to Lehigh County was in the summer of 1814. A British fleet was sighted in the Chesapeake Bay and concern spread that Washington or Baltimore would be a target. Governor Snyder feared Philadelphia would follow.

The cannon at Marcus Hook were never fired in anger. After burning the White House and the Capitol Building, the invaders were defeated at Baltimore. As they retreated, the body of their commander, General Robert Ross, killed by an American sniper, was preserved in a barrel of Jamaican rum for future burial.

Philadelphia was saved. But not everyone returned home. On November 30, 1814, the Lehigh County men at Marcus Hook, their numbers reduced by dysentery and other diseases from 600 to 400, were ordered to Philadelphia. They began returning to Lehigh County on December 5. On December 11, 1814, a service of thanksgiving was held for them at Allentown's St. Paul's Lutheran Church.

On February 28, 1815, word reached Lehigh County of General Andrew Jackson's defeat of a British Army on January 5, 1815, at New Orleans. Knowledge that the war had been over since December 1814 didn't dim the local celebration that greeted the news of Jackson's victory with a torchlight procession led by a brass band and lots of cannon fire.

As the cannon smoke dissipated, tranquility returned to Lehigh County. The county was still almost entirely agricultural, although no longer on the American frontier. As for Allentown, in 1840 historian Isaac Daniel Rupp, himself a Pennsylvania German, used these words to describe it: "Inhabited by a few wealthy and unenterprising Germans, and cut off for many years from the different post routes, by the influence of the neighboring towns, it remained inactive a long time."

The County Courthouse

Despite Rupp's image of the area as a Rip Van Winkle snoozing away its existence, things were changing. In 1816 Lehigh County's judiciary moved from temporary quarters at George Savitz's tavern, where they had been meeting since 1812, into their new $24,936.08 courthouse at the northwest corner of Fifth and Hamilton streets.

Proudly, county residents admired the Federal-style building modeled after the Lycoming County courthouse, which was in turn based on the Dauphin County courthouse in Harrisburg where the state legislature was meeting until the capitol building was finished. A committee of three prominent local citizens had gone to Williamsport, Lycoming County's seat, and returned with a glowing report of that building's elegant design.

At last Lehigh County had public buildings to reflect its status. Along with the courthouse, $8,420 had been spent in 1813 on a county jail in the 500 block of Linden Street. But change beyond anything anybody in the county could have imagined in 1816 was just over the horizon.

*David Thomas, the Welshman who built the first furnaces in Catasauqua for the
Crane Iron Company and in 1854 founded the Thomas Iron Company.*

CHAPTER TWO

Lehigh County 1812–1912

Charles Rhoads Roberts, a descendant of Judge Peter Rhoads, one of the founding fathers of Lehigh County, was a man of strong views, particularly where local history was concerned.

For him, as secretary of the new Lehigh County Historical Society and editor of the *Anniversary History of Lehigh County*—the official county centennial work published in 1914—it was about the struggles and triumphs of the early pioneer families, many of which were his ancestors. These sturdy Pennsylvania Germans were his people.

Like many Americans, Roberts apparently saw himself as fighting a rear-guard action to protect the past. Seeing immigrants pouring into America from Eastern Europe and Italy, and watching an industrial age change more and more of the country they knew, they thought of themselves as defenders and preservers of a way of life that was under siege.

Perhaps because of this, Lehigh County's African-American residents and the recent arrivals from Eastern Europe and the Middle East were given only a passing mention in Robert's history of the county. More-obscure ethnic groups didn't even get that.

In 1885, for example, the Allentown city directory recorded the arrival of Sammy Lee, who opened a Chinese laundry at 20 North Eighth Street. Whatever his actual Chinese name, he was in all probability Lehigh County's first Asian resident. By 1910, along with the laundry, Lee was running the American-Chinese Restaurant at 524 Hamilton Street, almost certainly the county's first Asian eatery. Entries in later directories suggest family members, apparently his brothers, had joined him here.

Coal, Railroads, Iron

The real changes that would lead people from all over the world to come to Lehigh County started in the second decade of the nineteenth century. A transportation revolution that altered Lehigh County in fundamental ways, big and small, began in the 1820s with farseeing Philadelphia businessmen Josiah White and Erskine Hazard. Among the first to understand the importance of anthracite coal as an industrial and home-heating fuel,

The Lehigh Navigation and river, across from the Geissinger (formerly Jennings) farm, two miles west of Bethlehem. Rufus Grider, 1851. (Moravian Archives)

they created the Lehigh Canal, a waterway that ran from the coal regions of Carbon County to Easton, to bring that coal to markets. The entrepreneurial dream of Thomas Penn and William Allen of using the local rivers as a commercial highway had come true. Previously isolated by poor roads and hills, Lehigh County was open to the rest of America in ways that it never been before.

The work force that dug the Lehigh Canal for White and Hazard was, as on most American canals, largely poor Irish immigrants. Anne Royall, a popular travel writer of the day, had these relatively sympathetic comments to make as she observed the Irish while waiting one morning for her stage coach to Allentown as she was passing through Mauch Chunk, now Jim Thorpe, in 1828:

> The poor fellows, fleeing from oppression to be free, grow rich in our country and make a short life and a merry one of it. I have been informed that they generally live eighteen months after coming to this country, and work and drink most of the time … In many instances, on some of the canals, they die so fast, that they are thrown into the ground from four to six together, without coffins.

On July 4, 1840, David Thomas, a Welsh ironmaster brought to America by White and Hazard, began production of iron at the Lehigh Crane Iron Company at Catasauqua, the first commercially successful iron furnace in North America to use anthracite coal to smelt iron. Thomas had been reluctant to leave Great Britain until his wife persuaded him that his five sons would have opportunities for a much better life in America than in Wales.

Widely recognized as the start of America's industrial revolution, the first puffs of smoke from Lehigh Crane's iron furnace changed Lehigh County forever. Furnaces using the same hot-blast technology as at Lehigh Crane were soon built in numerous locations in the country. Iron became, for the first time, abundant and affordable. This led to revolutions in agriculture and transportation. New generations of farm equipment could now be mass-produced, unleashing the imaginations of local inventors. Transportation began its transformation from horse and buggy to the iron horse as investors extended railroads throughout the country.

All along the Lehigh River, from Parryville just north of Lehigh County to Easton and Glendon in Northampton County, stacks were rising along the Lehigh Canal. Canal boats loaded with anthracite brought their cargo to the furnaces, while farmers transformed their fertile farm fields into iron mines and limestone quarries, carrying the raw materials in wagons drawn by teams of horses to the new industrial towns. While many of the managers and directors of the new iron companies had British backgrounds, many also were Pennsylvania Germans, as were most of the workers—farm boys who moved into the new towns to work in the new industry.

Pig beds in the casthouse floor at the Macungie Furnace, c 1885. Iron flowed out of the furnace and into the pig molds in the sand on the floor.

While industries were rapidly developing in Lehigh County during the 1840s, two major events took place that shocked county residents. One was the collapse in 1843 of the Northampton Bank; the second was the Great Ascension Day Fire of 1848 that destroyed Allentown's business district.

The Northampton Bank

The Northampton Bank was Lehigh County's first major financial institution. Founded in 1814, it opened that August on North Seventh Street in Allentown, a few doors down from Hamilton Street, and occupied a two-story stone building that had been the store of Peter Snyder. It was a small-scale operation by the standards of Philadelphia, but served the needs of local officials, who deposited the county's tax money there. Peter Rhoads, Jr., the son of Judge Peter Rhoads, ran it quietly and conservatively for twenty-two years.

John Rice, a member of a leading Moravian family in Bethlehem, was its cashier, the man who ran the bank's day-to-day business. At that time there was no national paper currency. The federal government minted only gold and silver coins. But banks, from the lordly Bank of the United States that operated out of a classical Greek temple in Philadelphia to the modest converted store home of the Northampton Bank, had the right to print paper money and that was the chief circulating medium of business. It was assumed that the bankers would be careful with this privilege and not print more money than they had gold and silver to cover. There was, however, no law commanding them to do so.

As records for the bank no longer exist it is difficult to know what Rice was thinking.

Apparently, like a great many small-town American bankers of the 1830s and '40s, he got caught up in the speculative wave of the day. Economic historian Edward Pessen notes that "large and quick profits" were the chief reason why banks' charters were sought from state legislatures. The way to make those profits, he adds, "was to invest as little capital as possible, issue as much paper money as they could get away with and speculate ceaselessly."

Among John Rice's major speculations was lumber, with his brother Owen, who managed the funds of the Moravian Church, which had large investments in sawmills and timber up and down the Lehigh Canal. In fact it was the development of the canal that opened up access to millions of feet of virgin timber. To fuel his speculation Rice used the banknotes of the Northampton Bank.

In1840, with the sudden death of bank president Jacob Eckert, Rice became the president of the Northampton Bank. By then he was so widely trusted that churches asked him to manage their money and widows made him trustees of their property. It was Rice's misfortune to be there when the music stopped in the game of musical chairs that was the American economy. The Panic of 1837 was already smashing one small speculative bank after another. In England investors were refusing to buy any more Lehigh Canal bonds, and a massive flood on the Lehigh Canal in 1841 wiped out many of John and Owen Rice's timber operations.

John Rice spent most of the year of 1842 attempting by fair means or foul to borrow money from brokers in New York and Philadelphia to keep himself and the bank afloat. Arguments among the heirs of those who had loaned money to John Rice were still attempting to collect through the courts on his IOUs. The house of cards collapsed on March 23, 1843, when the bank's directors claimed it was closing for a month. It never opened its doors again.

An investigation was launched and it was quickly discovered that there was little but loose change in Northampton Bank's vault. Lehigh County's tax revenue was gone, although eventually some of it was recovered. The funds of the First Presbyterian Church and all those trusting widows were gone. John Rice was burned in effigy in Center Square, but managed to escape to New York. There he would live until the late 1860s. Stricken by a stroke, Rice spent his final years unable to clothe or feed himself.

Lehigh County had barely recovered from the collapse of the Northampton Bank when on June 1, 1848, another disaster struck.

On that Ascension Day, traditionally a day off in the Pennsylvania-German community, two stable boys on North Hall Street, an alley between Hamilton and Linden streets, who had been forced to work that day, so the story goes, decided to get back at their boss by starting a fire.

This might not have amounted to much if there had not been a drought, and a stiff

Cutting face at the Blue Mountain Slate Quarry near Slatington.

wind had not been blowing. The flames quickly spread from the stable to Hamilton Street. It turned the buildings on the north side of the street between Seventh and Eighth into a sheet of flame. Houses, businesses, and a hotel burned rapidly. The bucket-brigade firefighting system of the time could not keep up with it.

The major loss was the newly completed Odd Fellows building, on the south side of Hamilton where the downtown campus of the Donley Center of the Lehigh Carbon Community College is today. From the Rough and Ready Oyster bar in the basement to the upper-floor meeting rooms, just completed at a cost of $6,000 the building was total loss, and there was no fire insurance.

The next day a committee was formed and the Allentown business district began to rise again. Three weeks after the fire ended a local newspaper was reporting, "several buildings are going up, the rubbish is being cleared away and preparations are being made for the rebuilding of every house in the burnt district."

An Industrial Mecca

The failure of the Northampton Bank and the Ascension Day fire were events that stood out as local disasters, but they did not interrupt the continuing evolution of the county into an industrial mecca. Immigrants were starting to come in increasing numbers to the county, having heard of the opportunities being opened by exploitation of natural resources.

Slate, discovered earlier but not exploited until water transportation became possible, brought experienced quarrymen from Wales and Cornwall to Lehigh County. Slate started

Looking north from Center Square in 1876, after the business center was rebuilt following the Ascension Day fire and before the monument was built.

to be quarried in earnest at several locations in Lehigh County in the 1840s. Kern's Mill, an early name for Slatington, was the early center of the industry and remained so during all of the nineteenth century. The Lehigh Valley deposits of slate were of high quality and were used for roofing slates, school slates and blackboards, as well as domestic furnishings and billiard tables. At the peak of slate quarrying in 1910 Slatington and the nearby communities of Emerald and Slatedale had twenty-five quarries and ten finishing factories that together employed 1,400 men. Only one quarry remains today, the Manhattan Quarry in Slatedale, operated by the Penn Big Bed Slate Company.

The North Pennsylvania Railroad grade, now abandoned, is being converted to a rail trail for walkers, bikers, and cross-country skiers. It will extend from Coopersburg to Hellertown. This is in the Upper Saucon Township section. (Upper Saucon Township)

During the 1850s railroads came to Lehigh County. First was the Lehigh Valley Railroad. Created by Asa Packer, a former carpenter and canal-boat captain, it opened between Mauch Chunk and Easton in 1855. It was built to compete directly with the Lehigh Coal and Navigation Company's canal, and quickly became the biggest carrier of "black diamonds" (anthracite) from the upper Lehigh River valley, and slate from Slatington. The railroad opened a spur to slate quarries in the Slatedale area in 1860 to serve that growing industry.

The North Pennsylvania Railroad, later part of the Reading system, was completed from Philadelphia to South Bethlehem in 1857. Now abandoned, a section from Hellertown to the Upper Saucon Township community center has been converted to a bike/walking trail. The North Penn was the only railroad from the Lehigh Valley directly to Philadelphia. The LVRR and the Central Railroad of New Jersey provided direct service to New York.

By the 1860s, what had been a two-day trip from Lehigh County to Philadelphia by stage coach as recently as the 1830s took two hours. For passengers this was a convenience. For commerce and industry, it opened endless opportunities. The 1869 Allentown City Directory notes that "direct and easy access is had with Philadelphia and New York, making Allentown the most central location for manufacturing enterprise in Eastern Pennsylvania."

The East Penn Railroad, for years known as the East Penn Branch of the Reading Railroad before it was merged into Conrail in 1976, opened in 1859 from Reading in Berks County to East Penn Junction in Allentown. It also was an anthracite railroad, carrying Schuylkill Valley anthracite. The Catasauqua and Fogelsville Railroad and the Ironton Railroad were the two major short lines in Lehigh County, serving almost exclusively the iron and later the cement industry. Both were in operation by the end of the 1850s and were expanded in the 1860s.

With the advent of railroads, coal could be transported in great volumes. Anthracite had become the fuel of the American industrial revolution, powering not just locomotives but industries of all kinds that had previously depended on waterpower or wood-burning steam engines. With unlimited supplies of anthracite coming down the rails, iron companies added furnaces and rebuilt existing ones to much larger proportions, greatly increasing capacity.

A symbiotic relationship between the iron and railroad businesses, each dependent on the other and each pushing growth in the other, developed in Lehigh County and the nation during this period of rapid growth.

The Civil War caused a burst of energy as the northern war machine needed iron for every possible task. At the start of the war in 1861, twelve furnaces owned by four iron companies along the Lehigh River in Lehigh County were producing pig iron. By the end of the war three additional furnaces had been built, others enlarged, and iron-company stockholders were making enormous profits.

With barely a hiccup the economic charge leaped into the post-war railroad-building boom. Allentown's city directory for 1869 noted that it was possible to read a newspaper at 3:00 a.m. by the light of the city's iron furnaces running around the clock. The furnaces extended upstream along the river from Allentown through Hokendauqua and Catasauqua in the greatest concentration of industry seen in the Lehigh Valley in the nineteenth century.

On April 10, 1869, with the driving of the golden spike at Utah's Promontory Point, the first transcontinental railroad was complete. The "iron horses" would not have gotten there without iron rails provided by the furnaces and rolling mills of Bethlehem Iron Company, located on the banks of the Lehigh River in South Bethlehem, a short distance from the Lehigh County boundary line.

After the Civil War, iron furnaces were built along the trackage of the East Penn Railroad in Alburtis, Macungie, and Emmaus by men eager to get in on what was clearly the most profitable industry of the day. The largest of these three was Lock Ridge in Alburtis, part of the Thomas Iron Company. A county park in Alburtis preserves the remains of two casthouses, a blast furnace, and several other buildings as a memorial to the largest industry of the nineteenth century.

Iron production changed the economy of the region, and transformed rural villages into small-scale industrial centers. Attorney E.R. Lichtenwallner, writing in 1884, recalled what the boom times that started in the late 1860s were like in Lower Macungie Township:

> … it seemed at one time as if almost everybody who owned a tract of land, however small, had been seized with the mining fever. Leases were made, shafts sunk, and the "hidden treasure" sought for everywhere. Ore-washeries and smoke-stakes seemed to spring up throughout the township like mushrooms in a hot-bed, while the fires from the chimneys of two furnaces and a foundry, erected within the confines of the township, lit up the night with their lurid flames. Although many beautiful farms were laid waste, the owners thereof reaped a rich harvest in the shape of royalties, and considered themselves amply compensated for the unsightly gaps in their land in consequence of mining the ore.

Industrial Diversification

Lehigh County's iron age continued even after the crash of September 18, 1873. The failure that day of a Philadelphia investment bank headed by Jay Cooke, America's richest man, led to bust in the market for railroad stocks. This in turn led to a national and worldwide depression that lasted the remainder of the decade.

The iron industry in Lehigh County felt the blow, but it was heavily invested in the manufacture of rails for coal mines, not railroads, and that business continued. Business slowed, and hundreds of men were put out of work, but furnaces continued to be built and rebuilt. Iron continued to be smelted in Lehigh County until the 1920s, but the immediate effect of the Panic of 1873 on the economy of the region was acute.

Concerned about the devastating effects throughout the economy of the region's dependence on one large industry, farseeing members of the Allentown Board of Trade found a solution in the desire of Paterson, New Jersey, silk makers to expand their business outside their home city. The Paterson interests liked the offer from Allentown's representatives, who even promised to build a new silk mill for the company. When the Adelaide

Coplay Iron Company furnaces, early 1880s, looking east. Wearing the high hat is Valentine Weygandt Weaver Jr., son of the superintendent. The Lehigh River is on the other side of the furnaces.

The Cinderella was one of the Thomas Iron Company's locomotives at the Lock Ridge works. Here she is outside one of the casthouse doors in about 1903, with some of the furnace crew. Her primary job was to haul slag from the furnace area to the slag dumts. Most of the men who worked here were local Pennsylvania Germans.

The Donaldson Iron Company (1882 to 1943) was one of many foundries in the Lehigh Valley that made products from pig iron produced by local furnaces. It was on the site of an earlier furnace. Donaldson made exclusively cast-iron pipe.

Silk Mills (named for a silk company president's wife) were completed in 1881, the city threw a party for the company, which included a dance in the Adelaide's building.

A success from the start, the Adelaide attracted many silk companies to Lehigh County and the Lehigh Valley. Allentown was particularly diversified, with mills that wove broad silk and ribbons, and numerous industries that supported them. Thousands of workers, many of them women and girls, were employed. By 1912 the Lehigh Valley was the silk-making capital of America, and Allentown was given the name "Silk City." Many former silk

The Macungie Silk Company was founded in 1908 by local investors. In 1909 it moved into a new factory where Allen Organ is in 2011. For forty years it produced silk ribbons and bindings there. (Macungie Historical Society)

mills still stand in communities throughout Lehigh County, some converted into apartments and condominiums, some used for light industry and warehousing, others vacant.

Other industries like furniture making followed, impressed by the craftsmanship and work ethic of local workers. Lehigh County, with its excellent railroad network, was positioned to attract industry. The American Steel and Wire Company, originally the Iowa Barb Wire Company, had been lured to Allentown from Easton in 1886. Known simply as "the wire mill," its enormous plant and 1,700 workers made barbed wire, nails, and other products made from wire. It closed in 1943 and was torn down in 1960.

Among Lehigh County's natural resources are bands of "cement rock"—limestone combined with chalk, clay and shale in the right proportions to make high-quality cement when

Mack Trucks: Born In Brooklyn, Grew Up In Allentown

The names William, Augustus, and Jack may sound like three guys in a musical trio. But put the last name Mack behind them and you know it's trucks and not tunes they would be singing.

One hundred and ten years ago, in July 1901, the three Mack brothers, then wagon makers located in Brooklyn, NYC, decided to expand their limited partnership and incorporate themselves as the Mack Brothers Company. It was a way of celebrating the fact that they had survived the Panic of 1893 and were now the leading wagon supplier to New York dairies, which used old-fashioned horsepower to see milk bottles found their way to the stoops of the city.

An even more exciting thing happened to the Macks in 1901. A friend of Jack had recently acquired a new gas-powered Winton automobile and invited him to go for a ride. As the big touring car glided down the street, the inventive mind of Jack Mack was working. Perhaps a gas-powered touring car was the future. It happened that brother "Gus," short for Augustus, had a friend who had been after him to build one for his tours of Brooklyn's popular Prospect Park. After much trial and error it was finished and became the talk of the city. By 1904 their touring-car business was taking orders from as far away as Havana, Cuba.

Now the Macks were in a tight but enviable position. They needed to expand. Brooklyn just did not have the room. Then, brother Joseph, who was in the silk business, told them about an empty industrial building in the bustling industrial community of Allentown. Jack, whose love affair with the internal combustion engine was to become legendary, embarked with Joe on a fourteen-hour car trip across the horrible dirt roads of New Jersey to see the Allentown building. That they could have done it in two hours by train was apparently not considered.

Jack took one look and decided that the building, in South Allentown along the banks of the Little Lehigh Creek and known as the old Weaver-Hirsh foundry, was ideal. It offered plenty of space, which, as they were going to make their own parts and motors, they would need.

Workers and machinery began arriving in December. On January 2, 1905, Mack Brothers Motor Company was registered at the Lehigh County Courthouse.

The Mack brothers probably would have been surprised if someone had told them they had just created an automotive legend. In those early years gasoline trucks were still considered untried vehicles. Wagon men would often get into fist fights with truck drivers for frightening their horses as they passed them on the highway.

(Kelly Butterbaugh)

Gradually the new trucks were taking hold. In 1911, finding local banks could not supply the capital they needed, the Mack brothers brought in investment banker J.P. Morgan, who arranged a merger with a Swiss firm called Saurer Motor Company and Hewitt Motor Company of New York to form the International Motor Company, a holding company that served as a selling and servicing division. It also led to the departure from the company of Jack Mack, who did not fit into the international structure. Gus also left the firm, with only William staying on to retirement in the 1920s.

These changes put Mack on the world stage and led to its reputation for quality. Like many Lehigh Valley companies, the outbreak of World War I in Europe brought contracts from overseas.

Mack was providing trucks to the British Army in 1915. The trucks, with their sloped hoods and low-slung lights, seemed to form a face. British soldiers were convinced they resembled a bulldog, their informal national symbol, and started calling them bulldog trucks. American doughboys adopted the name and, in 1932, so did the company. The symbol was designed by Alfred Fellows Masury, Mack's chief engineer, one of the last things he did for the company. A year later Masury was among the seventy-three passengers who lost their lives in the crash of the U.S. Navy's airship Akron off the coast of New Jersey.

The recession of the early 1920s was a hiccup for Mack. Their plants expanded. By 1925 Mack's 5-C plant was rising on the south side of Allentown. That year the company was running half page newspaper adds touting a million feet of factory space in their Allentown plants. Steam shovels were turning earth that only a few years before had known only a plow. Hundreds of workers would find jobs building the buses and fire engines that became part of Mack's legend. "Business men," read a Mack ad from the 1920s, "who have closely followed its progress and development still regard it as an infant industry with a tremendous future before it."

The Great Depression of the 1930s slowed Mack. But by the mid-thirties it had begun to revive. In 1936 the International Motor Company changed its name to Mack Manufacturing Corporation.

The approach of World War II led to a flood of government contracts. When the U.S. entered the war in 1941, Mack once more became a heavy-truck manufacturer to the U.S. Army. By the time the war was over, Mack had supplied the Allied forces with 4,500 five-ton, four-wheeled trucks and almost 26,000 six-wheeled trucks.

The post-war years brought even more changes to Mack, including highs and lows. Plants have been opened and closed and foreign ownership of Mack created controversy.. Its primary manufacturing plant remains in Lower Macungie Township.

The 2009 announcement of the departure of Mack's headquarters from Allentown to Greensboro, North Carolina, stunned many. But all that was far in the future the day 110 years ago that Jack Mack took a ride.

A scaling crew is stripping the walls in the zinc mines.   (Mayo Lanning)

crushed, burned in kilns, then crushed again into a fine powder. All along this Jacksonburg formation, cement companies started quarrying stone and erecting kilns in the decades after David O. Saylor's discovery of the process for making portland cement in the late 1860s. The small town of Coplay is where portland cement was first made in America. Vestiges of early-generation cement kilns still stand there. Cement was transported out of the area by canal and railroad.

Lehigh Portland Cement, founded in 1897, was the largest of several cement companies. Fortunes were made by those who ventured into this business, and a number of the mansions on Hamilton Street in Allentown credit their construction to cement money. Coplay, Cementon, Ormrod and Fogelsville housed many cement workers; Egypt, one of the earliest villages in the county, expanded greatly after the American Cement Company was established there in 1885.

By 1912, Lehigh Valley cement was being sent to the greatest construction project of the era, the Panama Canal, and for projects throughout the United States.

Among the early investors in cement was Harry C. Trexler, perhaps the county's wealthiest businessman. His fortune was based on the growth of his family lumber business and shrewd investments in electrically powered streetcar lines that, along with cement, were the cutting-edge industries of the early twentieth century. As the county observed its centennial in 1912, county residents were following the progress of the massive concrete toll bridge Trexler and his partners were building over the Little Lehigh Creek at

Construction of the Allentown and Reading Traction Company's line at Dorneyville, 1898. This line went into Dorney Park, then to Wescosville, East Texas, Kutztown, and Reading.

Eighth Street. The new bridge, the largest concrete bridge of the day, shortened the high-speed trolley trip from Allentown to Philadelphia and linked Allentown with fast-growing South Allentown when it opened in 1913.

Three major companies were founded to provide heavy equipment for the cement and mining industries. McKee, Fuller and Company in Catasauqua, founded in 1868, grew out of the Lehigh Car, Wheel and Axle Company, a supplier to the railroad industry. It made crushing and grinding equipment for the cement industry. Its name changed to Fuller-Lehigh in 1918, and to The Fuller

A major flood in early 1902 caused damage along the Lehigh River and its tributaries. The Hamilton Street bridge was destroyed and trolley service disrupted. A temporary bridge was constructed until a new permanent bridge could be opened in 1905.

Company in 1926. Bradley Pulverizer Company established a company in Allentown in 1886 to make crushing and grinding machinery, and the Traylor Engineering Company was founded in 1902 by Sam Traylor, a young mechanical engineer, to make quarrying, mining, and smelting machinery.

Zinc is the last of the major mineral industries in Lehigh County. While jasper, slate, iron ore, limestone, and cement rock all were processed within the county into commodities, zinc was not. Zinc ores in the Friedensville area of Upper Saucon Township, considered the best source of zinc in Pennsylvania, were mined starting in the 1850s and taken to what became South Bethlehem for smelting and manufacturing. National attention was focused

The Emperor And The Lady: Royalty Comes To Hokendauqua

Lehigh County has often played host to some major figures in world history. But only once did a reigning emperor with the bluest of blood ever stop in for a visit—to Hokendauqua. Dom Pedro II, emperor of Brazil, was full of surprises, and that he visited in part to please a young local woman only adds to his mystique.

Despite his Bourbon, Hapsburg, and Braganza (the ruling family of Portugal) ties, Dom Pedro was no reactionary stuffed shirt. Although he carried himself with regal bearing, this monarch was the most open-minded of men. Dom Pedro enjoyed nothing more than the study of industrial arts and sciences that he could use in turn to instruct his own people and modernize his country.

In the spring of 1876, Dom Pedro was in America to join in the celebration of the country's 100th birthday being held in Philadelphia. He helped open the event with President Ulysses Grant by starting the giant Corliss engine that powered the exhibition's many machines. Told how many revolutions per minute, one hundred, that the Corliss engine could turn, he said, "That beats our Latin American Republics!"

His movements were followed closely in the newspapers, which were so impressed with the energetic, intelligent Dom Pedro that they christened him "Our Yankee Emperor." At the end of June the emperor, at the invitation of Lehigh Valley Railroad founder Asa Packer, came to South Bethlehem. Despite the blazing heat, the emperor placed himself at the head of a delegation of Bethlehem Iron Company officials, dressed in the required black suits and tall coats of formal court dress. Full of questions, he often embarrassed his hosts who did not know the answers.

While he going down the receiving line at a formal reception, a young woman curtseyed to Dom Pedro and caught his eye. Something about her was familiar, but he could not place it. Finally he asked his hosts who she was. He was told she was Gertrude Thomas, daughter of ironmaker Samuel Thomas of Catasauqua. His father, David Thomas, had created the first successful anthracite-coal-fueled iron furnaces in North American in Catasauqua in 1840.

For her part, Gertrude was trying place Dom Pedro, who looked familiar to her. Only after another introduction and more conversation did they remember their exotic meeting place, several years before atop the Great Pyramid in Egypt. Dom Pedro, traveling incognito under one of his many titled aliases, had not made himself known to her. Gertrude had no way of knowing who he was until that moment.

Craig L. Bartholomew Iron Collection

56

With the empress on hand and their age difference—Gertrude was roughly the same age as the 50-year-old emperor's eighteen-year-old daughter Izabel—there was no hint of a royal romance. But there was clearly something that motivated Dom Pedro to tell his flustered aides to cancel plans for a royal visit to Easton. They were going to Hokendauqua to look at the Thomas Iron Works.

Telegraphic keys clicked as the imperial private railroad car sped out of Bethlehem. In Easton there was shock and dismay. Disappointed crowds lined College Hill. Some spotted an elegant carriage that carried two Brazilian court officials (sent out to plan the now-suspended parade's route) and a local reporter who accompanied them. The reporter had to tell them repeatedly he was no monarch, so there was no reason to keep on demanding to shake his hand.

In Hokendauqua there was delight. Gertrude took the lead in giving the emperor a tour of the Thomas Iron Works. At one point she stopped to introduce the Emperor to two mechanics in grease-stained overalls. They were her brothers, who were getting to know the family business from the bottom up.

Almost as fast as it had begun the tour was over. The train, disappointing a crowd gathered at Allentown's railroad station hoping to catch a glimpse of Dom Pedro, returned swiftly to Bethlehem in a blur and then went on without stopping to Philadelphia.

Dom Pedro was to be Brazil's last emperor. Overthrown in a coup in 1889, he died in Paris in 1891, a heartbroken man. But he would surely be pleased to know that today Brazil has become a growing industrial giant.

As for Gertrude Thomas, she married a Philadelphia doctor and raised a family. And just maybe, when she was trying to get her children to go to sleep, she told them the story of how she had once entertained an emperor.

Craig L. Bartholomew Iron Collection

on the large Ueberroth Mine when the largest pumping engine of its type, a Cornish beam engine, was installed there in 1872 to remove water from the depths of the mines. In this area, as in other parts of Lehigh County where special skills were invaluable, experienced men immigrated and made their homes where the new industries needed their knowledge.

Zinc mining stopped in 1893. The abandoned mines sat idle until the 1950s, when the New Jersey Zinc Company reopened the deep mines near Friedensville to supply ore to its smelters in Palmerton, Carbon County. Zinc mining ceased in 1983.

By 1912 several other large industries were major players in Lehigh County's economy. Shoemaking and cigarmaking were among the consumer-oriented industries that employed many.

Transportation

This was also a time of change in transportation. Horses, still used for personal transportation and local deliveries, were competing for space on roadways with automobiles during the early years of the twentieth century. Lehigh County's Henry Nadig, a talented Allentown mechanic, is said to have created his own horseless carriage as early as 1889, which makes it the oldest in America, ahead of Charles E. Duryea's 1893 automobile that is generally considered the first car made in the United States. Nadig's vehicle is currently owned by former Lehigh County Executive David K. Bausch, who purchased it from the Nadig family a number of years ago. It is on permanent loan at the America On Wheels transportation museum on Front Street.

The Eighth Street bridge was built 1911–1913 across the valley of the Little Lehigh Creek. It was used by the Lehigh Valley Transit Company for trolley service. Other vehicles paid a toll until the 1950s.

After the turn of the century, roads in the city started to be paved for sanitary reasons and to provide a better surface for cars. Almost all freight haulage was by railroad, some by trolley, and a few agricultural items and some coal by canal boats. Anticipating, and promoting, major changes in transportation, the Mack Brothers Motor Car Company came to Allentown in 1905, where they made buses and motorized delivery trucks. By 1911 they were the largest producer of heavy-duty trucks in the nation. The name of the company was changed to Mack Trucks, Inc., in 1922. Ownership has changed, and the headquarters are no longer in Allentown, but Mack trucks are still manufactured in Lehigh County.

A significant and visible change that swept Lehigh County over 100 years ago, and one of which there is little sign today, was the electric streetcar or trolley. Streetcars powered by electricity were introduced in Lehigh County in 1891 by Boston investors. By 1900 the county's largest streetcar line was the Lehigh Valley Traction Company created by Albert Johnson, a nationally known streetcar developer from Cleveland, Ohio. Johnson's abrupt death in 1901 at the age of 39 forced the line into bankruptcy. Acquired in 1905 by Trexler and his partner Colonel Edward Young (also one of Trexler's partners in the Lehigh Portland Cement Company), it was renamed the Lehigh Valley Transit Company. Soon trolley service spread to the countryside. By 1912 it was not uncommon for farmers to load milk cans and sacks of potatoes onto a trolley to travel rapidly to market.

In 1910 Lehigh Valley Transit launched its Liberty Bell Line service between Allentown and Philadelphia. Cartoons in the next day's newspapers showed two figures dressed in eighteenth-century garb and labeled Father Allen and Father Penn shaking hands and recognizing the joining of the cities.

The tracks may have been removed, but the trolley system left permanent results. Trolleys operated by Lehigh Valley Transit and the Allentown and Reading Traction Company made it possible for people in outlying rural towns to travel directly into Allentown as well as increasing development of the city's Hamilton Street retail district west beyond Eighth and Hamilton streets. A resident of Macungie could step on a streetcar at noon, travel to

Henry Nadig's horseless carriage, built in Allentown in 1889. (Lehigh County Historical Society)

A wealthy family such as that of John Greenall could afford a car such as this 1904 Franklin. He was a partner in a prosperous foundry and machine shop.

Milk was delivered by wagon long after cars and trucks became common. With frequent stops, horses provided ideal motive power.

Allentown, buy a new hat at Hess Brothers, enjoy a matinee at the Lyric, stop for an ice-cream soda, and be home by suppertime.

Communities that had been isolated now were connected to others in the county. In the days before paved streets and automobiles, for the cost of a trolley fare workers could travel to jobs far from home, rural students could attend high school in Allentown or Bethlehem, city and rural students could further their education at Kutztown Normal School. Families could spend Sundays at Dorney Park or Central Park, and they could make an easy trip to the Great Allentown Fair, an annual event when all available trolleys were put in service, running non-stop from the fairgrounds to outlying towns. Hundreds of new homes were built along trolley lines, linking places like East Allentown and West Bethlehem and changing some small villages such as Wescosville—a sparsely settled crossroads village on the old King's Highway from Easton to Reading—into thriving communities.

With new technologies came new problems. In May 1906, trolley workers, seeking higher wages and the right to organize a union, announced a strike against Lehigh Valley Transit. It lasted over a week. A state trooper wounded a 16-year-old boy in the leg, and only the personal intervention of a popular alderman prevented the officer from being killed. Eventually the company agreed to hire back the men and agreed to a small raise.

The 1906 strike was a symptom of how even a conservative Pennsylvania-German place like Allentown could be subject to the changes industrialization had wrought on the community. As villages and towns sprouted from the farmland, the region went from one of self-sufficient farmers to industrial workers dependent on others for their income. Development of municipal services did not keep pace with the region's growth. Sanitary sewers were non-existent, garbage service limited, and waste from industry and outhouses poured freely into rivers and streams. Alleys choked by livery stables swarmed with flies. In 1900 Hazelton newspapers wondered how Allentown could call itself a city when it did not even have one mile of paved streets. The Allentown police force that year consisted of just two five-man shifts, with no police coverage at all between 3:00 a.m. and 11:00 a.m.

Religious Diversification

For many the morals of the population, particularly of young people, seemed to be in peril. Farm boys and girls, lured to the bright lights of the "big city," found themselves prey to saloons offering entertainment that made righteous—some would say hypocritical—Victorians shudder.

Young women who found jobs outside the home in the silk mills had independent incomes. They sometimes defied their parents, who depended on them to support the family. In 1903 Mabel Bechtel, a vivacious young mill worker in her twenties, was found brutally murdered behind her Allentown home. The case attracted national attention with reporters from New York and Philadelphia newspapers flocking to the Lehigh County Courthouse.

A detailed account of the Bechtel case appeared in the 2002 issue of the Lehigh County Historical Society's *Proceedings*. Most clues pointed to Bechtel's mother and older brother, both supposedly infuriated when she rejected their choice of a respectable but dull man as a suitable husband. Mabel's favorite beau was from South Bethlehem, a dashing fellow in a fancy "turnout" who drove her around town, lavished gifts on her, and who, to the horror of her vocally anti-Semitic mother, was Jewish. Her family's dependence on Mabel's income (her older brother's drinking was said to prevent him from keeping a job) increased the tension. The case ended unresolved, but it sent a shudder through Lehigh County.

Another unsettling change was the increasing diversity of immigrants that arrived in Lehigh County in the late nineteenth and early twentieth centuries. In the 1850s and '60s these had been German, Irish, English, and Welsh iron, railroad, and canal workers. From the1890s to the 1920s newcomers came from Eastern and Central Europe along with Russian Jews and Italians, seeking work in the cement and silk industries.

Lehigh County's relatively small nineteenth-century Jewish community was concentrated in Allentown. Almost all of its members were of German background, so fit in with the vast majority of the population. Until the 1880s those who wanted to practice their religion attended services at the Congregation Brith Shalom (Covenant of Peace) founded in 1842 in Easton. It is the third-oldest synagogue in Pennsylvania and tenth-oldest in the United States. Newspaper accounts from 1883–84 are the first to mention anything resembling regular Jewish services in Lehigh County, which were held on the second floor of a retail building in the 700 block of Hamilton Street. In 1888 the congregation held a Purim Ball that was widely covered in the local press. Fairview Cemetery then included a section for Jewish burials.

When the first Russian Jews arrived in relatively large numbers in Allentown's Sixth Ward in the early 1890s, local press coverage of them was not at all favorable. They were accused of being dirty, uncouth, and, most unsettling of all, not being German. Many became peddlers who arrived in Allentown and then traveled to outlying Lehigh County towns, sometimes by wagon, sometimes on foot, with a sack on their back and "notions" to sell.

Sam Grossman of Allentown, who has vivid memories of the lively Sixth Ward Jewish community of his boyhood in the 1920s, remembers his family members going into the coal region with horse and wagon in the early twentieth century. He recalls that their knowledge of Eastern European languages helped them in dealing with the many ethnic communities, and Yiddish, a dialect of German, with the Pennsylvania Germans.

It was among these immigrants that Allentown's first Orthodox synagogue, Agudas

Achim (A Gathering of Brothers and Sisters), came to be in 1892. Its building in Allentown's Sixth Ward, still standing, was the focal point of the religious life of that early Jewish community. Across the street in 1916 another synagogue, Congregation Shaare Shalom, was formed. It merged with Agudas Achim in 1950. Agudas Achim closed in 2004.

In 1906 Allentown's first Reformed synagogue, Keneseth Israel, opened on Thirteenth Street. Charles Klein and Max Hess, Sr., leading Allentown merchants, were among its most prominent members. Its location was just around the corner from Max Hess's large Hamilton Street home.

On September 10, 1909, the Orthodox Jewish community celebrated the opening of Congregation Sons of Israel's synagogue at Sixth and Tilghman streets. With its solid stone walls and gold domes it was considered worthy of the attention of the leaders of the community who attended, and it received very favorable coverage in the local press. Among the congregation's officers in 1909 were Max Rapoport, Jacob Schattenstein, and Max Senderowitz, all successful members of Allentown's business community.

A unique aspect of the immigrant mix was the arrival of Christian Syrians in the early twentieth century. Settling largely in Allentown's Sixth Ward with the other ethnic groups, they were regarded as particularly exotic in the early days.

The link between Lehigh County and the Middle East began when Presbyterian missionaries from Allentown had gone to Syria in the mid-nineteenth century. When the Syrian and Lebanese immigrants came to America they came to Allentown as a place they knew. The Syrian Christians traced their roots back to the ancient church of Antioch. There, according to the Acts of the Apostles, was the first place the Christian gospel was preached to non-Jews and the first place the disciples were called Christians. Some Syrian Christians accepted the missionary's message and became Presbyterians. To this day there is an Arabic service on Sunday afternoon at Allentown's First Presbyterian Church.

By the 1900s many who came to Lehigh County brought their Orthodox form of Christianity with them. In the early spring of 1916, fifteen families in Allentown formed St. George Antiochian Orthodox Church, breaking ground for a small church building at 1011 Catasauqua Avenue. The church was built at a cost $5,000. According to the church history, male members of the congregation, using horses and wagons, did much of the labor. Over the years the congregation grew into an integral part of the county's ethnic life.

Although never a huge part of the county's population, immigrants from Eastern Europe and Syria were visible and brought suspicion by what were seen as their exotic customs. Newspapers of the day casually slurred these newcomers. Although there were sometimes tensions that boiled over into violence, in general Lehigh County's ethnic immigrants groups were met with general tolerance if not always acceptance.

The building of a church in 1912, and the sale of its original Sixth Ward chapel, reflected better than anything else the changing nature of the population of Lehigh County and Allentown.

Allentown's Grace Episcopal Church had been founded in 1865 with a mission to increase the church's outreach to the large numbers of British immigrants then flocking to the area's booming iron industry. Episcopal services were not unknown in Lehigh County even before the creation of Grace Church. At a time when most local families were either Lutheran or Reformed, some members of the founding Allen-Livingston family attended services in the Lehigh County Court House when a circuit-riding minister from Easton's Trinity Episcopal Church passed through.

Interest in outreach to industrial workers was encouraged by members of the Episcopal Church who in the late 1850s came to Bethlehem and founded the Church of the Nativity. Lehigh Valley Railroad founder Asa Packer, one of the founders of Mauch Chunk's St. Mark's Episcopal Church, and his chief aide Robert H. Sayre, one of the founders of Bethlehem Iron (later Steel) Company, were very active Episcopal laymen.

An Episcopal Sunday School was established in 1863; it met in the office of Levi Horace Gross, superintendent of the rolling mill of the Allentown Iron Works, a Pennsylvania-German convert to the Episcopal Church and a member of Grace.

In 1869, at 803 N. Front Street, at the corner of Front and Furnace streets, Episcopalians opened a small but handsome stone sanctuary called the Episcopal Church of the Mediator, named after a church in Philadelphia. Its senior warden was Moses Leach, an immigrant from Yorkshire, England, who was the foreman of the Allentown Rolling Mills. His tombstone in the Old Allentown Cemetery, alongside that of his wife Martha, reads: "Moses Leach is my name/England is my nation/Allentown is my resting place/And Christ is my salvation."

The Rev. Eliphalet Nott Potter, son of the Rev. Alonzo Potter, Episcopal Bishop of Pennsylvania, was Mediator's first rector or pastor. Young Potter had played an important role in establishing the Episcopal Church in Bethlehem. He believed that the future for the church in America was to act as a missionary to industrial workers as well as to factory owners.

The collapse of the railroad-building boom in 1873 and of the iron industry that depended on it hit Mediator hard. Concerned about its own congregation and iron workers generally, who were taking out their frustrations on their families, Mediator offered its building as a space for games like checkers and added a lending library to keep men out of the saloons. It regularly advertized in Allentown's *Daily Chronicle* newspaper that it offered workers these forms of recreation. This was not enough; as the furnaces cooled and went dark, many in Mediator's congregation fled. Some sought work in the coal regions, some went West. In the early 1880s a railroad spur was placed in front of the sanctuary's door. Eventually the Mediator chapel was used only for occasional services.

By the early twentieth century, when Mediator was almost forgotten, the Rev. Ethelbert Talbot, whose last charge had been as bishop of the Diocese of Wyoming, was named the first bishop of the recently created Episcopal Diocese of Bethlehem.

Talbot took among his first tasks the revival of Mediator. Despite some promising attempts from 1906 to 1911, he discovered that it was impossible to have an Episcopal church without Episcopalians. Most of them, primarily the sons and daughters of iron-company managers, had long ago moved out of the Sixth Ward—by then populated by an ethnic mix of Russian Jews, Syrian Orthodox Christians, Italians, and Slovaks—to the city's upper-middle-class neighborhoods. If Mediator were going to be revived it was not going to happen in the old Sixth Ward neighborhood where it had been born.

Talbot selected a new location for the congregation at Turner Street in what was then Allentown's far west end, near newly created West Park. Land was purchased for $25,000 and small chapel was built in 1912. Today the Church of the Mediator occupies a modern building constructed on the same site in the late 1950s.

The old chapel on Front Street was sold. On July 8, 1912, St. Mary's Orthodox Ruthenian Church, a growing Eastern Orthodox congregation in Allentown's Sixth Ward, purchased the Church of the Mediator's former sanctuary for $9,000.

Health Care

Among the greatest changes in Lehigh County from 1812 to 1912, medicine is high on the list. In 1812 doctors were still using methods like bleeding with leaches that had been used for thousands of years. With no concept of the germ theory of disease, doctors poked and pulled at their patients. It was not just the poor or destitute that suffered. In 1798 Elizabeth Allen Tilghman, the second daughter of James Allen, and among the most well-off citizens in then Northampton County, died in childbirth at Trout Hall. Roughly twenty years later the daughter she gave birth to on that day also died in childbirth.

By 1912 Lehigh County's health care was about as up-to-date as in any other region of its size in the country. Allentown Hospital, founded at Seventeenth and Chew streets in 1899, was taking care of a number of patients. Not only medical ills but industrial accidents caused by the many machines in the growing number of factories were being treated there.

Photos from the time show a well-lighted operating room with doctors and nurses in clean white gowns. It would of course look primitive today, but was about as good as it got at the time. If sometimes the bill was paid in sacks of potatoes rather than cash, they were always appreciated by the hospital's kitchen.

Doctors were plentiful even in the countryside. If there were many who stuck to the old Pennsylvania-German pow-wow remedies, those seeking modern medicines could find them—and if they could afford it, specialists in health care in New York or Philadelphia were only an hour or two away by train.

The year 1912 was witness to an important step in local health care. The outbreak of a diphtheria epidemic in Allentown among the German and Austrian immigrant poor of the city caused Father, later Monsignor, Peter Masson, pastor of Sacred Heart Church, to call for six Sisters of Mercy to come from their convent near Reading to care for them.

At first confined to the church's former rectory at 417 Pine Street, a side street near the church, in 1915 the nuns took over the mansion of Judge Edward Harvey at Fourth and Chew streets, thanks to the aid of the St. Aloysius Young Men's Society, a Catholic lay organization.

Built in the early 1860s by Jonathan W. Grubb, a wholesale merchant and real-estate investor, the home stood on a large lot and was one of the most prominent dwellings in the city. It had been purchased in 1877 by Harvey from the estate of Stephen Gould, who occupied it from 1864 to his death in 1876. Gould, a native of New England had, with his brother Isaac, built his fortune on vast acres of virgin timber he harvested in Lycoming and Carbon counties. The Harvey home was gradually replaced by a modern facility named Sacred Heart Hospital.

Schooling

In the Lehigh County of 1912 the one- and two-room school house still held sway. As they had been since about the 1860s, reading, writing and arithmetic were taught. Six grades were the norm for most scholars, although many others seldom got beyond fourth. This lack of formal education was not regarded as a drawback. In Roberts' *Anniversary History*, many of the biographies of Lehigh County's leading men state they had received only "a common school education." Sometimes this was coupled with a business-school course in double-entry bookkeeping or accounting.

Harry Trexler, arguably the county's leading citizen, had little more than that. However, he acquired a large library in which he could be found many an evening reading. By his own self-discipline and training Trexler was probably better educated than many college men of his time.

For those growing up in Lehigh County in 1912 the situation was a little more mixed. Pennsylvania's Free School Act was passed in 1834, but included a provision for local option. Voters in every municipality in the county except Hanover Township and the borough of Allentown voted down the law. A sea change in attitudes was underway: the

Cleaning the school at Kiechel's one-room schoolhouse on Lower Macungie Road, in the Lower Macungie Township School District. On the last half day of school the students cleaned the classroom. April 1916. (Lower Macungie Township Historical Society)

Students and teacher at the Claussville one-room schoolhouse on Route 100. Lehigh County Historical Society owns the building now and operates it as a working museum for students from area elementary schools. (Lehigh County Historical Society)

Students and teacher pose outside the Limeport School in 1910. (St. Paul's Lutheran Blue Church)

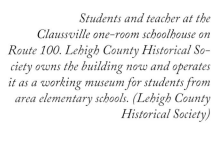

The children who attended the Blue Church School in Upper Saucon Township learned lessons in both German and English. The school was built in 1867. (St. Paul's Lutheran Blue Church)

Students at the Allentown College for Women, Fourth and Turner streets, leaving for a Muhlenberg College football came, circa 1910. (Lehigh County Historical Society)

The Macungie School is now a community center called the Macungie Institute, the original name for the school. (Macungie Historical Society)

controversy over the Free School Act finally caused education to be considered a right rather than a privilege. By the end of the 1850s residents in all township and borough school districts had voted in favor of free public schools.

County superintendents of education were authorized in an 1854 law. Lehigh County's longest-serving superintendent was James O. Knauss, a dedicated educator who was appointed in 1871 and served for twenty-one years. His first priority was improving the quality of the teachers hired by local school boards. Normal schools had been training teachers since the 1850s, but prior to that time few were trained for teaching. After the Civil War a building boom in school houses took place. Many of the old brick school houses seen around the county date from the late 1860s and later.

Of particular significance in Lehigh County was a new school code enacted in 1911, which may have been the talk of the town as it was put into effect in 1912. Among its many provisions were that the Pennsylvania-German dialect may no longer be used in teaching (although teachers continued to use it to assist the many youngsters who started school with no knowledge of English), and that school directors had the right to shut down one-room schools and transport students to larger schools. Instead of repairing old schools, directors were for the first time required to erect modern ones suitable for consolidating schools and properly grading classes.

Each municipality still had its own school district in 1912. It was not until the 1950s that today's consolidated districts were formed, the impetus being the need for additional high schools. Allentown had had a high school since the 1850s, as did Catasauqua, Emmaus, and Macungie. Alburtis and Slatington established their grammar and high schools later in the century. Students from township schools often attended a borough or city high school after eighth grade, with their education and transportation costs subsidized by their township board of education. Those who attended high school for all four years were rare.

Hospital Corps 4th Regt. U.S.P. 10/19/05

The Civil War

For those who looked back in 1912 at Lehigh County's past, the biggest event they recalled was the Civil War. Every Memorial Day aging veterans in fading blue uniforms marched in fewer and fewer numbers keeping the memory of the 1860s alive. In 1987 Mahlon Hellerich, Lehigh County's archivist, estimated that one out of every five Lehigh County families had a man in uniform during the Civil War. "Clearly on this basis alone the Civil War was a searing experience for many Lehigh Countians," he wrote.

Among those on whom it had an impact was Harry Trexler. When he was an impressionable pre-teen boy, his uncle Charles was killed serving with the 151st Pennsylvania Volunteer Infantry Regiment at Gettysburg. Throughout his long business career Trexler would often surprise associates with his vast knowledge of even the most obscure Civil War skirmishes.

Lehigh County had a particular kinship with the Civil War. Days after the firing on Fort Sumter on April 12, 1861, Captain Thomas Yeager, a young militia officer and local businessman, gathered his unit, the Allen Infantry, and prepared to go to Washington in response to President Lincoln's request for troops to defend the capital from possible attack by the slave states that surrounded it on all sides. Yeager was from Allentown; many of the members of his unit hailed from other parts of Lehigh County.

On April 17 the men left Allentown by train for Harrisburg. There they were joined by militia units from Pottsville, Reading, and Lewistown. The state adjutant general gave them non-functioning muskets. Asking what he was supposed to do with them, Yeager was told they could be used as clubs. In order to get to Washington the Pennsylvanians had to change trains in Baltimore, a tough pro-rebel town. When the Pennsylvania men arrived at Baltimore they were confronted by a mob. Greeting them at the station was Captain

John Pemberton, a regular U.S. Army officer, with a small contingent of troops. Their orders were to offer protection to the militia at least part of the way to the train that would take them to Washington.

In one of history's ironies, shortly afterward Pemberton, a West Point graduate and Philadelphian from an old-line family whose ancestors went back to colonial times, at the urging of his southern-born wife, resigned his commission in the U.S. Army and became a Confederate general. On July 4, 1863, he surrendered the fortress city of Vicksburg, Mississippi, to General U.S. Grant, causing Lincoln to write, "the Father of Waters again goes unvexed to the sea." After the war Pemberton returned to Pennsylvania, where in the 1870s he got a job as an inventory clerk at an Allentown iron furnace.

Pemberton's escort duties ended on a side street that turned off in the direction of Fort McHenry. From there the militia, ever after called the First Defenders, were supposed to be escorted by Baltimore city police, who were clearly in sympathy with the mob. Rocks, bricks, bottles, the contents of chamber pots, and the occasional bullet found their target. In response to taunts from the mob asking where he was going, Yeager simply replied "for my country."

Several soldiers were badly injured. Among them were Ignatz Gresser, a German immigrant and Allentown shoemaker, and Nicholas Biddle, a Pottsville African American who served as the orderly to one of the militia officers.

Later that day the First Defenders arrived in Washington. Assigned to take up quarters in the unfinished Capitol building they were greeted by Lincoln, who ordered the men's wounds be attended to. After their initial three-month enlistment was up, many of the Pennsylvanians re-enlisted in other units. Yeager was killed at the battle of Fair Oaks, Virginia, in 1862. Gresser received the Medal of Honor after capturing two Confederates and rescuing a wounded fellow soldier at the battle of Antietam that same year. Both are buried in Allentown.

Although Lehigh County men played a role in many Civil War battles, the most significant battle that they fought in as a unit was the battle of Cedar Creek, Virginia. It was the biggest single military action by Lehigh County troops as a unit. It took place on October 19, 1864, in Virginia's Shenandoah Valley. It was here that the men of the 47th Regiment of Pennsylvania Volunteer Infantry under the command of Union General Philip Sheridan helped turn back an attack by Confederates led by General Jubal Early. Ever thereafter, local Civil War veterans gathered to remember on what they regarded as their special day. For that reason Lehigh County's Soldiers and Sailors Monument at Center Square in Allentown was dedicated on October 19, 1899.

James Hauser's 1902 *History of Lehigh County* records 2,063 Lehigh County men as having served in the Civil War. This was out of an 1860 population of roughly 43,000. Of that number, 83 were killed in battle and 64 were wounded. Those who died in camp numbered 233, apparently from a wide variety of diseases, 257 were POWs, and 49 were missing in action. Including those who died or were wounded in non-combat actions, the total Lehigh County loss was 1,218.

Like most of the country, Lehigh County was deeply divided by the Civil War. In general Allentown, with its industrial base, supported the pro-industry Republicans. Holding the union together and keeping the tariff high to protect local industries from cheaper products from Europe were what drew their support. Slavery was a side issue.

In the rural countryside Democrats held sway. Some were War Democrats who wanted to see the war through to save the Union. Ending slavery was not an issue they supported. Others, if not pro-Confederate, wanted a compromise peace that would let the South form its own country.

Tempers flared and strong Lincoln supporters like Fogelsville pastor Rev. William Helffrich often found themselves a target of verbal abuse by those who blamed the president for the war and felt their sons were dying in a useless struggle. The so-called "Knights of the Golden Circle," a group of Southern sympathizers in the north who worked to undermine the Union cause, were said to be active in rural Lehigh County.

Lee's surrender and Lincoln's assassination in April 1865 meant victory and, most important, the end of the draft. Rev. Helffrich noted that there were a few hot heads in his neighborhood who, after Lincoln's death, were heard to say, "now he knows what it feels like to get shot." But Allentown held a large public memorial service for the slain president. The outpouring of grief was no less genuine than it was across the rest of the country.

By 1912 anger over the Civil War among whites had long ebbed. An example was the inclusion of a Confederate soldier on Lehigh County's Soldiers and Sailors Monument, erected in 1899. Linked arm in arm with a Union figure, the statue stands atop a niche that reads "ONE FLAG ONE COUNTRY." The model for the rebel was James Crader, an Allentown Union veteran of Gettysburg who was Allentown's police chief in the 1880s. One of the few Civil War memorials north of the Mason-Dixon Line to include a Rebel soldier, it uniquely reflected national sentiments about a reunited nation.

The unfinished business of the Civil War, represented most vividly in 1912 by the sixty-one lynchings of African Americans that took place across the South that year, was regretted by some and largely ignored by most as a local issue about which nothing could be done without upsetting the spirit of reconciliation between North and South.

Rev. Stephen Albion Repass, pastor of Allentown's St. John's Lutheran Church, was the local embodiment of this spirit. During the Civil War, Repass, whose Pennsylvania-German

Teddy Roosevelt spoke on behalf of progressive candidates, including Gifford Pinchot, at the Hotel Allen on October 26, 1914. He is getting into a car to return to the Allentown Terminal Railroad.

family had moved to Virginia in the early nineteenth century, served as an officer in the Confederate Army. Severely wounded at the Second Battle of Bull Run or Manassas on August 29–30, 1862, he recovered just in time to take part at the battle of Gettysburg in July 1–3, 1863. On the third day of the battle Repass participated in Pickett's Charge, the so-called "highwater mark of the Confederacy." He was one of a handful of rebel soldiers to survive withering Union fire and make it over the now iconic stone-wall defense line only to collapse into the arms of its Northern defenders. A POW until 1865, at war's end, to fulfill a vow he had made to his mother, Repass entered the Lutheran Seminary in Philadelphia. He was called to be St. John's pastor in 1885.

Repass's reputation as both a scholar—he taught at Muhlenberg College and served on its board as president—and compassionate pastor was widely known. With his long, patriarchal snow-white beard he looked the very image of a nineteenth-century Lutheran clergyman to his congregation and the community at large.

Repass never talked of his wartime experiences unless asked, and then only reluctantly. But when the cornerstone for the monument was laid, Repass was called on to offer prayers. And on the day of its dedication in 1899 he gave the benediction. For residents of late nineteenth and early twentieth century Lehigh County, Repass embodied national and local reconciliation. He died in 1905 and was buried in Fairview Cemetery.

Ed Wilt: Allentown's Sailor Of The Civil War

How many have wondered why there is a statue of a sailor on Lehigh County's Soldiers and Sailors monument in Allentown's Center Square? After all, Allentown isn't exactly a seaport. There is no mystery; it is there to honor Edward Wilt, Lehigh County's Civil War sailor hero.

Wilt was born in Allentown in 1836. His father was a saddle maker named Abraham; his mother's name is unknown. No one is sure why, but as a boy Wilt became fascinated by tales of the sea. When he was seventeen Allentown could hold Wilt no longer. After packing up his few belongings, he set off walking to New Bedford, Massachusetts, made immortal by Herman Melville's Moby Dick. Wilt saw the place in its heyday, when real salty sea dogs like the novel's peg-legged Captain Ahab walked the decks of whaling ships.

Wilt soon learned the life of the sea was far from a child's picture book. His first captain was a ruthless character he later called "a tyrant." Wilt rebelled and jumped ship in New Zealand. Then he signed on to a whaler headed back to New Bedford.

Despite his experiences, the lure of the sea remained strong and Wilt joined the crew of a whaling ship bound for California. He would uncannily discover on a beach in Baja California the grave of a friend from Easton who had left to discover gold in California, only to die when the steamer he was aboard, the *Independence*, burned and sank.

For a time Wilt disappeared into the gold fields of California but had no luck. He returned to sea, traveling on one whaling voyage touching every country, he told friends, but Greenland and Iceland.

After the Civil War broke out in America, it found Ed Wilt in 1862 in the Spanish port city of Algeciras. Nearby, the U.S.S. *Kearsarge* was undergoing repairs. Eager to go to sea and to serve his country, Wilt signed on. He soon was a master of the ship's rigging and sails. Although a steamer, she had sail and rigging enough to keep him occupied. Wilt's other task was more military: he was member of the crew that fired the ships forward was a big pivot gun. One expert has described watching the crew of the gun as like watching a well-rehearsed ballet.

Two years later, on June 19, 1864, the *Kearsarge* and Wilt stepped into U.S. naval history. That day the CSS *Alabama*, a rebel commerce raider commanded by Captain Raphael Semmes, sailed out of dry dock at Cherbourg, France, and toward the Union warship. The ships were so close to shore that French vacationers with opera glasses could watch the battle unfold. Semmes was a skilled seaman and his men tried veterans, but this time the rebel fox had underestimated the tenacity of the Union hounds. After a vigorous battle the outgunned *Alabama* was sent to the bottom. In the official reports following the battle, Ed Wilt was mentioned for his "deliberation and coolness" with the pivot gun crew during the battle.

When the *Kearsarge* returned to America that fall, Ed Wilt took up the government's offer to accept an immediate discharge. He received a bounty of $800 for his service and returned to Allentown, married, and had a child. But he was quickly bilked out of his money by scam artists, and his son died as an infant. He took a job in a boiler factory then, when he began coughing up blood, he got a job as a night watchman for the railroad, sharing with all who would listen his tales of the sea.

Death came for Ed Wilt on the snowy morning of February 2, 1882. He rests, as he has since then, in Allentown's Union and West End Cemetery. Binoculars and cutlass in hand, he still stands guard at Center Square.

Lehigh County Soldiers And Sailors Monument

For 111 years the Soldiers and Sailors Monument of Lehigh County has offered a reminder to citizens of the region of the ultimate sacrifice that local men and women have made, and are still making, to keep our nation free.

But the historical record shows that getting this monument built and keeping it in Center Square has not been easy. Although Catasauqua was one of the first places in the state and country to honor Union troops, dedicating its monument in October of 1866, getting things done in Allentown took a little longer.

Like many places in America, the war that divided the nation divided Lehigh County. Some thought it should have never been fought; others felt it had been fought for the wrong reasons. Allentown and Lehigh County had voted strongly in 1864 for Democrat George McClellan, the Union General and presidential candidate that advocated a negotiated peace with the South. Even Union victory under Lincoln did not automatically change those feelings. There was also the issue of cost. If a monument was going to be erected, who was going to pay for it, Allentown or Lehigh County?

These issues got caught up in local politics and repeatedly ended in deadlock. But every year, as the ranks of local veterans grew thinner, pressure to do something increased. Finally, in August of 1896, thrity years after the Civil War was over, a petition was circulated to do something most counties in the state had already done—build a monument to its Civil War veterans. The results were overwhelming favorable and presented to county officials by Medal of Honor winner and Civil War hero Ignatz Gresser. County and city politicians, citing the "who-is-going-to-pay-for-it?" argument, promptly turned it down. When a new petition was submitted a few months later, the county commissioners, perhaps finally feeling some heat from veterans and voters, accepted. They agreed that the county would pay for it and the city would maintain it.

The Pennsylvania Monument Association of Philadelphia was chosen for the work at a sum of $39,000. Its president, Edward Gallagher, Jr., oversaw the project designed by his staff artists Bartholomew Francis Xavier Donovan and Henry F. Plaschart.

Then the struggle over the location began. Veterans wanted it in Center Square, but that would require moving recently installed streetcar tracks. Allentown City Council agreed with the veterans, but when another group emerged wanting to move it to the south side of the square, they backtracked. After twice reversing itself, the council settled on Center Square.

In May of 1899, the streetcar tracks were removed. On June 26, 1899, the cornerstone for the monument was laid. Taking part in the services was Rev. Stephen Albion Repass, the pastor of St. John's Lutheran Church and a former Confederate veteran who had fought and been captured at Gettysburg. He was one of the few members of Pickett's Charge to make it over the fabled stone wall later known as the "high water mark of the Confederacy."

A box placed at the monument's base included a cannonball from the battle of Bull Run, local newspapers and magazines, and several other items of memorabilia.

The monument was finished on September 2, 1899. Decorators from Koch Brothers clothing store covered the statues in bunting, but the Goddess of Liberty at its summit had her shroud shredded by the wind. Harry Smith of Allentown climbed up the scaffold around the column and removed the strips of cloth, leaving Liberty unveiled.

At the insistence of veterans the date for the official dedication was October 19, the date selected to recognize their role in the battle of Cedar Creek, Virginia, on October 19, 1864. The

47th Regiment of Pennsylvania Volunteers, the largest regiment of Lehigh County troops, took an active role in that battle. Organizers had wanted an earlier date out of fear of bad weather, but the veterans would not budge.

Fortunately, the day was cool and cloudless. Photos taken at the time show a crowd of thousands or perhaps hundreds of thousands. Governor William E. Stone headed a state delegation. The chief speaker of the day was George F. Baer, president of the Reading Railroad and personal advisor to investment banker J.P. Morgan. His long speech was typical of the time, but since few beyond the first three rows of the audience could hear him, most had to wait until reading the text in the next day's newspaper to know exactly what Baer had said.

Another speaker, Lehigh County solicitor and former Congressman C. J. Erdman, a Democrat who as a Gettysburg College student in 1863 had heard and briefly spoken to Lincoln when he gave the Gettysburg Address, noted that the monument was "an enduring tribute to the valor and patriotism of our soldiers so that the memory of great and mighty deeds may never fade, yet with no tinge of bitterness against the one time foe."

Eight young women, Hannah Young, Ruth Shelling, Dorothy Trexler, Althea Kline, Eda Holman, Salome Helfrich, Lulu Schneck, and Fannie M. Walters, all granddaughters of Civil War veterans, pulled the bunting away.

The crowd was thrilled at what they saw. The base was 29 feet high, the granite column 49 feet, and the Goddess of Liberty 21, feet making a total of 99 feet from the street to the top of the goddess's Phrygian cap. The cap was a symbol of revolt against authority that went back to ancient times and was worn as a badge of liberty by newly freed slaves. Around the base were eagles, and statues representing the infantry, cavalry, artillery, and navy. Facing east was a Union Soldier and a Confederate above the word, "One Flag One Country."

The *Allentown Leader* newspaper gave credit for the idea of adding a Confederate to monument

(Private Collection)

designer Gallagher in recognition of the recent Spanish American War in which northern and southern men had fought side by side against a common foe. But it might not have been accepted quite so easily if Rev. Repass, a former Rebel, had not been such a beloved and respected figure in the community.

The model for the Confederate soldier was James Crader, a local Union veteran of the battle of Gettysburg and Allentown's police chief for a time.

At the 100th anniversary of the monument in 1999, Crader's granddaughter, Ethel Bixler Spring, over 100 years old herself and a resident of Florida, came to Allentown carrying a photo of Crader taken in the 1890s. It bore a striking resemblance to the figure on the statute. Gazing at the figure as it was undergoing restoration work at Wenz Monument Company, Spring, who was 11 when her grandfather died in 1910, noted "it looks just like he did when he was asleep."

The sailor on the monument was added to honor Ed Wilt. An Allentown man and former harpooner on a whaling ship in the 1850s, he joined the Union Navy in Algeciras, Spain, in 1863 and played a major role on the U.S.S. *Kearsarge* in her battle with the rebel raider Alabama off the coast of France in June,1864. Wilt died in Allentown in 1882 in his forties, apparently of tuberculosis. When word got out that plans for the monument were underway his many friends insisted a figure of a sailor be included in his memory.

Plaques showing battle scenes and portraits of famous Pennsylvania military commanders Winfield Scott Hancock, John F. Hartranft, George Gordon Meade, and George F. McClellan were included.

One of the most frequently asked questions about the monument is, why does the Goddess of Liberty face east? No one can say for sure but the most plausible explanation is that it was done so that troops, who went off to war and returned by train, would be able to see her facing them as they marched up Hamilton Street from the city's railroad stations.

Everybody seemed so pleased with the monument that day that they did not seem to mind when Gallagher presented his bill, now raised to $43,000. But there was some unhappiness expressed in 1901 when several bronze castings on the monument were discovered to be rusting, which bronze does not do.

According to an article that appeared in the *Allentown Chronicle and News* in 1901, as was common with most Civil War monuments of the day, they were not totally bronze but had simply been covered with bronze paint. Gallagher pointed out to the outraged Lehigh County Commissioners that if they looked closely at his contract he had promised "bronzed" (with a "d") figures, not solid bronze.

The year 1906 marks the first attempt, this one by the county, to move the monument from Center Square. Outraged veterans promptly accused officials of a disrespect for their dead that bordered on treason. The county backed off. In 1913 it was the city's turn to have its plan to move the monument to West Park shot down by the militant former members of the Grand Army of the Republic.

Another suggestion to move the monument was proposed in 1933 when the Goddess of Liberty was undergoing repairs. Strapped for cash in the middle of the Great Depression, neither the city nor the county wanted to have to go before voters at election time and explain why they had spent taxpayer dollars on such a project.

In the 1950s the "move-the-monument" folks put forth a prolonged effort, strongly supported by *The Morning Call*. Civil War veterans were gone; they could no longer complain. This was encouraged in 1957 when the Goddess of Liberty was found to be dropping parts. She was removed from her perch in 1958 and eventually taken to the scrap yard. Rumors that her head may have been saved are still heard today. As recently as 2008 one with a superficial resemblance to the first Goddess of Liberty surfaced for sale on E-bay. A quick check with contemporary photos suggested at the very least a case of mistaken identity.

Morning Call editorial writers argued that in the automobile age the monument was a traffic hazard and that Allentown, with a Civil War monument at its center, looked more like a "hick town" than the third-largest city in Pennsylvania. The newspapers were full of ideas about what to put in the monument's place, among them cutting the column in half and replacing the goddess with a lighted transparent globe. Another showed the statues and eagles removed and replaced by figures in mid-twentieth-century military uniforms. A third suggested an ancient sighting instrument known as an armillary sphere be put in the statue's place.

The weight of tradition was on the side of keeping the monument right where it was, looking as it always had.

At Allentown's 200th anniversary celebration in 1962 the monument received renewed attention. A group called Brothers of the Brush polished up the statues until they shined like new pennies. Also that year the move-the-monument issue was apparently resolved for good. On November 6, election day, the public at large finally got a chance to weigh in and voted by 40,619 to 20,841 to keep the venerable icon right where it was.

Two years later a new Goddess of Liberty was returned to the place her sister had vacated in 1958. She was unveiled on Memorial Day, 1964, and the monument was re-dedicated to all county veterans, not just those of the Civil War era.

Immediately, the new statue was attacked as ungainly, not at all like her graceful predecessor, and *The Morning Call* groused that for the $50,000 used to restore the statue the monument could have easily been moved to West Park. One source claimed that the statue's designers, the Rambusch Decorating Company of New York, thought the column was twenty-five feet taller than its actual height, so the statue's details would need to be extra large just to be seen.

This was all forgotten by 1999 when the Soldiers and Sailors Monument turned 100. All arguments were over, and she was honored as a treasured icon of the region's past. She has reigned for 111 years. May she continue to reign for many, many more.

Lechauweki Springs

Lechauweki Springs Resort was one of the showplaces of Lehigh County in the late nineteenth century. The resort took its name, Lechauweki, from the Indian word from which the word Lehigh was in part derived. Opened in 1873 by South Bethlehem businessman John Smylie, Jr., in what was then Salisbury Township, the resort was made up of three hotels with a total of 120 rooms set in a 63-acre site of beautiful grounds.

From the start its spring waters were praised by dyspeptic Victorians from Philadelphia and New York. For those who hoped for something more vigorous than sipping water in a rocking chair, there was lawn tennis, croquet, and dancing every Wednesday and Saturday night.

Guests were encouraged to bring their own horses, and a stable was provided for that purpose. Strolling on the grounds, genteel ladies and gentlemen often picked ferns that surely found their way to be pressed in the pages of those outsized albums beloved by the time. By 1876 the resort was attracting large crowds of guests who used it as a stop-off place after attending the national centennial exhibition then taking place in Philadelphia.

At the height of its success in 1881, an outbreak of smallpox in South Bethlehem caused Lechauweki Springs to be put under quarantine restrictions. Apparently the fashionable spa-going crowd, feeling that a health resort under quarantine was no longer fashionable, went elsewhere that season, perhaps Saratoga Springs, New York. At the end of the disastrous 1882 season the Smylie family decided to close its doors for good.

Lechauweki Springs never lost its place in the hearts of local people, who continued to frequent the grounds for nature walks. Today, as a part of the Borough of Fountain Hill and located at the top of Lechauweki Avenue, the grounds of the resort are a public park. Restored in part during the borough's 1993–94 centennial, Lechauweki Springs Park retains what it never lost, its natural beauty.

(Ed Redding)

Progressivism

What was on many minds in 1912 was the intense three-way political race for president that election year. Theodore Roosevelt, the immensely popular former president, was battling with his colorless successor, William Howard Taft, Roosevelt's former Secretary of War, for the Republican nomination for president that year. Woodrow Wilson, the former president of Princeton University and current governor of New Jersey, was the Democrats' nominee.

In April the hotly contested Pennsylvania Republican primary brought Roosevelt to Lehigh County in a feverish campaign swing. Arriving at Allentown's Lyric Theater on April 12, he was greeted by a tumultuous welcome. Popular in Allentown, he was less so outside the city in traditionally Democratic rural Lehigh County. Wilson had campaigned earlier at a rousing speech to a capacity crowd at the Lyric Theater that February.

Although Taft had his supporters in Allentown, among them Harry Trexler and much of the business community, he did not campaign in Lehigh County. Democrat Wilson, the ultimate winner in 1912, carried Lehigh County with 10,834 votes. Roosevelt, who failed to get the Republican nomination and was running as a third-party Progressive, got 7,580 votes. Taft came in a distant third with 2,722. A surprise in conservative Lehigh County was the 1,056 votes garnered by Socialist Eugene V. Debs, the best showing a socialist candidate for president ever recorded in Lehigh County.

Both Wilson and Roosevelt ran on Progressive-oriented reform platforms and Debs offered even more of a radical departure from the norm. In this, Lehigh County was in line with the rest of the country. The national mood wanted to shake things up. Corruption in both business and government were issues that were making headlines and the public responded well to calls for reform.

The chief voice of reform in Lehigh County in 1912 was Fred Lewis, a Republican and strong Roosevelt backer. He even bore a striking resemblance to Roosevelt, one which he played up by dressing like his hero, including using the old-fashioned pince-nez eye glasses that hung from a string around his neck. Lewis was to serve three terms as Allentown's mayor, the last time being in the early 1930s.

His father, ironmaster Samuel Lewis, was a founder of the Allentown Iron Company in 1846. His mother Mary was an active supporter of many community causes. Chief among them were attempts to establish a public library in Allentown. As far back as the 1870s she had been encouraging it but with little success. On an October night in 1893 the few books that survived from these attempts to create a library, temporarily housed at a building at Sixth and Hamilton streets, were destroyed in a fire.

A series of unforeseen events was to see the Allentown Public Library finally come

Postcard view of the entrance to the fairgrounds, 1909. (Kurt Zwikl)

Entrance to the Great Allentown Fair, ALLENTOWN, Pa.

into existence in 1912. The behind-the-scenes force in the library's creation was Max Hess, Sr., a German Jewish immigrant who had come to Allentown in 1897 with his brother Charles. They opened a dry-goods store in a hotel at Ninth and Hamilton streets and by 1912, through skillful use of advertizing and showmanship, Hess Brothers was the fastest growing retail establishment in Lehigh County.

Very much in tune with the Progressive spirit of his time, Hess was to play a leading role in a number of philanthropic projects before his tragically early death at age 59 in 1922. As a young man he had attended Cooper Union in New York. Founded by businessman and philanthropist Peter Cooper, it offered a tuition-free scholarship and a high-quality education for young people who could not afford one. Its major tenet, practiced and advised by its founder, was that those who had done well should also do good. Perhaps Max Hess learned the importance of philanthropy there. Like Harry Trexler, Hess did not believe in personally touting his good works.

Entertainment

The last half of the nineteenth century and the early twentieth century saw the creation in Lehigh County of a number of forms of entertainment.

Until this time Christmas, a much bigger festival among the Pennsylvania Germans than it was with their non-Dutch neighbors, the Fourth of July, and Fair Week were about the only times other than Sundays that farm work was suspended. Taverns, inns, and saloons were plentiful, some even managed by women, but most were regarded as strictly a masculine domain.

Farmers all across the county eagerly anticipated Fair Week. In 1854 the Lehigh County Agricultural Society created the Lehigh County Fair, which was known since the 1880s as the "Great Allentown Fair." It moved in 1888 from its space near Liberty Street, which was becoming overcrowded, to former farm fields at Seventeenth and Chew streets, then regarded as the far west end of the city. It offered everything from horse races featuring nationally known Dan Patch to shooting galleries and the slightly scandalous hootchy-kootchy

girls of farm-boy dreams. In 1911 a new enlarged grandstand was created to cater to the growing racetrack crowds. But the fair, open only one week a year, hardly slaked the thirst for summertime entertainment.

Recreational sports in the form of baseball arrived in Lehigh County in the 1860s. Sources show that baseball was being played by a team formed at Lafayette College in 1860. Local newspapers recorded games played between a Philadelphia team, an ancestor of the Philadelphia Athletics, against a Mauch Chunk team at Mauch Chunk in the early 1860s. By the close

of the Civil War the Mauch Chunk team was playing a South Bethlehem team on a semi-regular basis.

Lehigh County's first baseball team, the Allentown Pioneers, was organized among Civil War veterans in December 1865. The leading citizens of the community joined in to manage the team, whose rules combined those of baseball and an older ball-and-base game known as rounders. The Pioneers' home field was a large pasture at Penn and Union streets that belonged to a farmer named William Fry. It was located where the Riverbend apartment complex is today.

Real baseball, following rules created by early New York teams, was brought to Lehigh County by William S. Young, Jr., whose father was a local entrepreneur. In his business life William S. Young, Sr., owned a German-language newspaper, *Der Lecha Patriot*, invested heavily in local real estate, and was a partner with Henry Leh (later the founder of Leh's Department Store) in a dry-goods business, Young & Leh. His home, where his son grew up, still stands at the corner of Penn and Walnut streets.

Miss Carrie V. Moyer of Macungie, circa 1906, a professional baseball pitcher in the early twentieth century. (Macungie Historical Society)

While attending Amherst College in the 1860s, Young, Jr., had apparently gotten to know members of the school's baseball team. Established by students from New York in the 1850s, the team, the "Lord Jeffs," calls itself "the oldest collegiate baseball program in the world." Their 1859 game against Williams College was the first intercollegiate baseball game ever played.

In 1866 Young organized a baseball team called the Allentown Stars. They were the first Lehigh County team known to have held regular games, both with the Pioneers and teams from Bethlehem and Easton. The Stars' uniforms consisted of a cap with a star in the center. As was common at the time, they had no baseball gloves. At a reunion of former Stars' players on June 23, 1909, they showed the local press the scars that their hands still bore from that time.

The Stars' ballfield was a large grassy meadow, now a parking lot, near Jordan Creek between Hamilton and Union streets. Rude benches, boards set on willow-tree stumps, were the bleachers occupied by the fans that came to root for the team. Barefoot local boys were deployed along the creek bank to retrieve balls. Hand-sewn in Philadelphia, the balls cost $1.50 each, the average daily wage of a laborer in the 1860s.

Although it began as a sport of the well-to-do, baseball quickly took fire in Lehigh County among all levels of society. By 1870 what the newspapers of the day called "baseball fever" was hot. Allentown alone had five teams, one of them, the Empire, being made up of Irishmen from the First and later Sixth Ward.

In 1877 Macungie was home to the Resolute baseball team who, according to their minute book, were ordering uniforms from Philadelphia and established a system of fines for players who did not show up for games or used profane language. Those who did not show up for team meetings were fined five cents. Those who were intoxicated before a game were fined a dollar. The team's president was O.P. Knauss who, as editor of the local newspaper, saw that team news got plenty of coverage.

By 1912, although few people at that time would have remembered it, the region had already made some baseball history. On July 5, 1898, Lizzie Arlington, real name Lizzie Stride or Stroud of Mahanoy City, became the first woman to pitch in a professional minor league base-

The iconic carousel of Central Park delighted both children and adults. (Robert Reinbold)

ball game. Playing at Reading for the Reading Coal-Heavers, she contributed to the defeat of the Allentown Peanuts. In the early twentieth century, the pitching abilities of Carrie Moyer from Macungie created a sensation as far away as Chicago.

Other than baseball and perhaps the old swimming hole, the two most popular forms of summertime recreation in Lehigh County were two amusement parks, Dorney Park and Central Park.

Dorney was the oldest. It had been established west of Allentown as a fishing weir and hotel in 1860 by Solomon P. Dorney. It offered a chance to catch a fish and have it turned into a dinner. Set in a bucolic meadow, it was a getaway from the noisy streets of Allentown. Dorney's slogan, "the Natural Spot," said it all.

For those seeking something more daring there was Central Park. Opened in 1892, it was the classic "trolley car park," a type rapidly sprouting all over America at the dawn of the twentieth century.

Postcard view of the Derby Racer, a popular ride at Central Park.

Central Park was owned by Lehigh Valley Transit in 1948. This is LVT car No. 812 on the Central Park line in 1948. (Robert Reinbold)

Located on the east side of Allentown and the western edge of suburban Bethlehem at a little place called Rittersville, Central Park was designed by the Lehigh Valley Traction Company to get the public of both towns to use the streetcar even when they didn't

The Dentzel merry-go-round at Dorney Park.

have to go to work or shop. The park led to what were known as "streetcar suburbs." A trolley line usually had a subsidiary land-development company associated with it. Amusement-park goers, it was hoped, would notice "For Sale" signs on a lot and decide such a site, with its access to ready public transportation, would be an ideal location to build a home. Some urban historians argue it was the streetcar that set the pattern for the automobile-fueled suburbs of the 1950s and '60s.

Central Park offered vast spaces for family and church picnics. "Monster Family Picnic Held" was a headline that appeared frequently in the local press at a time when "monster," for most people, meant something large, not an imaginary movie menace. It was popular with many local ethnic groups as the location for club gatherings, offering popular amusement-park rides and fun houses such as might be found in Philadelphia's parks or New York's Coney Island.

Theatrical productions like George M. Cohan's flag-waving song fests or slapstick comedy by vaudeville acts like the Marx Brothers appeared at Central Park's outdoor theater. In 1912 the Lehigh Valley Transit Company printed a brochure touting both the up-to-date thrill rides Central Park offered, and the easy access by streetcar.

During the twentieth century the parks were to undergo a role reversal. Starting in the 1930s, Central Park would be plagued by a tragic series of fires that destroyed many of its rides and eventually led to the park's closing in the early 1950s. Today Westminster Village, a nursing home, occupies most of what was once Central Park.

Dorney Park, following the addition of a roller coaster in the 1920s and its dance pavilion, Castle Garden, was to take its place as the region's amusement mecca. Today its "thrill rides" eclipse anything that could have been imagined in 1912. Transportation may have been a factor in this change. Tied to the streetcar, Central Park went into decline with the end of the trolleys. Dorney, with ample parking space for cars, flourished.

Nothing that might possibly be called a theater, a place where entertainment could be had all year round, existed in Allentown before the Civil War. The first was the opening on the 800 block of Hamilton Street of Hagenbuch's Opera House. Named after its founders,

Allentown and Bethlehem Rapid Transit Company car no. 4 stopped outside the Geo. Weidner's Rittersville Hotel on August 2, 1891, its inaugural run. The trolley company developed Central Park nearby, and opened the land between Allentown and Bethlehem for development. The line became part of the Lehigh Valley Transit system in 1894.

brothers Benjamin J. and C.H. Hagenbuch, it was a combination of first-floor shops and a second-floor playhouse that could hold up to 1,400. Designed in the style that originated in Europe and today is known as Second French Empire, it opened on December 26, 1870.

The building hosted both local and national talent. Among the big names that appeared there was Mark Twain, who spoke on October 17, 1871. Local critics in both Allentown and Bethlehem were not impressed with the young author, who had just started on the lecture circuit. Another was Tony Pastor,

The Manhattan Hotel (formerly the Rittersville Hotel) in 1911. (Robert Reinbold)

one of the best-known New York impresarios of the 1870s, '80s, and '90s. He is often considered the father of vaudeville, a series of family-oriented variety acts that made the stage suitable for Victorian women and children.

Pastor ran a popular New York theater and had a traveling troupe of actors that would travel to places like Allentown. One of his biggest discoveries was a buxom actress named Lillian Russell, "Diamond Lil." She was very popular in Allentown and went on to be a national hit, and could still draw a crowd at her last appearance in Lehigh County in 1920, when she lent her support to the Republican presidential campaign of Warren G. Harding in a rally at the Lyric Theater.

In 1873, an early play by western author Ned Buntline called "The Scouts of the Prairie" attracted large crowds to the Opera House. Among its stars was a former Indian scout Buntline had persuaded to go on the stage. He was named William Cody. A few years later he

The Pergola movie theater at Ninth and Hamilton was the first in America that showed color movies regularly. It and adjacent buildings were torn down in 1926 to be replaced by the PP&L tower.

would return to Allentown at the head of a circus-type Wild West show under the name that would be known around the world, Buffalo Bill.

Perhaps because of its German roots there was a strong appreciation of music of all kinds in Lehigh County. Among the best-known musical organizations of the day that appeared at the Opera House was the Mendelssohn Quintette Club of Boston. These were European-trained musicians based in Boston who toured America, bringing the chamber-music works of Beethoven and other classical composers to places that would not ordinarily hear them. The club appeared at least three times at Hagenbuch's in the 1870s. Surviving programs in the Lehigh County Historical Society archives show they performed a mix of classical and popular music during their appearances.

Hagenbuch's closed in 1886 and was taken over by John Bowen, a retail and wholesale grocery merchant that some credit with being the first to sell bananas in Allentown. The Academy of Music, a much larger building, quickly opened at the northeast corner of Sixth and Linden. Until a fire swept it in 1903 it was a very popular playhouse. One of its most-repeated musical shows was a version of the Gilbert and Sullivan operetta "H.M.S. Pinafore" in the Pennsylvania-German dialect.

In 1899 the Lyric Theater, today Allentown Symphony Hall, opened for legitimate plays and musical performances including opera. Originally constructed as the Central Market Hall it was to be an indoor farmers' market. Having become used to setting up on Center Square rent free, the thought of having to pay for space hit frugal Pennsylvania-German farmers the wrong way. So it was decided to use the space to hold meetings and concerts. These proved to be wildly successful, and by the late 1890s it was being converted into a musical hall and later a theater. The first play shown there was a comedy loosely based on the life of eighteenth-century Prussian King Frederick the Great. In 1911 an English-language version of Puccini's opera "The Girl of the Golden West" packed the theater as a crowd in formal wear paid top price of $3.25 for tickets.

The Lyric became the primary community gathering place for visiting notables and politicians. In 1912 presidential candidates Theodore Roosevelt and Woodrow Wilson both gave campaign speeches there. Among many other national figures to appear at the Lyric in

Allentown: Home Of The First Halloween Parade

Every year toward the end of October, Lehigh County and the Lehigh Valley region are alive with Halloween parades and related Halloween events. Newspapers carry stories and local television offers footage of parading children in costume, fire trucks, a politician or two, and bands from local schools playing away.

Newcomers to the region, who think of Halloween as exclusively a holiday celebrated by trick-or-treating children on October 31, are surprised to find it transformed into a movable feast, with parades being held as long as two weeks before the actual holiday, some at night and some during the day.

The reason the celebration is so focused around parades here may be that Allentown in Lehigh County had the first recorded Halloween parade in America over 100 years ago.

How far back the celebration of Halloween goes in Lehigh County is unknown. Scholars still argue over its ties to pagan Celtic, Roman, and early Christian holidays. It did not become really popular in America until large numbers of Irish immigrants, following the potato famine of the 1840s and '50s, brought their folk customs here.

Whatever its origins, the holiday was being celebrated in Lehigh County in the late nineteenth century. At least some people were not happy with the way it was. Perhaps their view was best summed up by the irate editor of the Allentown Chronicle and News in a November 1, 1892, editorial:

> When young hoodlums walk boldly up to a man and dash a handful of corn violently into his face, to the imminent risk of his eyes; when drunken loafers deliberately empty bags of flour over the dresses of ladies utterly ruining them; when door bells are pulled out by the root; and steps smashed and carried away, it is time to call a halt.

Apparently without intending to, it was the Pioneer Band of Allentown that took the first steps toward changing the holiday into the ritual it has become in Lehigh County today. On a warm October day in 1905, the band's historian Matt Cascioli told The Morning Call in 2001, band members decided to leave their stuffy rehearsal space and practice outside. Soon, a group of listeners, some of them children, had gathered and before long were following the band around. People liked this so much the band did it again the following year, this time awarding costumed children small prizes like a ball or a box of candy.

Ten years later, in 1915, the Allentown Halloween parade had become big enough to attract the attention of the national press. The parade that year was two miles long, took nearly two hours to run, and had an estimated 5,000 to 6,000 participants, not all them children. More and more, those taking part were young adults. At least fifty young men competed that year for the best Charlie Chaplin costume. The movie-star comedian had recently skyrocketed to public attention in his popular favorite role as the "Little Tramp," and everybody wanted to imitate him.

Bethlehem held its first Halloween parade in 1921. By then the idea of holiday parades was spreading around the Lehigh Valley. It really took off in the 1950s and '60s when huge numbers of baby-boom kids began to come on the scene.

So popular is the Halloween parade today that when a freak October 29 snowstorm prevented the city from holding the parade in 2011, Allentown's city fathers decided to hold it in November, after the official holiday, rather than cancel it entirely.

The movie "Circus Days" was shown at the Rialto soon after it opened in 1921.

Interior of the Rialto, 935 Hamilton St. Allentown. (Library of Congress)

The Lyric Theatre, today Symphony Hall, at the beginning of the twentieth century. (Kurt Zwikl)

the first part of the twentieth century were, in 1902, African-American educator Booker T. Washington, and in 1911 Socialist Party presidential candidate Eugene V. Debs.

Next door to the Lyric, Keith's Orpheum Theater opened in 1906. It was a part of a national chain of vaudeville theaters that belonged to Benjamin Franklin Keith of Philadelphia. His "refined vaudeville," as it was known, was popular up and down the east coast. Many years later the Radio Corporation of America would buy out the Keith chain and use the theaters to show films made by a movie studio they created. It was called Radio-Keith-Orpheum and known by its initials RKO. In the 1920s Allentown's Orpheum Theater would be taken over by Wilmer and Vincent's State movie-theater chain.

Movies came to Lehigh County about 1905. The first theater was in Allentown, a small one named the Nickelette. It was favored by young male audiences who liked westerns. In 1907 James Bowen, a prominent local attorney and entrepreneur, opened the Pergola, a combination penny arcade, bowling alley, and billiard parlor at 902 Hamilton Street where the PPL tower office building is today. Four years later he tore out the penny arcade and built a fifty-seat movie theater. He added a theater organ, the first known in Lehigh County, to provide background music for silent movies.

The Palace movie theater opened in 1909 in Emmaus, and the Majestic in Catasauqua the same year. Each replaced an earlier Nickelette. The manager of the new theater in Emmaus, Edward H. Buss, assured the townspeople at the time that although only a few years earlier the Nickelette theater had run riot, flaunting its blatant and sensational picture entertainments, "the new films have driven out the immoral and rotten shows and are fast putting the salon out of business. … A world of romance and art is brought before your eyes … fit for the young and old to see without any demoralizing results." Furthermore, in a reference to Allentown, "You will notice that the management of the PALACE THEATRE is keeping up well with our Neighboring Metropolis in showing big things."

Attracted by the new technologies of his day, James Bowen was fascinated when he heard about a new color movie process called Kinemacolor, created in England and being promoted by Charles Urban. Kinemacolor had made its debut in America on December 11, 1909, at Madison Square Garden, where it attracted a great deal of attention. It excited Bowen who went to London with his business partner Gilbert Aymar, an actor turned promoter, and purchased five of the Kinemacolor movie projectors. Four of them were used in attempts to raise money by showing them to potential investors in New York, Philadelphia, Boston, and Chicago.

Bowen used the fifth Kinemacolor projector to show films at the Pergola, which became the first theater in America to show color movies on a regular basis. Admission was a nickel, ten cents for a reserved seat. That December the great French actress Sarah Bern-

The Emaus Band (founded 1892) is standing in front of the entrance to the new Palace movie theater on Main Street in 1909. (Emmaus Historical Society)

hardt, then appearing on tour at the Lyric Theater, insisted on seeing this new wonder, colored movies.

In 1961 John Y. Kohl, longtime theater critic for *The Morning Call*, recalled having seen as a teenager in 1911 color films of the Delhi Durbar, a ceremony in British-ruled India that year to welcome King George V and Queen Mary. Filmed by Urban and a staff of eight, and running over two hours, it was the first major color movie known.

According to Kohl, the Pergola's bread and butter were westerns and melodramas. The former were very popular in that era during Saturday matinees when they were shown continuously. D. Ellsworth Knorr, the Pergola's manager, in 1961 fondly remembered escorting Sarah Bernhardt on his arm to see the Kinemacolor films. He also recalled his far less glamorous task of answering the phone calls of worried mothers looking for their children on Saturday afternoons at the turn of the last century. These "cowboy movies" were simple films, many done in the wilds of New Jersey and acted by unknowns.

It was not until 1915–16 that Charlie Chaplin became the first recognized "star." So popular was Chaplin that his name ran bigger than the title of the film in Allentown newspaper movie ads.

West Park

Entertainment came not just from the movies or on the stage. It was on September 17, 1908, that West Park, Allentown's first public park, was born. The process began in the late nineteenth century when the slice of property from Fifteenth to Seventeenth streets between Linden and Turner streets in Allentown was being discussed as a future site for the city's much-needed reservoir. It had been acquired by the city for that purpose in the 1880s. But when a standpipe, a high vertical pipe, was added at the Waterworks at Thirteenth and Lawrence streets in 1900 to balance water distribution, the reservoir was made unnecessary.

By 1900 the lot had become a vacant, bramble-covered dumping ground. A part of the property had been reclaimed by some local baseball teams who turned it into a ballfield where they played on weekends. During the week small boys emulated their heroes by playing baseball there. It was not unknown for a ball to find its way through the window of a nearby home. Perhaps its high point as a baseball field came in 1905 when the Cuban X Giants, one of the leading teams in the segregated Negro Leagues, defeated in a close game an Allentown team, the Franklins.

The future of the site was changed in 1902 when Allentown Mayor Fred Lewis established the city's parks department. At the same time it was brought to his attention that a group of South Allentown developers was using city water without paying for it. Lewis went to Harry Trexler, the head of the South Allentown Development Co., and told him about this.

Trexler said he was unaware of this practice and would put a stop to it. To compensate the city, he would take over the water-department land between Linden and Turner and turn it into a park. From 1906 to 1908 Trexler and the city worked together to create a park on the site. Trexler donated almost $14,000, including $3,600 for its band shell.

The band shell was created by the Philadelphia architectural firm of Horace Trumbauer, a Pennsylvania German and one of the leading architects of the day. Some sources suggest the band shell was actually designed by young African-American architect Julian Abele, who had just joined the firm in 1906. He was one of the first professionally trained African-American architects of the time. According to the notes of Allentown city engineer Harry Bascom, the Allentown band shell was based on one Trumbauer's firm had done for Willow Grove Park outside Philadelphia. Whatever the source it was popular with local people as a band mecca, and a place to sleep when summer heat was overwhelming.

The trees and shrubs came from Philadelphia landscape architects Thomas Meehan and Sons. Among their previous work had been the Quaker City's Fairmount Park. Thomas Meehan had died in 1901; his son, J. Franklin Meehan, oversaw the work for West Park. He would later design the grounds of the Little Lehigh Parkway, Trexler's country estate of

Allentown Public Library: Reading Along With The Times

Step into the Allentown Public Library any given day and you are sure to find it busy. The current building, at Twelfth and Hamilton streets, never seems to be at rest.

In the second floor microfilm room, genealogists are busy trying to find Aunt Sadie. Downstairs, every computer is in use, helping redefine the knowledge revolution. Nearby, in a reading room, folks read their way through newspapers and magazines.

As an institution, the Allentown Public Library is a youngster of 100 years old and easy to take for granted. But the prologue of its history was a long one.

Seven hundred and ten was the population of Allentown when its first library opened. Those that gathered at 7 o'clock on Saturday, December 22, 1810, at the home of leading citizen Colonel George Rhoads were responding to a newspaper advertisement to form the Allentown English Language Circulating Library. That evening was spent drawing up bylaws and writing a constitution.

In 1810 there was no such concept as a free public library. In a place as small as Allentown, where many people worked at farming or a trade from morning until night, leisure time to read was the privilege of a very few. There was the added concern of opening an English library in a community where German was the most widely spoken and read language. The ad for the English language library was placed in a German-language newspaper, the only paper in town.

Among other early Allentown libraries was the Library Company of Northampton, Northampton having been Allentown's official name until 1838. There was also the Fratres Literarium, Latin for "Brothers of Literature," which opened in 1848 and existed until the 1870s. It was founded by Professor Robert C. Chandler of the Allentown Academy.

The real impulse for what would become the Allentown Public Library did not begin until after the Civil War. Local women, many the wives of leading citizens, took up the cause. Chief among them was Mary Lewis, the wife of iron maker and banker Samuel Lewis. She was also the mother of Fred Lewis, later a three-term mayor of Allentown and Congressman.

Lewis kicked off her efforts as early as 1874. She used the unique fundraising technique of offering, on New Year's Eve, a game supper based on a successful hunting trip a local taxidermist had recently made out West. The menu included buffalo, deer, and bear meat. Local ladies dressed in colonial costume served, and a "hop" with dancing followed. Everyone raved about the party, but, alas, the sad state of the national and local economy due to the Panic of 1873 that had brought to a halt the iron industry on which the county's prosperity depended led to empty pocket books and the idea died.

Mary Lewis and other local women persisted nonetheless. They gathered the few books they could find from the Brothers of Literature collection and made them available to subscribers. They got the Odd Fellows fraternal order to agree to house them at their meeting rooms at the B&B (Breinig and Bachman) building at the southeast corner of Sixth and Hamilton Streets. The low point of their efforts came on October 13, 1893, when these books were destroyed in a fire that reduced the B&B building to ashes.

Even before the fire, Allentown woman were working toward a public library. Lewis organized the Woman's League, whose goal was to create a library for all people. Balls, bazaars, and other events raised $1,200. With this handsome sum the League began to buy books that they placed in a building on South Seventh Street in 1893, after the fire. This was the start of the Allentown Public Library's first collection.

It was the twentieth century before the actual founding of the Allentown Public Library came about. In 1907 the female employees of Hess Brothers Department Store formed the M.U.M.

Circle, short for Members Until Married. Max Hess, Sr., the store's founder, was a firm and strong supporter of community causes and may have privately given his encouragement.

The club's leader, Blanche Phifer, was looking for a cause and found it after Mary Lewis told her of the decades-long efforts of Allentown women to create a public library. It was about time, they both agreed, that it should happen.

M.U.M quickly went into action with a series of fundraisers, among them a car raffle and a roll of honor on which those who gave anywhere from $1 to $1,000 would find their names. M.U.M. put the $5,000 made from these efforts toward a $10,000 mortgage on a building at 914 Hamilton Street. As renovations were being made, tragically, Blanche Phifer, now married as Blanche Phifer Travena, died. The newspapers gave no cause for her death.

The same year that Travena died, 1912, the library she never lived to see became reality. It was helped over the top by the efforts of the Allentown Chamber of Commerce as a part of the 100th anniversary of Lehigh County celebrations then going on. The chamber launched a fundraising campaign that raised $12,000 from the business community, enough to pay off the mortgage. The chamber also promised to establish its own headquarters in the library.

Opening day was November 25, 1912. The high point came when Mary Lewis walked forward and gave to Dr. George T. Ettinger, Muhlenberg College's dean and head of the Allentown Public Library Association, books she had signed out just before the fire of 1893, and the old charter of the Fratres Literarium.

From that day in 1912 to 1978 that Georgian-style building at 914–916 Hamilton Street was home to the Allentown Library, and generations remember it fondly even today. But by the late 1960s the building was coming to be regarded by some as cramped and dowdy.

Real change came in 1972 when Morning Call publisher Donald Miller came home from an overseas trip and noticed that the Asbury Methodist Church at Twelfth and Hamilton had been destroyed in a fire. Deciding it would be a perfect site for new library, Miller began a massive fund drive that poured a great deal of his family money and that of other community leaders into its building. The task took up so much of Miller's time that one of his newspaper executives was heard to say he would be glad when the library was finished "and I can get my publisher back."

He got his wish in 1978 when the current library finally opened. It stands as a monument to both Miller and its former longtime executive director Kathryn Stephanoff, who worked with him in planning it.

(Reprinted with permission of The Morning Call. All Rights Reserved)

93

Springwood, now Trexler Memorial Park, and the Brookside Country Club.

With the opening of the new space, officially called City Park but popularly known as West Park, in 1908, the crowds flocked to see it. The Allentown Band offered the first concert in the band shell. Throughout the following week the city's other bands offered a full evening of entertainment. Trexler was not present for any of the events. Presumably he just let the park speak for itself. It was the first in the city's park system. Turner Street along the park became one of the most desirable upper-middle-class residential areas in the city when the West End Development Company built a row of handsome townhouses facing the park. The development company was run by Harry Trexler; the homes were built with materials from the Trexler Lumber Company.

A whole series of industrial and technological marvels, from railroads to automobiles to electric lights, were transforming Lehigh County. Jobs were plentiful throughout the county. If many people in the rural areas in 1912 still went to bed with kerosene lamps and plowed their fields with old-fashioned horsepower, even they recognized change was coming.

End of an Era

With all of the marvels that the new twentieth century seemed to promise, there was also fear that the world was moving too fast. Where was it going?

On the morning of April 15, 1912, the residents of Lehigh County were as stunned as the rest of the world when they awoke to the startling news that the luxury liner RMS *Titanic* had plunged to the bottom of the North Atlantic.

A paragon of modern industrial technology, the largest floating object ever built, one that was declared "virtually unsinkable," had, the night before, rammed an iceberg on its maiden voyage to New York, taking with it 1,503 lives. Among them were John Jacob Astor IV, the richest man in America, Major Archibald Willingham Butt, military aide to President William Howard Taft, and poor immigrants from Russia and Italy seeking a better life in the New World.

Over the next several weeks the local newspapers would tell of a 24-year-old Syrian immigrant woman, Mary Abraham, engaged to a local man who worked in the cement industry, who was saved. Also a survivor was Lillian Cribb, the 17-year-old daughter of a butler from Bournemouth, England, who was the niece of Mrs. John Moser of Bethlehem. Cribb was returning with her father to America, where he had worked for several wealthy employers and planned to relocate his family. He placed the girl in a lifeboat, and died when the ship sank.

One local person who did not survive was Annie C. Funk, a 37-year-old Mennonite missionary on her way home to Bally, Berks County, from India to aid her gravely ill mother.

On April 12, 1912, Funk celebrated her 38th birthday on the *Titanic*. She was about to step into a lifeboat when the woman next to her shouted, "my children! my children!" Funk stepped away and let the children take her place. Hereford Mennonite Church, her home congregation, conducted a special memorial service in Funk's memory. Although her body was never found, a stone was raised to her in the church's cemetery and is still there today.

The horror over the sinking of the *Titanic* had barely left the public mind when something far worse suddenly appeared on the horizon two years later.

On long summer days in 1914, as the Old World seemed to be going mad, Lehigh County watched and waited. The June day an Austrian archduke died in Sarajevo, a headline in *The Morning Call* read "Rain Fails to Mar Catasauqua Home Coming Week."

For a time things appeared to quiet down. European diplomats in shiny top hats on the front pages of *The Morning Call* appeared to be saving peace. No one in Lehigh County was reading the diplomatic cable traffic between Berlin, St. Petersberg, Paris, and London. There was still hope.

Perhaps Victor de Journo, French immigrant, Allentown soap maker, and baseball fanatic, would be able to take the Allentown Tri-State league club and an all-star team picked from other clubs to tour Europe at the close of the 1914 baseball season.

Maybe there was no need for Charles Hess, then in Paris learning about the latest in French fashions for Hess Brothers' French Room, to hurry home to America before the fashionable crowds gathered for the fall races at Longchamp.

Should the elderly members of Allentown's beer-brewing Neuweiler family, then touring the fatherland on a long-planned visit to their native Germany, cut the trip short? Europe had come so close to the brink before and always pulled back, surely it would do so again.

But with a startling suddenness toward the end of that July, war talk broke out into the open. Across the front page of *The Morning Call* headlines almost seemed to shout:

July 28: AUSTRIA DECLARES WAR ON SERBIA.

July 29: CZAR ORDERS GENERAL MOBILIZATION IN RUSSIA.

August 1: FRENCH GENERAL MOBILIZATION IS ORDERED.

August 2: PEACE HANGS BY A THREAD.

August 3: GERMANY DECLARES WAR ON FRANCE.

August 4: ENGLAND DECLARES WAR ON GERMANY.

Now there were no more doubts. War had come to Europe. What would it mean to America? As they were across the country, people in Lehigh County watched and worried.

Hamilton Street, Allentown (PPL Corporation)

CHAPTER THREE

FROM WAR TIME TO SWING TIME: LEHIGH COUNTY 1914-1940

Historians have come to call the period after 1914 "the short twentieth century." The years from the start of World War I to the collapse of the Berlin Wall and the end of the Cold War in 1989 are said to form a discrete time period. Two world wars and the 45 years of uneasy peace between the United States and the Soviet Union that followed are the big defining moments.

At first Lehigh County people hoped that the European War, as it was called from 1914 to 1917, would have no real impact locally. Foreign travel, of course, was disrupted. The Allentown baseball team never made it to Europe. Charles Hess hurried back from Paris and the Neuweiler family later gave a harrowing story to *The Morning Call* of what it was like getting out of Germany before the borders closed.

One Lehigh County resident, Annie Weaver, was to see the start of World War I up close. The daughter of an Allentown furniture store owner, her tour of Germany, Switzerland, and France had begun that fateful June of 1914.

The first hint something might be wrong was in Berlin when her tour group returned to their bus-like touring car. They found a circular on all the seats noting the assassination of Archduke Franz Ferdinand, heir to the throne of Austria-Hungary, in Sarajevo, Bosnia, by Serbian nationalists, but no one seemed too upset by what would later be regarded as the spark that ignited World War I.

Weaver knew something was clearly going on when early one July morning in Heidelberg, an ancient German university town, she awoke just before daybreak to the sound of hobnailed boots striking cobblestones. Looking out the hotel window she saw companies of German soldiers marching in full uniform. Since there had been no sign of them during the day, she wondered later if the Germans had secretly mobilized their troops at night.

Weaver was in Paris on August 3 when Germany declared war on France and Russia. The city was suddenly full of soldiers. Two waiters were the only male staff left at her hotel. "Everywhere we saw men bidding goodbye to their families," she recalled.

All over Paris shops were shuttered. The only really busy places were railroad stations as people stood in long lines trying to buy tickets out of the city. She and the rest of her tour group were forced to get passports, until then not required for international travel, in order to leave. Helped by a young Englishman and a French Boy Scout, she was able to get to England but could take little luggage.

Once in England, Weaver found her way to Liverpool and after an uneventful crossing of the Atlantic she was back in Allentown. Several months later a package arrived from her Paris hotel with the clothes and other things she had been forced to leave behind.

Lehigh County residents' first reaction to World War I was to thank God for the Atlantic Ocean. "America can think itself lucky that it has no entangling foreign alliances," wrote *Morning Call* Editor David A. Miller. Before 1914 was over a stalemate was already shaping up between France and Germany. The most popular song in the country was "I DIDN'T RAISE MY BOY TO BE A SOLDIER" with its lyrics,

> *There'd be no war today,*
> *If mothers all would say,*
> *I didn't raise my boy to be a soldier.*

As much as Americans wanted to stay out of the war, the world had become too complex for that. Lehigh County farmers could now follow the rising price for food in a world no longer able to buy Russian wheat. And though fears of unemployment and layoffs had rippled through the economy at the war's outbreak, by the end of 1914 local factories were booming with orders for war-related products.

War Production

Local industry played an important role during World War I. In 1915, Bethlehem Steel CEO Charles M. Schwab turned down a $100 million dollar offer from Kaiser Wilhelm II of Germany for a controlling interest in the company. "Gentlemen," he is said to have remarked to the German ruler's representatives, "I have given my word to the British … that I would maintain my personal control of the Bethlehem interest, and there are no sums you can offer me to get me to go back on my word."

Two months after the war had begun, Schwab contacted British First Sea Lord Winston Churchill, promising that he would do all he could to aid the Allied cause. When Churchill told Schwab in a personal request that he needed submarines, the steel man willingly agreed. Not only did he speed production up from 14 months to 5½ months, but in order to get around the USA's neutrality laws that forbade the export of such weapons to nations at war, Schwab had the parts shipped from America to Canada, where they were assembled. By 1917 Bethlehem Steel was the largest single supplier of arms and munitions for the Allied cause.

In 1918, when the U.S. had officially joined the Allied cause and Schwab had been placed in charge of managing shipbuilding for the government he received the following note from Churchill: "I am delighted to learn of your appointment which will enable you to turn your wonderful energy and unique experience to an urgent and vital task. Remembering our work together at the Admiralty at the beginning of the war and the way in which you surmounted every difficulty and successfully completed every undertaking, I feel complete confidence now."

One Lehigh County industry that had a direct connection with the World War I battlefield was Allentown's barbed wire works. Located on the east side of Lehigh Street, just south of the Little Lehigh Creek, it had opened in Easton as the Iowa Barb Wire Co., and in 1886 was moved to Allentown where, because of more level terrain, it could add additional facilities more easily. In 1892 it was acquired by speculator John "Bet-A-Million" Gates (this nickname came about when Gates bet $900,000 on a horse race and won; newspaper headline writers, apparently because it sounded more dramatic, supplied the inflation). Gates renamed it the American Steel and Wire Company and sold it for $50 million in 1901 to U.S. Steel Corporation.

From the beginning, a mini-town grew up along the wire mills. The heart of it was known as Wire Street. Here immigrants from Europe and local Pennsylvania-German workers mixed. It started with 300 men. By 1917, when World War I was at its height and the city's population was almost 54,000, it employed 1,200 workers.

At the start of the war, since the U.S. was neutral, the wire mill supplied both sides. As the war ground to a stalemate there was a huge demand for barbed wire on the Western Front to protect troops in trenches. Around the clock, steel ingots were sent by rail from Pittsburgh to Allentown where they were melted, rolled, and drawn into barbed wire, galvanized wire, and nails of all shapes and sizes.

After the United States entered the war in 1917 the wire works could no longer sell to the Germans. But there was already plenty of it on the much-fought-over fields of France.

A group of nurses in France during World War I. Utie Kleibscheidel of Catasauqua, one of the first women to reach the rank of Lt. Col. in the U.S. Army, is in the center, holding a book. (Catasauqua Public Library)

Mack "Bulldog" trucks stored along Lawrence Street in 1918, awaiting shipment to Europe. (Lehigh County Historical Society)

Years after the war at least one Lehigh County doughboy recalled his dismay at crawling toward a German trench under barbed wire that bore a tag "Product of Barb Wire Works, Allentown Pa." Before 1917 no one harbored those feelings but rather admired it as a fine example of local industry. Many in Allentown set their clocks and watches by the whistle that marked shift change at the works.

The wire works had its own police force, fire company, and medical staff. But what apparently impressed contemporaries most was the telegraph-order operations room. The telegraph keys clicked wildly and ran non-stop as the company's wire-making machines, recording orders from all over the globe. Globalization, not yet a word, was in full swing at the Barb Wire Works.

What seemed like a herald of the future in 1917 proved in reality to be an echo of the past. When the war ended the works limped along and really felt the Depression. The decision by U.S. Steel to transfer its operations to a new plant in Ohio and close the Allentown works in 1943 sounded its death knell. It gradually became an eyesore and was torn down in the 1960s.

Mack Trucks, then known as the International Motor Company, was another local company that had its identity shaped by the war. The company had come to Allentown in 1905 from New York and was headed by the Mack brothers, Jack, William, and Augustus or "Gus," and was already well known as a maker of buses and trucks. By 1914 it had merged with a number of other truck companies and become the International Motor Company.

Its major contribution to the war effort was the sturdy, rugged Mack AC truck. In 1917 about 150 of these trucks, with their distinctive front that resembles a face, were sold to the British. Seeing in it a look similar to their own national pet, they called it the "bulldog" truck. Thousands of AC trucks, built in Allentown, served the Allies during the war. Soon the Mack Bulldog was so well known that in 1932 it became the company logo. With its combination of toughness and durability, by the time the war was over Mack had created a world-wide legend.

August 1914 to April 1917

From 1914 to 1917, the United States was technically neutral. During that phase of World War I there were young men who left Lehigh County to serve in the German Army. When the war broke out in 1914, *The Morning Call* recorded Allentown's ethnic Sixth Ward witnessed many local immigrant men jamming the railroad station to return to their regiments in Europe. In 1915 the newspaper printed in full a letter one of them wrote to his parents while serving with the Kaiser's army on the Western Front.

Unlike World War II, Germany at the start of World War I was not regarded by most Americans, particularly the German-oriented Lehigh Valley, as being as alien as the Third Reich would later be. Many were proud of Germany's transformation from a collection of small bickering states to an emerging world power. Beyond that, there were strong cultural ties that went back to the eighteenth century. German was a required course at Allentown High School, as it had been since the 1850s. The text book used to teach the course in the early twentieth century was titled "Im Vaterland" (In the Fatherland). Despite the strong German background of the county German classes were dropped in Catasauqua in May 1918, and became an elective in Allentown High School that same month.

World events began to change attitudes toward the war. Among the biggest to do so was the sinking of the Cunard liner RMS *Lusitania* on May 7, 1915. Hailed as the fastest ship on the high seas, she was hit by two torpedoes from a German submarine, without warning, off the coast of Ireland. She sank in roughly fifteen minutes, taking 1,153 passengers, among them 128 Americans, to their deaths. When the German ambassador noted that a statement had been placed in major American newspapers days before the Lusitania sailed, warning Americans they sailed on Allied ships at their own risk, it only made the situation worse. Americans were outraged that an unarmed passenger ship had been sunk without warning.

The next day's *Allentown Chronicle and News* offered an interview with Captain Harold S. and Mary Ormrod MacLaine, who had sailed frequently on the *Lusitania*. Captain MacLaine, a native of Belfast, Ireland, was an officer in the Royal Irish Rifles. His wife was the daughter of George Ormrod, an English immigrant to Lehigh County. Ormrod had made a fortune in investing in local coal, iron, and cement businesses. His home at 1227 Hamilton Street, built in 1897, would later be purchased by General Trexler.

Newsreel footage of the *Lusitania* sailing out of New York for the last time was being shown at Allentown's Orpheum Theater four days after the sinking. Lehigh County was only the second place in the country to see that newsreel; the first was New York. And, in an event that would have been comic if the reasons for it had not been so serious, two local men got into a heated argument over who was to blame for the sinking, which led to a fist fight with the pair rolling down dusty Hamilton Street to Penn Street. "When they [the press] got there Germany was on top and seemed to have the advantage," recorded the *Daily City Item* newspaper.

The Morning Call, which less than a year before had been blessing the fact that the U.S. had no entangling alliances, was taking a firmer tone following the death of American civilians on the *Lusitania*. "The United Sates will find it increasingly difficult as time goes on to keep out of the European war snarl. The war gods have envied the peace of our nation. [President Wilson must] weigh well and act firmly when the right course has been determined [but] the incident cannot pass by unnoticed."

The sinking of the *Lusitania* was a wake-up call to America and Lehigh County. There could be no neutrals in a world of global war. Throughout 1915 and 1916 the sinking of cargo ships bound for Britain by German submarines were a staple of war news that crossed the front pages of Lehigh County's newspapers.

In 1916 two major war-related events sent shock waves into Lehigh County. The first took place that April. In a raid on the New York office of the German military attaché Wolf von Igel, three FBI agents uncovered a treasure trove of documents. Among them, it was later disclosed, were letters from a Dr. Theodore Otto, an Allentown children's doctor and German immigrant. They included information on lax security at the Traylor Engineering Company in Allentown, then making shells for the British. "In supplying information for use by the German government he told of the number of foreign inspectors at the plants, the type, quality, caliber and quantities of guns ordered by foreign governments and the efficiency of the shops," wrote the Associated Press. Otto would later protest his innocence and was never prosecuted. Even though this information was not disclosed by the press until after the U.S. entered the war in 1917 it fed into the national feeling that even while the country had been at peace, German agents were in operation.

Another war-related act that had a more immediate impact on Lehigh County than the sinking of the *Lusitania* occurred of July 30, 1916. At 2:08 a.m. the large pier in Jersey City owned by the Lehigh Valley Railroad exploded with a roar. Known as the Black Tom Explosion, after the name of the island on which it was located, it shattered windows and popped 100 rivets in the torch-holding arm of the nearby Statue of Liberty.

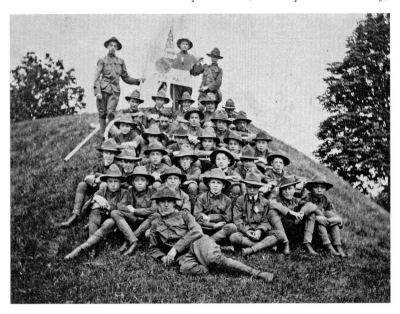

More importantly, much of the munitions on the pier had been made by Traylor Engineering, Bethlehem Steel, and other Lehigh Valley companies. After World War I was over it was proven that German sabotage had indeed been involved, and Germany paid the Lehigh Valley Railroad $50 million in damages in 1953. In 1916, Black Tom's major impact was another blow at the belief that America could continue to help arm the Allies while remaining out of the conflict.

Local industries, however, were not about to stop the boom that was providing handsome profits and good wages for Lehigh County workers. Things did not always run smoothly. Traylor, thanks to faulty engineering, had problems with the quality of the shells it produced in its first order for the British. Many were rejected as duds. This so enraged General Trexler, who was an investor in the project, that he exclaimed at a conference both he and Traylor were attending at Bethlehem Steel, "I wish I had never gone in with that damn Traylor outfit." Furious, Traylor told Trexler he would gladly buy him out if he was not happy. But Trexler knew he had gone too far. He offered an apology to Traylor in private. Traylor accepted and began major changes at the plant that vastly improved the quality of the shells it produced. "Afterward [Trexler] and I got along splendidly," Traylor wrote in his autobiography.

Lehigh County during the War

Against this background, it was quickly becoming clear as 1916 became 1917 that America's entry into the war would not be long delayed. On April 6, 1917, President Woodrow Wilson declared that America was going to war against Germany, Austria-Hungary, and other Central Powers to "make the world safe for democracy."

An editorial in *The Morning Call* noted that this was not a war against the German people, "but with the Hohenzollerns and their tools who have betrayed the German people … People in a community like this appreciate this fact more than those who live in communities where there has been less German influence. Everybody practically knows the excellent character of the Germans, their high qualities, their noble virtues, their excellent citizenship." Lehigh County joined the country in an explosion of patriotic fervor. Huge flags were flown from factories and local colleges. On April 21, a Saturday, Allentown held its first patriotic celebration with more than 1,500 children, most of them high-school students.

Young men began to volunteer for the military in large numbers. By May the Selective Service was recording 13,769 Lehigh County men signed up for the draft, 7,356 from Allentown. Many local troops would serve in France. Two hundred and one Lehigh County citizens, 200 men and one woman, died serving their country in World War I. The lone woman was nurse Anna Marie McMullen, a 1915 graduate of the Allentown Hospital School of Nursing. She died in October 1918, while serving overseas as a nurse in a military hospital.

The first citizen of Lehigh County to be killed in World War I was Herbert Paul Lentz. A native of Friedens, he was born in 1899. At the start of the war he was living with his parents and brother Gordon at 125 S. Jefferson Street in Allentown. He had moved with his family into the city and taken a job at Traylor Engineering. Lentz left his job in 1916 and joined the U.S. Navy, serving first on the battleship USS *Arkansas*. Decades later, on December 5, 1943, *The Morning Call* ran a story about Lentz. It included an interview with Howard A. Moyer, a native of White Haven then living in Allentown, who had served in the Navy with Lentz aboard the destroyer USS *Jacob Jones*. The ship, named for an American naval hero of the early nineteenth century, was then on convoy duty in the Irish Sea.

It was 4:20 p.m. on December 6, 1917. The *Jacob Jones* was returning from the French port of Brest to Queenstown, now Cobh, Ireland. Lurking in the water was the German submarine U-53. Spying the *Jones* through his periscope, the U-boat's commander, Hans Rose, gave the order to launch a torpedo. It went 3,000 yards, the longest successful torpedo shot on record. The unfortunate *Jones*, the first U.S. destroyer lost in combat, went to the bottom in seven minutes.

Of the crew of 122, forty-four survived. Most of those who died were killed by the release of the *Jones's* own ammunition. "The *Jacob Jones* was loaded with many depth charges and when it sank, those charges exploded, killing many of our men in the water," Moyer recalled.

Lentz had made it to the relative safety of a life raft. But without thought for his life he left it and, being a powerful swimmer, began to rescue his fellow sailors, Moyer among them. "He became very excited," Moyer recalled. Lentz had gotten three of them in the life raft and was going for a fourth when he disappeared under the water and was not seen again. Some U-boat captains would have left the area as soon as possible, but this was not Hans Rose's style. He treated the sailors of the *Jacob Jones* with what could only be called chivalry. The U-53 surfaced and after getting information that he needed about the destroyer, Rose took a wounded member of the *Jones* on board his vessel and sent an SOS message to the British at Queenstown giving the location of the *Jones's* crew. Six of the men died of exposure before they were rescued the next day by the British destroyer, HMS *Camellia*.

When the American Legion was formed in March 1919 in Paris, among those present was Colonel Henry A. Reninger of Allentown. That June, he became the co-founder of the Herbert Paul Lentz American Legion Post 29, among the oldest, if not the oldest, in Lehigh

Catasauqua raised more money per capita than any other community in Lehigh County for war bonds during World War I, and received the first Honor Flag in the United States for its citizens' contributions to the third Liberty Bond drive. This is a Liberty Loan parade in 1918. (Catasauqua Public Library)

Allentown had recently removed clutter of all kinds and enhanced the appearance of Hamilton Street, and refused to allow small booths for selling war bonds along the beautified commercial corridor. This large kiosk was built as the location for bond drives and many other events during World War I. (Lehigh County Historical Society)

Members of the U.S. Army Ambulance Corps drilling on the racetrack at Camp Crane at the Allentown Fairgrounds, 1917–18. The fair was suspended during the war. Some of the ambulances the young men learned to drive are on the right. (Kelly Ann Butterbaugh)

USAACs practice carrying a stretcher at Camp Crane at the Allentown Fairgrounds. (Library of Congress)

County, and among the oldest in the country.

To support the war service of men like Lentz and Moyer, Lehigh County business people formed a Committee of Public Safety to organize the selling of U.S. government bonds, known as Liberty Bonds. Max Hess, Sr., a German immigrant himself, was selected as the group's treasurer.

Bond drives were a regular sight throughout Lehigh County during World War I. They were held in every community and in Allentown at the Lyric Theater, West Park, and kiosks on Hamilton Street. Among the most prominent kiosk was the one erected in Center Square in Allentown near the Soldiers and Sailors Monument. It was used particularly during the flu epidemic of 1918 because it was assumed to be safer to hold bond rallies outside.

Companies throughout the area encouraged their workers to buy Liberty Bonds, as did the government and the newspapers. "Over the top," a common phrase used in reference in trench warfare in World War I, was frequently adopted to encourage civilians to exceed their goal or quota in the purchase of Liberty Bonds.

Within weeks after the declaration of war, the U.S. government announced plans to open a training camp at the fairgrounds in Allentown for the U.S. Army Ambulance Service. The camp was named Camp Crane, named for Charles Henry Crane, the U.S. Surgeon General from 1881 to 1882. At first there was concern about the establishment of a military camp in the city, and the bad moral influence of thousands of soldiers. But it happened that the ambulance corps tended to attract some of the best-educated and socially connected young men in America. Instead of having to protect their daughters, local families were thrilled when an Ivy League student arrived for dinner. In a number of cases marriages grew out of relationships that began at Camp Crane.

The Lehigh County Agricultural Society canceled the annual Great Allentown Fair for the duration of Camp Crane, but Romper Day continued, sponsored by the USAACs, as the members of the U.S. Army Ambulance Corps were known. In addition, the many entertainments took place throughout the county to raise money for war bonds provided some forms of recreation in compensation for the loss of the fair. The USAACs trained to drive ambulances and to carry stretchers on the fairgrounds' racetrack and learned how to live in trench-warfare conditions in dugouts near Guthsville. An auxiliary camp at Kern's Mill near Slatington had to be opened in September of 1917 due to the large numbers of men in training.

Toward the end of the war the camp became a pre-embarkation camp for regular troops heading for Europe. The social activities of the USAAC period were no more.

Spanish Flu

If Camp Crane was the most enjoyable part of World War I for Lehigh Countians, the arrival in September 1918 of the worldwide flu epidemic was the worst; it is estimated to have killed between 50 million and 100 million people, three percent of the world's population at the time. The first reported U.S. case was in Fort Riley, Kansas. At the same time, an outbreak began in Europe. Because Spain, a neutral country during World War I, did not censor its press, the first accounts of the epidemic started there and it was dubbed the Spanish flu.

The first news of the pandemic reached Lehigh County in *The Morning Call* on September 13, 1918, in a report saying that the flu had swept Europe and was being seen in U.S. coast cities. The article noted, wrongly as it turned out, that the impact was short, and had no permanent results. By early October cases were first being seen in Lehigh County.

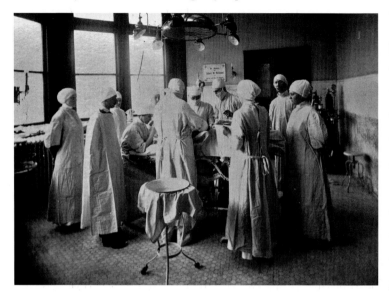

Uniformly it was young people, in their 20s, 30s, and 40s who seemed to be dying from the disease. Doctors were horrified to discover that victims' lungs virtually dissolved.

At first Lehigh County municipal officials thought that requests from state and federal health officials that schools, churches, saloons, and theaters be closed were an overreaction. Allentown Mayor Albert Reichenbach said Allentown was a clean city, not dusty and dirty like South Bethlehem, and so had nothing to fear. Public officials across Lehigh County quickly discovered disease germs were no respecter of municipal borders. On October 7, 1918, when over 200,000 case of flu were being reported statewide, Reichenbach and city council gave in to the closing order, but even then not all businesses went along.

It was only when many prominent people were struck down that the full impact of the flu was admitted. Among them were Lehigh County District Attorney Warren Miller, age 35; George A. Miller, burgess of Slatington and a state representative, age 31; and Francis R. Crispen, secretary and director of Traylor Engineering, age 36. All three died.

These were the names in local headlines. But a lot of other people were ill also. From October1 to October 22, 2,084 cases were reported in Allentown. On October 27 alone, 397 cases were reported. This epidemic marked a turning point in the public's acceptance of hospitals. Up to this time, most families would care for their ill in their homes with doctors and nurses visiting as needed. The demand for health-care services became so great that this was no longer feasible, and hospitals had to find additional beds to accommodate all who were ill.

The orphans that resulted when both parents died or were incapacitated by the flu became an issue of great concern. Although not as bad as Philadelphia, where flu orphans numbered in the thousands, Allentown and Lehigh County had their share. Among the many local service clubs who took on the challenge of the orphans locally was the Allentown Kiwanis Club. On October 29, 1918, Mrs John F. Saeger, a civic-minded member of one of the oldest families in Lehigh County, turned over her former mansion at Fourth and Walnut streets to the Kiwanis for what was called the Temporary Children's Protective

The Macungie Band posed for a photograph on November 7, 1918, after performing during the impromptu celebration of what the nation believed was a signed, official armistice. (Macungie Historical Society)

Home. General Harry C. Trexler donated $500 a month for every month the home was in operation, and Samuel Traylor gave $1,000. Donations from all over Lehigh County of mattresses, sheets, blankets, and pillows were recorded.

The home opened on October 31, 1918. The same day, city health officials reported a monthly total of more than 3,000 cases in Allentown with 996 still active and over 200 deaths. Officials admitted that probably only 75 percent of the cases in the city for that month were recorded. Allentown's working-class Sixth Ward alone had 476 cases and 33 deaths.

By early November 1918, county health officials noticed the numbers begin to drop. Although cases would continue to appear until early 1919, the plague seemed to recede as quickly as it had come.

The Temporary Children's Protective Home that had offered refuge to almost forty children at its height at the first week in November was closed by year's end. In many cases those who had relatives were adopted by aunts and uncles, no longer afraid that the children might be carrying the disease.

The War Ends

With the end of the epidemic also came the end of the war, amidst much confusion.

On November 7, 1918, a cable from war correspondent Roy Howard of the United Press came clattering into newspapers across the country, among them Allentown's Chronicle and News. Written in a shorthand style known in contemporary slang as "cablease," it read as follows:

```
UNIPRESS - NEW YORK

URGENT ARMISTICE ALLIES GERMANY SIGNED ELEVEN SMORNING
HOSTILITIES CEASED TWO SAFTERNOON SEDAN TAKEN SMORNING BY AMERICANS.
```

Lehigh County soldiers returning from Europe in 1919. (Lehigh County Historical Society)

Lehigh County troops returned from Europe, marching in the Victory Day Parade, June 15, 1919. (Reprinted with permission of The Morning Call. All Rights Reserved)

William "Bud" Tamblyn, later a photographer and cartoonist for the *Evening Chronicle* and *Morning Call*, was a teenager at the time and would often recall how word was received via United Press and published in the *Chronicle and News* that the war was over. "Everybody was running around screaming and jumping and driving their cars like crazy in the streets," Tamblyn said. Allentown's many bands flooded the streets with instruments playing Sousa marches and, over and over again, "There'll Be A Hot Time In the Old Town Tonight." Bars that had remained closed under the flu restrictions reopened.

The Lehigh Valley and the rest of the nation awoke on November 8 to discover the newspapers had jumped the gun. Although peace was clearly in the air it had not hap-

pened yet. Some American military officials had gotten erroneous information from the U.S. embassy in Paris that an armistice, an agreement to end fighting, had been signed between Germany and France. Wanting to "scoop" the Associated Press, U.P.'s great rival, reporter Howard, with the permission of high-ranking American military officers in Brest, France, sent it out. To this day no one can say for sure how this misunderstanding came about. But it left the U.P., and by extension the *Allentown Chronicle and News*, with a great deal of egg on its face. *The Morning Call*, a client of the AP, included an editorial the next day reminding its readers where they could go for accurate news in the future.

The war's end meant Lehigh County boys would be coming home, but most did not arrive until April, May, and June of 1919. Towns around the county built victory arches, and held parades to welcome them home. Photos of the time show streets bedecked with flags of America and her allies, Britain, France, Italy, and Japan. As returning troops marched up Hamilton Street from the railroad station they were greeted by cheering crowds lining the sidewalks three and four ranks deep.

The names of over 200 Lehigh County residents are listed on the Roll of Honor of those who died in the Great War of Democracy.

"Floating On A Sea Of Booze": Lehigh County During National Prohibition 1919-1933

The late William "Bud" Tamblyn, longtime Allentown newspaper photographer and cartoonist, remembered a lot about life in early twentieth century Lehigh County. One topic it was easy to get him going on was the Prohibition era. After regaling a listener with one tale after another from what one social critic has called "the era of wonderful nonsense," he declared emphatically, "during Prohibition Lehigh County floated on a sea of booze."

The Eighteenth Amendment to the Constitution, which forbade "the manufacture, sale or transportation of intoxicating liquors" was ratified in January of 1919 and went into effect a year later. It was the result of years of lobbying by "dry" forces who claimed it would lead to a more moral and upright America. For Tamblyn and many of his generation, Prohibition was nothing more than the work of self-righteous killjoys intent on preventing them from having a good time. And the more effort that was made to stop them from drinking liquor, the more they would do to find it and drink it.

Born in 1905, Tamblyn was a young man in the Roaring Twenties with money to spend. The thirty-five gold-backed Coolidge dollars he made each week designing fashionable japanned furniture for Allentown's Yeager Furniture Company afforded him the ability to help his widowed mother pay the mortgage on her home and have enough left over to enjoy the "speakeasies" of the region.

"Now, the roadhouses out in the country were not bad," he recalled one day in the early 1980s. "At least you knew the homemade applejack wouldn't kill you or make you blind. But the hangovers from it had quite a kick." Lehigh County had a taste of what Prohibition would be like during World War I, when war-time rules forbade the use of grain for making distilled liquor and the county's two commercial distilleries, in New Tripoli and Pleasant Corner, had to close. Soldiers were forbidden to drink either in or out of uniform, and regulations shut down twenty bars in October 1917, and twenty more in 1918.

Lehigh County's five large breweries stopped making beer in December 1918 and made Ice cream and soda instead. Some charged that the brewers continued making beer and sold it secretly. Allentown's brewing Neuweiler family tells the story that when gangster Dutch Schultz attempted to foist such a deal on them he was told, "we have always made honest beer" and was ordered off of the property.

Tamblyn's supply of country applejack probably came from the many illicit stills that could be found all around the county. Homemade liquor was stored under bridges, in barns, even in abandoned mine shafts. He talked of houses lining the edge of a cliff above Lawrence Street (now Martin Luther King Jr. Drive), overlooking a factory district. The chief function in apartments here seemed, to him, to be to produce bathtub gin. "I remember walking in and seeing them [bootleggers] actually mixing it in a bathtub," he recalled.

Like most young men of the day he carried a hip flask to have something to mix with the bottles of ginger ale or other mixers that were featured in ads for respectable local restaurants. Tamblyn remembered the house detective at the Hotel Traylor being not too happy with him and several of his "three sheets to the wind" friends when they arrived to dance at the hotel's popular roof-garden restaurant in 1929. But the man made no effort to stop them from drinking.

There were many people in Lehigh County in the 1920s whose lips never touched liquor, bootleg or otherwise, or walked into a smoky speakeasy, and would never have thought to go on a drinking spree. But there must have been something behind the observation made by a local newspaper columnist in 1921, when Prohibition's thirteen-year reign was still in its infancy: "If all the energy expended in Allentown 'making your own' could be concentrated there'd be enough generated to change the course of the Jordan in a few hours."

The overwhelmingly tolerant attitude toward alcoholic beverages in Lehigh County, where many of the people had German roots and brewing was a major industry, was bound to make the very idea of prohibition a hard one to sell. When a follower of nineteenth-century Midwestern saloon smasher Carrie Nation attempted smashing kegs of beer in Allentown, she was firmly sent out of town. This tolerance was not simply among the working class. General Harry C. Trexler, Lehigh County's leading citizen, told a reporter for a Philadelphia newspaper that Prohibition did nothing but criminalize a formerly non-criminal behavior. Trexler said it took control of the liquor trade from perfectly respectable citizens and turned it over to the worst elements of society.

Attempts to enforce Prohibition were subject to much kidding in the local press. One article in The Morning Call all but laughed at attempts by local "dry" agents to surround their doings in secrecy, comparing it to the mumbo-jumbo of a college fraternity rite. When an Allentown city councilman attempted to gain publicity by taking part in a raid of a still hidden in an empty factory off Lawrence Street, he was depicted as a comic dupe of the agents when they found nothing.

One "gangland" crime related to that era occurred in Allentown in 1926. Louis Genovese, a rising realtor, was gunned down when a gang of men broke up a poker game he was playing at a friend's house. No one was ever found guilty for this crime, which the newspapers covered with banner headlines and vague slurs about the ethnic Italian nature of both the victim and the accused perpetrators.

Speakeasies, underground bars that required a password, sprang up all around. One incident involved critic and beer lover H.L. Mencken, and was recorded by him as having taken place in South Bethlehem. After a performance of Bach's Mass in B Minor, he and his publisher, Alfred Knopf, went searching for a beer. Spotting the words "seafood" over a door, which Mencken knew as the "universal euphemism for beerhouse" in Pennsylvania and Maryland during Prohibition, they knocked and were given the once-over by an eye gazing at them through a peephole. To prove he was not a "dry" agent, Mencken held up his Bach score. With that, both men were admitted, given two glasses of German beer, and had to run to catch their train back to New York.

With the collapse of the economy in 1929 and election of Democrat Franklin Roosevelt in 1932, the demands for Prohibition's repeal grew ever louder. Petitions circulated all over Lehigh County, including at the Allentown Fair. Finally, despite the efforts of Gifford Pinchot, Pennsylvania's militant prohibitionist governor (the man who gave the state the state-store system), the Eighteenth Amendment was repealed and speakeasies re-emerged as cocktail lounges. On that day Tamblyn, by then having lost his job in the Depression and driving a horse-drawn bread-delivery truck, pulled over to the side of the road and gazed at the celebrating crowds. Happy days, in the words of the popular song of the day, were here again.

Post-War Changes

Many industries, in both Lehigh County and elsewhere, had assumed that the troops would fight until they entered Berlin. The sudden end of fighting brought abrupt economic dislocation. Orders for war materiel were dropped by the government. It would take time for industries to beat those swords into ploughshares and return to peacetime production. The result was a recession that would begin in 1919 and last until 1923.

Another product of the war that sparked fear in many was the Bolshevik Revolution in Russia. Many Americans were sympathetic when the autocratic Czarist regime was replaced by a republican provisional government. But its overthrow in turn, and the coming to power of a communist regime that wanted to overturn capitalism and whose rhetoric argued for a worldwide workers revolution troubled the conservative Lehigh Valley, as it did most of America.

Before the war there been a small but active group of Lehigh County socialists who saw nothing un-American about supporting socialism. Their leaders were more apt to quote Christ and Lincoln than Marx. In May 1911, an overflow crowd gathered at Allentown's Lyric Theater to hear a talk by Eugene Debs, the best-known socialist in the country. The hysteria of the war years and the Bolshevik Revolution tainted socialism, which became seen as a plot by bomb-throwing foreigners.

The labor issues in 1919 were a national steel strike to recognize steel unions and reduce the 12-hour day to 8 hours. It sent shock waves through the country and particularly at Bethlehem Steel. Full-page ads in *The Morning Call* branded the strikers as Communists and socialists, whose real goal was to attempt to establish socialism in America, which was now suddenly un-American.

In an attempt to find a solution for the strike deadlock, former president Taft, a conservative Republican considered a fair-minded person respected by both sides, stepped in to lead negotiations. Eugene Grace, Bethlehem Steel's president, would not be moved. He told Taft he would talk to individual workers "but not as union men." The strike failed nationally and it would be twenty years before unions were seriously considered at Bethlehem Steel.

Coupled with the steel strike was what became known as the Big Red Scare. From 1919 to 1921 a number of bombings against high-profile American officials and institutions, apparently sparked by anarchists, alarmed the country. The first was on May 1, 1919, targeted at A. Mitchell Palmer, the U.S. Attorney General. Although the only one killed by the bomb was the hapless bomber himself, Palmer, a former Democratic congressman from Northampton County who was known as the "Fighting Quaker," saw this as a reason to launch raids against suspected Reds. The raids were headed by a young man named J. Edgar Hoover. The last bombing occurred on September 16, 1920, when a wagon with a bomb attached blew up on Wall Street, killing one and wounding seventeen. Gradually the scare wound down.

One victim of the bad economic times was the Lehigh County Courthouse itself. In 1864 the original 1816 structure was discovered to be too small for the county's needs. It was enlarged and expanded under the direction of civil engineer G.S. Aschbach. A German immigrant, he had fled his troubled country following the unsuccessful revolutions of 1848, and died young due to malaria he contracted while designing fortifications along the Ohio River for the North during the Civil War. Lehigh County's growth had become so great that by the second decade of the twentieth century the county commissioners were thinking of tearing down the old building and replacing it with a much larger structure. It was to be done in a rather grand style called Second Renaissance Revival, made popular by the architectural firm of McKim, Mead and White.

The first wing of the new court house, designed by local architect Henry Anderson, was begun in 1914 and completed by 1916, at a cost of $199,000. So confident were the commissioners of the eventual completion of a new building that postcards were available showing the finished structure. But the entry of the U.S. into World War I in the spring of 1917 put a halt to almost all civilian construction. Shortages and the allocation of construction materials to the war effort brought work on the courthouse to a standstill.

When peace returned in 1919 it brought a combination of inflation and recession. Not wanting to go to the voters for a tax increase, the county shelved its plans and never took them up again, leaving Lehigh County with a courthouse with its architectural feet in two different eras. It was the 1960s before a completely new Lehigh County Courthouse was built.

Silk Magnate D. George Dery

The recession of 1919–1923 that followed World War I had several local victims. D. George Dery of Catasauqua may have been the most prominent. Desiderius George Dery, originally spelled Deri, was born the son of Hungarian landed gentry in the empire of Austria-Hungary in 1867. "They were not nobility but just below it," recalled Dery's son-in-law, Lehigh University English professor Dr. Carl Strauch, in 1985.

Dery's youth was spent in Vienna, the capital of a multi-national empire called the Dual Monarchy. Founded the same year as Dery's birth, Austria-Hungary was a compromise that gave Hungary a higher status within the Austrian Empire than the rest of its many nationali-

Postcard view of the Dery Silk Mill in Catasauqua. It was the nation's leader in fine silk manufacturing around 1900. (Kelly Ann Butterbaugh)

ties. As a result, the emperor of Austria was also the king of Hungary.

Vienna was one of the most sophisticated, culturally attuned cities in Europe. Here Dery acquired the Old World charm, good manners, and love of the arts that he retained for the rest of his life. But Austria-Hungary was not a place where an ambitious young man like Dery could thrive.

Dubbed by historian Edmond Taylor "the fossil monarchy," it was largely a collection of medieval fiefdoms held together by loyalty to the Hapsburg dynasty, the empire's ruling family. Sharp-eyed old emperor Franz Joseph, a largely benevolent despot when not crossed, kept close watch on the all-important genealogical bloodlines that governed who was and was not *hoffähig*, that is, acceptable at court. Even members of the nobility who had less than sixteen quarters of nobility, which means eight pairs of ancestors who were noble in both the male and female line, were not *hoffähig*. The emperor had personally rejected the admission of a countess who had only twelve quarters and disinherited from the throne the children of his son and heir Archduke Franz Ferdinand when he had the temerity to marry a mere countess, and a Czech countess at that!

For Dery, the mere son of Hungarian gentry without powerful friends at court, there was little room for advancement. So, after studying the art of industrial silk making at the Vienna Textile Academy he left for the New World in 1887. After running his own silk mill in Paterson, New Jersey, then the silk-making capital of America, Dery came to Catasauqua with his wife Helen in 1897. Soon he had a mill under construction. After considerable expansion, by 1900 it had 400 employees. By 1914 Dery was employing 3,600 people at his fourteen silk mills. D. George Dery's local office (the corporate office was at 295 Fifth Avenue in New York), occupied the entire seventh floor of the Allentown National Bank building, a Beaux Arts Classical office building just off Center Square.

Dery's biography in Robert's 1912 county history mentions that, along with his silk business, he had recently begun a major real-estate investment near Muhlenberg College's new location (in 1904 the school had moved out of the Fourth and Walnut street property at Trout Hall it had occupied since 1867), with his business partner, State Senator Arthur

DeWalt. Dery had also just purchased Harry Trexler's home at 926 Hamilton Street, the dwelling occupied by the general from 1881 to 1912, and owned "several hundred acres of fine farm land in Northampton County." Unlike other biographies of the local self-made men, Dery's makes no mention of his background in Hungary, or having once been an immigrant, even if a well-off one. As these biographies were based on items submitted by the subject this was apparently the way he wanted it.

Like the eighteenth-century Allen family, Dery held at least in part to the Old World view. His business was not an end but the means to an end, cultivated leisure as an educated gentleman. His home in Catasaqua, perhaps the most lavish ever built in Lehigh County, was a showplace. From its columns of Colorado limestone to the massive indoor swimming pool to the roof observatory where Dery engaged in the gentlemanly science of astronomy it took the breath away of locals.

Added to this was Dery's personal art gallery. Strauch described Dery's taste as good but sentimental. "If he had put himself in the hands of an art expert he would have been able to acquire Impressionists for almost nothing," he said. But Dery's taste did not apparently incline him to "radicals" like Monet, much less Cézanne. What arrived by the crate at Catasauqua, purchased by Dery on his many trips to Europe, were seventeenth-, eighteenth-, and nineteenth-century landscapes and portraits by Dutch, English, German and French artists.

Coquettish milk maids, to judge from descriptions in the press, were a seemingly popular subject. Surveying the paintings in the Dery collection in 1923 *The New York Times* said "they are of the kind that fine decorator, the late Stanford White, picked up wherever he found them and used in interiors with delightful results." Among the real gems of objets d'art in the collection were a sixteenth-century bronze font, a seventeenth-century reliquary of Christ on the Cross, and a Carrara marble statue, the "Blind Girl," based on a character in Bulwar-Lytton's nineteenth-century novel *The Last Days of Pompeii*.

By 1919, with 42 mills, an estimated total of 6,500 looms and 10,000 workers, and valued at near $20,000,000, Dery was called in the business press the single largest private manufacturer of silk in the world. But the slender threads that held the empire of silk together were more fragile then anyone knew.

In 1920 Dery attempted the ultimate coup. He tried to "corner" the international silk market, in other words to get control of enough raw silk to set the world price for it. Perhaps he hoped to take advantage of the general worldwide economic distress in all markets that followed the abrupt end of World War I. Whatever the reason, it was an extremely risky move. Market "corners" are almost immediately targets of other speculators and seldom last.

Cornering a market required vast amounts of capital, more than even the single largest private silk maker in the world had at his command. Apparently Dery borrowed it from others, among them E. Gerli (pronounced girlie) Co., Inc., a raw silk commission merchant with strong links to the Japanese silk trade. Dery signed trade acceptances, promises to repay at a certain date the loans with Gerli and other creditors.

At the same time Dery was attempting his corner, Paolino Gerli, the 30-year-old nephew of E. Gerli's president, Emanuel Gerli, was in Japan dealing in silk for his own personal account. Whether the younger Gerli, later a leader in the silk business and a skilled market trader and Wall Street short seller, was working for or against Dery's interest at this time is unknown. What is known is that Japan, one of the largest exporters of silk in the world, dumped large amounts on the market, "breaking" Dery's attempt at a corner.

By 1922 Dery's trade acceptances with E. Gerli were coming due. To meet this obligation, Dery authorized the issue of $4,000,000 first mortgage 7 percent sinking fund gold bonds through brokers Redmond & Company and Janey & Company to cover the debts. The value of those bonds, however, was apparently based on a false evaluation of the Dery Corporation's assets, one deliberately involving corporation officers. In a footnote in the official history of the influential Wall Street law firm of Cravath, Swaine & Moore, the author, firm partner Robert Swaine, claimed there was "a bald fraud upon the accountants who verified the balance sheet upon which the [Dery] bonds had been issued."

According to Swaine, "every night after the accountants who were counting the bolts of silk checking inventories had left, certain Dery officers took a large number of bolts from the shelves which had already been counted and put them onto shelves yet to be counted. As a result the inventory was overstated." The estimated size of this overstatement, it was later disclosed, was $1,250,000.

On March 27, 1923, *The New York Times* reported that, the day before, E. Gerli had the federal court appoint three receivers, George A. Post, Joseph M. Proskauer, and John P. McGuire, to take over the Dery Corporation's assets. "The receivership, it was announced, is preliminary to a reorganization to protect the assets," the *Times* noted. The receivers also informed the court, "it was not advisable to employ D.G. Dery, President of the corporation, and he is not at this time connected with the organization." Dery protested he had known nothing about the fraud and had in fact told the receivers when he learned of it. Apparently, rightly or wrongly, no one believed him.

On August 29, 1923, before the reorganization became complete, the Dery Corporation was renamed Amalgamated Silk Corporation. It was to last until 1930 when, as a result of the oncoming Great Depression, it declared bankruptcy. Dery was left with four silk mills that he continued to run in the 1920s. But the Great Depression and a strike at his silk mills in 1934 was the end. "That finished him off," Strauch recalled.

Dery left his mansion and moved in with his daughter in a much smaller home across the street. In the late 1930s he could still be seen walking the streets of Catasauqua in a formal morning coat with gray flannel pants and gray spats, his little dachshund "Zig Zag" at his heels. Occasionally Dery would give talks to local groups on his perspective on the coming war in Europe, nineteenth-century Vienna, or astronomy. In 1941 when Otto von Hapsburg, the heir apparent to the no-longer-existent Austria Hungary, having fled the Netherlands just ahead of the Nazis, came to speak at Lehigh University he is said to have talked to Dery.

Feeling ill and always troubled with a heart condition, Dery left Catasauqua to spend a few days with his daughter, like her mother named Helen, and her husband at their home in Bethlehem. He died there at age 74 on March 5, 1942.

Swindler Martin Kern

Perhaps even more significant for Lehigh County than Dery's fall was the collapse of the fortunes of Martin Kern, Allentown banker/entrepreneur and confidence man, in 1922.

Although there were many Kerns in Lehigh County, this Martin Kern was not a native. He arrived in the Lehigh Valley in 1909 with wife Mary Jane and mother Marie. An insurance salesman for the Mutual Life Insurance Company of New York, he got an office in the Allentown National Bank's Beaux Arts Classical building on Center Square.

From the first, Kern was different. It is hard to know exactly how local people 100 years ago thought an insurance agent should act, but, apparently, someone who wore spats, carried a cane, flaunted a fresh gardenia in his buttonhole, and tilted his derby at a rakish angle was not what they had in mind. When asked about his past, Kern would respond in smooth-as-silk, central-European-accented English that he was Swiss by birth. He had come to America, he said, as a child with his parents and an older brother Edward. Unfortunately, his brother had turned to a life of crime, causing his mother much grief. Old Marie Kern would sometimes become confused and refer to her son Martin as Edward. Most people just wrote it off as a sign of her advancing age.

Kern aimed high. He sold insurance to Joe Mack and Jack Mack. Although Joe Mack was not involved with the truck business, Jack Mack was. Kern received a large block of Mack Truck stock in payment for the premiums. Within a year he was a vice president of the company. In 1911 Kern talked the Mack brothers, who were seeking loans to expand but getting nowhere with conservative Allentown bankers, to go to Wall Street, primarily to J.P. Morgan. How big a role Kern played is unknown, but in October the creation of the International Motor Car Company, a merger of Mack with Saurer Motor Co., a Morgan-backed Swiss truck concern, was announced. A year later the Hewitt Motor Company would be added to the new concern. According to newspaper accounts, Kern made $100,000 on the deal.

Kern did not stop there. After selling two insurance policies for $1 million each, he formed a bank, the Penn Counties Trust Company. The same year, 1912, he purchased Joe Mack's big home at Sixteenth and Walnut streets. Shortly thereafter, Kern became a fixture on Walnut Street as he headed downtown in either a chauffeur-driven Rolls Royce town car or a fire-engine-red Stutz Bear Cat sports car. His lavish parties at the Lehigh Country Club and on railroad trains to and from Atlantic City, which included Broadway showgirls, were the whispered gossip of the Lehigh Valley.

Kern's biggest coup occurred during World War I. Using his influence in both Washington and on Wall Street, with well-honed contacts at the highest level of both the Democratic and Republican parties, and putting up little of his own money, he managed to buy Bosch-Magneto, the maker of ignition systems for almost all the automotive vehicles in the world. As a German-owned company it had been confiscated by the U.S. government as enemy property. The official in charge of selling enemy property, known as the "Alien Property Custodian," was A. Mitchell Palmer, the former Northampton County congressmen who would soon be named U.S. Attorney General. Mitchell and Kern shared adjoining summer homes at Blue Heron Lake in the Poconos.

Business ethics were not what got Kern in trouble, at least not directly. Enjoying the company of beautiful women after his wife died in 1915, he was a frequent customer at New York's New Amsterdam Theater. This was the home of the Ziegfeld Follies, the popular variety show founded by impresario Florenz Ziegfeld. It featured showgirls that fit a certain highly stylized ideal of feminine beauty known nationwide as the Ziegfeld Girl. On the theater's roof garden, wealthy "stage door johnnies" gathered for a risqué floor show, "naughtier" than the Follies, known as the "Midnight Frolics."

It was at the New Amsterdam's roof garden, so the story goes, that Kern spotted Marion Davies, a former Ziegfeld Girl turned movie actress, and mistress of newspaper publisher William Randolph Hearst. Hearing Davies request a glass of champagne, Kern had a bottle sent to her table with his compliments. Apparently this was the start of an affair between Kern and Davies, most details of which are unknown. But one which, in light of later events was to have dreadful consequences for Kern and was still circulating in Lehigh County many years later.

Hearst supposedly learned of the affair and was outraged to discover that Kern had spirited Davies off to his home at Blue Heron Lake. Enraged, he ordered his chauffeur to drive there immediately. Among the most powerful, wealthy, ego-driven men in the country, one whose opinions on many things were the gospel of millions in editorial pages across the nation, and who had even been mentioned as a possible presidential candidate, Hearst was a force to be reckoned with. He was said to be not at all pleased at being two-timed by his actress girlfriend and some person he had never heard of from Allentown, Pennsylvania.

When Hearst arrived at the Kern home he found it dark. He is said to have seen a shadowy figure hiding behind some slightly moving curtains when he looked up at an upper-story window. "Kern! I'll ruin you for this!" Hearst is supposed to have shouted before getting into his car and heading back to New York.

Whether the details of this story are true or not, ruin Kern is exactly what Hearst did. He hired a private detective named Felix Unger to dig up all the details on Kern that could be found. In this he had ready allies in the former owners of Bosch-Magneto, who were furious at what they saw as a corrupt deal between the government and Kern to deprive them of their property.

When the Kern bombshell burst on January 26, 1922, it was a sensation. There was, the Hearst newspapers said, no Martin E. Kern. There was, however, an Edward Kern, a thief and con-man with string of aliases and a criminal record that went back to the nineteenth century.

The front page of the *Allentown Record* featured a photo of Martin Kern; next to it was the one that graced the New York City police department's "Rogues Gallery" as number 3874. An independent newspaper not run by Hearst, the *Record's* editor was Charles W. "Bud" Weiser. He was later to have two sons, Nelson "Nels" Weiser and Charles "Bud" Weiser, Jr., who would become leaders of local journalism.

A longtime newspaper man, Weiser had always distrusted Kern. Some of his business deals had left a bad taste in Weiser's mouth. The so-called Bethlehem Motor Truck Company, which despite its name was located in Allentown, had been created by Kern during World War I. "Government contracts for this company were said to have been good bait for the selling of stock, large numbers of conservative 'Pennsylvania Dutch' buying shares," wrote *The Morning Call*.

The stock dropped from $40 a share to a fraction of a dollar. The company's 200 employees lost their jobs and many investors their life savings. Lawrence Rupp, Kern's attorney and a leader in the Lehigh County Democratic Party, told Kern that people would see him as "morally culpable" for their loses. His only reply was that "business is business."

Kern's private life, including his parties, came under the *Record's* microscope. Weiser thundered in the *Record* that those who attended these show-girl-studded events were no better than moral lepers. "Tales are afloat of wild Parisian parties held in a bungalow owned by Kern in the almost primeval part of the Pocono Mountains," said the *Record*. "Girls from

Allentown have been taken to those parties by Kern and his friends and certain photographs in circulation here following those parties indicate the nature of those parties."

Kern was the owner of the *Allentown Chronicle and News*. Under the editorial headline "Character Assassin," it blasted the *Record*. Only a Hearst publication, "or its imitators [would have] the audacity and shamelessness to publish an article [that] cast a cloud of suspicion against a man through coupling his name and picture with that of a brother, now deceased, who brought dishonor on his family ..."

Weiser fired back with both barrels: "Intimations of libel suits will not deter the Allentown Record from telling the people of Allentown the truth. There is a lot more coming." That "more" came in the form of the detective work of Felix Unger, who discovered that Kern's father, Edward Kern, Sr., had been killed in 1901 in a railroad accident in upstate New York. Kern's mother had sued the railroad and received $1,500 in a settlement.

In going over the records the detective discovered a sworn document by Marie Kern saying she had only one son, named Edward Kern, who was then "currently residing in Auburn, New York" at Sing Sing Prison. More importantly, the document noted Edward Kern's birthplace as Mühlhausen, Alsace, Germany, in 1871, not Switzerland. It also noted that Kern had never applied for U.S. citizenship. By the rules of the Alien Property Custodian, Kern was therefore himself an alien and could not legally purchase Bosch-Magneto.

When this news broke, Martin/Edward Kern was far away in Europe. On January 18, 1922, days before the first articles appeared, he had sailed to France on the S.S. *Paris*, pride of the French Line, and was now in his suite at the high-toned Hôtel Meurice, since 1814 the preferred lodging of European royalty and American millionaires. Friends had been told he was on a secret economic mission for the U.S. government at an international conference in Genoa, Italy. Others had been told he was to receive the title of count from the Italian government.

Whatever his hopes, tea with Mussolini was not in Martin Kern's future. He was in fact apparently ankle deep in transatlantic cables in his hotel room from his associates in Lehigh County telling him the jig was decidedly up.

Kern did not deny the charges about his past life and resigned as president of Penn Counties Trust Bank. But he was still hoping to rescue his control of Bosch-Magneto. He cabled Lawrence Rupp, his attorney and a leader of Lehigh County's bar, to contact his connections in Washington. "Why don't all the interests take [Secretary of War John W.] Weeks and [Attorney General Harry] Daugherty and put a quietus on this?" It is not known if Rupp ever did this, but a few years later both Daugherty and Weeks were caught up in the major scandals that plagued the Harding Administration.

In a long letter to Rupp, later published in full in local papers, Kern admitted to being a liar, "and who would not once he got a chance to live a better life and get ambitions … I am convinced my days in Allentown are over … What a house of cards! What a crash!"

When Kern finally returned to the U.S., he admitted to being involved in bootlegging and other illegal activities. Despite a Congressional investigation, Kern was never charged with anything other than falsely swearing to be a U.S. citizen. He was fined $2,000 and released. Perhaps Bosch-Magneto was such a political hot potato for both powerful Democrats and Republicans that they were willing to let it die. But Kern did resign as head of the company.

In 1925 Kern traveled to Florida, where he made and lost a fortune in the giant real-estate scam known as the Florida land boom. By 1927, out of cash and out of luck, Kern returned to Allentown, where he stole $90,000 from a business he once owned. Rupp, so the story goes, followed him to New York and demanded he return the money. Kern agreed but wanted to make a deal first. He demanded Allentown businessmen pay him $1,000 a month for life to keep him out of Lehigh County forever. No details are known but apparently, according to *Morning Call* reporter Fred McCready, who wrote about it in 1956, the deal was struck. Allentown never saw Martin Kern again.

What Kern did thereafter is a mix of rumor and legend. One story stated that in 1939, under the name Emil Metzler, he traveled to Nazi Germany to offer his services as a spy. Apparently the Third Reich was less than impressed and turned him down. As practiced con-men and gangsters themselves they probably knew they were being taken.

On January 17, 1947, a well-dressed man walked into the Robert Treat Hotel in Newark, N.J., registered as Edward J .Marsden, and was given a key to room 827. The next morning he was found dead, a suicide victim of cyanide poising. It was nine years later that Essex County, N.J., traced his past back to Sing Sing Prison and Edward E. Kern, Jr.

Prosperity Returns

By 1924, as the Kern scandal was beginning to disappear from the newspapers, the country was finally coming out of the post-World War I recession. Lehigh County, like the rest of the country, was beginning to boom.

Pennsylvania was not in the forefront of the recovery. With the exception of Bethlehem Steel, which glowed far into the night producing H-beams for the iconic skyscrapers of the era, most production by heavy industry was modest. "Coal, textiles and agriculture—all conspicuously sick industries in the 1920s," write historians Philip S. Klein and Ari Hoogenboom in their 1973 History of Pennsylvania, "were basic to the state's economy. … Pennsylvania did little more than hold its own throughout the decade."

What helped Lehigh County was the diversity of its industries. The silk industry continued to thrive and grow throughout the 1920s. Mills, found in almost every community throughout the county except the smallest villages, employed many women and men. Martha Capwell Fox, the historian of the silk industry in the Lehigh Valley, writes that "dozens of other industries supplied equipment and other mill necessities, such as harnesses, reeds, oil soaps, bobbins, belts, shuttles and even the rabbit fur that cushioned the quill in the shuttle." Allentown had the largest number and greatest variety of silk mills, some large ones integrating all production processes in one large complex. The number of mills in the city increased from twenty-eight in 1916 to sixty in 1927, the peak of the industry's presence in the county. That year, Capwell Fox notes, the value of silk production in Lehigh County was over $53.6 million, nearly twice that of any other county in the state. It was the biggest industry in the county by a substantial amount. By 1927 some of the mills were weaving rayon, which had started to displace silk as a fabric, but silk was not as hard hit as wool or cotton. Silk stockings were wildly popular among the era's flappers, and as skirts grew shorter the demand for silk stockings grew.

Mack Trucks, its AB and AC trucks having proved themselves in Europe during the war, was another industry that kept the Roaring '20s on the move in Lehigh County. The metals products industry, which included foundries, pump manufacturers, and trucks, was the second-biggest business in the county in 1927, with a value of slightly over $41 million.

Along with a number of innovative products, such as an aluminum container for economical shipment, Mack Trucks had created a dynamic sales force instructed to try to meet the needs of the customer. The company was growing just at the time when paved roads were being built throughout the United States and demand was growing for highway trucks as well as local delivery trucks—although horses continued to be used for local deliveries for some decades. John B. Montville, in Mack's official history, *Mack: A Living Legend of the Highway*, writes:

Production and financial figures reflected the high quality and teamwork that brought

widespread public recognition of the Mack product line during the 1920s. Total Mack chassis output went from about 5,000 in 1919 to over 7,500 in 1927. Sales in 1919 were reported as $22,143,699, which resulted in a profit of $1,983,469. But by 1927 sales had more than doubled to $55,270,295, resulting in a net profit of $5,844,307, which was before payments on preferred stock of about $1 million.

Cement, represented by the Lehigh Portland Cement Company, founded in 1897, the American Cement Company, founded in 1883, Coplay Cement Company, the first producer of "portland" cement in the nation, and Whitehall Cement Company, founded 1899, was in greater demand than ever. When Progressive Republican Governor Gifford Pinchot launched a road-building campaign in 1922 "to get the farmers out of the mud," he was using a great deal of local cement to do so. Lehigh County's leading industrialist, General Harry C. Trexler, who, despite his membership in the same political party, thought Pinchot a Progressive-type radical, noted to his aide, Nolan Benner, that the governor would have been furious if he knew how much of Lehigh Portland's cement was going into his road program. In 1927 the Lehigh Cement District, which includes major mills in Northampton County and in New Jersey and Berks County in addition to Lehigh County, was producing 43,732,278 barrels of cement, just over 77 percent of the state's total. At almost $17 million, it was the third-largest business in the county in terms of economic value that year, after silk and metal products.

Fourth in value in 1927, at almost $12.5 million, was agriculture and food products. Tobacco products—cigarmaking was a major business throughout the county—were rated number fifth, at slightly over $7 million. The former undisputed number-one industry in the county, primary metals (mostly pig iron), had dropped to sixth place at $6,173,500.

With these resources Lehigh County was out ahead of the rest of Pennsylvania. The prosperity of the mid-1920s encouraged rural-to-urban migration in Lehigh County. "Almost certainly the increase in the local population in Allentown in the 1920s was based primarily on internal rural to urban migration," notes Dr. Robert Schoen, professor of family sociology and demography at Penn State University.

The Great Limeport Raid Of 1925

As Lehigh County's chief law man in the Roaring Twenties, county sheriff Mark Sensenbach had his work cut out for him. It seemed every roadhouse had become a speakeasy, and every car an occasion for sex. Things had gotten so bad that Lehigh County Court Judge Richard Iobst had declared from the bench that these "automobile mashers," as he called them, had to be stopped.

In the summer of 1925 Sensenbach had been hearing rumors of something about to take place in a Limeport hotel that would put everything else in the shade. There were reports about girls being brought up from Philadelphia who were going to put on a "show." As the saying went at the time, these city women were said to be "hot stuff."

By 1925 several such shows had already been held in hotels and old, vacant one-room schoolhouses. The tickets cost as much as $2 for a good seat, and they were getting out of control. They had to be stopped. That is what brought the sheriff and his deputies in the early morning hours of August 29, 1925, to the three-story Limeport building. Approaching quietly, they discovered an open field filled with cars. Carefully they climbed the stairs to the third floor, hearing the sound of a player piano and the excited shouts of a crowd, estimated to be 350 men, growing louder as they did so. Then, standing in front of locked doors, the sheriff shouted to his men to break them down.

The deputies pounded and pounded and with a smash charged into the room. Every head turned toward them. Recalled one who was there, the 350 men had but one thought: what will my wife, girl friend, or mother do to me if they find out.

Acting as one, the crowd charged windows, doors, and whatever other exit they could find. Some even jumped from the windows to the second floor porch roof, rolled to the ground, and ran.

Apparently no one was killed or seriously hurt, and the sheriff made no real effort to stop them. They were last seen as a blur of Model-T Fords disappearing over the horizon in a smoky haze of 5-cents-a-gallon gas. What was left behind were the two male promoters and the four female dancers. They were quickly scooped up and arrested.

On September 30, 1925, in a courtroom the press described as packed to suffocation, most of the spectators being women, the trial began. The details of the dancers' striptease were described by *The Morning Call* as being "against all decency." There was talk of the women being naked and the men "fooling around with the girls."

By the time the defendants came forward the court had gone into a night session. The young women dancers claimed they were not naked but did a Charleston and walked around in a sort of see-through costume. One of the dancers, an African American who claimed to be from Bethlehem, brought the house down with laughter by her witty responses and caused Judge Claude Reno to gavel several times for order. When the assistant district attorney asked her what the music was like she replied, "It was very bum, It was rotten," which caused a huge laugh and more banging of Judge Reno's gavel.

The trials ended with the conviction of the women for public lewdness. They received four-month prison sentences and $200 in fines. The male promoters were let go and the owner of the hotel only paid court costs.

Within days the newspapers were reporting on sheriff's raids on other country roadhouses. Perhaps because of its size or the sensational court case that followed, the Great Limeport Raid of 1925 remained in the public memory for a very long time.

Lynn Township's population went from 2,021 in 1920 to 1,924 in 1930, and Lowhill Township's population dropped from 581 to 538. In this Lehigh County reflected what was happening across the nation. In 1900, 60 percent of the American population lived in small towns and on farms. By 1920 that number had been reduced to 49 percent and by 1930 to 43 percent. At the same time, agriculture remained an extremely important part of Lehigh County's economy. Increased mechanization on farms reduced the need for extra farm hands, while improvements in fertilizers and the sciences of crop rotation and disease prevention increased yields. In 1916, the new Lehigh County Farm Bureau had hired Al Hacker as its first county agent. Among his many achievements, improving potato production was one of the most economically important for Lehigh County, already a major potato producer. The county became the biggest potato producer in the state, and sixteenth in the country, after farmers adopted his recommendations.

Allentown's rapid rate of growth in the late nineteenth and early twentieth centuries led local officials to believe they were looking at a trend that would make it a city of 100,000 by 1930. From there the sky was the limit. "Barring any catastrophe which might cause the line of growth to break," noted *The Morning Call* on May 19, 1928, "and providing Allentown's population increases at the same rate it has over the past 78 years, in 1940 it will reach 160,000, in 1945 there will be 192,000 in the city and in 1946 the population will have increased to 200,000." Because the older figures were an exception, not the rule, and future population changes are not predictable, the optimistic figures predicted in 1928 were never achieved.

Inflation, fueled in part by higher wages, was increasing, along with Allentown's population, in the 1920s. On October 1, 1925, the *Allentown Chronicle and News* printed a story about the problem local merchants were having in getting and keeping employees. One Allentown businessman, who refused to give his name, described his encounter with the problem:

I had two young boys from high school come to the store to ask for a position. Since we do an extensive wholesale trade dealing largely in smaller household accessories and farmhouse supplies I told them I could place them and give them excellent insight into that line business. I offered them eighteen dollars a week to start. But they sniffed at it. Thirty dollars a week was the price they set for their services.

What this merchant and others were up against were the general wages paid in local factories. The city's Yeager Furniture Company, which among other items turned out japanned furniture, highly prized in the 1920s for its design work, paid the artists who worked for the company $33 a week. *Morning Call* cartoonist Bud Tamblyn, then an unmarried man in his mid-20s, recalled supporting his widowed mother, younger sister, and himself comfortably on that income.

Lafayette Hotel Fire Was Allentown's Jazz Age Tragedy

In 1926 the subject of a new hotel was much on the minds of Allentown's civic boosters. In 1921 the Hotel Bethlehem had opened and in 1924 the Hotel Easton. It was not right, Allentown's city fathers said, that the region's largest city still lacked a modern fireproof building like its rivals. Unfortunately, it took a tragic fire for the city to finally get one.

When critics pointed to Allentown's inadequate lodgings, the Lafayette Hotel at 133–137 N. Seventh Street was the kind of place they had in mind. The oldest hotel in the city, its roots went back to 1809, when it had opened as the Black Horse Tavern. Its heyday was in the Victorian era as a simple place popular with farmers and traveling salesmen.

In a burst of entrepreneurial enthusiasm for the Lafayette's 100th anniversary in 1909, the hotel's owners, brothers Elmer and George Guth, added two stories to the three-story building. Although their names were still on the Lafayette's side in 1926, they had sold it in 1924 to businessmen Louis Genovese and W.D. Cassone. Whatever plans the pair may have had for it, they were never able to carry them out.

The early morning hours of January 23, 1926, were bitterly cold ones in the Lehigh Valley. Most of the forty-five guests at the Lafayette Hotel had long gone to bed, but on the building's fourth-floor annex at least one was still awake, smoking a cigarette. For reasons unknown, the smoker threw the still-smoldering butt down a wooden clothing chute.

City fire-department investigators believed this was the spark of the horror that soon followed. Encouraged by the drafty chute, the cigarette butt burst into flame. Eating their way through the

Icicles are hanging from exposed surfaces on the morning after the fire.
(Reprinted with permission of The Morning Call. All Rights Reserved)

128

wooden walls, the flames moved quickly to the narrow space between the annex and the main building. With frigid winds blowing on them, they turned the slit between the two walls into a flue, lit, the official fire report said, "as from the end of a burning torch."

At 2:20 a.m., the Lafayette's night-desk clerk, Ralph Lehman, was startled out of his conversation with *Morning Call* linotype operator Melanchthon Usaw with cries of "Fire!" from upstairs.

Almost before both men knew what was happening, smoke began pouring down the lobby's ancient wooden staircase. They charged up the stairs, only to be forced back by an inferno. Lehman was able to get the elevator to take him as far as the second floor and managed to get the guests who were staying there out of the building. But it was impossible for him to go any higher.

Out in the street, late nighters were horrified as they saw people on the fourth and fifth floors of the Lafayette jumping or attempting to jump from the building. The fire department's hook and ladder men arrived to find guests hanging outside by their fingertips from the window ledges of the Lafayette. "Get us out for God's sake, we are burning up!" they cried.

Traveling salesmen E.R. Learner awoke in his fourth-floor room to the smell of smoke. He ran up and down the hall banging on doors. One man did awaken but could not get the door open, and Learner was forced back by the heat and flames. From somewhere, Learner could hear a woman screaming, but could not get to her.

Wearing only his underwear and an overcoat, Learner stepped out onto the roof ledge. With his hand he broke a window in the building next door and was helped by its occupants to safety.

Not everyone was so lucky. Guests were now jumping from their windows and falling to their deaths with what *The Morning Call* recorded as "a sickening thud." One fire fighter was carrying a man to apparent safety when he slipped on an icy ladder and fell with his burden to the ground. The hotel guest, elderly, frail, and already weakened from smoke inhalation, died. Sitting on the ground in tears was the firefighter. "I should have held him," he kept repeating over and over again.

Nineteen-year-old Henry Geiger, just starting out as a traveling salesmen, was trapped on the Lafayette's top floor. After banging on the elevator button and getting no response he hung out the fifth-floor window. By the time the firefighters got to him he was burned over much of his body. "Where is my mother? Tell my mother about me!" he screamed repeatedly.

It was 5 a.m. before the Lafayette Hotel fire was finally out. Gutted like a building that had been bombed, the remains were grotesque and presented a challenge. It was decided the next day to try what a later generation would call an "implosion." C.V. Weaver, demolition expert with the DuPont Powder Company, was brought in to handle the job. As crowds watched at a safe distance, he pushed the plunger. For a moment the Lafayette's walls shuddered, staggered, and then fell to the ground in a heap of rubble. The 117-year history of the Lafayette Hotel was over. For many people, the fire would never be over.

Thirteen guests had died. Some were so badly burned that relatives had to use dental records to identify them. Thirty-nine were injured, some of them with wounds so severe they never really recovered. There was one other legacy from the tragedy of the Lafayette Hotel fire. Allentown tightened its fire code. When the Americus, Allentown's first modern hotel, opened the following year, its owners could not repeat often enough that their building was fireproof.

It was not just about money. Lehigh County was being transformed by a technological and cultural revolution sweeping the country. The automobile was given the blame by many. As early as 1921, it was clear to some that the "closed car," as opposed to the open convertible, was transforming morals.

That year the State Federation of Women's Clubs held their annual meeting in Allentown. Asked by a reporter of the *Allentown Chronicle and News* what was the major issue facing the federation, president Mrs. H.H. Corson of Scranton said it was the auto's impact on morals. "I notice at home and in other cities I visited that girls with low necklines, short skirts and near silk stockings are given to make motions to have men in autos take them for rides. Their mothers would be shocked if they knew." Since skirt lengths in 1921, according to *The New York Times*, were all of nine inches off the ground, Mrs. Corson might have been overreacting. As a lady, she had to be careful with her words. In 1924 a judge of a juvenile court in Muncie, Indiana, was blunter. He called a closed car "a house of prostitution on wheels."

Whatever its impact on morals, the automobile was also changing Lehigh County in a lot of other ways. Rural areas that had once been isolated were drawn even closer to the network of the city. This isolation was not nearly what it had been. Trains and trolley cars were popular and widely used. If you wanted to go into Allentown or Slatington for shopping you could either hitch up a horse, and there were many people in the 1920s still doing that in Lehigh County, or you could get a scheduled train or trolley. But with a car you could come or go when you wanted, not when the railroad or the streetcar line allowed you to. With gas between 5 and 10 cents a gallon it was clearly cheaper than any other form of transportation except the horse, and you did not have to harness a car.

Radio comes to Lehigh County

Radio was a new form of technology that changed Lehigh County. At the decade's start no one thought of it as an entertainment medium. In fact, in 1920 the word "radio" was almost never seen in the local press. Most people called it the rather English-sounding "wireless" or, after its inventor, the "Marconi device."

Although radio broadcasting began in East Pittsburgh at the Westinghouse Company station KDKA, it is highly doubtful that many people in Lehigh County were listening to it in its very early days. There appear to have been no references to radio in the local press in 1921, although there may very well have been some who had homemade crystal sets.

On Saturday March 19, 1922, the *Chronicle and News* broke the silence on radio. It announced a nationally syndicated feature, "Radiographs." Sponsored by the U.S. Bureau of Standards, part of the Department of Commerce, it gave operators at home tips on how to deal with problems making your own radio and problems with static. This suggests that radio already had a following in Lehigh County, one that the newspaper felt could be a potential readership and market for advertisers with radio-related products.

By April 1922, Lehigh County was home to its first radio club in Allentown. By that June it was attracting major national figures like Captain Walter Hinton, pilot of the NC-4, the plane that had completed the first history-making flight across the Atlantic in 1919. On January 18, 1923, the club inducted its first woman member, Gertrude Mitchell of 506 N. Seventh Street. "Miss Mitchell is no novice in the field of radio," noted *The Morning Call* that day. "She has the distinction of having constructed her own receiving set which works admirably."

Freeman's was one of several dealers who sold and serviced radios.

Though the jargon of "Radiographs" may have appealed to Lehigh County's radio tech-heads of the 1920s such as Mitchell, it must have proved a little overwhelming for those who did not have the time or talent to create a radio of their own. Soon, however, commercially produced radios in large numbers would be available for the masses.

On March 25, 1922, the *Allentown Chronicle and News* published the first regular list of scheduled radio programs seen in Lehigh County. It included only two stations, Pittsburgh's KDKA, and WJZ of Newark N.J. The broadcast day began at 11 a.m. and consisted mostly of classical music. KDKA'S broadcasts were by live studio musicians, a twelve-piece orchestra made up of Westinghouse employees. The founder of KDKA's music program, along with being the conductor of its orchestra, was Victor Sudek. He wanted to use radio as a way to encourage interest in classical music. In 1965 his son Robert recalled how

131

distressed he was when a postcard from a distant city arrived with the message "Program Coming In Fine. Please Play 'Japanese Sandman,' " a popular show tune of the day.

Along with music there were a few simple programs. At 7 p.m. WJZ had a fashion program titled "Budget for Beauty." This was followed at 8 p.m. with a 15-minute talk by Newark's public health officer on "Contagion." The last feature on WJZ's evening schedule, starting at 8:15, was an English-language performance of the opera "Martha" by Friedrich Von Flotow.

At the same time KDKA offered "a talk by the prominent businessmen of Pittsburgh" and a live program that featured a soprano and the Fellows Club Quartet of Pittsburgh. Both stations went off the air at 10 p.m. with the Arlington Time Signals from Washington, when everyone set their watches and went to bed.

Roughly a month later, on April 18, 1922, Hess Brothers' Department Store really got the ball rolling. In a full-page ad featuring an illustration of a family sitting around a radio with a big speaker horn coming out of its center, the store announced that it was selling radios: "Radio, the most fascinating science of our time, has taken the country by storm."

Lehigh County took its own plunge into commercial radio in 1923 when WSAN, the county's first commercial radio station, opened in Allentown. This encouraged local people to get into the listening habit. At least they would be able to get better reception.

There are no statistics on how many people in Lehigh County purchased radios in the 1920s. National figures on the sales of radios show that in 1922 Americans spent $60 million for the new invention. By 1923 the amount had leaped ahead to $136 million, and by 1924 had soared to $358 million. Until the Great Depression of the 1930s, the hottest stocks on Wall Street were radio and radio-related. It was the high-tech industry of the day.

Radios were not a cheap item. A look at Christmas holiday ads in the *Allentown Morning Call* for 1927 showed the cheapest one at $68. Those who wanted to go all out could purchase the Spartan, "its cabinet of beautiful American crotched walnut," for $375.

What enabled average people to buy such a pricy item was the introduction of installment buying. For $5 down and $5 a month, customers could enjoy the cutting-edge technology of the day. By the decade's end there were probably plenty of second-hand radios on the market.

Movies

Movies, which had first appeared in Lehigh County before World War I, underwent explosive growth. Movie palaces like the Colonial in Allentown, which opened in 1920, set the tone for a fantasy palace of theaters. By 1929 there would be so many places to watch movies in Allentown alone that not all of them weathered the Depression.

The arrival of talking movies in 1927 was big news. The first all-talking movie was Al Jolson's "The Jazz Singer," but for unknown reasons that was not how local audiences first heard talking movies. The talkies arrived in Lehigh County on December 16, 1927, with the opening of the Earle Theater in Allentown. There was some doubt about how the public would take to what the *Allentown Chronicle and News* called the "latest novelty." People were used to getting their movies with generous doses of organ music. Would conservative Lehigh County audiences go for this change?

At the Earle that evening, after a concert consisting of some selections from Victor Herbert operettas was played on the theater's organ, the big screen filled with the face of Will R. Hays, former postmaster general and at that time president of the Motion Picture Owners and Distributors of America. As Hays opened his mouth in greeting, the audience gasped. "There was a synchronization between motion picture and sound," noted an amazed reporter for the *Chronicle and News*, "that made it plain that Mr. Hays was speaking."

Once Hays was done, the new medium was put through its paces. A film short followed, featuring grand-opera tenors, ukulele players, cheerleaders at the Yale–Army football game, Niagara Falls, and some Baltimore and Ohio Railroad steam locomotives sounding off. By the time the feature film began, "The Prince of Headwaiters," a romance starring Lewis Stone (later famous as the father of Mickey Rooney of the popular Andy Hardy films of the 1940s), talkies had arrived in Lehigh County.

Rise of the Suburbs

Movies, radio, and changing mores, while significant, did not change Lehigh County nearly as much as another phenomenon of the late 1920s, the rise of the suburbs, made possible by the automobile. Along with freeing the average citizen from railroad and streetcar timetables, it began to undermine the city itself. Towers of concrete and steel, like Allentown's Pennsylvania Power and Light Company skyscraper building, which rose 322 feet above a sidewalk, were considered fine places to work. But a home of faux Tudor or in the Colonial-Revival style with its own lawn, however small it might be, and a garage for the car away from downtown was the way more and more people wanted to live. Row homes, fashionable and popular from the middle of the nineteenth century into the first decade of the twentieth, began to lose their allure.

College Heights, the creation of the real-estate firm of Kaeppel & Kester, was in South Whitehall Township when the subdivision was first planned in 1916–17. Charles W. Kaeppel was an attorney; Earl S. Kester had done everything from running a billiard parlor to performing as a song-and-dance man on vaudeville stages up and down the East coast.

Ninth and Hamilton St., 1905. (PPL Corporation)

On May 6, 1923, they announced the creation of the College Heights Improvement Company (the "college" apparently being Muhlenberg College) to develop land north of Liberty Street and west of Seventeenth with building lots for sale to the upwardly mobile upper middle class. Newspaper ads for the new neighborhood showed well-dressed young couples gazing longingly at a rose-covered cottage. "Own Your Own Home!" it read, "The Fulfillment of a Dream!"

"Every young couple builds 'air castles' and one of the dreams has to do with owning one's own home," the promotion read. College Heights was "free from the annoyances of an undesirable neighborhood." In College Heights, homes would be assured of the rising values "that a high class location affords." There was a sense created by the real-estate sections of the local newspapers that failure to get into College Heights now would be regretted later. "The constant and unremitting fashion in which fine new homes are being built at College Heights," noted *The Morning Call* on June 10, 1923, "is proving the well-known slogan of the ideal suburban development, 'Allentown's New West End,' to be no idle boast."

College Heights, which was annexed to Allentown in 1924, turned out to be quite successful. Soon other housing developments followed. By mid-1929, as the residential real-estate boom was already fading both locally and nationally, small homes were sprouting on the east side of Allentown's North Lafayette Street between Liberty and Allen. Still there today, these faux-Tudor cottages, much smaller than their rivals built earlier in the decade on Liberty and Chew streets, were selling for $5,000 to $6,000. The average price of a new home at the time was a little over $7,000.

The collapse of the stock market in 1929 and the Great Depression of the 1930s that followed stopped almost all private residential development in Lehigh County. It would not resume in any real way until the end of World War II.

Electricity and PP&L

None of the growth in radio, movies, and extensive use of electric-powered home appliances could have been accomplished without large electric utilities. In fact in those early years utilities also sold appliances. The private utility company that fulfilled this role in Lehigh County and the surrounding region of eastern Pennsylvania was called the Pennsylvania Power & Light Company, then PP&L, now simply PPL.

Created in June 1920 out of a series of smaller private utilities, PPL's rise was due in part to the desire for business consolidation, a hallmark of the 1920s. Although a large part of the capital for the utility's creation was from New York investment banks, General Trexler was its primary local supporter. As head of the Lehigh Valley Transit Company, whose streetcars moved on electric power, Trexler had large generating capacities at his disposal. He was already involved with a number of local utilities when the merger took place.

As the prosperity of the 1920s advanced, so did the growth of the company. Home appliances like washing machines, refrigerators, stoves, vacuum cleaners or "Hoovers" and many smaller appliances were becoming fixtures in more and more households. These items were creating an increasing demand for electrical power. Lehigh County residents, now the owners of electric-powered washing machines (many of which were sold to them by PP&L), wanted more power than had satisfied their fathers and grandfathers.

This led PP&L to embark on the first of two major projects in the 1920s: the creation

Pennsylvania Power and Light skyscraper.
(PPL Corporation)

of Lake Wallenpaupack for hydroelectric power, and the building of its skyscraper tower headquarters building in Allentown.

Starting in 1924, PP&L began to purchase properties in and around the small town of Wilsonville on the border of Pike and Wayne counties in order to build a dam on the Wallenpaupack Creek. About 100 property owners were paid $20 an acre for their land. Seventeen miles of roads and telephone lines were rerouted, trees were cut down, and one cemetery was relocated. Most of the buildings were razed or moved, but some remained. A stream was temporarily diverted while the dam was built.

Construction began in early 1924 and took 2,700 men two years to complete. Along with the dam, a power-generating plant was built. A giant wooden flow line built to carry water from the lake to the plant, located three and a half miles away, was among the largest pipelines in the world at the time. Made of 500 board feet of Douglas fir, it was transported by ship from the state of Washington.

When Lake Wallenpaupack was completed in 1926 it was 13 miles long, had 52 miles of shoreline, and was 60 feet deep at its deepest point. At the time it was the largest man-made lake in Pennsylvania. It increased PP&L's power-generating capability by 25 percent. An Allentown Chamber of Commerce pamphlet published two years later, in 1928, recorded that PP&L had five large steam plants in addition to its hydroelectric plant, with a total capacity of 280,000 kilowatts. It had established interconnections with adjacent power companies, which gave its customers access to one million kilowatts of power. In the ten years between 1918 and 1928, it had increased its number of customers 230 percent, along with a phenomenal 325 percent increase in consumption. Over 23,000 houses in Allentown were wired for electricity, and service was already provided to 590 of the over 2,000 farms in the county. This was substantially more than the number of farms with indoor bathrooms or running water.

The same year that it finished construction of the Lake Wallenpaupack dam, PP&L began work on its headquarters building in Allentown. Since its creation in 1920, the company had taken over the upper stories of many Hamilton Street retail stores as office space. When a proposal was made for a new headquarters building, Trexler argued successfully in favor of its location in his home town rather than in Hazelton. According to one story he had wanted it built on the southwest corner of Ninth and Hamilton streets, the current site of the Holiday Inn. He had not counted on the refusal of a Mrs. Martin, an elderly widow from a prominent family who had a stately Victorian home that occupied the site. As she was almost blind she knew where everything was in her house, she said, and did not want to move. Whether the story is true or not is unknown, but construction of the building was begun on the opposite side of the street.

That the PP&L headquarters building would be a skyscraper was probably never in doubt. Across the country in the late 1920s power companies were building skyscrapers to house their office workforces. What was something of a surprise was the choice of an architect.

Harvey Wiley Corbett (1873–1954) was not just any building designer. Born in San Francisco, trained in the U.S. and Europe, he was to build only a handful of buildings. Corbett's primary contribution was as an educator and visionary. From 1907 to 1937 he lectured at the Columbia University School of Architecture.

Here, generations of young architects would receive Corbett's teachings and be shaped by them. One of the most significant of these was that modern buildings should have their own style, reflecting modern times. Many skyscrapers before the mid-1920s were built by classically trained architects who felt uncomfortable if they didn't place a pseudo-Greek temple at the top of a 30-story building. Corbett thought this did justice neither to classical architecture nor to the modern concept of the skyscraper. He favored generous use of setbacks that emphasized the monumental qualities of tall buildings, calling the effect "sculpted mountains."

Work on the PP&L tower building began in October 1926. Lehigh County had never seen anything like it. Before the building began a deep foundation was dug. Caissons were driven down past the fractured Lehigh County limestone to bedrock. The building rose to a height of 322 feet above the pavement, towering over Mrs. Martin's Victorian home, Hess Brothers store, and everything else manmade in Lehigh County. The rattling of rivet guns, remembered by many, were a rhythm that seemed like the beat of modern times.

Corbett believed a modern building should showcase modern art. To do this he picked Alexander Archipenko, the most avant-garde sculptor in America. Born in Ukraine, then a part of Russia, he had gone to Paris where he became influenced by a variety of art trends, particularly Cubism.

On arriving in America in 1922, Archipenko was ridiculed by conservative critics who

Summer scene along a dirt road in Lower Macungie Township.
(Lower Macungie Township Historical Society)

considered his work outrageous. Although the relief sculptures around the base of the PP&L building were not Archipenko at his most radical, they introduced what was almost certainly the first modern sculpture seen in Lehigh County.

Archipenko was able to blend Cubist art forms successfully with PP&L's mission as a utility in ways that were strange to the eyes of Lehigh Countians in the late 1920s. Angular Cubist fish are shown beside a large gear wheel while a wave of water pours over it, probably included to highlight the company's recent creation of Lake Wallenpaupack's dam and hydroelectric power. Another relief shows a tunic-dressed native of some distant tribe carrying an outsized light bulb over her head. On the opposite side a man in Native-American dress, a simple loin cloth, carries a large gear.

When the PP&L tower opened in June 1928, Lehigh County saw nothing but a rosy future before it. The January 1, 1929, special issue Prosperity Edition of the *Chronicle and News* told of the terrific success of the many businesses from cement to electricity that made the region great. The section was introduced by a large illustration depicting an Allentown and Lehigh County covered with giant skyscrapers. Near it a figure in a Roman-style helmet mounted in a chariot rode skyward. The caption under it read "With Giant Strides the Great Spirit Of Progress rides toward a Greater Lehigh Valley."

Lehigh County's spirit was America's spirit. As historian Frederick Louis Allen noted in 1931, in 1929 everyone predicted a future of unending growth and prosperity:

> Roads swarming with millions upon millions of automobiles, airplanes darkening the skies, lines of high tension wire carrying from hilltop to hilltop the power to give life to a thousand labor-saving machines, skyscrapers thrusting above one-time villages, vast cities rising in great geometrical masses of stone and concrete and roaring with perfectly mechanized traffic—and smartly dressed men and women spending, spending, spending with the money they had won by being far-sighted enough to foresee, way back in 1929, what was going to happen.

This was not what the future had in store.

The stock market crash of the fall of 1929 did not, at first, hit Lehigh County hard. Local newspapers and most opinion makers seemed to feel that the market had been over-inflated and that it was good that things would now go down to more respectable levels. Unlike the Panic of 1873, when the region was tied to the iron industry, the economy in Lehigh County was much more diverse than it had been. "The collapse of prices in recent days," noted *The Morning Call* on October 29, 1929, "has not removed a machine, it has not destroyed a single pound of materials, raw or finished in the country … All things of intrinsic value remain just as they were before the smash. … It will be a harsh readjustment for hundreds of thousands, perhaps millions. But it is to be hoped it will prove a useful and profitable readjustment in the end."

On the surface that logic made sense. But it failed to take into account how interdependent both the world and the national economy had become. The same system that made Lehigh County so prosperous, that had made its Lehigh Portland Cement and Mack Trucks commodities sought after across the country and the world, could make them vulnerable to economic conditions far from home.

Still, it was easy to see why, at first, the stock-market crash seemed a far-distant event for many people in Lehigh County. Pennsylvania Germans had a reputation for frugality that was legendary. A story recorded by General Trexler's aide Nolan Benner at the start of the Depression sums up well how Lehigh County's saw itself. Trexler, seeing an elderly Pennsylvania-German woman that he knew, asked how she was getting along during the hard economic times. "Well all right. You know, General, I always lived like there was a depression."

Those values were believed to be rooted in the self-sufficient rural way of life of many of the Pennsylvania-German farmers in Lehigh County, from which most of the local population had sprung.

Farm Life before the Crash

Charles B. Lichtenwalner, whose family farmed in Lower Macungie Township for many years, recounted, in an essay written for his family, what life was like on a local farm. He grew up in the 1920s on what was a 117-acre property on Brookside Road, just north of Brookside Country Club. His father, Charles A. Lichtenwalner, was one of the most respected farmers in the county. In 1940 the senior Lichtenwalner became the third farmer from Lower Macungie Township and sixth from Lehigh County to receive the Master Farmer Award given by the magazine *Pennsylvania Farmer*.

Looking back, young Charles recalled what his life was like on an average day in the 1920s. It began at 5 a.m. with milking two to three cows by hand, seeing that the hogs

William S. Weaver on his 1915 McCormick tractor, circa 1920. Weaver was a prominent citizen of Macungie, a well-known orchardist, and a Master Farmer. (Macungie Historical Society)

were fed, and making sure the laying hens had scratch feed. It was only when those chores were done that a hurried breakfast was eaten and clothes were changed. Once this was done he left home for a three-quarter-mile walk to school.

"The little red school house was our source of the 3 R's," Lichtenwalner writes. "If you were fortunate you attended a two room school house of 4 grades each, instead of a one room school house of eight grades."

After returning home from school, Lichtenwalner's first task would be seeing the wood box was filled. When that was done he had to milk the cows he had milked in the morning. Then it was time to feed the hogs once more, and see they had water. These tasks would last until 6:30 p.m.

The 1943 Farmall tractor replaced a team of mules used on the Yost Farm. (Evelyn Yost)

Supper was the main meal of the day, with lots of meat, potatoes, vegetables and desserts, "for mother loved to bake." Lichtenwalner recalled doing homework after dinner and often falling asleep over it. He adds that he was fortunate that his mother had once been a school teacher and could help him and his siblings with homework, while she peeled potatoes for the next day's meal.

Lichtenwalner wrote that most Lehigh County farms in the inter-war years of the 1920s and '30s were between 100 and 120 acres in size and were valued between $12,000 and $15,000. The average farm also included eight to ten horses, about 300 chickens, ten to fifteen milk cows, mostly for butter and milk, and ten to fifteen hogs for home slaughter and

140

family use. Equipment included two to three plow tractors for plowing and preparing the seed bed and providing belt power for grinding or threshing grain. The land was usually planted in a five-year rotation: corn, oats, hay, potatoes, and wheat. Extra money was made by selling butter, eggs, vegetables, and potatoes on a weekly route in Allentown.

In the mid-1920s, the period Lichtenwalner was describing, over 70 percent of Lehigh County was in farmland and the county had the highest value of crops of any in the state. The principal crops county-wide were potatoes, corn, wheat, oats, peaches, apples, and hay.

Change was certainly not unknown on Lehigh County farms of that day. As Lichtenwalner remembered it, electricity had come to the family's Lower Macungie Township farm about 1922–23. The tractors of the 1920s, he says, had steel lug wheels. "Horses pulled the planters, grain drillers and cultivators, usually hitched in teams of two or three together," he recalled. A big transformation came in the mid-1930s when, along with rubber tires, tractors with self starters became common. One other big change was the arrival of a two-row tractor cultivator because "horses need to rest while working but tractors could be worked continuously." The new equipment enabled farmers to plow more land, raising the size of an average Lehigh County farm by 1940 from 200 to 300 acres. It also apparently spelled the end for the horse and mule as farm animals. By 1935 they joined the ox, which had been the chief draught animal on Lehigh County farms from the eighteenth century to the Civil War, as part of the county's agricultural past.

The 1930s

If rural Pennsylvania-German values were as strong as ever, even they could not fully blunt the economic tidal wave that engulfed the world. Those who lived on farms may have fared better than those who were employed and dependent on a cash income.

Since Allentown was the industrial heart of the region it felt the collapse earlier than the rest of the county. Among the first to lose his $30-a-week job was young Bud Tamblyn. A designer of fashionable "japanned" furniture for the Yeager Furniture Company, he was laid off in one of the first kickbacks from the great collapse. "The salesman came out from New York and told us in a meeting that the bottom had dropped out of the japanned furniture market," Tamblyn recalled many years later.

Until 1937, when, thanks to his friend and fellow Allentown High School classmate and *Morning Call* newspaper executive Donald P. Miller he was finally able to get a job as newspaper photographer, Tamblyn, sole support of his mother and sister, barely survived with one part-time job after another. Until he died in the 1980s he never forgot having almost lost the family home until a New Deal program saved it.

Tamblyn was certainly not alone. Men were being laid off from one place and another. Bethlehem Steel, which had been working around the clock to provide wide-flange steel beams for the white-hot skyscraper market, slowly fell silent. By 1932 its chairman emeritus, the normally ebullient Charles M. Schwab, was shattered. "I am afraid, every man's afraid. I don't know, they don't know, whether the values we have today will be worth anything tomorrow."

From 1932 until government defense contracts started to come in just before the outbreak of World War II in Europe, Bethlehem Steel was operating at reduced capacity. Company president Eugene Grace, convinced that the steel industry would be among the first to revive, created a "Share The Work" program that redistributed hours so that at least his skilled workers could be kept on the job, albeit with reduced hours. Some worked only two or three days a week, as needed. The plant was kept in top-notch running order, and men were kept busy on improvements projects, such as making and installing four new blowing engines and an electric furnace.

Layoffs, foreclosures and other economic woes sent a panic through the county as it was feared "runs" on local banks would lead to a collapse of the region's economy. Here the unique nature of Lehigh County did indeed prove significant. Many local bankers had close ties as fellow Pennsylvania Germans and as longtime associates. Working to save both themselves and the community, they formed The Clearing House Association. It encouraged mergers between weak banks and strong ones. Only three banks collapsed in Allentown during the Depression and eventually the depositors were able to receive back a substantial part of what they almost lost.

Even the best efforts to aid the banks left many in Allentown and Lehigh County without work. By October 1932 the Lehigh County government's Emergency Relief Survey found 11,000 heads of families alone without work. The city and county did what they could to create jobs, the county providing road work to needy men. But they were hard pressed and were skimping by. Marches and demonstrations, the size of which had not been seen in Allentown since the Panic of 1873, were frequent.

In February 1933, 9,000 unemployed protested in front of the Lehigh County Courthouse demanding either work or relief. Another large but peaceful demonstration of the unemployed took place at Center Square that May. It had been preceded the previous month by a crowd estimated at 2,000 that "besieged" Red Cross workers distributing clothes and bedding. It was not until later that year, when the state created the State Emergency Relief Board, known by headline writers and the general public alike as "the SERB," and New Deal programs began that an unemployment system was able to cope with the huge numbers of those thrown out of work by the Depression.

Local private relief agencies were either brought down by the economic collapse or only hung on due to government aid. The Allentown Rescue Mission was a case in point. Founded in 1900 by Obadiah Becker, a recovered alcoholic, and his wife Rose it was a privately run Christian charity offering aid and comfort to those down on their luck. Unusual for its time, it accepted men and women of all races and faiths. But nothing could have prepared the Beckers, then in their 70s, for the Great Depression.

Traditionally, the Allentown Police Department had been the chief "refuge" of transient men passing through the city. In 1929, for example, the police reported 324 men used its municipal lodging room as a shelter for a night before being given a breakfast of a pastry and a cup of coffee and sent on their way. In October 1930, a year after the stock-market crash, that number had risen to 726. By February 1931 it had reached 1,095. Ernest B Fricke, in his 1974 study of Depression-era Lehigh County, puts the total number of transient men who found temporary lodging with the Allentown police in the winter of 1931 at 5,696.

Fearful of being overrun again the police prepared for 1931–32 by arranging to use an empty building at the southeast corner of Fifth and Hamilton that was scheduled to be torn down when construction of a new post office began. The facility, made up of fifty cots, was supervised by the National Guard. Heat, light, and water were provided by local utilities. As a stop-gap measure it seems to have worked, but it was torn down in January 1932.

Seeking a more permanent solution the city turned to the Rescue Mission, which was paid 15 cents a day to house and feed transients. The same arrangement was worked out for the winters of 1932–33 and 1933–34. But the 15 cents was far from covering the increased cost, and there were no available sources of money that could be raised privately.

In October 1934, the state decided to step in. The SERB's Bureau of Transients and Homeless began to quietly send clients to the Rescue Mission. On December 5, 1934, local newspapers announced that the SERB had reached an agreement with the Beckers to take over the management of the facility under a new name, the Obadiah Lodge. The Becker family, Obadiah and his son Harold, would run the day-to-day affairs of the organization.

The Obadiah Lodge was one of three organizations for homeless men that the SERB ran in Allentown. The first, Parkway Lodge, the former YWCA at 411 Walnut Street, had

Max Hess: Lehigh County's Merchant Prince

It was 2008, but Wolfgang Otto, master artist and window display designer, remembered the details of a day fifty years before like it was yesterday.

A young immigrant from Germany, Otto was busily engaged in creating a window display for his new employer, Allentown's Hess Brothers department store. A very careful man with an artistic flair that would become his trademark, Otto's work strove for a perfection that was, one day, to mark him among the leaders of his profession and win him a position as a vice president of Hess's.

On that 1950s afternoon his concentration was suddenly shattered by a loud voice shouting his last name. Turning toward the general direction of the voice, he saw a man behind him in a wrinkled London Fog-style raincoat, thick rimmed glasses slightly askew. The man, whom he had never seen before, began giving him directions as to exactly how the window should look, and then, turning abruptly, walked away.

Not at all pleased, Otto held his tongue as the man disappeared out of earshot and then turned to a nearby colleague, wanting to know who this impertinent stranger had been. "That," his fellow employee replied, "was Mr. Hess."

Otto's introduction to his boss, Max Hess, Jr., the merchant prince of Lehigh County, was unusual—but then a lot about the man was. As Otto would soon learn, his employer, although certainly as aware of the importance of making money as any business person, was no mere department-store owner. From his taking over the store fully in 1946 to his sale of Hess's to businessman, art collector Philip I. Berman in 1968, Max Hess was the impresario of a commercial fantasy and his stage set was at Ninth and Hamilton.

Born in 1911, Hess was the son of Max Hess, Sr., the German-Jewish immigrant who had founded Hess Brothers with his brother Charles. From its opening in 1897, the store was recognized for its flair. In 1909 it had a restaurant with a trout stream flowing through it. In 1912 its French Room, the creation of Charles Hess, brought high-style fashions direct from Paris to Lehigh County.

Max Hess, Sr., died in 1922, his brother Charles in 1929. In 1932, when the Depression was at its height, young Max left Muhlenberg College and took over the store. Hess made his first major change in 1936–37 by giving Hess Brothers a streamlined "Art Moderne" façade. But until the end of World War II building restrictions made him unable to do too much.

In 1946, with America on the verge of post-World War II prosperity, Max Hess made a splash by installing New York-style escalators. In 1947, just at the start of the Christmas season, he installed a huge sign, said to be the largest of its kind between New York and Chicago. And in 1951 the Patio Restaurant, with its outsized plates of food and strawberry pie, was born. For a Depression-scared, World War II-era generation who finally had money to spend, Max Hess rolled out the red carpet.

Along with bargains, high quality, and fashion, Hess's offered the stars. Where else could you go and maybe run into TV and movies celebrities? In 1956 George Reeves, television's Superman, even went door to door with a Hess's delivery truck. Who else but Max Hess would send out not just some costumed employee but the "real" superhero to deliver your sweater?

Reeves was one of many. Under the elegant chandeliers of Bohemian crystal they passed—Zsa Gabor, Barbara Eden, Rock Hudson, Hugh O' Brian, Troy Donahue, James Garner. The list seemed endless. Like Louis B. Mayer, MGM's studio head in its heyday, Hess could boast that he hosted "more stars than there are in heaven."

With the stars came the spectacle—flower shows, exotic art works, mechanical toys. Gerry Golden, Hess's fashion czar, toured the world, coming home to Allentown with fashion secrets known only to Sophia Loren or Princess Grace of Monaco. When topless bathing suits made their scandalous splash in 1964, Max Hess had them first. If that didn't do it for you, there were the bargain sales to end all bargain sales. To this day veterans of those shopping wars recount their shopping coups with lamps that still decorate suburban recreation rooms.

To top it all, Hess had his West End home, where he entertained lavishly in his own personal nightclub. Alligators were said to share the pool at fancy parties, and in 1952 when his pet kangaroo got loose there were headlines. As much as they loved it, sometimes guests couldn't see what he saw in some of this new entertainment, like the evening one told him that these young hippy singers Sonny and Cher, would never amount to anything.

So with all this it came as a total shock to the community when Max Hess announced in 1968 that he was selling Hess's to Berman. No reasons were ever given. It was even more of a shock a year later when Max Hess Jr. died suddenly.

Although Berman created a different experience, in some ways more sophisticated than Hess's, with modern artists and political figures, the great gaudy show of Max Hess could not be duplicated any more than the early 1960s era that inspired it can be reborn.

At least for now, the memories Hess's shaped live on.

(Private collection)

(Lehigh County Historical Society)

145

opened in December 1932. The Williams Lodge at 377 Union Street, which was primarily used by African Americans, opened roughly at the same time. At the same time Agudas Achim, the city's oldest Orthodox Jewish synagogue, ran a private space for Jewish transients.

A little over a year later, January 4, 1936, *The Morning Call* announced that the federal government, which funded the state's aid programs including the SERB, had decided to shift its focus to a work-relief program, the Works Progress Administration. In response, the SERB ended its transient program and began to register residents with the WPA.

The Parkway Lodge and the Williams Lodge were closed. The Obadiah Lodge remained open but was struggling. In March of 1935 it had closed for three weeks as major repairs were undertaken.

Needing a place to house those in its WPA relief program, the city decided to purchase the former Lewis Mansion at 506 Hamilton Street. It was estimated to be able to provide 200 beds. The only problem was that by taking it over the city would have to eject the current tenants, a unique institution known as the Community Cafeteria that provided low-cost and free meals for the unemployed.

The Community Cafeteria was supposedly based on an idea from Fred Lewis, then Allentown's mayor. The building had been owned by his family. But the real organizers of the cafeteria were the Rev. Joseph Burke and his wife Sadie. Both had long been active in the field of social work.

Sadie Feather Burke was a native of Allentown whose family had maintained the city's Fairview Cemetery for many years. She had met her future husband at a Bible college they attended and they were married in 1910. For twelve years they had run the Allentown YMCA. After that they opened a restaurant where they gave aid to disabled World War I veterans.

On May 23, 1932, the Community Cafeteria opened. The unemployed were provided with free meals. Those who were partially employed were asked to pay a nominal fee like 10 or 15 cents per meal. The food was provided through donations from restaurants and grocery stores and from a 41-acre farm in Lyons Valley, Berks County, managed by Sadie Burke.

Although they were not required to, many of the unemployed volunteered to work on the farm in exchange for free meals. Among the tasks they performed was canning the farm's vegetable produce. On its opening day the Community Cafeteria served seventy meals. Within a month it was serving 500 to 700 a day and by 1933 it had increased to 1,000 meals a day.

Not wanting to lose this important and useful community institution, Allentown Mayor Malcolm Gross and other civic leaders began to look for a new location. They contacted the Obadiah Lodge and worked out an agreement. It allowed the city to rent out the building for a nominal fee. The Burkes would manage it as the new location of the Community Cafeteria.

The Beckers were allowed to continue to live in their apartments in the building. Rose Becker died in February 1936. Her husband stayed on until 1941, when the Burkes were named supervisors. He died in 1951.

On April 26, 1936, the building was renamed the Allentown Rescue Mission and the Community Cafeteria took over the basement as their space. On May 10, the cafeteria reopened in a special ceremony that included the Boys Haven Harmonica Band, a program to help local youth. More than 500 meals were prepared that night.

In 1939 *The Morning Call* featured a detailed article on the workings of the Allentown Rescue Mission and the Community Cafeteria. Since 1932 they had provided 1.43 million meals. Of that number 452,000 were without charge. "A typical 10 cent meal," the *Call* noted, "consists of a meat course, two vegetables, a salad, bread, butter and coffee." One family of ten had been eating at the Community Cafeteria every day for a year.

In 1938 the Rescue Mission provided lodging for 14,522 homeless transients without charge. Besides its location on Fourth Street, at the height of the Depression the Mission maintained three annexes, at 426 and 433 Hamilton Street, and 380 Linden Street.

Some thought of those using these services as shiftless freeloaders. Sadie Burke begged to differ. "Many people have a miscalculation of our work," she told the *Call*. "It is generally thought we are housing a shiftless group of man and women—derelicts. This is far from true. Of the hundreds passing through our doors we have less than a dozen of this type.

"Our population comprises men and women out of jobs; men unable to buy food because of a delay in their relief checks, WPA workers whose checks fail to come through on schedule and, of course, transients coming into our city. We are sort of the 'first aid station' filling the gap that comes between the time of the application for relief and the time the checks come through. We take care of the borderline cases which do not get consideration by the established agencies."

Less than a year after Burke gave this interview, World War II would begin in Europe; in 1941 the U.S. would enter the war. On November 25, 1942, almost a year after Pearl Harbor, Sadie Burke was telling the *Call* that only three or four transients were seeking food and lodging at the mission, compared to the thousands it had seen just four years before. For every transient that was now working in a defense plant or, as the Andrews Sisters sang, "whose number came up and was gone with the draft," there were people flocking into Allentown from rural Lehigh County seeking jobs. She reported the mission was housing nine families with a total of thirty to forty children. There was no affordable housing in the city.

In 1946 Sadie Burke suffered a heart attack while walking on Hamilton Street and died in the back of the police car taking her to Sacred Heart Hospital. She was 62. Her husband resigned from the leadership of the Allentown Rescue Mission a year later. Shortly before Sadie Burke's passing she had told *The Morning Call* that from 1936 to 1946 the Allentown Rescue Mission had served 1,500,000 meals to men, women and children, most from Lehigh County, who might have gone hungry without them.

Harry C. Trexler

Interestingly, in some ways Lehigh County was better prepared for the Great Depression than most parts of the country. Far back in the 1920s General Harry Trexler, who had served as the head of Allentown's planning commission from 1916 to 1923, had experts from Philadelphia draw up plans for a park system, largely what became Little Lehigh Parkway. "The years of design work by the City Planning Commission and the establishing of a political consensus in favor of parks," writes historian Peter Hall, "paid off as the city had in hand detailed plans of what it intended to do with federal funds once they were available."

Trexler, deciding it was fruitless to wait while politicians dithered, was going ahead. Using his own checkbook he was buying so much property he did not easily remember what he had purchased. In the early 1930s, driving past a small farm on what would later become part of Little Lehigh Parkway, Trexler, his wife, and his aide Benner noticed a beautiful blooming lilac bush. As lilacs were her favorite flower, Mary Trexler had chauffeur Charlie DeLong stop the car. Going up to a girl sitting on the steps of the farmhouse she

asked how much it might cost to pick some for a bouquet.

Unawed by the rich lady or the big car with chauffeur, the child responded like Mary Ann Jackson, the wise-cracking freckle-faced child actress with a Dutch-boy haircut in the era's popular Our Gang comedies. "Ain't our lilacs, Colonel Trexler's lilacs," she said curtly. It was only after a quick consultation with Benner that Trexler realized the child was correct. He had recently bought that farm.

Allentown was not the only place where Trexler owned property. According to Benner, at the time of his death he was among the largest land owners in Lehigh County.

The Trexler Game Preserve, begun as part of an effort to save the buffalo from extinction, had attracted many visitors. Trexler had begun the process in 1906 by purchasing small farms in the low hills south of the Blue Mountains. By 1923 he had purchased thirty-six farms and tracts on both sides of a public road between Schnecksville and Weidasville. Trexler enclosed 1,170 acres of the property with a 6½-foot wire fence. According to Benner, a written request arranging for a time between the months of May and October was all that was required to visit the game preserve. By 1927 the size of the buffalo herd had increased to the point that Trexler had to reduce the herd by giving some away.

No one can say for sure how these park projects envisioned by Trexler would have come to pass if a tragic event had not shaped their outcome.

On the evening of November 16, 1933, Trexler was returning to Lehigh County from a business trip to New York. His black Cadillac Town Sedan glided along the William Penn Highway headed to Allentown. Trexler had told a business associate before he left that he had promised his wife he would have dinner with her.

As was his custom, the General was sitting in the front seat next to Charlie DeLong, his longtime chauffeur. Bolt upright, the General would pound his cane on the floor when he wanted DeLong to pick up speed. He may have done just that as they passed the Taylor Wharton Company plant and entered a slight dip in the road. DeLong, who was fighting a head cold and feeling somewhat groggy, recalled later that he had just raised the car's speed to forty miles an hour.

Invisible to them on the top of the rise in the road was a stalled fuel-oil truck driven by William Krick of Fullerton. The battery on his vehicle had given out and he was waiting for the Miller Motor Company in Bethlehem to arrive with a new one. Although he had gotten the truck as far over on the shoulder as was possible, Krick also waved a flashlight to warn drivers who might not see him of his location.

Perhaps because of his cold and the darkness, Krick's flashlight did not register with DeLong until he was almost on top of the fuel truck. The Cadillac caught the left wheel hub of the fuel truck and the car's right side slammed into the stalled vehicle. The almost 80-year-old Trexler took the full force of the impact. When the car finally came to a stop its front and rear doors were hanging open and broken glass was everywhere.

DeLong and Krick flagged down a passing car and took Trexler to Easton Hospital. To the surprise of everyone Trexler walked out of the car and into the hospital without assistance. But on examination the doctors saw he had a shattered collarbone, several broken ribs, and massive internal injuries. So they made him as comfortable as they could, hoping the General's cast-iron constitution would heal him.

News of the accident spread and Benner and Mary Trexler rushed to the hospital. Benner later recalled the General was conscious when they entered the hospital room, "and recognized us with a nod of his head." At 3:55 a.m. on November 17, without uttering a sound, Trexler died holding his wife's hand.

The news of Trexler's passing sent shock waves through Lehigh County. At the height of the worst economic crisis anybody could remember the county had lost its leading citizen.

On November 21, as the procession of cars returned across Allentown's Eighth Street Bridge from Fairview Cemetery following Trexler's funeral, a changed world greeted those who had worked closest to him. Perhaps none had been closer than two men, his aide Nolan Benner and Allentown's mayor "Mal" Gross, and one woman, his wife Mary.

What surprised and delighted the community was the creation of the Trexler Trust by the General's will. Here was a plan that would benefit the city and county and provide money to help pay for it. The contribution was something that required the city and county to play their part as well. As it was the middle of the Great Depression, when schoolteachers were being laid off and private money for charitable purposes did not exist

One of the WPA-era playgrounds in the city was this one behind Trout Hall.

(despite the fact that he was a very conservative investor Trexler had taken a hit in the stock market that had reduced the value of his fortune by Benner's estimate from $50 million to $10 million), it seemed the plan would not ever come to fruition.

At the same time, the new Democratic administration in Washington was trying very hard to come up with programs to put people back to work. Three of the agencies the New Dealers came up with were the Civil Works Administration (CWA), the Public Works Administration (PWA), and the Works Progress Administration (WPA).

The CWA was created to provide temporary employment. It was phased out on March 31, 1934. The PWA planned projects that were built by private construction companies who used their own workforces, which they hired on the open market. The WPA, created in 1936, hired and paid the unemployed directly.

General Trexler, a very fiscally conservative Republican, was already on record stating that government work programs were not something he approved of. If he had remained alive these programs might never have been tapped into, and perhaps the park system never built. Then again, Trexler was a pragmatic man who just might have gone along with the government to see his projects completed. But now he was gone.

The following year Mary Trexler passed away. Her most significant action between her husband's death and her own was giving the money he had promised for the start of a building for St. James AME Church, a congregation with a long history in the local African-American community.

Benner and Gross were left to take up Trexler's legacy. Benner, who lived until 1980, would spend the rest of his life overseeing the legacy of his former boss. As head of the Trexler Trust, a board made up of community notables, he was uniquely positioned to serve that role.

Gross's role was also extremely important. As a mayor of Allentown in the 1920s he had worked closely with Trexler on his agenda for the city. Gross believed strongly with Trexler that the development of a park system was not only an asset to the citizens but

Construction of the stage area at Union Terrace park, a 1933 WPA project.

an important economic tool that would draw business to Allentown. Out of office when Trexler died, Gross was re-elected mayor in 1935, narrowly defeating Harry Dubbs, a Republican newcomer. Mayor Fred Lewis decided not to run after the Dime Savings Bank of which he was president failed.

Gross knew the city and county could provide the labor for the parks and knew the government was looking for projects to keep WPA workers busy. And he knew better than anyone else what those properties would mean to the growth and development of the city. So when Gross was able to show New Deal planners a blueprint for just the sort of community improvement projects that they were hoping to fund, they immediately agreed. Although he was already a passionate advocate for federal aid to the city, his efforts were helped by the fact that they had already begun under his predecessor.

According to historian Peter Hall, the first CWA money to come into Lehigh County arrived in January 1934. These funds were used for work on city parks and playgrounds and the completion of a field house at Allentown High School. "In May, 1935," writes Hall, "following the settlement of the Trexler Trust the government established the first Civilian Conservation Corps camp—at the Trexler Lehigh Game Preserve. Its task was to transform the general's private preserve into a publicly accessible park, a task that would not be completed until April of 1937." In June 1937, *The Morning Call* estimated that $3.9 million of federal money had been spent in Lehigh County between 1933 and 1937.

The WPA was to have a major role in the creation of the city's park system. Even the Republican-leaning *Morning Call*, which backed Franklin Roosevelt's rival Alf Landon in the 1936 presidential election, was impressed. "W.P.A. Gives Reality to Park Plans Dreamed for a Quarter of a Century," was the headline over an article that appeared in the paper in 1937. In the late 1930s the parks system project was in full swing.

"Within two years of the initiation of these programs," Hall writes, "Mayor Gross could proudly point to a nearly completed system of parks which included (moving from east to west) the Irving Street Playground, Riverfront Park, Jordan Park, Allen Park, Fountain Park, the Little Lehigh Parkway, West Park, Union Terrace, Cedar Pool and the gem of the system,

Trexler Park, which had been laid out at Trexler's Springwood Estate."

Even with the success of getting federal money and jobs to Allentown's unemployed, Gross had his critics both in the city government and among the general public. The idea persisted that public money was "wasted" when it was spent on parks. In 1940 the *Evening Chronicle* noted that an often-heard cry among his critics was "All he thinks about is parks." Others referred to the park system as "Gross's Folly."

When Gross created a more streamlined management system to manage the parks he was attacked by city councilmen. Since the early twentieth century Allentown operated under a "commission" form of government with a mayor and four council members, each of whom ran a municipal department. Whatever its virtues may have been, this system made the city council very protective of their agencies, which some of them used to dispense patronage.

In 1938 Gross voted against the city's budget in protest that $19,000 was moved from the Parks Department and divided between the councilman who controlled the Fire Department and the councilman who controlled the Streets Department. "Council was making a statement," his grandson writes, "that parks were to be downgraded in favor of other councilmen's departments." In spite of this, Gross generally felt that the good the park system did for the community spoke for itself. Just before leaving office he called Allentown's park system the "ace in the hole" for competing with other towns of its size. "No other city can touch it," he told the *Evening Chronicle*.

Apart from all its many problems, Allentown had plenty of things that made life in the Depression era, especially if you were lucky enough to have a job, enjoyable and inexpensive. There were many downtown movie houses. Although some, like the Embassy and Capitol, did not survive, the Colonial, Earle, and Rialto were extremely popular.

The Nineteenth Street Theater, which was built at a cost of $500,000, had opened to much fanfare in September 1928. But it had closed that December when its owners declared bankruptcy, and remained dark for two years. Then on September 8, 1930, a small article appeared in *The Morning Call* saying the theater had been purchased and would reopen later that week. The new owner was Amusement Incorporated of Pennsylvania, a Williamsport-based company. Now equipped to show sound movies, it was a second-run house whose admission of 25 cents was marginally affordable to a Depression audience. The first film shown was "Common Clay," a tearjerker whose star, Constance Bennett, was mistaken for Greta Garbo in *The Morning Call's* article about the re-opening. The theater prospered until the arrival of television.

Radio was more popular than ever. Few people had the money to afford even the 25-cent admission price at the Nineteenth Street Theater. But they could always "tune in" to

Hamilton Street was the busiest shopping district in the greater Lehigh Valley for decades. This photo by William Zwikl shows busy shoppers and a bus at Seventh and Hamilton in the winter of 1940. Europe was engaged in war at the time, but the United States remained neutral. (Kurt Zwikl)

dance music featuring performances by both local big bands and national figures.

In February 1935, Allentown was the site of a live national broadcast of "Amos 'n' Andy," the most popular national radio program of the time. It is said that in most American towns of the day, on a warm summer evening it was possible to walk down just about any street and hear the program through open windows without missing a word.

Other popular radio performers in the Lehigh Valley were comedians Jack Benny and Fred Allen, whose radio "feud" was a long-running feature in the 1930s and '40s. And, like most people in the nation, Lehigh County residents in October 1938 were caught up in the invasion of Earth by Martians as a result of a panic brought on by Orson Wells' Mercury Theater radio drama, "War of the Worlds." People flooded the police and *The Morning Call* with phone calls claiming they could "see" Bethlehem Steel and South Mountain burning as a result of fires set by the Martians' flame-shooting death ray.

The 1930s were also a great time for local theater. The Civic Little Theater, an amateur group founded in the late 1920s, drew on the talents of many in Lehigh County. The driving force behind it in the 1930s was John Y. Kohl, Sunday editor of *The Morning Call* and devout theater fan. Other amateur theater productions, like those sponsored by the WPA and local church groups, were common.

Big bands were not just heard on the radio. At Mealey's Auditorium in downtown Allentown and at Dorney Park's Castle Garden ballroom some of the best-known music makers of the day performed. With excellent railroad service and some spare change it was possible to travel to New York to see a Broadway show and spend the night. In 1933 New York's Plaza Hotel was offering single rooms for $5 a night.

One national event that marked the decade for that generation of Lehigh County residents was a visit to the New York World's Fair of 1939–40. Fifty years later, in 1989, Dr. John F. "Jack" McHugh, former Allentown High School principal and then a Lehigh County

Commissioner, recalled the wonder he had felt as an eight-year-old boy on his trip to New York's Flushing Meadow for a glimpse of what was billed as "The World of Tomorrow."

McHugh's father was working on the fair's Midway promoting a number of acts. His feature performers were Benny and Betty Fox, a Lehigh County dance team who had perfected the art of dancing on a 12-foot disk high in the air.

Young Jack and other family members toured the fair. "They had televisions, the first we had ever seen," McHugh remembered. "Everybody stood there and kept trying to figure out how they could fit all those people on such a little screen. In 1939 the idea of television in every home seemed far in the distant future."

Although a lot of people remember the big General Motors exhibit or the towering pointed Trylon and huge oval Perisphere, symbols of the fair, it was the home appliances that transfixed McHugh. "Pop-up toasters, electric irons, vacuum cleaners and electric stoves, these were things that could change everyday life," he recalled. His uncle, Joe McHugh, who was helping his father at the Midway, remembered seeing frozen food for the first time. "I looked at it and remembered thinking how could you possibly freeze food and get it to taste like anything," he recalled.

The McHughs were not the only ones in Lehigh County caught in World's Fair fever. Allentown hairdressers were advising potential customers that they had "the styles of tomorrow," just right for a visit to the fair.

Service stations were reminding those driving to the fair that it was time to get a tune-up if they wanted to get there safely. One Lehigh County furniture store promised that the first five lucky winners who could put together a jigsaw puzzle of the fair would receive free living-room suites. Second-prize winners would receive one of 400 free tickets for the fair. As the admission fee was hefty 75 cents, these were undoubtedly highly prized.

The World of Tomorrow that glimmered so brightly those summer nights of 1939 in Flushing Meadow could offer only a momentary distraction from distant world events that would, as they had in 1914, plunge the world into war. On September 1, without warning, Germany attacked Poland. By September 3, England and France had gone to war against Germany. World War II had begun.

CHAPTER FOUR

LEHIGH COUNTY: ARSENAL OF DEMOCRACY 1940-1945

Unlike 1914, the onset of war in Europe in 1939 took few people in Lehigh County or many other places by surprise.

"This is not peace," French commander Marshall Ferdinand Foch, on whose private railroad car at Compiègne the armistice that ended the fighting was signed in 1918, had said one year later, "it is an armistice for twenty years." He was off by only two months.

By the early 1930s many could see the next war coming. In 1933 British journalist Philip Gibbs interviewed some residents of Geneva, Switzerland, about the hope that the League of Nations, whose new headquarters building was rising on the shores of Lake Geneva, would prevent another war. "First we hoped, then we cried, now we laugh," was their reply.

The cover on the November 1933 issue of *Vanity Fair* magazine summed up the mood of the day. It showed top-hat-wearing diplomats on a globe turned into a gigantic time bomb with a slowly burning fuse. Predictions of war were like heat lightning on the horizon. China and Japan had been at war since the invasion of Manchuria in 1931; Mussolini had invaded Ethiopia in 1935; and the Spanish Civil War of 1936–39 all belied the "peace" of that time.

The Munich Agreement that gave Hitler Czechoslovakia's German-populated Sudetenland was signed by Germany, France, Britain, and Italy in September 1938. Britain's Prime Minister Neville Chamberlain called it "peace in our time." Not everyone agreed. "You were given the choice between war and dishonor," said Winston Churchill in the House of Commons, "You chose dishonor and will have war." War came on Sunday, September 3, 1939, when England and France declared war on Germany over the German invasion of Poland two days before.

That Sunday, Bethlehem Steel's CEO Eugene Grace was standing with his usual golf foursome of company executives outside the Saucon Valley Country Club's clubhouse. One of those executives, George Hurd, would recall many years later that when he heard war had broken out, Grace turned to them and said succinctly, "Gentlemen, we are about to make some money."

Grace's words sound callous, but he was just stating a fact. Wars made big profits for steel companies. Three days later, on September 6, 1939, *The Morning Call* carried an Associated Press story under the headline "Steel Prepares for Boom: War Opens New Markets Despite Neutrality Act." It began by noting some facts: "The American industry's capacity is 2½ times that of Germany, Britain and France combined. The Bethlehem Company alone is rated equal in capacity to the entire industry of Britain and France together."

The German-American Bund

Few people in Lehigh County wanted to see America go to war. If the nature of the Hitler régime led to less ambiguity as to who was right and who was wrong in the conflict than had been the case in 1914, very few people in Lehigh County in 1939 wanted to go to war, as the saying then went, "to pull England's chestnuts out of the fire."

Yet the smell of those burning chestnuts would not leave the nation and Lehigh County alone. The same Sunday, in Sellersville, Bucks County, Fritz Kuhn, the *fuehrer* of the pro-Nazi German American Bund—estimated membership between eight and ten thousand—was scheduled to speak at the Deutschhorst Country Club. The club had become a mecca for like-minded, pro-Nazi Americans. They came to drink German beer and take rifle practice.

When the press got word that Kuhn was going to speak that day, it was news. He had already generated "newspaper ink" the previous May when a car carrying him and his aides through the Lehigh Valley was spotted being followed by detectives from New York District Attorney Tom Dewey's office. A grand jury had charged Kuhn with stealing almost $15,000 from the Bund's treasury. Supposedly, $14,000 of it was to pay off a blackmailing former mistress. Cornered in a Krumsville, Berks County, gas station, Kuhn gave up without a struggle. "Where's your friend?" Kuhn asked, chiding the New Yorkers about Dewey's night clubbing that was a regular feature of newspaper gossip columns. "I bet he's at the Stork Club—that's where I am always running into him." Despite his theft the Bund refused to press charges against the leader they called "our Fritz." Three busloads of Bundists from New York pulled up at the Deutschhorst Country Club to hear Kuhn. Bert Baum, a son of painter Walter Emerson Baum, lived nearby. He had gotten word from the *Philadelphia Bulletin*, for

which he worked part-time as a "stringer," that Kuhn was coming. Slipping a small 49-cent camera into his pocket, Baum left his home. *The Morning Call* had also gotten word of Kuhn's speech and sent reporter Gordon Fister and photographer Bud Tamblyn to Sellersville.

Baum headed for the field and was surprised at the large crowd. The few local people who held memberships in the club, like he did, claimed they did so only to drink the good-quality German beer it provided. A speaker's platform had been set up, draped with Bund banners and American flags. Men, women, and children milled about. There were storm-trooper types in full uniform "sieg heiling" each other and singing Nazi marching songs.

Tamblyn and Fister soon arrived. As he was taking pictures of the crowd, Tamblyn was attacked by a storm trooper. "You are a spy," the Nazi shouted. "He's a spy, throw him in the river," the crowd began to shout, pointing to a nearby creek. The storm trooper yanked the camera out of Tamblyn's hands and pulled the plates out of it, destroying the photographs. The crowd chased him back to the car, where they also found Fister. It was only because Baum had a membership in the club that they were not driven away or beaten up.

A crowd of 2,000 was on hand to cheer as Kuhn arrived and began to speak. He spoke, in German, of Jewish warmongers, reminding his followers that they should be strictly neutral while claiming "Hitler will lick the whole of Europe." When his boss had finished Kuhn's press aide, Gerhard Kunze, replaced him at the microphone.

It was common in the late 1930s for Nazis, and anti-Semites of all kinds, to imply by slurring his name that Roosevelt was Jewish. Kunze did just that: "We hope F.D. Rosenfeld is thrown out of office next year," he shouted. "[The Bund] hopes a white American will be elected president." Fister, who understood German, was jotting notes using the stub of a pencil he had concealed in his suit-coat pocket.

After his speech Kuhn allowed Tamblyn to take his picture. Baum, who had managed to get a shot off without being seen, got it to the Bulletin, which then put it out over the Associated Press newswire. The next morning, over their orange juice and toast, millions of

Americans were viewing Baum's grainy photo of the rally.

Kuhn let the press ask a few questions. He told them Hitler would get all the raw materials he needed from the countries he would conquer, and that Japan would soon join Germany and Italy as Axis powers. "I wouldn't want to be in England's shoes for nothing," said the American *fuehrer*.

For all his bombast and bluster, Kuhn's reign was short. In December 1939 he was sent to prison for tax evasion and embezzlement, and was shipped back to a shattered Germany in 1946. Kunze, who took over the Bund after Kuhn's arrest, was later imprisoned for advising young men to avoid the draft. Both died in West Germany in 1951.

None of Our Business

To many people in Lehigh County in 1939, the German American Bund was a group of fanatics. Most were convinced that this affair among Europeans had nothing to do with them. Among them was Lehigh County's Republican Congressman Charles Gerlach. "If nations like Norway, Sweden, Switzerland and others can remain neutral in time of war," he told *The Morning Call* on September 1, 1939, "I see no reason why we, 3,000 miles away, cannot stay out of Europe's 'real estate deals.' " Gerlach was right about Sweden and Switzerland. But when Hitler invaded Norway the following year it found how little its neutrality meant to Nazis.

On September 2, 1939, the *Evening Chronicle* asked Lehigh County readers if they thought the U.S. would be drawn into a war. "I don't think so," a man from the village of Stiles said. "There's no reason why we shouldn't be able to keep out of the European mess. We're not being attacked nor are we being even threatened. If we just mind our own business and stay strictly neutral in any conflict we will be all right." An Allentown man agreed: "I do not see why we should become involved in the European situation. No one over here is interested in Danzig or the Polish Corridor. It is none of our business what's going on over there. We know better how to stay out because of our experience in the last World War."

Only one interviewee, school teacher Harold German of Neffs, felt that sooner or later America would be involved in World War II. "Eventually we will be drawn into a European war," he said. "The United States has too many financial interests in foreign countries to enable us to stay out. The possibility of acts being committed against our merchant marine is great. We probably won't enter a European war the first year of fighting however."

Lehigh County citizens who had been vacationing in Europe that summer began to come home. Among them were Allentown schoolteachers Julia Kramer and Adelaide Richards and their escort Eleanor Barba, wife of Preston Barba, Muhlenberg College professor and German folk-culture expert. The women recalled fleeing a Europe of blackouts, air-raid sirens, and troop movements.

Their voyage home had been on the German liner S.S. *Bremen*. The women were probably unaware of it, but two days before they reached New York the *Bremen's* captain had received orders, as had German passenger ships around the world, to return to Germany because war was imminent. The captain ignored the order and let his passengers off in New York. The German liner sailed back to Europe two days later, empty.

The most headline-grabbing local return from Europe was that of Charles Schwab, chairman emeritus of the board of Bethlehem Steel. He had been in England, and was recovering from a heart attack. The personal intervention of U.S. Ambassador Joseph P. Kennedy got him a stateroom on the overcrowded steamer S.S. *Washington*. Schwab arrived safely, but died in New York on September 19.

A perceptive and detailed account of what Hitler's regime was really like came in *The Morning Call* shortly before the war. Helen Brendle, a schoolteacher who had grown up the daughter of Rev. Thomas Brendle, a German folk-culture expert and Reformed pastor of a church in Egypt, Whitehall Township. A 1931 graduate of Whitehall High School, she had signed up for a ten-week course to study at the Weimar-Jena Institute. She stayed at the home of a German countess who was a cousin of former German Field Marshall and last President of the German Republic, Paul von Hindenburg. During her stay Brendle, who was fluent in German, met Germans from all walks of life. Some in the upper-class circle of her hostess regarded Hitler as an Austrian upstart. "We did not have to salute Bismarck or the Kaiser so why do we have to salute Hitler," they complained.

Others, like the family Brendle was forced to stay with overnight when she could not find a hotel room in Munich, almost worshiped Hitler. The master of the house greeted her with a brisk "Heil Hitler" that Brendle felt obliged to return. Later, sitting at a kitchen table "shrine" of twin photos of Hitler and Mussolini, he told her he loved his wife and daughter very much, but if he had to choose between them and Hitler he would choose his *fuehrer*.

On July 26, 1939, Brendle and fellow American students from the institute attended a performance of Wagner's opera Parsifal at Bayreuth, at which Hitler was present. She recalled his arrival and the 600 uniformed SS men that saluted him. Dressed in a cashmere sports jacket and Bavarian-style gray hat, Hitler appeared to her more like a movie star greeted by adoring fans than a political figure. The dictator's skin was very pale but his eyes were what scared her. "They were decidedly different. He seemed to have a far-away look." During breaks in the five-hour-long opera, Hitler would go to a window where he would gaze at the crowd below. Children greeted him with songs and flowers.

Brendle noted that everywhere in German restaurants and hotels were signs reading "Jews Forbidden." And the Germans, who claimed to love America, said that President Franklin Roosevelt was "a friend of Jews" and that "America and England will have the same trouble with their Jews as Germany within the next ten years."

Brendle returned home just before the outbreak of war and later served as a translator with the U.S. Army. Even sixty-one years later some things about that time in Germany, in particular the man in Munich, haunted her. "I still wonder sometimes whatever happened to him, his wife and his daughter."

Industry Gears Up

As they consumed all this European news, Lehigh County residents could not help but notice a direct benefit from the conflict: the revival of industry. Foreign and federal government defense contracts began to flow to Bethlehem Steel, Mack Trucks, and other local industries. As early as 1939 Mack had been working on tank transports ordered by the French government. When France fell to the Nazis in 1940 the transports were sent to British forces in North Africa. "Mack engineers, working closely with British military staff," writes John Montville in the company's official history, "then developed the model NR 6x4 series, with the object of overcoming specific problems found in the Middle East."

As Bethlehem Steel's Eugene Grace had predicted, the steel company was making money. In fact work had begun to pick up at Bethlehem in 1938 and was doing even better in 1939. Many of the steelworkers lived in Lehigh County. Wally Herman, who operated Wally's Newsstand on South Sixth Street in Allentown for over fifty years, recalled in 2005 that it was the streetcar loads of local men headed to Bethlehem Steel and stopping at the corner of Sixth and Hamilton in the World War II era and just after to buy a newspaper that convinced him to buy the business from previous owner Meyer Kerson in 1953.

While Bethlehem Steel was being hailed in *Fortune* magazine as having "geared every unit of its empire to a functional efficiency that Adolf Hitler might envy," things were not well on the shop floor. Even *Fortune* felt labor conditions at Bethlehem had a long way to go: "In terms of the social responsibilities of modern American industry, Bethlehem management is provincial. Socially they are like characters in a majestic Götterdämmerung."

What had really changed in the 1930s was labor legislation. The National Labor Relations Act of 1935, better known as the Wagner Act after its author, U.S. Senator Robert F. Wagner, gave workers the right to be represented by a union of their own choice, and could not be prohibited by their employers from doing so. Under this act the National Labor Relations Board was created to see that its provisions were enforced.

Beginning in 1919 Bethlehem had something it called the ERP, Employee Representation Plan. It was top-down device created by management to give the workers what management thought they should get. In August 1939 the NLRB announced it refused to recognize the ERP as a legitimate union and told the company they would not recognize it. Bethlehem

appealed, and in early 1941 it was still
being fought in the courts.

On March 24, 1941, the company
announced that it was going to go
ahead with ERP elections. Pro-union
workers were furious and threatened a
strike. The Northampton County sheriff called in the state police, and the
next four days were marked by labor
strife that at times crossed over into
violence. Non-strikers and managers
attempted to keep the plant running,
but there was not much they could
do. State and federal mediators were
brought in. On March 28, an agreement was announced that included
the right of the workers to select their
own union. In August 1941, the workers
picked the Steelworkers Organizing
Committee (SWOC), which soon became the United Steelworkers (USW).
The following year the first contract
was negotiated.

Women working at Mack Trucks during wartime.
(Lehigh County Historical Society)

Production of Mack EH cargo trucks for the military
was close to 4,700 from 1940 to 1944.
(Lehigh County Historical Society)

World War II brought the return of
women to Bethlehem Steel. Although
the idea of women working in a steel
mill sounded odd to a lot of people
in the 1940s, it had happened before.
During World War I Bethlehem recruited women to do "man's work" when
the doughboys were off licking the Kaiser. Most of the women were hired in subsidiary
companies that made shells and other armaments. But, except for some photos, women's
contributions to the Great War have been largely lost.

Pearl Harbor brought the entry of the United States into the war, and the departure of
the men. American industry once more turned to women to fill the shortage. Over five million women worked in the country's mills and factories during World War II. Of that num-

ber, 25,000 were working for Bethlehem Steel Corporation, 2,200 of them in the Bethlehem plant. Many of them were not unfamiliar with working in industry; since the nineteenth century many women had had jobs in local cigar, silk, and garment industries. Local newspapers carried articles in March 1942 that upward of 10,000 Lehigh Valley women would be needed, bringing a large number of them to the doors of Bethlehem Steel.

Some were country people who had seldom been far from home before. One, Anne McLauglin Cassium of Jim Thorpe, recalled many years later how scared she was in her first days at Bethlehem Steel. She described herself as a "skinny connected thing" who found herself encumbered in sixty pounds of safety gear. Other women discovered that long hair, then fashionable, had to go. It was easily caught in machinery, with sometimes-fatal results.

Veronica Lake, a movie idol of the early 1940s who had made peek-a-boo bangs her trademark, publicly had her locks shorn for the war effort. As a result, her career took a nose dive from which it never really recovered, but also as a result many women were spared from serious injury.

Once they had been trained and became accustomed to the different working environment of a steel plant, the women generally enjoyed and were good at their work. By March 1944 the company's newsletter was pointing out that women were filling fifty-three types of manual-work positions. They also served as members of Bethlehem Steel's internal police force. "They called us the pistol-packing mamas," one remembered.

It was still not always easy for the men they had to work alongside to get used to the presence of women. One woman remembered that the man she worked beside had developed a habit of frequent use of profanity in the formerly all-male environment. "He'd be standing next to me and apologize for every third word he said. Finally I told him he really didn't have to do that since I had heard them all before."

One complaint that the women at Bethlehem Steel heard constantly from their male co-workers was that they were taking jobs that should have gone to men. As essential war workers, men who worked there during the war were exempt from the draft. The many who left to join the military were volunteers, and the company was expanding rapidly to be able to produce government orders. Women were needed to keep the plant running. Nonetheless, the negative attitude toward them persisted until the war ended. "Now you girls can go home," one woman at Bethlehem Steel remembers hearing a male colleague yell at her on V-J Day.

The facts that there was a labor shortage while production was booming, and that women were only there because men were off fighting, did not stop this constant friction. That the women were paid 10 to 12 cents less an hour than men, for similar jobs, made it even harder for them to take. To aid women in their adjustment, Bethlehem hired female counselors and matrons. It was their job to offer advice and sometimes comfort to the many young

Operation #16
Cap Hardness
Testing

women who worked there.

Although the enduring image of "Rosie the Riveter," the poster icon that was widely known in the war era, was mostly as a single woman, significant numbers of the female work force at Bethlehem were married with children. Many of them had husbands in the service. Many were able to leave their children in the care of a relative; others needed different arrangements and a movement started among the workers for child care. On March 8, 1944, a petition signed by 529 working mothers was presented to the Bethlehem School Board by the AFL-CIO Child Care Committee, asking for a mixture of child-care facilities for those up to twelve years old and a social center for teenagers. Before these suggestions could be acted on, the war was over.

Bethlehem Steel was not the only local industrial company that hired women. Among others were Mack Trucks and machine-tool maker L.F. Grammes. Even the introduction of women was not enough to offset the wartime labor shortage. In 1943 the Allentown office of the United States Employment Service reported that local war plants needed an additional 12,000 workers. "The scarcity of labor was the result of several factors," noted Lehigh County archivist Mahlon Hellerich in 1987, "the heavy draft calls, the reluctance of many men to leave steady jobs in the non-essential or less essential industries, and the reluctance of housewives to leave the home." Despite efforts to hire and train women the shortage persisted, forcing the government to insist that essential war-industry workers work a 48-hour week.

At the same time Bethlehem Steel workers were voting for the SWOC, the situation in the Pacific between the U.S. and Japan was looking serious. Japan was deeply involved in China and its admirals and generals were looking around for more natural resources to fuel its war machine, like the oil and rubber in the former French Indo-China, now Vietnam and Cambodia, and the Dutch East Indies, now Indonesia. Since Japan's Axis ally, Germany, now occupied the mother country of these colonies, the U.S. feared they would be turned over to the Japanese and threaten American possessions in the Pacific, particularly the Philippines.

As the summer of 1941 headed toward the fall, Lehigh County's Arsenal of Democracy was humming. Streetcars loaded with workers headed for Bethlehem Steel, Mack Trucks, and other defense-related employers were seen moving through the streets early in the morning and heading home in the evening. At long last the stranglehold of the Great Depression seemed to have been broken. Folks from far rural corners of Lehigh County who had seldom traveled away from home were arriving in Allentown and renting apartments in some of the big older homes that had been divided into rooms.

At War Once More

Entering the war seemed more and more of a possibility, although isolationist feelings were far from dead. Congressmen Francis E. "Tad" Walter, a Northampton County Democrat, refused in 1939 to give the Navy any money to expand its bases in the South Pacific, despite the growing militancy of Japan. As late as August 1941, while speaking at a convention of the conservative Patriotic Order of the Sons of America in Stroudsburg, he declared, "I oppose with all my strength any attempt to send another AEF [American Expeditionary Force, the name for the U.S. Army's European forces in World War I] to Europe … I don't think American blood should ever be shed in any foreign land."

His counterpart in Lehigh County, Republican Congressman Charles Gerlach, was equally opposed to U.S. military involvement in Europe or Asia. In fact, he thought the whole thing was a ruse. On the evening of Saturday December 6, 1941, Gerlach told a gathering of local journalists, "I have it on good authority, the Japs are only bluffing."

The day Gerlach made his remarks was cloudy and slightly overcast with evening fog in Lehigh County, but the weatherman promised sunshine with mild weather in the mid- to upper fifties for Sunday. Shoppers flocked to Hamilton Street to take in holiday bargains. Many, for the first time in a long while, had a little extra to spend for Christmas.

There were movies to take in, from "Keep 'em Flying" with Abbott and Costello to "A Yank in the RAF" with Tyrone Power and Betty Grable. The Hotel Traylor in Allentown was offering Roxy Reif and his orchestra, while out at the Royal Hotel on Route 222 the Swingettes All Girl Orchestra was appearing.

At 12:53 p.m. the next day, December 7, 1941, as most people in Lehigh County were sitting down to Sunday dinner, or possibly nursing hangovers, radio broadcasts of football games were interrupted by frantic announcers claiming that some place called Pearl Harbor in the Pacific had been bombed by Japanese planes. The next day President Roosevelt would declare before a joint session of Congress what everybody knew. The United States was at war.

Many Pennsylvanians were in the military in 1941, a lingering effect of the joblessness of the Great Depression. One young sailor who would later live in Lehigh County, Walter

Popejoy, recalled that serving on the battleship *West Virginia* was the first steady paycheck he had ever had. "I got $21 a month and I was able to send half of it home to my mother," he recalled.

Russell Rutman from Egypt in Whitehall Township joined the Navy because there was no work. Most mornings he would join other young men who went out to see if they could get jobs as day labor picking crops in a farmer's field. "The boss would stand on the back of the truck and say 'I want you, you, you and you. The rest can go home.' " Deciding a Navy enlistment had to be better, Rutman joined up after high school. December 7, 1941, found him at Pearl Harbor, a sailor on the cruiser USS *New Orleans*. He was a member of the ship's baseball team and one of its best players. "We were beating everybody in the fleet," he recalled. The day before the attack, Rutman got word from his captain that on December 8 he was going to be assigned to the USS *Arizona* at the request of her captain, who wanted him primarily because of his baseball skills. "I still can't believe how narrowly I missed that one," he said in 1991.

Rutman was up early on the morning of December 7. Wearing his baseball uniform, he was eating breakfast in the mess room with the rest of the team. "We were scheduled to play three games that day … In about ten minutes we were supposed to be in a motor launch in the center of the harbor." Suddenly the loudspeakers aboard the ship all came on at once. "General Quarters! Go to your stations! This is no drill!" Rutman quickly ran to his anti-aircraft gun and began firing. Unfortunately, all of the ammunition boxes on the ship were locked. Rutman's fellow sailors were swinging fire axes in desperate attempts to open them. The *New Orleans* was in dry dock and covered by a huge crane, which prevented the Japanese fighter plans from flying too low.

At the height of the battle all of the power on the *New Orleans* went out. The cause had nothing to do with the attack. Apparently an over-excited sailor attempting to cut the ship loose with an ax sliced into what he thought was the rope keeping her tied to the dock. It was actually the cable to the shore-side generator that provided electricity to the ship. This meant that ammunition for the ship's five-inch gun had to be hauled by hand.

Leading the men in this task was the ship's Protestant chaplain, Rev. Howell M. Forgy. "He was our baseball officer," recalled Rutman. Asked by a sailor what they should do now, Forgy replied, "just praise the Lord and pass the ammunition." When songwriter Frank Loesser heard this story he set it to music. Soon "Praise the Lord and Pass the Ammunition" became one of the first popular American hit songs of World War II.

For Rutman, Pearl Harbor, as horrible as it was, opened up his world. He was to serve in several major naval battles in the Pacific including Midway, be sent to the Atlantic for the D-Day invasion of Europe, and sail on the same ship, the cruiser USS *Quincy*, that took FDR to

Yalta for the summit meeting with Churchill and Stalin. He recalled crying quietly to himself when he saw how sick the commander-in-chief, whom he greatly admired, had become. And he was there in Tokyo Bay on September 2, 1945, to watch Japan surrender.

Anna Mae McCabe Hays

Lehigh County had many sons, fathers, and brothers who went overseas to fight in the war. Daughters, wives, and sisters served also. The best known of them was General Anna Mae McCabe Hays, who came to Allentown from Buffalo, NY, as a child with her parents, Daniel J. and Matie McCabe, both officers in the Salvation Army. "From them I learned the importance of hard work and service to others," Hays said in an interview that appeared in *The Morning Call* on September 5, 1997. It was her desire for service that took this 1939 graduate of Allentown High School into nursing. Two years later, in 1941, Anna Mae McCabe graduated from the Allentown Hospital School of Nursing with highest honors, the first graduate of the school ever to do so.

When the U.S. entered the war Hays decided she wanted to serve as a U.S. Army nurse. In May 1942 she went to the old Allentown police station on Linden Street between Sixth and Seventh streets and was sworn in as a second lieutenant in the Army Nurse Corps Reserve. A week later she found herself on a Liberty Bell Line streetcar bound for Philadelphia.

After undergoing training in Camp Claiborne, Louisiana, Hays (then nurse McCabe) thought she would be sent to Europe. She was surprised when she learned that she had instead been assigned to India. The trip required a 43-day crossing of the Pacific Ocean, swarming with Japanese submarines and planes, on a troop transport carrying 7,000 men. "It was a strange mix of fear and excitement," she said. "For someone who had never really been away from home before it was like an adventure."

Hays arrived safely in India, then still the jewel in the crown of the British Empire. After a long train ride on a narrow-gauge railroad and a boat trip up the Brahmaputra River, she was at her post at Assam in the rear of the Ledo Road. Although not far from enemy action, she does not recall being under fire—but snakes and malaria were a constant threat. She remembers meeting the legendary American commander Gen. Joseph "Vinegar Joe" Stillwell and the Supreme Allied Commander for Southeast Asia, Lord Louis Mountbatten. McCabe's task in part was overseeing the health of workers who were building the Ledo Road. Built with great difficulty, it was designed to move supplies to China after Japan seized the lower part of the Burma Road to the south.

When Hays finished her tour of duty, she returned to Allentown and was here on V-J Day. Deciding she wanted a career as a military nurse, she decided to stay in the Army. In

1950, during the Korean War, Hays traveled with the 4th Field Hospital to Inchon, Korea, arriving shortly after MacArthur's invasion at Inchon. "We had no water. It was so cold we wore all the clothing we could. And because there was no firewood it was almost impossible to keep warm," she recalled. She spent long hours in the operating room. "Sometimes we had to get along on as little as three or four hours of sleep a night.

In the late 1950s, Hays was one of three nurses assigned to care for President Dwight Eisenhower following his ileitis attack. She and Eisenhower became friends, and several times Ike and his wife Mamie had her as a guest at their Gettysburg farm. "I felt highly honored that a graduate of the Allentown Hospital School of Nursing had been chosen for this position," said Hays. It was during this period that she met and married William A. Hays, who directed the Sheltered Workshops in Washington, D.C. He died in 1963.

Just before her retirement on June 11, 1970, Hays was made a brigadier general. She was the first woman in the U.S. Army to be given that rank, making her a significant historical figure on three levels: county history, women's history, and national history. "If I had it to do over again, I would do it longer," she said.

One Down, One Dead

Air aces, pilots that shot down enemy planes, were among the stand-outs of the war. One Lehigh County airman who is credited with destroying five enemy planes was Frank Speer, later a resident of Emmaus. He had developed a passion for flight early. Speer was married and working for Bell Telephone Company in Allentown when Pearl Harbor was attacked. He enlisted in January 1942 in the Army Air Force, received basic training in Texas, and graduated as a fighter pilot.

In 1944 Speer crossed the Atlantic in a British ship and joined the U.S. Army's 8th Air Force in England after further training. He flew P-51 Mustangs with the 334 Fighter Squadron, 4th Fighter Group, whose job was to protect the American bombers that were pounding the Third Reich into rubble. In *Wingman*, one of three books he wrote about his wartime experiences, Speer recalled one event in particular: he had just shot

Air ace Frank Speer.

down a German plane, its top popped open, and the Luftwaffe pilot parachuted out. "There, not 50 feet to the side of me he hangs under his huge white canopy, resplendent in his uniform, his medals clearly visible on his chest, and the sun glinting off his highly polished knee-high black boots. As I roar past him he smiles and waves, a salute to the victors. He can well smile, since he is over his homeland and tomorrow he'll be up again in another plane. That is a far different fate than would await us were the tables turned."

Speer was soon to know that fate. On May 30 his plane was shot down over Poland. He was discovered and placed in a German POW camp. In January 1945, as the Red Army was getting close to his prison camp, Speer's German captors decided it was time to move the prisoners. Many of his fellow captives died on the 77-hour forced march through deep snow. On a later march to a different POW camp, he and a friend escaped but were recaptured. Their second attempt to escape met with more success. This time, they were able to join a group of French forced laborers who hid them during the day and fed and protected them at night. From their hiding place, with no idea of the progress of the war, they witnessed Germans retreating and even accepted the surrender of one contingent of Germans. They were found by American troops, who locked them in an abandoned schoolhouse until their identities could be verified. They remained there only a short while until an artillery barrage forced them to flee. They hitchhiked to Nuremberg, by then under American control. Moments before their hospital ship departed for the U.S., an announcement came over the loudspeaker of unconditional surrender by the Germans.

Lieutenant Colonel Thomas J. Lynch was one Lehigh County serviceman of World War II who didn't come back. A celebrated air ace, he was born in Hazleton in 1916 and grew up in Catasauqua. His parents were William and Alice Lynch. He was good looking, bright and athletic, an Eagle Scout with a winning smile. In 1940 Lynch graduated from the University of Pittsburgh with a degree in engineering. His father wanted him to join him at Bethlehem Steel, but shortly after graduation Lynch joined the Army Air Force. After training he was assigned to the 39th Pursuit Squadron. He was one of the first American pilots to reach Australia shortly after Pearl Harbor.

Lynch's first two victories came on May 20, 1942, when he shot down planes about to attack Port Moresby, New Guinea. A third came on May 26, 1942. On June 26, 1942, Lynch was shot down but parachuted to safety with only a broken arm. By December he was up and flying again, shooting down two enemy planes on December 27 and another on December 31. In 1943 Lynch scored victories on January 7, March 3, May 8, and June 12. On August 20 he shot down two more planes, and another on August 21. Before the year was out he would shoot down two more, one on September 4, the other on September 16.

That October Lynch returned to Catasauqua to marry his girlfriend, Rosemary Fullen, whom he had met in college. Asked during that visit home by *The Morning Call* his secret for success as an air ace, Lynch's reply was simple: "All you gotta do is see them first. If you see them first you can get in position. If you see them coming up your tail it's too bad—you've seen them last."

Lynch's return to the Pacific in 1944 led to a new victory on February 10, two victories on March 3, and another on March 5. On March 8, while flying with his fellow ace Richard Bong over New Guinea, Lynch swept low over a group of Japanese barges. He had not counted on the enemy's anti-aircraft fire ripping open his plane. Lynch tried to parachute out but was apparently too close to the ground and it failed to open. His body was never found.

Later Bong would fly to Allentown to speak to Lynch's family. His mother and sisters asked Bong if there was any possibility that Lynch could have survived. "Quite frankly — no," he replied. On August 6, 1945, the day the first atomic bomb was dropped on Japan, Bong was killed while test piloting an experimental plane.

A Soviet Spy from Emmaus

The foreign correspondent became a renowned World War II figure, memorialized in a movie Alfred Hitchcock made with that title in 1940. The Lehigh Valley had one of their own in the form of Stephen Laird of Emmaus. A dashing figure to some, he seemed part of the great world outside the small town. It was a shock many years later, the Cold War over and Laird dead, when it was claimed that he had been a minor-league Soviet spy.

Born August 1, 1915, his name at birth was Laird Lichtenwalner. His father, Fred Lichtenwalner, was a dentist with an inventive turn of mind who had created an early movie theater in Emmaus. "He rigged up a phonograph with couple of loudspeakers so he did not have to pay a piano player," his son recalled many years later. As he grew older, Laird found life in Emmaus rather dull. His only favorable memories of his childhood were the strawberry sodas. "To tell you the truth it was rather boring," he said in 1986.

Laird graduated from Emmaus High School in 1932. One of only two graduates who went on to college, he entered Swarthmore. He was a fairly good athlete and was on the football team; also on the team was Oleg Troyanovsky, son of the first Soviet ambassador to the United States. "The coach told me to teach him American football and I did," Laird remembered. It was supposedly Troyanovsky who recruited Laird as a spy.

On graduation Laird got his first job with the *Chester* (Pennsylvania) *Times*. It was while working there that he changed his name to Stephen Laird. "I would call and say 'this is Lichtenwalner of the Times' and they'd say, 'Can you spell it?' It just ended up taking too long."

In 1937 Laird's journalism experience landed him a job with *Fortune* magazine, one of the gems in the crown of publisher Henry Luce's Time-Life-Fortune periodicals, at the princely sum of $35 a week. By 1939 he had his own column and was making $75 a week. When the war in Europe broke out Laird was told to switch to *Time* magazine, which he promptly did.

In 1940 Luce decided that he wanted a correspondent in Berlin, and that Laird would be that person. With him was to be his wife and fellow reporter, Lael Tucker. Their hopes seemed dashed when federal passport officials claimed it was too risky, and refused to issue her a passport. As Laird remembered it, Luce himself decided they would go the other way—across America, the Pacific, and Stalin's Russia, to Germany.

In 1986 Laird recalled some of that eventful trip to *The Morning Call*. It included a stop in Tokyo, after a trip across the Pacific in a Japanese liner, where they were quizzed by the secret police in the guise of journalists; a trip across the Japanese-occupied Chinese province of Manchuria on a railroad freight car loaded with Japanese soldiers; and an outbreak of plague during which they were forced into isolation for days by Soviet doctors. "It was pretty rugged, let me tell you," he recalled.

On arriving at the border between Soviet-occupied Poland and German-occupied Poland—the two countries had divided Poland as part of the Hitler-Stalin pact—they were ordered off the Soviet train. "We had to walk a couple of miles with our suitcases until we finally got the train to Berlin." The German capital was both exciting and boring. The Nazis wanted publicity, but did not want Americans to report the war without clearing everything with them first.

Laird's two major experiences in Germany were an interview in an air raid shelter with the Luftwaffe head, Field Marshall Herman Göring, and uncovering suspicious troop movements that made it clear that instead of launching a cross-channel invasion of England, Hitler was going to move east and invade the Soviet Union. In order to publish his "scoop," Laird and his wife had to travel to neutral Switzerland. After ten days of Nazi red tape they finally got there and he filed his story. On June 22, 1941, when Hitler's forces crossed into

Russia, *Time* was on the newsstands with Laird's article.

Unable to return to Germany, Laird and his wife settled in Geneva where he met CBS radio man Edward R. Morrow and agreed to do some broadcasts. He also encountered the American super spy Allen Dulles, who would later found the CIA. Eventually they were able to travel through unoccupied Vichy France and reach Lisbon and a Pan Am Clipper to America.

Laird and his wife separated, and he was sent to London to head *Time's* bureau there and make more broadcasts for Murrow. From 1943 to 1944 he had a number of desk jobs in *Time's* New York office. Finally, becoming frustrated over the magazine's refusal to send him overseas, Laird gave it all up and went to Hollywood to become a screenwriter, eventually a producer. He had a big home with a swimming pool and hobnobbed with movie stars.

One day Murrow came for visit. After a week in Hollywood, on the day he left he told Laird he was wasting his life: "Steve, there is just one thing I can't understand. After all we had in London, how could you come back and live in this flimsy world?" Laird protested it was *Time's* fault for not allowing him to go overseas. Murrow offered to take him on at CBS as a radio broadcaster; Laird, realizing that you did not say no to Edward R. Murrow, agreed.

In the late 1940s and early 1950s Laird headed CBS's bureaus in Paris, Berlin, Nuremberg (where he saw Hermann Göring sitting in the dock with the other Nazis at the war-crimes trials), Warsaw, London, and Geneva. In the mid-1950s Laird gave up day-to-day journalism, retired to France, married a French woman, and raised a family. He wrote occasional articles for French magazines. On a brief return trip to Emmaus with his wife Jackie, she scandalized his mother by asking if it was all right if she swam topless—it was certainly not all right.

Laird's return to the Lehigh Valley in 1986, without his family, was brief. He claimed he had come to stay, and had a friendly German shepherd named Daisy Mae with him. John Gould, former owner of Gould's Pharmacy in Emmaus, had known Laird since childhood and offered him a place to stay in his home if he put the dog in a kennel. "But you never could tell Laird anything and he showed up with the dog anyway," he recalled in 1999. Laird stayed with friends in New Tripoli, then rented a small apartment in Allentown where he told his life history to *The Morning Call.* Eventually he went to Swarthmore where he became ill, then returned to France.

Laird died in Europe in 1990. About ten years later, when long-secret American National Security Agency records of spying were released and published in a book, Laird was named, code name "Yun," as having been a spy for the Soviets in the mid-1940s, starting while he was in *Time's* New York office. He was one of several *Time* journalists who were Communists. He continued spying in Hollywood but apparently stopped shortly thereafter.

Laird's long-time friends in Emmaus were shocked. "It took us all by surprise," says

Assembly line of the TBY-2, the Seawolf, at the Consolidated Vultee plant.
(Lehigh County Historical Society)

Gould. "Laird was eccentric, a little free with advice but never in a nasty way," he re-called. Other friends said Gould "didn't think Laird could find his way out of a closet with a spotlight."

Vultee Aircraft Corporation

Back in Lehigh County the big war news continued to be the impact of World War II on the local economy. Nothing brought bigger headlines than the announcement that an airplane factory was to be opening in Allentown. "Part of Mack Plant to Be Taken Over by Vultee Aircraft For Construction of Navy Bombers," read the headline on December 16, 1942. The story in *The Morning Call* noted that Vultee Aircraft, a California company, had recently been given a contract for a new type of torpedo bomber. The federal War Production Board, acting as a go-between, had leased Plant 5C from Mack Trucks, Inc., for Vultee.

According to the newspaper article, this plant had manufactured buses for General Motors but had not done so since America had entered the war. The *Call* noted that up to $100 million in contracts were being offered by the Navy. Up to $11 million was to be used for construction of a hangar, office building, and airport. The site chosen was a 32-acre plot off Lehigh Street known as Mitchell Field that had been used as a grass landing strip for small aircraft since the mid-1920s. In the 1940s it was considered on the far edges of Allentown.

Gloria Kuhns, center, worked at Vultee Aircraft Corporation as a riveter on the TBY-2 "Seawolf" folding-wing torpedo bomber at the Mack Trucks 5C plant. After the contract ended, she operated a drill press for Mack Trucks, drilling holes in large hinges for PBY Catalina flying boats, as well as components for the BT-13 "Valiant" Trainer and B-24 "Liberator" Bomber. She worked at Mack until men coming home from the war displaced the women. In 1945 she began work at the new Western Electric plant in Allentown, initially etching crystals to a frequency for radios used by the Navy. (Lower Macungie Township Historical Society)

Wartime security made details scarce. It was not until March 1943 that construction began. Over the winter Vultee merged with Consolidated Aircraft Corporation, a Connecticut-based company, to become Consolidated Vultee Corporation. Due to problems with sinkholes, which seemed to open up the moment one was filled, and labor disputes, it was September 12, 1943, before the airport, dubbed Convair Field, was ready for dedication.

Tight security kept the crowd that day down to about 2,000. Admiral Ralph Davison, chief of the Navy's Bureau of Aeronautics, was on hand to represent the government. He told the crowd for the first time that the plant would build the TBY-Seawolf, a torpedo bomber. "This plane has everything we have learned about planes of this type," Davison said. "It carries the deadly tin fish [torpedo], which the Japs make a futile effort not to catch [sic], or a load of bombs which makes them equally unhappy."

The most meaningful moment for the crowd that day came when 20-year-old Marine Private Edwin Bastian of Trexlertown rose to speak. Bastian had been severely wounded on Guadalcanal on August 20, 1942. He was still being treated in a Philadelphia hospital and

walked up to the platform on crutches. He told how the Grumman Avengers cleared the bay—officially Sealark Channel, but it contained so many sunken ships that GIs nicknamed it "Ironbottom Sound"—of Jap submarines when wounded Americans were evacuated, and urged the people of the Lehigh Valley to help the company that would be making more planes for America's fighting forces, "planes that will clear more sea lanes of wolfpacks." This was the nickname given to a team of German submarines that hunted the seas during World War II to destroy convoys of Allied ships.

The Consolidated Vultee project attracted a large number of workers, both men and women. Among them was Allentown's Gladys Rader. Her father saw an ad in the paper offering a drafting course for those who would work at the aircraft plant. "He said, you get out there and apply for this right now," she recalled in 1994. "You sometimes need a little push and my father provided it." The course, offered at Raub Middle School, was part of the Pennsylvania State University Extension Program. Out of work since graduating from Allentown High School in 1939, she leaped at a chance use the drawing skills she had learned in school.

Gerry Snyder, a local professional photographer, was hired to head the photography department for Consolidated Vultee from 1942 to 1945. As part of his job he regularly took part in test flights. "I would go up with the test pilots," he said in 1994. "We would take off and fly out over the Atlantic Ocean carrying dummy torpedoes." Once a plane was over the ocean off the New Jersey shore, the pilot would sweep low over the test zone and drop a torpedo. Snyder, movie camera winding away, would be recording it all for Navy brass. "When we flew off of Atlantic City the beaches would be crowded with people watching us from a safe distance. We put on quite a show."

Despite these very public displays of the Seawolf's prowess, rumors both during and after World War II ran through the Lehigh Valley that the plane never flew, or that the whole

thing was some sort of government boondoggle. The reasons for this, Rader, Snyder, and several others who worked on the Seawolf believe, were the Navy's demands for tight security and the constant second-guessing from planners in Washington as to exactly what kind of plane they wanted to produce. One of the revisions was a primitive form of radar, shaped like a small dome, that was located on the plane's right wing. "There were daily, almost hourly changes," recalled plans department worker Margaret Sopper in a 1982 interview. "Everybody was working really hard to get things done." Kenneth Bogert, who worked in construction illustration, was particularly frustrated. He said in 1982 that he often had no plans from which to draw: "I had to try and show a plane that I hadn't even seen."

Despite these delays, by late 1944 Consolidated Vultee and its workforce were turning out seven planes a day. Vultee Street was used as a taxiway. Because of gas rationing and the location of the site there were never any problems with traffic when this was going on.

To the east of the airport the federal government built housing for many of the technical employees who came from other parts of the country to work at Consolidated Vultee. Today the neighborhood of small brick homes remains. Some of those streets—such as Liberator and Catalina, named for other Consolidated Vultee airplanes—are all that remain of its links to the World War II era.

In early August 1945 it was announced that the Seawolf was ready for combat and a large flight of the planes was flown to California in preparation for the long-anticipated invasion of Japan, during which most sources speculated that perhaps a million Americans would be killed by die-hard Japanese soldiers and civilians. It was assumed that the war would not end until 1947 at the earliest. But the dropping of atomic bombs on two Japanese cities and Japan's agreement to unconditional surrender on August 15 put everything on hold. Suddenly, production of the Seawolf ceased. Despite the protests of local business leaders and public officials the project, which by one estimate had cost the government $110 million, had not led to the establishment of the much-hoped-for new industry in the county. Snyder's last assignment for the Navy was taking pictures of scrapping the Seawolf. Jet technology would soon begin to replace planes of World War II vintage, making the high-tech marvel of 1945 an antique by 1950.

Writing in 1987, Lehigh County historian Mahlon Hellerich noted local feelings about the Seawolf project that made Lehigh County citizens feel they had been betrayed:

> The failure of the Vultee experiment was a bitter disappointment. Many people had looked upon it as a new industry which would add substantially to the city's prosperity in the future. They had hoped that it would provide Allentown with an aircraft plant to complement the Mack truck plant, thus giving the city one base in the automobile age and another in the aircraft age. They were frustrated by the fact that the failure was due to factors which they could not control and that an out-of-town management had used poorly the loyalty, skills and labor of thousands of local workers.
>
> If Lehigh County was never to become a major producer of military aircraft, it did undergo a major revival. Photos of smiling, grease-stained workers being awarded Navy E pennants by suited executives for exceeding production quotas were a major feature of the local press during the war years. It also marked the end of the pervasive unemployment of the Great Depression era.

By 1945 Lehigh County officials, believing that the war would last at least another two years, were fearful that a labor shortage would be their chief problem. With the sudden end of the war a new concern developed: would there be enough jobs for veterans when they returned? Many still remembered how the sudden halt in war production in 1919 had led to a sharp recession that lingered into 1924 and led to labor unrest. They feared a repeat might be in the offing.

This was far from the minds of most local people who, along with the rest of America, wanted the war to come to an end. They would let the future worry about itself.

Relief and Joy

Although news of the end of World War II was not quite as confused as it was when World War I ended, it had its moments. On April 28, 1945, a report flashed over the radio that the war in Europe was over. This was denied the next day by President Harry S. Truman, who had been FDR's vice president and had come into office following Roosevelt's death on April 12, 1945. On Monday evening, May 7, at 9:30 p.m. the unconditional surrender was announced over the radio. Officially, V-E Day was May 8, 1945, and it was so announced by the White House.

Still, most Americans regarded the job as only half done. Japan was not beaten. The attack on Pearl Harbor was still not avenged. The anticipated invasion of Japan was expected to be a

bloodbath that some were estimating would leave a million American servicemen dead, and would not end until 1948.

When reports of dropping an atomic bomb on Hiroshima were broadcast on August 6, 1945, most did not know what it meant, but hoped there would be no need for an invasion of Japan. But it was not until August 14, after a second atomic bomb was dropped on Nagasaki and more diplomatic wrangling, that Japan agreed to the unconditional-surrender terms.

Across Lehigh County the feeling of relief and joy when the announcement was made by President Truman was as great as it was across the nation. Church bells rang, cars drove in a tight procession

up and down the streets, and crowds thronged the sidewalks. The bars were closed but alcohol wasn't necessary for most of those who wanted to feel good.

Of those from Lehigh County who had served in the war, 517 men and one woman (Lt. Dorothy M. Berger) would not be coming home alive. For their families the war would mean many years of an empty place at the table and a photograph of a forever-young face in a uniform. Seventy were listed as missing in action, and 1,115 wounded. For at least some among the injured, World War II would never end. It would be with them every time they moved their bodies or coughed.

The sacrifices of all living and who had died was praised by *The Morning Call* in an editorial proclaiming that the residents of the Lehigh Valley should thank God, "who has blessed our arms with victory and who thereby spared our country, our peace and our institutions for that greater destiny and helpful influence in world affairs which this victory has brought."

CHAPTER FIVE

LEHIGH COUNTY 1945-1970

As the guns of World War II fell silent the people of Lehigh County, for the second time in twenty-five years, waited for their sons and daughters to come home.

Questions about the future hung in the air. Some were personal. What will my children be like now that they've been in a war? Will they marry? Will they have children? Will they be able to find a job? Others were economic. The end of the last war brought economic dislocation and a severe recession. Now that this war is over, will it happen again? With millions of men leaving the service, will there be mass unemployment? Where will the country find housing for them all? Where will their children be educated? With government contracts being canceled every day, what will happen to the workers in war industries? Will there be strikes and economic chaos?

Then there were questions that were national and international. When will the government lift price controls and rationing? If they do, will it cause inflation or a depression? What is this new atomic bomb? Will our enemies get one and use it on us? Who will those enemies be? We beat Germany and Japan: Is humanity really headed for a time of peace? Or will something happen that could lead to another war?

Despite the many questions, in a lot of ways World War II had not changed Lehigh County. There was still a fairly sharp physical if not cultural divide between the city, Allentown, and the countryside. Very little residential building had occurred in recent years. The red-hot housing boom of the 1920s had been stopped dead in its tracks by the Great Depression and World War II, leaving behind crumbling foundations and empty lots.

The GI Bill

Before World War II, a college education was beyond the reach of most Americans. This changed immediately after the war when, thanks to the GI Bill of Rights, college campuses here and throughout the country saw a massive influx of new students. Through the GI Bill, officially the Servicemen's Readjustment Act of 1944, any returning serviceman could have a college education. For the first time, the federal government agreed to pay for veterans' high-

er education, including tuition, books, and living expenses.

These new students were of a type that local campuses had never seen before. Muhlenberg College, a school with deep roots in the county's past going back to the 1840s and long known as a place for those interested in a solid education, had participated in a training program for naval aviation cadets starting in 1942. Now, it was seeing many who came because of the GI Bill. In 1946, more than 1,200 new students were enrolled at the college. Most were veterans who had experiences that the average college freshman of 1940 had not. The pranks that were the staple of college life in the pre-war era did not interest these serious men, many married with young families.

Space for classes and offices was limited. The situation became even more stressed in 1947, the result of an event that had nothing to do with the crush of new students. On the evening of May 31, commencement weekend, college watchman Elmer Frey and Howard MacGregor, Muhlenberg's treasurer, who was working late, smelled smoke coming from the clock tower of the administration building, now Ettinger Hall. It was the first building occupied by the college when it moved from downtown Allentown in 1904. It also housed many books, documents, and other items that were significant, including those of prominent professors Preston Barba and J. Edgar Swain.

Firefighters arrived quickly but because it was at one of the highest points of the city, water pressure was low. By the time the fire trucks were pumping water, flames were bursting through the building's roof. Alumni, who were attending a party at the Hotel Traylor, raced to the college to attempt to help rescue what they could. The next day the building, looking like something out of recently bombed Europe, was a gutted ruin. Fortunately, the diplomas that were scheduled to be given out that weekend were among the items saved.

The college asked for help from its neighbors in the community and it was received. Allentown's Art Deco Nineteenth Street Theater was turned into a classroom and Cedar Crest College also offered help. Later, Quonset huts, pre-fabricated, semi-circular structures of galvanized steel created for the Army during the war and now war surplus, were used as classrooms. The college also provided some apartments in temporary housing south of Chew Street for veterans' families. By 1950–51 most of the World War II veterans were gone and the all-male college returned to its regular routine.

New People, New Industries

Allentown in the late 1940s was still a Pennsylvania-Dutch metropolis. The city, 105,781 strong by the 1950 federal census, was almost as ethnically homogeneous as the countryside that surrounded it. Anyone who doubted it could tune in "Assebe un Sabina," the popular local radio comedy program broadcast by WSAN from 1944 to 1955. Featuring rural characters speaking in the distinctive dialect that been a part of Lehigh County's heritage for over 200 years, it had a following that stretched from the row homes of Allentown's center city to the many farms of Lower Macungie Township.

Although their numbers were small and shrinking daily, there were still residents of rural regions of Lehigh County in 1945 who read by kerosene lamps and plowed their fields with old-fashioned horsepower.

Latinos were barely visible then among Lehigh County's ethnic groups. An article in the September 28, 1952, issue of *The Morning Call* noted that the Allentown police had been called in as a result of a ruckus among three Puerto Rican brothers. Although no one was seriously hurt, the police could not talk to the men because they did not speak Spanish nor did they know anyone who did. Hearing that there were Spanish-speaking nurses at Sacred Heart Hospital, they went there. Although they apparently could not find a nurse, they did find Francisco Fuentes Suarez, one of the very few Puerto Ricans in the Lehigh Valley, who was waiting for his wife Lillian to give birth to their daughter. At the urgent request of the police he agreed to go to the prison and help translate for them. From then on, his wife later recalled, Suarez grew accustomed in the 1950s to getting calls from the police requesting his services as their informal translator.

Things were changing, employment opportunities among them. Several new large industries were established in Lehigh County in the late 1940s and 1950s. General Electric built a large manufacturing plant in Allentown; Air Products, which had moved from the Midwest to Emmaus in the 1940s, expanded into Upper Macungie Township in the 1950s; Western Electric was perhaps the biggest change of the time.

Western Electric's arrival on the Lehigh Valley industrial/manufacturing scene began with a toothache. Sometime in 1945, Warren Deifer, a former resident of Allentown, an engineer for Western Electric in New York City, returned to the Lehigh Valley to see his longtime dentist, Dr. George Diefenderfer, about a tooth that was giving him trouble. As dentists do, Diefenderfer began by trying to make small talk with Deifer.

"So how are things going at Western Electric?"

A room full of "girls in white" assembling vacuum tubes at Western Electric, Allentown. (Lehigh County Historical Society; Gerald P. Snyder photographer)

"Well, I've heard they are thinking of moving out of New York and are looking around for a new location." Deifer replied.

When Deifer left the office, dentist Diefenderfer put on his "other hat" as a member of the Allentown Chamber of Commerce. He knew there was a lot of concern about the unemployment that might arrive with the end of the war. The failure of Consolidated Vultee, the airplane maker, to stay in Allentown and establish a modern airplane industry in Lehigh County had been a real blow. Now here was a chance, he told his fellow Chamber members, to make up for that by attracting a big employer that would offer a lot of jobs in the city. But they had to act fast before some other community contacted the company.

Shortly thereafter the president of Western Electric, responding to an invitation from the Chamber, was driving through the streets of Allentown in his chauffeured limousine. Four members of the Chamber were with him. They had already found four sites that, after careful discussion, they thought would be ideal. They planned to show them to their visitor that day.

They were rather surprised when the visiting executive spotted an empty forty-acre site on Union Boulevard, one that was not on their list. "That's a nice piece of property," he said. "Well, that's just the spot we were going to show you," Chamber officials responded without missing a beat. The man from Western Electric was so in love with the space it was the only one he would even consider looking at that day.

On October 11, 1945, with the ink barely dry on the peace agreement signed by Japan ending World War II, Bob Wolfe, a former *Morning Call* reporter and secretary for the Allentown Chamber of Commerce, organized a press conference that announced the new plant. The next day, October 12, the front page of *The Morning Call* told the story of the city's first post-war industry under the headline "Western Electric To Build Plant in Allentown."

The move of Western Electric out of New York did not make everybody happy. Engineer Howard Tooker recalled in 1996 his feelings when the announcement was made: "I liked living in New York. I walked ten minutes to work. The Lehigh Valley was a lot different in those days. I found the Pennsylvania Dutch accent very difficult to understand."

Western Electric's leadership had particular reasons for wanting to leave New York. In 1944 an explosion in the company's vacuum tube division was a wake-up call. Company executives feared a really severe industrial accident in the densely populated metropolis could be a major disaster. They needed a space far from the overcrowded city. War-time restrictions on construction materials and labor were still in place, and any kind of new civilian building projects had to wait. But Western Electric did what it could. It began by sending employees to Allentown and putting them in temporary buildings. These included a four-story former cigar factory on Franklin Street, a one-story structure on East Susque-hanna Street, and the Leh Building at 310 Hanover Avenue, named for the Leh Dry Cleaning Co. that had built the building in 1926, and apparently leased part of the structure to Western Electric.

Allentown's leaders confidently predicted Western Electric would have its new building open by October 12, 1946, but conversion from wartime to peacetime production took longer than anyone had anticipated. In March 1946 the federal Civilian Production Board put a freeze on any new construction that did not involve easing the national housing crunch. Plant construction was further delayed due to shortages of materials after this order was lifted in April.

Although the building was completed in 1947, it was not until October 11, 1948, that the company was willing to show it off to the public. The next three nights, more than 4,000 people toured Western Electric. Some compared it to the futuristic exhibits they had seen at the New York World's Fair in 1939.

"The 'open house' for the huge industrial palace along Union Boulevard is being held in order to give residents of Allentown and vicinity an idea of the importance of Western Electric's local establishment to the nation and world," wrote *The Morning Call*. At a dinner given for company executives at the Hotel Traylor, Allentown Mayor Donald Hock expressed the community's thanks: "You liked us because you found us to be progressive and because of our fine people. We are hard working people."

Western Electric was like nothing Lehigh County had seen before. Smokestack and resource-extraction heavy industries had risen and fallen in the region since the 1840s. In those 110 years the people of Lehigh County had adjusted to many changes. Electronics of the type represented by Western Electric was something new.

A June 30, 1948, article in the *Evening Chronicle* managed to catch the Buck Rogers-Flash Gordon-The Shape of Things to Come wonder of it all, declaring that "Allentown may play a strong part in revolutionary development of the electronics industry." The device that would make this possible was something called a transistor. Described as a "tiny metal

device about the size of a shoelace tip, [it] serves nearly all the functions of a conventional vacuum tube." The promise was held out of "someday bringing television into the home over ordinary telephone wires."

On October 1, 1951, the world's first transistor production began at the Allentown plant. On February 12, 1953, *The Morning Call* reported that Western Electric engineer Tooker was on the verge of creating a radio the size of a cigarette pack. By the early 1960s, the transistor radio was as ubiquitous as the cell phone is today, pouring everything from John Glenn's orbit of the earth in 1962 to the hit of 1960, "She Wore An Itsy Bitsy Teeny Weeny Yellow Polka Dot Bikini," into the ears of a listening Baby Boom generation. "We are living," an *Evening Chronicle* editorial writer noted in 1955, "in an age of miracles."

Population Growth

By the late 1940s Lehigh County, like the rest of the country, was bursting at the seams with babies. Sylvia Porter, a business columnist for the *New York Post*, was apparently the first to give it a name. In a May 4, 1951, column titled "Babies Equal Boom" she wrote: "Take the 3,548,000 babies born in 1950. Bundle them into a batch, bounce them all over the bountiful land that is America. What do you get? Boom. The biggest, boomiest, boomy, boom ever known to history."

Thus the era of the Baby Boomers, that huge "bulging mouse in the demographic python" as University of Missouri demographer and sociologist Rex Campbell called it, an event that would change the course of late-twentieth-century American history and culture, had begun.

Lehigh County added its share. In 1945, 4,160 babies were born here. In 1946 the number rose to 5,613. By 1947 it reached 6,439, then dropped off to 5,998 in 1948, 5,736 in 1949, and 5,638 in 1950. There was a spurt to 5,918 in 1951, and in 1952 the number of births reached 6,300.

Lehigh County was never to see birth statistics quite this high again. But by 1964, when the baby boom officially ended, the nation's population had increased from 157,553,000

in 1952 to 191,833,000. From 1950 to 1960, Lehigh County's population increased from 198,207 to 227,536.

Interestingly, these figures showed a remarkable shift. Whereas center-city Allentown had been the focal point of the county's growth for the first half of the twentieth century, this was changing. The city's population in 1950 was 106,756, but by 1960 it had grown only to 108,347. "The combined neighborhoods of the first ten wards," writes historian Richard Krohn in the Lehigh County Historical Society's 1987 history of Allentown, "the oldest sections of the city, lost population." Now the city's growth was to the west and southwest: the 17th and 18th wards. "These wards were enlarged with a series of annexations that, combined with rapid suburban development, helped triple their population," Krohn states.

A similar phenomenon was taking place in rural Lehigh County, where the population grew by 31 percent from 1950 to 1964. This was not due to a sudden back-to-the-land movement. "The boroughs of Emmaus, Coopersburg, Coplay and Macungie and the surrounding townships of Salisbury, Upper Saucon, Lower Milford, Upper Milford, Lower Macungie, Upper Macungie, North Whitehall, South Whitehall, Lowhill and Hanover," Krohn notes, "which soared [in population] a combined average of 37% between 1950 and 1960, could all be considered 'suburban,' regardless of each community's age or type of housing or street pattern. If anything, Lehigh County had become less rural."

One hundred years earlier, many Lehigh County farmers leased the mineral rights to their land to iron companies or their agents. In later years, quarries for cement rock and slate were sold outright to the slate and cement companies. All of this was part of the changing land uses and economic transformation of the region in the mid-nineteenth century that marked its development. In the 1950s some farmers were selling land to housing developers who were hoping to attract those wanting to enjoy the new American ideal of suburban life, "country" living with all the technological advantages of the city. Some of this was so-called strip development, with farmers selling a strip of land along a road. Houses were built while the farmer continued to farm the land behind the houses. In other cases, estate or death taxes led to whole farms being sold to real estate developers and speculators who often rented the land to farmers and developed it later.

The new "normal" was no longer the center-city row house or working rural farm that had long predominated in Lehigh County, but the suburban developer's rancher or Cape Cod.

From the late 1940s on, the demand for housing across Lehigh County was part of a national tidal wave. In early August 1946, 500,000 homes were under construction across America and an estimated 1,200,000 were estimated to be completed before the year was out. The prices on an average home rose from a little over $6,000 in 1941 to almost $10,000 in 1946.

Eric Weiss, for many years head of Allentown's building-code inspections, grew up in that era and remembers moving out of the city in the early 1950s with his family to the south side of Allentown. "There was almost nothing out there. A gas station, a small grocery store, a few scattered houses and farms was about it." Weiss recalls it was a great place for boys to ride their bicycles virtually unimpeded on the runways of the old Consolidated-Vultee testing airfield, which was not yet Queen City Airport. "There was no Route 309 out there yet so we could ride without worrying about it. We would ride on the runway until somebody would come out and tell us to get off the property."

Hess's Department Store

Despite the suburban movement to Allentown's West End and deep into the country-side in the 1950s and early 1960s, the city was still the major retail draw of eastern Pennsylvania outside of Philadelphia. What kept Allentown's downtown vital when many other medium-sized cities were already seeing decline could be summed up in one word: Hess's.

Started as Hess Brothers—a name it officially retained until 1965—in 1897, the store was better known than any other local retail outlet. Baby boomers from as far away as Delaware and Maryland, many now in their fifties and sixties, can recall being dressed in their childhood finest by their parents and driven many miles to partake in the spectacle of Hess's during the Christmas season.

From the 1940s to his tragically early death in 1969, Max Hess, Jr., dominated the retail business environment of Lehigh County from his store, part commercial business, part stage set, at the northwest corner of Ninth and Hamilton streets. Born in 1911 as the son of store founder Max Hess, Sr., he was too young to play any role in the family business when his father died in 1922. Max Jr. was just starting Muhlenberg College in 1929 when his uncle Charles died. The business was then taken over by Sol Hoffman, longtime business associate of Max Hess, Sr.

When the Depression arrived, shortly after Charles Hess's passing, the retail environment of the region went into a tailspin. There are no surviving records to offer positive proof of how Hess Brothers fared at that time. It could not have been easy for Hoffman and the other longtime store executives who had gotten used to running the store one way to change the way they had always done things.

Hess Brothers store before the major renovations undertaken by Max Hess, Jr.

As he did not leave behind any written statement, it is not possible to know exactly what motivated Max Hess, Jr., at the time. But his actions speak volumes. In 1932, with less than a year left before he would graduate from Muhlenberg, Hess left school and took over a position at the family business.

If he had some grand strategy for rescuing the store, 21-year-old Max did not reveal it right away. In 1936 an article appeared

Hess Brothers in the early 1960s. The pre-war façade improvements made by Max Hess, Jr., created a unified front. The large sign was installed in 1947. (William Zwikl photo)

in *The Morning Call* in which he announced an entirely new look for the store's exterior. Since its birth roughly thirty-nine years before, Hess Brothers had expanded by annexing one Victorian neighbor after another. Those who walked around the store's interior would sometimes find themselves walking up and then down as they went from one building to another. The façade in the early 1930s was one long, disjointed building with only a coat of white paint to unify it.

Hess decided his store needed a new look. The popular design-theme buzz word of the day was "streamlining." From the French Line's *Normandie*, launched with much fanfare in 1935, to Chrysler's Airflow model cars that debuted the same year, everything in the mid-thirties was to be "streamlined." So Max Hess decided to give Allentown and Lehigh County its first "streamline" department store, an architectural style known today as Art Moderne or Streamline Moderne. When the project was finished in 1939, at a cost of $100,000, it had

Thanks for the Memories: Bob Hope Visits Allentown in 1950

To those over fifty, the name Bob Hope brings back many memories. There are some who recall his classic movies from the 1940s and 50s, regarded as masterpieces of comedy even 60 years later. Others remember him entertaining American troops from WWII to Vietnam. Still others recall his star-studded Christmas specials.

In his early career, Hope was also on stage. It is quite possible he might have appeared at Allentown's Lyric Theater, now Symphony Hall. Bing Crosby, his old comedy colleague in the famous Road pictures, is known to have performed there. It was in a different venue, Allentown School District Stadium, now J. Birney Crum Stadium, that a crowd estimated at 8,000 saw Hope on the chilly night of September 6, 1950.

Hope came to Allentown that year at the urging of Manny Davis, then the manager of the Lyric. Davis knew that Allentown Osteopathic Hospital was planning a fund raiser and felt it could use someone like Hope to make it a success. That June Davis had used his theater connections to get himself backstage at Philadelphia's Academy of Music, where Hope was appearing. Davis spotted Hope standing among a group of stage hands. He walked over, introduced himself, and told the comedian what he wanted. Hope responded that he was currently in the middle of making a movie, "The Lemon-Drop Kid," and had decided to restrict himself to few personal appearances that year. But he did tell Davis that he would try.

As they spoke, Davis asked him if he would mind speaking to his young son Michael on the telephone in Allentown. Hope agreed and ended up getting so involved telling the boy jokes that he forgot all about the performance he was supposed to give. Frantic stage hands were whispering to him that he was three minutes late. Just before he hung up, Hope told Michael Davis the words his father had wanted to hear. "I'll see you in Allentown, son," he said before dropping the phone into the receiver.

Davis did not pursue this with Hope. Two weeks later, he got a phone call from Hollywood. Hope was on the other end of the line, and agreed to appear in Allentown. Because of his filming schedule, he told Davis, the only day he could possibly be there would be September 6. The comedian concluded the conversation by telling Davis that his stop in the Lehigh Valley was one of only four personal appearances he would make that year.

When the word leaked out that Bob Hope was coming to Allentown, the press went into overdrive. Articles about Hope, his wife, his family, his movies were all over the entertainment sections of the newspapers. Interestingly, several articles focused on speculation that Hope would bring Fred Waring, the noted choral director, and his chorus, the Pennsylvanians, with him. In 1950 Waring, who was born in Tyrone, Pennsylvania, had one of the most popular television

Construction of Allentown School District stadium, now J. Birney Crum stadium.
(Kurt Zwikl)

programs around and had had a popular radio program long before that.

Since Waring's resort, Shawnee on the Delaware, was nearby, he seems to have been regarded as a local boy who made good. It was also known that Hope and he were friends. Apparently, it only seemed natural that they would get together in Allentown. There was almost a tone of disappointment in the press when it was revealed that Waring was not coming.

On September 6, Hope arrived about mid-day in Allentown along with big band leader Bob Chester with his orchestra and "songstress" Helen Forrest. There is no account of exactly how they got to Allentown although it might have been by train. Hope was driven up Hamilton Street to the Americus Hotel. A crowd of what the press called "about 800 autograph seekers" were milling around Hamilton Street, hoping to see the movie star, but local police decided to take Hope in through the Sixth Street entrance. By the time fans had charged around the corner, he was already safely in the building.

Sometime near the dinner hour, a number of Hope's fans were allowed in to meet him and get autographs. Two of them, Marjorie Rujek and Janet Baltrame, were shown with Hope in a photo in the next day's *Morning Call*. Shortly thereafter, Hope and his party got into automobiles and were driven out to the ASD Stadium. As they rode through the streets a squad of police motorcycles acted as an escort.

When they arrived at the stadium the crowd of autograph seekers had gotten there first. Hope waded into it, signing as many things as he could and keeping up comic patter of one-liners as he did so. Before he went on, Hope told an interviewer from WSAN radio that he was very impressed that a town the size of Allentown had a football field that big. "For a minute I though we were coming into Soldiers Field [in Chicago]," he quipped.

Unfortunately, there was no record in the newspaper the next day of what jokes Hope told the crowd that night, or even how they were received. A sudden change in the weather swept Allentown, turning what should have been a balmy late summer evening fall-like. Photos of the crowd show the men and woman in overcoats and hats. This may have kept the size of the crowd down. Hope's departure or how much money he raised for the hospital was not recorded.

Hope returned to the region again in 1973 at the Pocono Fair and 1983 at Lehigh University's Stabler Arena. He was at Stabler to cap off the inauguration of university president Peter Likins. The comedian was greeted warmly at both locations. After his 1983 appearance Hope was taken to Allentown and spent the night at the former Hilton, now the Holiday Inn at Ninth and Hamilton, perhaps remembering the night he slept up the street thirty-three years before.

An Industry Built On Air:
The Story Of Leonard Parker Pool And Air Products And Chemicals

Throughout his life Leonard Parker Pool was many things. The words salesman, innovator, and industrialist might all be applied to him with equal accuracy. Two more might not come immediately to mind: visionary and dreamer. His consummate skills in his business life enabled Pool to pursue his larger goals.

Pool's first dream was to be a doctor. This was a tall order in early twentieth-century America for the son of a railroad boiler maker. An education in medicine cost time and money, of which he had little. "He wanted to become a doctor," his brother Walter told *The Morning Call* in 2000, "but financial problems made that impossible." He put that dream aside, but did not forget it.

Pool quickly decided whatever ambitions he had could not be resolved without money, more than he could ever make working for the railroad. So he became a salesman, a super salesman. As the 1920s roared Pool was going door to door hawking the virtues of Pillsbury Pancake Flour. Frugal by inclination and necessity, he soon acquired a nest egg to help him on his next venture. In 1929 he decided to start up a company selling welding and cutting equipment as well as cylinder oxygen and acetylene. Pool had had some background with them working in railroad repair shops as a welder. That same year he met and began courting Dorothy Rider, a college professor who taught French and was six years his senior. They were married on December 19, 1931.

Pool's company was so successful that it was bought out. He was made an executive by the new owners, but he wanted more. His big idea was the creation of small generators of industrial gases that he could lease to the many customers who could not afford what the big companies charged. The oxygen would be paid for at a metered rate, like natural gas. Pool called it leasing "the cow" (the generator), while selling "the milk " (the gas).

Engineers Frank Pavlis and Carl Anderson, Pool's first employees, created the small generator. On September 30, 1940, the company was formed and after a few false starts was named Air Products. Anderson said later that some companies start with a shoestring, "but to tell you the truth we didn't even have a shoestring."

World War II gave Air Products its first big boost. Early contracts with the military for small-scale generators led to more and more contracts. By 1945 its involvement in the Lend-Lease program to aid America's allies had made Air Products' generators known as far away as Russia. In 1946

Air Products arrived in Lehigh County, relocating from Tennessee to Emmaus.

By the 1950s and '60s Air Products was doing a thriving business overseas with its generators. At the same time, at the height of the Cold War it was developing liquid oxygen to fuel the U.S. military's growing guided-missile force. It was also developing agricultural chemicals like anhydrous ammonia to increase crop yields. The so-called Green Revolution of the 1960s, sponsored by the Ford and Rockefeller foundations, encouraged the use of these chemicals and pesticides on farms in the Third World.

With the aid of top executives Ed Donley and Dexter Baker, the company continued to prosper. In 1960 Air Products' success led to a cover story in *Business Week* magazine with Pool gracing the cover. In 1961 the company's stock was listed on the New York Stock Exchange and its name was changed to Air Products and Chemicals, Inc.

For all his business success, Pool was also to see tragedy in the 1960s. Most important was the long struggle with lung cancer that took the life of his much-loved wife Dorothy in 1967. It convinced Pool that his adopted home of the Lehigh Valley needed better hospitals. If he could not become a doctor, he could at least make a contribution to medicine, his first love, and honor his wife as well with the Dorothy Rider Pool Health Care Trust.

Unfortunately, Pool's efforts sparked a controversy that pitted him against the local hospital community. Although the modern hospital he envisioned did finally come to fruition, it was a long-drawn-out battle that included disagreements with the Rev. Joseph McShea, the Roman Catholic bishop of the Diocese of Allentown. The issues around it became so complex that in 1980 *The Morning Call* published a book-long special section on the controversy.

Another important contribution Pool made to the community was the Pool Wildlife Sanctuary. The 77.5-acre tract along the banks of the Little Lehigh Creek in Lower Macungie Township was given by Pool in 1975 to the newly formed Lehigh Valley Conservancy, now known statewide as Wildlands Conservancy. Much more than a recreational and educational environmental organization, the Conservancy's mission is also to protect, restore, and enhance natural areas, primarily in the watershed of the Lehigh River. The grounds of the sanctuary feature a pavilion, a bird blind, an arboretum, ponds, nature trails, and educational buildings. It is used by many school groups to teach their students about the environment in Lehigh County and to foster a general appreciation of nature.

Pool died in 1975. Dexter Baker, asked to describe his boss, said "He was a man of great tenacity, with an abiding faith in his own vision. He really encouraged us and got satisfaction from doing so. Leonard would always say, "How can we do it better?"

(Wildlands Conservancy)

193

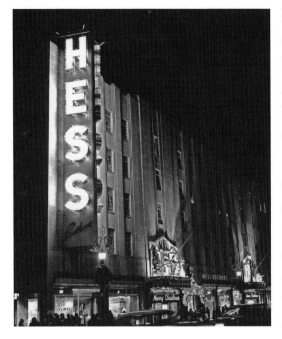

Hess Brothers giant sign, 1947–1973, seen here during a Christmas shopping season. (William Zwikl photo)

banished the mishmash of Victorian façades and created a sleek, elegant façade, comparable to what might have been found in a major American city of the day. It also let the public know that a new generation with a modern outlook was now running Hess Brothers.

The new façade Max Hess put on his store could not change the international and national realities that shaped the economic environment at the time. No sooner had government defense spending finally broken the back of the Depression than the U.S. entered World War II. Government-imposed restrictions led to the rationing of a wide variety of civilian-related products, clothing and shoes among them. It was not until 1947, as wartime rationing was phased out, that the long-pent-up demand for consumer goods could finally be met. Hamilton Street's three department stores, Hess Brothers, Leh's, and Zollinger-Harned, were beginning to see more and more shoppers with money in their pockets who wanted to spend it.

To catch his share of the customer's dollar, Max Hess decided to make another addition to the store by installing escalators. Never doing anything in a small way, his escalators were top-of-the-line models that a New York department store of the era might have installed. This was followed a few weeks before Christmas by the arrival of the iconic Hess's sign. It was a forty-five-foot tall, eight-ton giant with letters seven feet tall. According to one story, Hess got the idea one day in New York when he saw the large sign that said BOND over a Fifth Avenue men's clothing store. Said to be the biggest retail sign between New York and Chicago, the Hess's sign's 2,250 light bulbs flashed out the name "Hess" in a way that could not be missed.

A flashy sign was one of many ways that Max Hess lured customers. In 1951 he created the Patio, the ultimate department store restaurant to replace the restaurant Hess Brothers had had as far back as 1909. Like the sign out front, Hess's Patio made a trademark out of abundance. For a Depression-born, war-weary generation that had undergone rationing it heralded a future of release from austerity and want. Mile-high strawberry pie, a special Patio dessert with lots of whipped cream, was a featured attraction. It was so filling it was often eaten by itself with coffee rather than as a dessert following a meal.

It was not just Lehigh Valley residents who were captivated by the strawberry pie.

Liberace, the flamboyant pianist/personality of the 1950s and '60s known for his razzle-dazzle playing style, wild suits, and guttering candelabra ("I don't do concerts, I do shows" he told complaining music critics) fell in love with them after visiting Hess's, and used special freezer packs to ship the strawberry pies to friends during the Christmas holidays.

Coupled with the triple-decker sandwiches and super-size menus, it marked Hess's Patio as a place where you did not have to worry about going away hungry, something many of the Depression survivors could understand.

Hess also expanded on ideas created by his father and uncle. Charles Hess's creation of the French Room in 1912 gave the store a touch of glamour and an association with exotic foreign fashions. Max Hess encouraged the trend, sending his buyers—at times going himself—to Europe. Hess's began having fashion shows outside the store at places like Longwood Gardens, a former DuPont family estate. By the 1960s, Gerry Golden, Hess's fashion guru, was showing fashions on special television shows broadcast from Philadelphia. Among other fashion coups was the introduction of Rudi Gingrich's infamous topless bathing suit of 1964. None sold, but that his store had them first and had gotten the publicity for it was what Hess wanted.

In the late 1950s Wolfgang Otto, a German-born window designer, went to work for Hess's. It was not long before Max Hess realized his talents. Soon, Otto's stylized window displays were reflecting the glamour of the Jackie Kennedy–Grace Kelly era and made Lehigh County and Allentown known throughout the world. By 1965, Hess's had offices in London, Paris, and Rome—nothing fancy, but they were there.

Store photographer William "Bill" Zwikl was another Hess's employee who helped add to Hess's aura of glamour. From the 1950s to the 1980s he worked at the store, taking pictures of the many celebrities who came to the store and of fashion trends that ranged from the staid Eisenhower era to the "mod" swinging London styles of the 1960s. In that same period Zwikl was sent abroad to accompany young women who had won Hess's "Trip of a Lifetime" contest. His expertly done photos made stay-at-homes envious, and added to the glamour that was Hess's trademark.

Center Square, looking south, in the winter at the end of the 1950s or early 1960s. The statue at the top of the monument has been removed. Leh's Department Store is where the Lehigh County Government Center was built in 1997.

In the 1950s and '60s Max Hess brought what might be called "star quality" to Allentown and Lehigh County. Stars of the big screen and the TV screen were at the top of their game in those decades, and the publicists of Hollywood made sure that their clients followed the image created for them by the front office. Hess knew that by bringing stars to his store he was letting the public know how important Hess's was, and by definition how important the residents of Allentown and Lehigh County were. "Back then," recalls one local baby boomer, Robert H. Wittman, Jr., "people saw it as much as *they* were coming to see *us*, as *we* were coming to see *them*."

As if to emphasize this, in 1956, when George Reeves, television's Superman, came to Allentown he not only appeared at Hess's but went out on delivery trips with the Hess's truck in full costume. A doorbell would ring and there would be Superman, not some lookalike but the "real" guy from TV, at the door with a recently ordered sweater. Perhaps today, more astonishing than Superman, was the idea that fifty years ago you could actually get a store to deliver items you had purchased, in person or by phone, to your door.

Hess's had two major department store rivals on Hamilton Street, H. Leh and Company and Zollinger-Harned. Both located in the 600 block, Leh's was the most senior. Its roots went back to the early 1850s when Henry Leh, a young canal boat mule boy and tailor, opened a dry goods store. Its first items were shipped in by canal boat.

During the Civil War Henry Leh acquired government contracts to make boots for the Union Army. The boot and shoemaking business was expanded after the war and helped put the store on a firm financial footing. In the 1870s and 1880s, according to a publication by the Allentown Board of Trade, no male citizen of Lehigh County felt his wardrobe was complete until he had been "rigged out" in a wool suit from H. Leh and Company. Later an intermarriage with the enterprising Koch family led to a very successful and well-run business that survived into the 1990s.

Zollinger's was founded in 1909 on the northwest corner of Sixth and Hamilton. Its roots went back to a small Sandusky, Ohio, chain founded by William Ruel Zollinger in 1900. It was located on the site of Lawfer's, an earlier department store that is generally credited as having had the first department-store Santa Claus in 1904. In 1924 Zollinger's rebuilt the store with a stately Colonial Revival façade. Zollinger's became Zollinger-Harned when it was taken over in the 1950s by the Harneds, an old Allentown family. It survived until 1978 and its space was later converted to offices. Of the three Allentown department stores of the 1950s, it is the only one whose building has survived.

That Allentown's Hamilton Street could support three department stores in its hey-day speaks highly of the commercial vitality of the city and county. In the mid-1950s, the Allentown Chamber of Commerce gave it the nickname the "Miracle Mile." Along with the department stores there were several movie theaters and a host of other merchants. Some were national or regional chains like Fanny Farmer's, a candy store chain, and Whelan's Drug Store.

Others, such as Farr's Shoe store and Young Hardware, were longtime family businesses that, like Leh's, went back into the middle of the nineteenth century. Others were more recent, such as Dobnoff's, a furniture store, and Bohlen Gross & Moyer, which sold men's suits.

J. Clinton Miller, a longtime Allentown church organist currently at the Episcopal Church of the Mediator, remembers coming to the city from New York City in 1963 for the first time when he was applying for a job at St. John's Lutheran Church. He recalls being impressed with the vitality of the retail sector of the community. "In those days Hamilton Street was like a mini-Manhattan."

Even its commercial rivals understood that Hess's was unique. Sylvia Lawler, TV and media critic for the *Evening Chronicle* and *The Morning Call* in that era, praised Max Hess's unerring eye for celebrity spotting: "He was very good at getting them for the store when they were on the rise and in the news." She gave part of the credit for the store's celebrity draw to Hess's skilled public-relations man, Max "Maggie" Levine.

Lawler recalled a particular Max Hess coup of 1954, when he brought to the store Porfirio Rubirosa, the Dominican heart-throb whose name in the newspapers of the day was always prefaced with the words "international playboy." Rubirosa was in the headlines that year for his whirlwind 54-day marriage and divorce from Woolworth dime-store heiress Barbara Hutton, known to gossip column readers of the day as the "Poor Little Rich Girl" for her many unsuccessful marriages, including one to Hollywood mega star Cary Grant.

Rock Hudson was a popular draw during the early 1960s, when he was making the

"Pillow Talk" movies with Doris Day. Hudson was a tall man, and photos by Zwikl show him towering over the women who came to see him that day. That Hudson was gay would not become publicly known until his death from AIDS in the 1980s.

Along with Hollywood, television was the source of many Hess celebrities. Among the shows and stars were "Ramar of the Jungle" with John Hall, Barbara Eden of "I Dream of Genie," and Chuck Conners of "The Rifleman" fame. Stars of the day would freely "plug" Hess's on television in return for Max Hess's hospitality. They would appear on "The Tonight Show" with Jack Parr and say something like "like my tie? I got it at Hess's in Allentown."

Max Hess seemed to understand instinctively that there was no such thing as bad publicity. In the mid-1950s, when the popularity of television quiz shows was at its height, Hess paid to have one of his employees appear on the popular "$64,000 Question" program. The employee later said he was told by company publicists he was to stay on the program until they got to the important $64,000 prize and then deliberately give a wrong answer. But the employee flubbed on the first question, never got any further, and was either fired or quit.

In 1959, due to reports that the quiz programs were rigged, Congressional investigations were launched. When the government man with the subpoena showed up at Hess's, a furious Max Hess took the document, stuck it into the man's suit-coat pocket, and personally shoved him out the door. But, thinking better of it, Hess agreed to appear. He was the first witness on the day the hearings opened, the moment of the most media coverage and public attention.

Hess turned his appearance into a commercial, of sorts, for his store. Yes, he had paid $15,000 to put his employee on the program. No, he had no idea where the money went. Hess said he was as shocked as the committee and thanked them for going after those crooks. With thanks from the committee chairman, Hess walked out of the hearing room a hero. "With that appearance he got more free publicity than he could have ever paid for," Lawler recalled.

Television Arrives in Lehigh County

Television, although invented as far back as the 1920s, burst on Lehigh County, as it did in the rest of the nation, in the late 1940s. At first screens were small and reception fuzzy, but the local love affair with the black box was as strong here as everywhere else. "You would walk up and down Hamilton Street, which in those days was a very busy street, and all the electric appliance dealers would have them on in their windows. And everybody was watching them," Lawler remembered.

Despite all this attention there was a lingering question in the minds of many in Lehigh County. Technology being what it was in the late 1940s, would reception from Philadelphia even be possible in a hilly region like Lehigh County?

The first test came with the first televised event known to be aired in Lehigh County, a basketball game between Muhlenberg College and the University of Pennsylvania. It was broadcast live from Philadelphia on December 21, 1946, and was carried by Channel 3, WPTZ. The game was watched locally on the TV set belonging to B. Bryan Musselman of Allentown, the vice president and general manger of radio station WSAN and one of the few people in Lehigh County at the time who owned one. The next day *The Morning Call* noted that "while the visual reception was not as clear as it could have been if the set had been in the Philadelphia area … it was a triumph for the local area inasmuch as it was believed impossible."

The problems with reception did not stop people from buying TV sets. In 1949 the *Evening Chronicle* noted that there were anywhere from 6,000 to 8,000 in use across the Lehigh Valley. Lawler recalled that one of the people who had one at the time was her uncle, meatpacker Walter Bastian. Like many people at the time, Bastian would invite family over on occasion to watch it. "We would get in the car and drive down to his home. It was a real event."

Throughout the 1950s clear television reception was erratic in Lehigh County. To improve picture quality, some adopted the latest technology, antenna rotators, which enabled set owners to move their antenna in any direction. Even that could help only so much. The rise of TV antennae from the Victorian rooftops of Allentown annoyed many because of the visual clutter. "There was this jungle tangle of high television antennas that looked horrid," recalled Lawler.

Lehigh County never got its own nationally affiliated television station. Part of the reason had to do with opposition from Philadelphia network affiliates, who saw the Lehigh Valley as their own growth area. According to Lawler *The Morning Call's* owners were also said to have played a role. They owned two newspapers and a local radio station, and Lawler said they did not want any challenge to their media monopoly of the region. There is nothing in the public record that supports this claim about the newspaper-owning Miller family, but it was widely believed in the community at that time.

It would be the 1960s before cable TV came into the region. Cable had started in Mahanoy City, Schuylkill County, when General Electric appliance dealer John Walson decided that he wanted to sell more television sets. If reception was bad in Lehigh County, it was virtually impossible in the hilly area around Mahanoy City. So Walson set up an antenna on top of a nearby mountain and in 1948 ran heavy-duty wire to the TV display in his sales shop. People were transfixed watching the popular "Kukla, Fran and Ollie" puppet program broadcasting as clearly as it might be seen in Philadelphia. Later he was able to add more cable and fed it into homes of people who were willing to pay for the reception. They paid

$100 for the hookup and $2 a month for the service, called CATV or Community Antenna TV. His Service Electric Company was the first cable TV provider in the United States, and by the time Walson died in 1993, his Service Electric Cable TV, Inc., served 210 communities in Pennsylvania, New York, and New Jersey and was the thirty-ninth-largest in the country.

News was a vital part of what television brought into Lehigh County. The 1950s and '60s were the height of the Cold War with the Soviet Union. Along with rest of the country, fear gripped the region during the Cuban Missile Crisis of October 1962. When *The Morning Call* and the *Evening Chronicle* ran a small map showing that Bethlehem Steel would make the Lehigh Valley a logical target for Soviet missiles based in Cuba, it seemed to put the region on the front line for nuclear destruction.

Later, coupled with the civil-rights movement of African-Americans in the South, the Vietnam War, and eventually the anti-war protests of the late 1960s and early 1970s, television both united and divided Americans in ways they had never been before.

Fellow Traveler or Patriot?

Long before 1962, the Cold War at its chilliest came into Lehigh County, in 1954, in the person of Herman Erwin Thomas, an Allentown businessman. In the late 1930s Thomas had briefly joined a local chapter of the Communist party. This was not illegal at the time, and Thomas left the party in 1939, perhaps disillusioned, as many were, by the pact signed between Hitler and Stalin—supposedly avowed enemies—dividing Poland between them at the start of World War II. In 1944 Thomas was asked by the FBI to rejoin the party to find who they were and what their plans were. This he agreed to do.

By then, under the Alien Registration Act of 1940—better known as the Smith Act after its author, Howard W. Smith, a conservative, anti-labor-union Democratic Congressman from Virginia—it was a crime punishable by fine and imprisonment to teach or advocate the overthrow of the government by force or violence. The act was used against both Trotskyite Communists and Fascists during World War II, and was later reinforced by the Internal Security Act of 1950.

The bombshell came at a trial of Communists being held in Philadelphia in front of Federal Judge J. Cullen Ganey, then a resident of Bethlehem. When Thomas admitted to having been a Communist from 1937 to 1939, it sent an immediate shockwave into the Lehigh Valley. The concept of "the enemy within" was a potent one to the World War II generation. Phyllis Guth, a young teenager at the time and later a *Morning Call* reporter, was a high-school classmate of Thomas's daughter Sally, and was concerned there might be violence against the family. "When she did not show up for class the next day we thought she was afraid someone would shoot her," Guth recalled in 1992.

Everything was cleared up on May 10, when Thomas once more walked into the Philadelphia courtroom and took the witness stand. "On Thursday you testified you joined the Communist Party in July 1937, and remained a member until 1939," said attorney Thomas J. Mitchell of the federal prosecutor's staff. "Will you tell us the circumstances of your return to the party?

"Yes," said Thomas. "Early in 1944 I was approached by the FBI and asked whether I would work with them. After some consideration I accepted." With those words Thomas was no longer a "Kremlin termite," as Allentown's *Evening Chronicle* called the "Reds," but a hero. The next day's newspapers featured a front-page picture of Thomas and his family that could have been a publicity photo for the popular TV show of the day, "Father Knows Best."

Thomas was suddenly the local version of TV's then-popular true-life spy drama, "I Led Three Lives." A best-selling 1952 book with the same title was among the most popular non-fiction works checked out of the Allentown Public Library that year. Its author, Herbert Philbrick, an FBI undercover informant, told how he had infiltrated Communist party "cells" across the country. The nationally syndicated program starring the jut-jawed actor Richard Carlson was broadcast into Lehigh County homes at 7 p.m. on Wednesday evenings on Philadelphia's channel 10.

Over the next several days, Thomas testified that in the 1940s he had attended meetings of Communist fronts with false names like "The Easton Fur Club." Here they were given books on Marxist-Leninist communist ideology to read, and others that explained how the overthrow of the U.S. government could be achieved.

The chief local target of Thomas's testimony was Joseph Kuzma, a Bethlehem Steel worker who lived in Easton. An *Evening Chronicle* editorial citing the FBI called Kuzma "the Mr. Big of the Communist Party organization in Eastern Pennsylvania and Delaware." Kuzma, who had been under arrest for quite some time, had never denied being a Communist and refused to admit he had done anything wrong.

In his testimony, Thomas mentioned by name several other local Communists or "fellow-travelers" he had met. Most said they had last attended meetings in the 1940s and were no longer Communists. Others claimed they never had been party members. One Allentown resident, who happened to have the same name as a person mentioned by Thomas, complained to the newspapers about the threatening phone calls he had received. Both *The Morning Call* and the *Evening Chronicle* ran articles the next day saying the man was not a Communist.

In December, 1954, Thomas was called to Washington, D.C., to appear before the anti-Communist investigating committee headed by Wisconsin Senator Joseph McCarthy. McCarthy, having recently been the subject of a vote of censure by the Senate, was not present for Thomas's testimony. Among his prosecution staff was a bright young man named Robert F. Kennedy, later the attorney general for his brother, President John F. Kennedy, and a noted liberal icon of the 1960s.

Most of the Thomas testimony, which was taken privately and not released in public until 2003, was used against Bethlehem Steel workers who had been active in union organizing in the 1940s. Some admitted to having belonged to the party but others denied it. Several said that they had merely attended a party meeting but had never become a member. But those who took the Fifth Amendment against self-incrimination were assumed to be Communists. If they worked for Bethlehem Steel they were fired.

In 1957 the U.S. Supreme Court found the Smith Act unconstitutional and the charges against many accused Communists were dropped. When Thomas, who had since left the Lehigh Valley, died in the 1980s, his brief newspaper obituary made no mention of his role in the trials of the 1950s.

A Revolution in Transportation

Even as Cold War hysteria was grabbing headlines, everyday life for Lehigh County residents was changing in more visible ways. With the growth of suburbs, the "car culture" that had come to the Lehigh Valley in the 1920s became all-important in how the region saw itself. The first six years of the 1950s were to witness the end of street-car service in the county. Several of the more-distant rural routes disappeared as early as the late 1920s, replaced by bus routes or just discontinued. In the late 1930s the Lehigh Valley Transit Company introduced lighter, modern streetcars and sold its old, heavy, turn-of-the-century equipment to scrap dealers, who in turn sold it to Japan.

Unknown to most Americans, a campaign was already underway that would not simply replace old streetcars but would do away with them entirely, replacing them with buses. In 1974 the U.S. Senate Subcommittee on Antitrust and Monopoly published a document titled "American Ground Transport." In some detail, it told how, starting in the late 1930s, Firestone Tire and Rubber, General Motors Corp., Phillips Petroleum, Standard Oil of California, and Mack Manufacturing Corporation (then a major bus maker), working through a corporation called National City Lines, bought up and destroyed streetcar lines in forty-two American cities and replaced them with buses. The allegations first came to light as part of a federal court case in 1949, United States v. National City Lines. The result was a guilty verdict and a $5,000 fine.

Gerhard Salomon of Allentown, a local watchmaker and jeweler, and a passionate trolley buff, said he and his friends had no idea that such a court case had taken place at that time but did have fears for the future. "We knew then that without rail transportation, the area—particularly the cities—was going to get clogged with vehicles," he said in 2003.

Even those who mourned the trolley's passing, like John Y. Kohl, *The Morning Call's*
longtime Sunday editor, were caught up in the always-better-tomorrow logic of the time.
"We hate to see them go," he wrote of the trolleys in a June 7, 1953, column, "realizing full
well, of course, that their passing is just another phase in the inexorable march of progress
in this fast-changing age." Since the future has to be better than the past, then buses have
to be better than the trolleys.

The Liberty Bell Line was among the first to go. Founded in 1912 to link Allentown with
Philadelphia, it had been LVT's pride and joy. In 1915 former President William Howard
Taft had taken the route in the company president's private car to speak at the dedication
of the Allentown Hospital's new school of nursing. By 1951 the company had received
permission from the state Public Utilities Commission to discontinue the Liberty Bell trolleys and replace them with buses. Only because they had gotten word from friends who
worked for LVT did local trolley buffs get word of the line's last run. That September they
were the last to travel it.

The formal end of Allentown's streetcars came on June 9, 1953. At 10:20 a.m. streetcar
No. 912, flag and bunting bedecked and full of local dignitaries, started the last ride through
the city. Most of the rest of the cars were already at Bethlehem Steel's scrap yard. Car 912
carried bigwigs, no trolley buffs allowed. Salomon was so outraged that he put some fire
crackers on the track. They exploded harmlessly. He did record the last official journey with
his camera. Finally, at noon, the trolley came to rest at Eighth and Hamilton streets. Shortly

thereafter, all the trolley cars were off the streets. On June 12, No. 912 made its very last journey, joining its sisters at Bethlehem Steel's scrap yard for a fiery end, caught by local trolley buffs with their cameras.

An editorial writer for *The Morning Call*, under the heading "Too Late For Tears," found all this sympathy for the passing trolley age odd. "It is strange situation in which the public, which slowly killed the trolley by abuse and lack of patronage (except during the foulest weather) now is weeping, figuratively speaking of course, at their demise." Even buses, the writer suggested, would join the trolley on the scrap heap unless they could deliver "adequate and punctual service." Left unsaid, the implication was clear: the future belonged to the family automobile.

Even as those last streetcars were being burned, the theme of highway progress was on the drawing boards. The old Route 22, which twisted its way though the Lehigh Valley around city streets and up and down hills, was by 1954 the butt of jokes. Nicknames for it included Old Cowpath, Suicide Highway, and Bad Dream Highway. The future promised something better, the new Route 22. Newspapers spoke of the future road as the "dream highway." Also known as the Lehigh Valley Thruway, it was to be a straight ribbon of asphalt into tomorrow.

"Allentown in 1953 was a city on the march," averred the *Evening Chronicle's* editor in the January 1, 1954, "Progress and Prosperity" edition, a tradition at that paper since the 1920s. "You could sense it everywhere in the deep stirrings of a community rapidly fulfilling its destiny as a great city." Highways were the key to the future, not just for Allentown and the Lehigh Valley but the nation. "In the studied opinion of experts on the subject," opined the *Evening Chronicle*, "50 billion dollars must be spent on United States highways within the next ten years, if they are to keep pace with the demand for more and better roads to meet the demands of a nation on wheels."

As early as 1953, the public had a view of that future when an eight-mile section of bypass between Kuhnsville and Route 145, also known as the Seventh Street Highway, was opened. "The new Route 22 visualizes routing of through traffic around the city rather than through its narrow streets," said the newspapers. No longer intermingled with local traffic, it would relieve "congestion of the worst sort." Throughout 1954 the growth of this new highway was followed in the press as if it were an army on the march.

On September 21, 1954, victory was proclaimed. Under a thin drizzle, a caravan of 1954 Cadillacs, proud tail fins on display, was led by one carrying Pennsylvania Governor John S. Fine. Others, with the mayors of Allentown, Bethlehem, and Easton close behind, glided from the Kuhnsville bypass to the Airport Road interchange. Around them was an almost bucolic landscape of open fields and trees.

With a pair of big shears Fine cut the ribbon, opening the "dream highway." A little later, at an official reception held in Bethlehem Steel's hangar at A-B-E- Airport, Lafayette College President Ralph Cooper Hutchinson compared the new Route 22 to the roads that tied the Roman Empire together.

In his remarks, Governor Fine expressed the hope that the new Lehigh Valley Thruway would remain open country with rolling fields, free as it was then of any billboards and roadside clutter. In this he was destined to be disappointed.

Apparently no one gave voice to the thought that the new highway would do the very opposite of what was claimed. By directing traffic outside the cities, new highways would encourage their decline and lead to the development of suburban shopping malls and a huge explosion of housing developments that would transform the rural landscape and the divide between country and city.

From 1954 to 1959 the highway's construction pushed on. Progress was not always smooth. At one point a farmer took to blocking a township road with sawhorses. At another, local business people along the old Route 22 complained about what would happen to their roadside stands and shops. Others, mostly residents of small towns, expressed relief that it would cut down on truck traffic on their village streets.

On March 22, 1959, the last link of the new Route 22, between Fogelsville and Kuhnsville, was completed. At last, *The Morning Call's* editorial writers declared, a modern four-lane road linked Allentown with Harrisburg. "It is the end of the worst stretch of highway in the state," they declared that day.

This optimistic view of the new highway lasted about a year. At the end of 1960, state highway officials were telling *The Morning Call* that "the Lehigh Valley Thruway between Allentown and Bethlehem gradually is nearing a saturation point at busy hours." Officials, who had assumed that the road would be more than adequate at least until 1970, were puzzled. According to their plans, the new Route 22 would be used largely by traffic going from Allentown and points east and directly on to Harrisburg or back to Allentown. It would take traffic out of the city and off the overburdened downtown streets. They were surprised to discover that many local drivers were using the thruway for short hops

The intersection of Route 100 and Route 22 at Fogelsville in 1959.
(Lehigh County Historical Society)

between Allentown and Bethlehem. Traffic that had moved primarily on local streets was now on the new highway, where it was mingling with drivers going to Harrisburg or heading to Allentown from there. "It is getting busier all the time," said state police chief Capt. Lawrence Sapudar.

Three years later it was no better. "The Thruway: 4 Lane Highway With 8 Lanes of Traffic" was the headline on *The Morning Call's* lead front-page story on September 29, 1963. The news peg for the story was the ten highway traffic deaths on Route 22 over the past year. Almost all of them had been caused by cars traveling too fast and ramming the backs of trucks.

The highway was sparking development and growth, leading more and more people to regard Route 22 as their lifeline to work, home, and school. When they drove it the road became more and more clogged. So began complaints about Route 22 that, even with the construction of Interstate Highway 78, plagues the local road system into the twenty-first century.

Air Travel

Roads and highways and the departure of the street car were not the only changes in local transportation. On September 21, 1910, flyer Glenn Curtiss, using Allentown's Nineteenth Street as a runway, took off for Philadelphia in the first airplane flight over Lehigh County.

His crude, noisy aircraft (it was only eight years after the Wright Brothers had shown the world how to fly) swept over an amazed crowd in the grandstand at Allentown's Fairgrounds, frightened a South Allentown woman hanging out her laundry when he waved to her, and looped over Bethlehem Steel to a shrill "serenade" by a cacophony of whistles. The next day's newspaper offered a front-page photograph showing Curtiss's plane as a winged dot over Allentown.

Before Curtiss could complete his historic flight, disaster struck. Suddenly, the little plane's engine began to spurt oil at him. Fearful that he would soon come crashing to the earth, Curtiss frantically began to look for a level place to set his aircraft down. There was none. Hills seemed to define the landscape, rising up around him at every side. Desperately turning back toward Allentown, Curtiss spied a small flat section of a farmer's field

Small airports were dotted all around Lehigh County. One of them was in Wescosville, behind the present elementary school. In 1938 airmail came to Wescosville for the first time. Local inventor and pilot Miles Erbor is holding the mail bag; postmaster Granville Guth is on the right. (Lower Macungie Township Historical Society)

near Rittersville and began his descent. The little plane slowed and hit the earth with a thud. Both man and machine were bruised but relatively unhurt. Even before he hit the ground Curtiss could see, heading in his direction, a speeding open automobile bouncing wildly over the rutted cow pasture, his assistant, a doctor, and the gentlemen of the press hanging on to it for their lives.

That evening at the Hotel Allen the slightly battered aviation pioneer told his rescuers he feared there was no future for aviation in the Lehigh Valley. There were way too many hills, he said, to ever make it practical.

Curtiss was wrong. Over the next twenty years aviation advanced and by 1929 Allentown had a small grass airfield, a U.S. airmail station with a 1,500 foot landing strip, a tower with a simple beacon, and a small shed. It occupied fifty acres out of a 316-acre farm in Hanover Township, Lehigh County, that the government had purchased several years earlier. That same year John Henry Leh, a scion of the Leh's department-store family, purchased from the federal government the entire 316 acres for the Allentown Airport Corporation. As part of the agreement, the federal government continued to operate the fifty acres of the property it was already using.

Leh wasted little time. Once he had achieved the endorsement of General Harry C. Trexler for his plan, the normally conservative Pennsylvania-German business community decided it was worthwhile. Then he began to build. The *Polk's City Directory* of 1930 noted the fledgling Allentown Airport, as it was then known, was equipped with a twelve-plane hangar complete with "mechanical service, gas, oil and other necessities at all times." Aerial photos of the day show a line of biplanes with the hangar with the word ALLENTOWN in capital letters on its roof.

Leh's interest in flying was not just business. He and his wife Dorothea were the second married couple in America to be licensed pilots. Dorothea Leh was also a founding member of the 99s, an organization made up of the first 99 women flyers in the country. Leh's

United, Eastern Air Lines, and TWA planes at A–B–E Airport. The passenger terminal opened in 1950. (Lehigh County Historical Society)

co-founder was her close friend, women's aviation pioneer Amelia Earhart, who made at least three visits by air to Lehigh County in the 1920s and '30s to help promote the airport.

Randolph Kulp, a local historian, remembered seeing and hearing the roar of Earhart's bright red Lockheed Vega monoplane as it swept over Allentown at that time. When the aviation legend disappeared over the Pacific in 1937 she was mourned by some local people who knew her not just as a newspaper photograph but a person they had heard speak, and had talked to.

By the 1950s, thanks largely to the work of John Henry Leh, who continued to be head of the airport authority, the airport was one of the most modern for its size in the country. On September 16, 1935, Leh had overseen the arrival of regular air passenger service by United Airlines. In 1938, thanks to the federal government's WPA program, a handsome Art Moderne-style terminal building was erected, and in 1948 it officially became the Allentown-Bethlehem-Easton Airport.

During the World War II era, when civilian and military air traffic increased dramatically, the airport was used in a number of ways by the military. It became the home of Group 312 of the Civil Air Patrol, whose primary task was to provide courier service for defense plants and to patrol the Atlantic coast. German submarines were known to have sailed into New York harbor during World War II. It was also at that time that a new runway was completed, and a U.S. Weather Bureau station was installed.

The post-war years saw the creation of the Lehigh Airport Authority to own and manage the airport. By the 1950s a new passenger terminal had been constructed and the runways expanded. United was joined by TWA and Colonial Airlines at what was now A-B-E Airport. During the 1960 presidential race, the national spotlight shone on A-B-E as candidates Nixon and Kennedy both flew into the airport. Later during the 1960s, A-B-E began jet passenger service and in 1975 opened a new terminal. Glenn Curtiss would have been amazed.

Baseball

Before Route 22 was luring folks out of Allentown to the suburbs, a sports venue had established itself in Whitehall Township. Breadon Field, home of the Allentown Cardinals, a minor-league farm team of the St. Louis Cardinals, was located where the Lehigh Valley Mall is today. Its at-times-erratic history says a great deal about local sports and its role locally and nationally in the 1950s and '60s.

Baseball has been a popular sport in Lehigh County throughout its history. The phase that launched Breadon Field began with a coin toss in 1943. That year Sam Breadon, owner of the St. Louis Cardinals, invited Alvin Butz, part owner of the Allentown Wings, the Cardinals' farm team, to attend the All Star Game in Philadelphia's Shibe Park. With Butz was his nine-year-old son Lee. "I remember Breadon well," Lee Butz recalled in 1994. "He was a tall, very distinguished man. He looked like what people in those days thought the owner of a professional baseball team should look like."

Despite his courtly appearance and demeanor, Breadon, a native New Yorker who had gone to the Midwest as a young man and made a fortune on his Pierce-Arrow luxury car dealerships, was known as a sharp and skilled baseball trader. Business was the major reason he had invited Alvin Butz to Philadelphia. As Lee Butz remembered it, Breadon wanted to buy the Allentown Wings outright. His father was willing to sell but they could not agree on a price. During talks in their hotel room, Breadon suggested they decide by a coin toss and that Lee be the one to flip the coin. Alvin Butz agreed to let his son do so. Lee Butz said he has no recollection who had "heads" and who had "tails," but he was never allowed to forget the result. "I ended up costing my father $1,000 that day … I never heard the end of it." The next day's Morning Call stated that Breadon paid $15,000 for the Wings.

In the fall of 1946, roughly the same time Western Electric was planning on coming to Allentown, the *Evening Chronicle's* sports writer, Dave DeLong, wrote an article announcing that the Allentown Wings, now renamed the Allentown Cardinals, would be getting a new stadium. DeLong recalled in 1964 that Bill Walsingham, Breadon's nephew, who "actively directed Sam's baseball empire" of twenty-four farm teams, told him about the

209

new ballpark. It would be built of concrete and steel, seat 5,000, cost $425,000 and be located on the Seventh Street Pike. Although Whitehall Township commissioners had renamed the road Mac-Arthur Road in 1942 after World War II icon General Douglas Mac-Arthur, *The Morning Call* was still giving it the older, more-familiar designation.

Work on the project went rapidly and on August 5, 1948, it was declared done. That evening Breadon flew into A-B-E airport for the next day's dedication. Gravely ill with cancer, Breadon had defied the advice of doctors by coming to Lehigh County to take part in the ceremony. "I am happy to be in Allentown, I am always happy to be in Allentown," he told waiting reporters.

The next evening, before a large crowd, Allentown mayor Donald Hock officially welcomed Breadon and dedicated the new ballpark "now and forever more" Breadon Field. Breadon thanked the mayor and the baseball fans for turning out, noting that the Cardinals had invested more money in its teams than any other baseball organization in the country. It was one of his last public appearances. On May 10, 1949, Breadon died of cancer at age 72.

The year 1949 was a very good one for Breadon Field. As part of the Inter-State League, the Cardinals played teams in Wilmington, Delaware, Lancaster, Reading, York, and Trenton, among others. More than 120,000 fans jammed the ballpark that year. The Cardinals had every reason to expect an even better year in 1950, but numbers sank to fewer than 50,000. The reasons are unclear but everybody had an opinion. Some claimed it was the arrival of televised baseball. Some that with people able to travel to Philadelphia and New York they preferred to see the major leagues than a home team. Others said the outbreak of the Korean War in June 1950 led people to be preoccupied with something other than sports. And it may have been that the quality of local baseball was just not as good.

In 1951 the Cardinals sent a young man named Don Dix to Allentown. He and his wife Edna Mae became very active in the community and created excitement around the Allentown Cardinals, even putting on a "Miss Allentown Cardinals" beauty contest. Numbers that year were up to 75,000.

Then, in 1952, Breadon Field seemed to sink back in its slump with fewer than 50,000

attending. Dix felt there were a number of reasons for that. "We lost 14 home dates—seven in a row, at one point—due to rain. Plus baseball on television was not just new it was a novelty for most people." Another blow came when teams in York and Hagerstown, Maryland, announced they were leaving the Inter-State League. When no class B team could be found to play against them, Allentown was left without a baseball season.

Meanwhile, things were not happy in St. Louis. With the passing of Breadon there seemed to be no one who was willing to make the commitment to his farm-team system. On February 3, 1953, Cardinals' president Fred Saigh announced he was selling the team.

In 1953 Breadon Field sat empty. The Cardinals main-

Max Hess bought Breadon Field in 1960 and renamed it Max Hess Stadium. (William Zwikl photo)

tained it, but just barely. Fortunately for Lehigh County fans, the Cardinals' new owner was Augustus "Gusssie" Busch, the president of the Anheuser-Busch Brewing Company. After discussions with Busch, Dix was sent back to Allentown with a commitment to acquire a franchise to field a Class A Eastern League team. The Cardinals took players from its other farm teams and re-created the Allentown Cardinals.

In the winter of 1954 Dix returned to Allentown to look over Breadon Field. According to a *Morning Call* article he found "a covey of quail in the high grass of center field, a dead raccoon and a groundhog in the grandstand and rabbits everywhere." But the structure was basically sound. In no time the "grundsow" and bunnies were routed and Dix had Breadon Field ready to play ball.

Looking back on it in 1994, Dix remembered the years from 1954 to 1957 as Breadon Field's golden age. "Those years were very good ones," he recalled. Season crowds averaged between 70,000 and 80,000. And the Cardinals organization under the hand of Busch seemed willing to do what it took to make Breadon Field a success. This included hiring young women as ushers for fans who owned box seats. Among them was Anita Rosenberger. "It was for the 1954–55 seasons," she recalled. "I was at Central Catholic in my sophomore and junior year." Attired in a simple uniform of cotton shirts and Bermuda shorts, the ushers would escort the fans to their seats and if requested get them hot dogs. Rosenberger recalled the unique method used to keep the grass trimmed between games: "They had a herd of sheep that would graze in the outfield to keep the grass short."

Among the coveted positions for young boys at the time was that of bat boy. Edward "Eddie" Miller, son of *Morning Call* publisher Donald P. Miller, recalled how fortunate he was to have been one. "There was usually one older player who had been in the minors forever. The rest of them were just 17-year-old kids but they seemed like gods to me." Miller, then thirteen years old, recalled in particular a visit by Gussie Busch to Breadon Field. He arrived in Allentown by train in his private railroad car. When all the bat boys assembled, Busch asked them what they wanted to drink. "Everybody said 'a Coke' till he got to me. I told him I wanted a Budweiser. I was just kidding of course but that really cracked him up."

However much he may have personally enjoyed his visit to Breadon Field, Busch was beginning to think about the business end of the Allentown Cardinals. "Basically what it boiled down to was they wanted to get out of the real estate business," Dix recalled. "There were taxes to pay and the upkeep on the property began to take its toll."

After some negotiating, it was announced in 1957 that three partners, Lehigh County District Attorney Paul A. McGinley, Brass Rail restaurant owner Philip Sorrentino, and New York attorney A.E. Robert Friedman, had purchased Breadon Field for $180,000. The new occupants of the field were a Boston Red Sox farm team that became the Allentown Red Sox.

Although there had been some concern that the public would be turned off by all the changes at Breadon Field, this was not the case. In the 1958 season almost 80,000 fans showed up to root for the Allentown Red Sox. In 1959 almost 90,000 fans were in attendance. It seemed that whatever ills had plagued local baseball in the early 1950s had been banished.

So it was an understandable shock in 1960 when it was learned that Max Hess, Allentown's prince of merchandising, had purchased Breadon Field for $300,000 and renamed it Max Hess Stadium. Since he was not particularly known as a lover of baseball, why Hess did this has been the subject of much speculation both at that time and since. Hess claimed

Lehigh County broke ground on September 6, 2006, for the new AAA baseball stadium for the home of the Philadelphia Phillies minor-league team, soon to be named the Lehigh Valley Iron Pigs. The photo shows the stadium in February 2008, two months before the scheduled first-pitch. (Lee Butz)

he saw the property as a possible future site for a shopping center. Others felt he feared a rival from outside the area, a national chain perhaps, might see the desirability of putting a store there that would lure the growing suburban market away from his downtown Allentown store.

Whatever the reason, interest in the Allentown Red Sox fell. In 1960 fewer than 50,000 fans attended their games. On December 5, 1960, Tommy Richardson, president of the Eastern League, announced that he had decided to move the team to Johnstown, where it drew over 8,000 spectators on opening night of 1961 in Johnstown.

After 1960 Breadon Field, aka Max Hess Stadium, was never to hear the words "play ball!" again. From 1961 to 1964 the newspapers were filled with accounts of this possible team or that possible team coming to Breadon Field. But none ever did. On May 7, 1964, Hess announced that Breadon Field was to be torn down. He claimed that, despite his best efforts, demands by major league teams for a guaranteed advance sale of 50,000 admissions were a non-starter.

Eventually Hess sold the property for $2.2 million to a developer who went broke. It was not until 1976, long after Max Hess was gone, that what remained of Sam Breadon's field of dreams disappeared under a parking lot.

The day he sold Max Hess Stadium, the department-store owner said there was no longer an interest in minor league baseball in the Lehigh Valley. While this may have been true in 1964, attitudes changed. After several attempts to establish professional baseball teams in the Lehigh Valley over the next several decades, success finally came in the twenty-first century.

On September 6, 2006, ground was broken for the 8,100-seat Coca-Cola Park, the home of the Lehigh Valley IronPigs, the triple A level minor league baseball affiliate of the Philadelphia Phillies. It cost $50.25 million to build. On March 7, 2007, naming rights were awarded to the Coca-Cola Bottling Company of the Lehigh Valley.

Since its completion in 2008, Coca Cola Park has become not only a popular spot for sports fans but for concert goers as well. A 2009 concert with Bob Dylan, Willie Nelson and John Mellencamp sold out to a crowd of over 10,000. With an inspired combination of sports venue and inexpensive outdoor family entertainment, the park's managers have created a success. Somewhere in baseball heaven Sam Breadon is surely smiling.

The Blue Laws

One reason Max Hess might have been concerned about the Breadon Field property had to do with a battle royal that engulfed Lehigh County in the 1950s, '60s and '70s—Pennsylvania's closed-on-Sunday blue laws. Eventually the issue would be taken all the way to the U.S. Supreme Court before finally being settled.

As far back as the eighteenth century, Pennsylvania, like many states, had on its books a law that did not allow buying and selling of items, opening of bars, or gatherings of a non-religious character like going to a play, or later a movie, on the Christian holy day of Sunday.

These so-called blue laws were said to have gotten their name because the laws first appeared in seventeenth-century Puritan Connecticut on blue paper. But no evidence of this has ever been found. It is most likely related to the eighteenth-century use of the word blue, as in "bluenose" for a rigidly moral person. Whatever their origin, they were an assumed part of the American way of life well into the twentieth century.

Hallowed by long tradition, the blue laws were sometimes more honored in the breach than in the observance. In 1940 voters in Allentown overturned a longstanding ban on Sunday movies, and by the 1950s Sunday baseball games had long been an exception. Sales of medicine and food were allowed. Since the laws provided at least one day of rest for workers who might not get one otherwise, Sunday business closings were accepted.

The blue-laws war in Lehigh County began with the opening of the county's first mod-

ern shopping center. "Chain-Store Will Build 7th Street Pike Shop Center," read a headline in *The Morning Call* on June 5, 1957. The anchor store was called "Two Guys From Harrison," a discount chain founded in Harrison, N.J., in 1946 by two brothers, Sidney and Herbert Hubschman. The Lehigh County store was located in Whitehall Township on ninety-four acres between Route 145 and Mickley Road.

To manage the Two Guys store, the Hubschman brothers hired Isadore (Izzy) Klitzner, a native of Slatington and a 1936 graduate of Muhlenberg College,

where he had been drum-major of the college band. Klitzner, who had an antiques business, had moved to Emmaus in 1950 with his family. Previous to running Two Guys, Klitzner was general manager of the Bargain Center in Allentown. His middle son was Chuck Kalan, who was later to have a career in dance and appeared on Broadway in a number of shows, including Fiddler On The Roof. He was also a director, and is now a leading figure in the Lehigh Valley's arts community. Kalan had a unique perspective on the controversy: "I remember when I first went out to the store after it opened. The traffic on MacArthur Road was unreal. Then there were these huge parking lots. In 1957 the Lehigh Valley had never seen anything quite like it."

There was no mention then that the store would be open on Sundays until that October. The immediate reaction of the business, legal, and religious communities was to fight it. The Greater Allentown Council of Churches asked public officials to enforce the Sunday-closing laws.

On the legal front, Irving W. Coleman, an Allentown attorney who happened to be Max Hess's lawyer, was also the owner of 100 shares of Two Guys stock. As a stock owner, Coleman said that by being open on Sundays the company was risking his investment. He urged local officials to enforce the closing laws.

As that suit was winding its way through the federal district court in Philadelphia, Hess dropped another bombshell on December 2. He said that he was going to open Hess's for three Sundays in December for the Christmas season. Zollinger-Harned's department store and Koch Brothers men's-wear store said they would also open on those Sundays; John Henry Leh II, owner of Leh's, said he was "studying the matter."

The religious community acted. Rev. Arthur Sherman, pastor of Allentown's Episcopal Church of the Mediator and president of the Council of Churches, promised a protest march to city hall. More of a visit than an actual protest, it included clergy representatives of the Protestant, Catholic, and Jewish faiths. Both verbally and in writing they stated their opposition to Sunday sales. They received support from Lehigh County District Attorney Paul A. McGinley, who said failure to uphold the blue laws would lead to a "moral break-down." He noted that "the public apparently wants existing law governing the sanctity of the Sabbath to be enforced. My duty as district attorney is not to determine whether the laws are good or bad but to enforce them."

In coordination with the state and Northampton County, arrests of blue-laws violators began. On December 8, 1957, 111 violators, 76 of them Two Guys clerks, were arrested. In Northampton County, eight employees of the Bargain Center in Freemansburg were also arrested. Those taken into custody did not go quietly. Detectives were met with shouts of "storm-trooper" and "Gestapo" as they led them away.

Among those arrested was store manager Klitzer. "Suddenly we were being told 'Daddy's in jail,'" Kalan recalled. "As a kid I could not believe it." Two Guys attorneys Morris Efron and George Joseph promised to fight the charges, which they called unfair. Kalan recalls the arrests of his father as almost a weekend ritual. "I remember how every weekend my father would get arrested and how George Joseph, who as a kid I was told to call "Uncle George," would come down to the prison to bail him out and they would go out to have cup of coffee together."

Raised in an Orthodox Jewish household, Kalan recalls looking at the whole blue-laws controversy from a different religious window. "As a child I found it strange that nobody ever tried to arrest my father when he got dressed and went out to run the store on Saturday, his religious holiday. It was only on Sunday."

Kalan's father left Two Guys in late 1959 to take a job as general manager of a discount store in suburban Philadelphia. In 1960 Joseph was placed in a position where he would have to start enforcing the blue laws when he took office as Lehigh County District Attorney, a post he held until his death in 1976.

Court cases continued. In the spring of 1958, Lehigh County Court Judge James F. Henninger upheld the ban on Sunday sales. That fall the state Superior Court agreed but issued a restraining order on arrests. A week later the issue was back in federal district court, which concurred with the Superior Court decision but lifted the restraining order, allowing arrests to begin again.

Hoping to clear up the matter, the state legislature passed a law in 1959 naming the items that could not be sold on Sunday. They included "clothing, jewelry, silverware, watches, clocks, luggage, furniture, housewares, home and office furnishings, household and office appliances, musical instruments, recordings, toys, building and lumber supply materials, tools, paints and hardware."

Despite the legislature's good intentions, the new law raised more questions than it answered. Failure to explain why some items had been banned and others had not led to questions about what sort of logic had been used to create it. The arrests continued.

On May 30, 1961, it appeared a final resolution had been reached. That day the U.S. Supreme Court decided, by a vote of 8 to 1, that a state had it in its power "to provide a weekly respite for all labor." The blue laws of Pennsylvania, Maryland, and Massachusetts were legal. "It was my baby from the beginning," said then-former District Attorney McGinley, "and I am delighted with the result."

But there are some things even an 8-1 decision by the U.S. Supreme Court cannot stop. Apparently the desire of American shoppers to shop any day they please, and the willingness of merchants to encourage them to do so by being open had become one of them.

As the 1960s progressed and more and more businesses defied them, blue laws were gradually becoming impossible to enforce. The public had become accustomed to shopping on Sundays and would go to a store that was open, resulting in a loss of business for those that were not.

In 1967 the state police informed Whitehall Township's commissioners that they could no longer enforce the blue laws and that the township would have to do so on its own. In 1976, when the Lehigh Valley Mall opened, a group of clergy and lay people attempted to enforce the blue laws. The response of the mall's manager was that it would be impossible. "The stores are filled to capacity on Sunday," he said.

In 1978, recognizing reality, the Pennsylvania Supreme Court decided by a vote of 5 to 2 that the blue laws were now so "riddled with exception after exception" as to be unenforceable and unconstitutional. In 1992 Irving Coleman, who had been there when the blue-laws battle began, agreed. "The laws were antiquated and no longer made any sense," he said.

The disposal of the blue laws into history's waste can was a small reflection of the changes gripping Lehigh County in the 1960s. The growth of housing developments around Allentown that began in the 1950s had accelerated at a terrific pace. The once-clear dividing lines between country and city were becoming blurred. Before 1957 no one would have thought of trying to build a shopping center like the one that developed around Two Guys From Harrison. The population pressure from the growing suburbs and the presence of new highways like Route 22 opened up the region to more and more development.

Shopping Malls

After the success of Two Guys, the arrival on the scene of the Whitehall Mall in 1965 was inevitable. This was the first indoor mall in Pennsylvania north of Philadelphia. The project first emerged publicly in January, 1963. Donnelly & Suess, a Philadelphia realty firm, announced its plans to build a mall, something of which many in Lehigh County were only vaguely aware, on forty-seven acres of farmland just north of Allentown on MacArthur Road.

For most, shopping meant going to shops on their closest town's main street, to one of the new multi-store shopping centers such as at Mountainville, Parkway Shopping Center, and Airport Plaza, or to Hamilton Street in Allentown. Now they were being promised a totally enclosed shopping space that would include shops, a supermarket, and a movie theater. There would be no need to fight for on-street parking. The mall would be sur-

rounded by huge parking lots designed to aid what were called "directional shoppers," that is, those who liked to see the store they were going to as they parked. Most importantly, it would be free of the tyranny of the weather. One would be able to shop in heated comfort in the winter and air-conditioned relief in the summer.

Despite the complaints of a few neighbors who were concerned about traffic, almost everyone hailed it as the wonder of the age. On April 12, 1965, with the last t crossed and the last i dotted, it was time for the groundbreaking. Readers of the *Evening Chronicle* were offered a unique picture of the day. Wielding a five-handled shovel, Leonard Mercer, vice president of Donnelly & Suess, Donald Vollmer, president of Zollinger-Harned department store, Charles Raab, general manager for Sears Roebuck in the Lehigh Valley, Whitehall Township Board of Commissioners President Arthur Wieand, and Allentown Mayor F. Willard Harper did the honors. At the conclusion of the ceremony, Commissioner Wieand and Mayor Harper joked over whether Whitehall had annexed Allentown or vice versa.

To judge from the article that accompanied the picture, few people at the time thought the new mall would have any real impact on Hamilton Street's status as the shopping mecca of the region. Vollmer, whose main store in the 600 block of Hamilton Street had been a fixture there since 1909, could not have expressed it more strongly: "Let me point out as emphatically as I can that we have no intention of closing our Hamilton Street store. We believe the growing economy of the Lehigh Valley will warrant two stores. In addition, I ask you to look at Zollinger-Harned's rapid growth over recent years. That growth demands expansion."

It was over a year before the Whitehall Mall opened. Zollinger's opened its store ahead of the rest on August 15, 1966. *The Morning Call* estimated that 25,000 shoppers jammed its aisles that day. It created such a traffic jam that Whitehall Township's police chief suggested shoppers try alternate routes. The mall's official opening on September 26, 1966, was if anything even more busy. The words "modern" and "futuristic" were used

In 1972– 73 the Hamilton Mall was built. Canopies placed over the widened sidewalks. (Lehigh County Historical Society)

repeatedly by both *The Morning Call* and the *Evening Chronicle* to describe it. Shoppers would be able to see "wildly creative and colorful lighting fixtures, stately fountains, tropical plants, cages with several varieties of exotic birds, disappearing store fronts and architectural forms." They were even reminded that the planters were modeled on those at the 1958 World's Fair in Brussels.

As a band called Kal's Kids played in the background, mall manager Mercer told the press what he had planned: "You know, I treat this thing as a Broadway production. It's something you've got to constantly promote and give tenants action at all times. We're going to run it as a gala. The mall will be open 24 hours a day, seven days a week, except an hour or so now and then while changes are being made. But it's big enough so that people can be in one end while they are cleaning up or making changes in the other."

It is not known what Max Hess, Jr., Allentown's prince of merchandising, must have thought when he read those words in the newspaper. Whether he intended it or not, however, Mercer sounded like he was issuing a challenge. Two years later, Hess would sell his store to businessman Philip I. Berman, who would begin an expansion that took Hess's into the malls.

At first the Whitehall Mall attracted huge crowds. Gradually it began to fade, and when the nearby Lehigh Valley Mall opened in 1976 it put its elder sister in the shade. The fountains were turned off, the exotic birds were removed, and the teenagers who came to hear Kal's Kids went elsewhere. By the 1980s the Whitehall Mall had become popular with senior citizens who appreciated the fact that they could walk about in a climate-controlled setting without a lot of crowds.

Hamilton Mall

In 1998 the Whitehall Mall was unenclosed. Without the cost of heating and lighting the vast public spaces, the stores there were once more economically viable— but all that was far in the unknown future in 1965. As supremely confident as Donald Vollmer of Zollinger-Harned was about the future success of his store, it is difficult to imagine that many of the Hamilton Street merchants of the day were convinced of his vision of what

Hamilton Mall in 1973, with widened sidewalks covered by canopies and one-way traffic eastbound.
The Zollinger-Harned department store, now on the National Register of Historic Places, is on the right.
(William Zwikl photograph; Lehigh County Historical Society)

the future might hold. By the late 1960s their concerns were realized. Allentown Mayor Clifford "Chips" Bartholomew noted in 1970 that Hamilton Street merchants had once paid fourteen percent of the city's taxes, and now paid only eleven percent. "This cannot continue," he added. Other civic boosters decried the fact that Mack Trucks' new World Headquarters, which opened on April 28, 1970, had been built on the city's suburban south side rather than downtown, where it could have added shoppers who would help merchants and increase tax revenues.

The county's largest city needed to act, and it did. Experts were contacted and studies created. Among the first appeared in 1969. Put together by David M. Walker Associates, a Philadelphia firm, it put its emphasis on the city's traffic patterns. Despite the fact that there were many parking lots in Allentown, they argued that traffic moved too slowly. In one memorable line, they described the route on Hamilton Street as taking "ten tedious driving minutes." Their suggestion was a tunnel under the monument at Center Square. Another proposal was the virtual rebuilding of part of the street's historical and eclectic buildings with something called "superblocks." Two were to be built on opposite sides of the 700 block of Hamilton and the third was to cover the south side of the 900 block. It would have brought almost 800,000 square feet of new office space, parking decks for 1,750 cars, and 380,000 square feet of new retail space along with an enclosed retail mall.

To say the Walker plan was ambitious is an understatement. It was far more than the

Tearing up Hamilton Street when the sidewalks and canopies were removed in 1997, looking southwest from the 800 block. (Carol M. Front)

business or political leadership of the city was ready to accept. Parts of it—the tunnel under the monument and the superblocks with the enclosed mall—were rejected.

One recommendation that survived was the creation of canopies over sidewalks. This, the report suggested, would encourage pedestrian traffic. The point was brought home forcefully on October 23, 1970, when an overflow crowd gathered at the Allentown Art Museum to hear Bernard Rudofsky, an Austrian-born architect from New York and author of a recent (1969) book "Streets for People." His original, thought-provoking ideas on design for everything from buildings to sandals had attracted a wide following.

At that point Hamilton Mall, as it came to be called, was still on the drawing boards. Rudosky refused to comment on something he had not seen. But he was willing to comment on what he thought was a general problem with urban design in America. He noted that the pedestrian always seemed an afterthought, in the way of the "all-powerful" automobile. "The street lives and dies with the people who inhabit it," he said that evening.

In the spring of 1971, plans for the new Hamilton Mall were unveiled to the public. The *Sunday Call-Chronicle* featured an artist's rendering of the proposed canopies, showing bushy-mustached men in aviator glasses greeting women in hip-hugging, bell-bottomed pants as they crossed under a canopy. It was hip, with-it architecture for a new hip, with-it generation.

Work on the first canopies began on August 8, 1971. For the next two years Hamilton Street was one large construction project. Photos from the time show it reduced to dirt and pipes. Dump trucks rumbled up and down and front-end loaders were busy moving piles of dirt from one place to another. Among the victims was the Hess's department store sign, Max Hess's pride and joy, the largest retail-store sign between New York and Chicago. On June 30, 1972, the Simpson Sign Company of Croydon, Bucks County, began taking down the iconic sign. It was cut into pieces. On July 1, 1972, a photo of the sign's badly battered letter H, deposited at the Sussman scrap yard, appeared in *The Morning Call*.

By the summer of 1973 the mall project was largely finished. It was dedicated on November 10, with Governor Milton Shapp on hand to watch and make a few remarks. The Allentown Band played selections from Hello Dolly, The Music Man, and Sounds of the Carpenters. City Council President Charles Snelling remarked that Allentown had realized a dream "that would make itself well and whole for the next century." Then, with a strong wind whipping the air to an unseasonable wind-chill temperature of twelve degrees, everybody went inside.

The Hamilton Mall seemed to revive the city's downtown, at least for a time. An event called Super Sunday, with activities up and down the mall, added to the spirit of revival for a few years. But by the late 1980s, what had seemed modern and "with it" in the 1970s had come to look dowdy and dated. A writer for the *Philadelphia Inquirer* described the canopies in a 1988 article as resembling oil drums that had been cut in two. Their clear coverings had become dirty and dingy despite the best efforts to clean them and, instead of offering protection from the elements, water dripped on those they were supposed to be protecting. They finally were removed in the late 1990s, with almost no sign that they had ever existed.

CHAPTER SIX

LEHIGH COUNTY: TODAY AND TOMORROW

By the 1970s Lehigh County was confronting many challenges. From a population of 177,533 in 1940 it had exploded to 255,304 a mere thirty years later. The clearly defined separation of city and small towns and farms that greeted the returning World War II GI had either disappeared or was fast disappearing.

Sprawling housing developments and shopping centers had started to suburbanize the once-agricultural townships, eventually growing more asphalt than corn. By the late 1970s the loss of farmland to housing developments, exurban shopping centers, and industry was attracting critical attention. A sewer interceptor designed to carry domestic and industrial wastewater from western Lehigh County to the Kline's Island wastewater treatment plant in Allentown would accelerate the change.

The Schaefer brewery and the Kraft plant, both off rural Route 100 near Fogelsville, were immediate beneficiaries of the sewer line. Village crossroads that had been largely passed by in the railroad era (and, thanks to the automobile, in the 1920s had sprouted a gas station with a couple of pumps) were becoming centers of population.

The city (in the case of Lehigh County this primarily meant Allentown) was not immune to the changes sweeping the region. Although scorned by 1940s intellectuals as a "monotonous red brick city," lacking the assumed character of a highly idealized countryside, for well over a century Allentown had been the economic agent that had given Lehigh County residents industrial jobs, a way of life that kept the region thriving. By the 1970s, the image of the city was changing rapidly. The largely homogeneous demography of Allentown, white northern Europeans and their descendants, together with a smattering of eastern Europeans and Italians and a very small number of African Americans, was beginning to undergo a sea change that continues to this day.

Immigrants from Latin America, at first from the U.S. territory of Puerto Rico and later from other Spanish-speaking lands in Central and South America, came to Lehigh County seeking jobs and a better way of life for themselves and their children. In 1972, the enrollment of Latino students in Allentown schools was five percent of the total; this became 15.2 percent by 1985. Today, in 2012, it is 64.4 percent.

In 1988 Lillian Suarez, an Allentown native of German-American heritage, recalled that in 1950, when she married her husband, Puerto Rican-born Francisco Fuentes Suarez, there were almost no Puerto Ricans in the region. "I think back in the late 1940s there must have been about 16 to 20 Puerto Ricans in the whole Allentown-Bethlehem area," she recalled. Although her husband was a skilled furniture maker, the only job where he could find work was as a laborer at Bethlehem Steel. "They were one of the few places that would hire Puerto Ricans at the time."

This began to change starting in 1952. That year Suarez's husband was used by the Allentown police to translate for them following a scuffle between three Puerto Rican brothers, none of whom spoke English. He began to be called in more frequently throughout the decade by the police. This inspired Suarez, in 1958, to create the Puerto-Rican American Cultural Society to foster better relations among Latinos and whites.

According to former Muhlenberg College history professor Anna Adams, whose 2004 book *Hidden From History: The Latino Community of Allentown, Pennsylvania* is the first work to study the subject in any depth, the industrialization drive of Operation Bootstrap in Puerto Rico in the 1950s drove many agricultural workers off the island and to the farm fields of the Lehigh Valley. Adams cites a newspaper story from the 1950s quoting Frank Mohr of Mohr Orchards saying what good workers Latinos were.

At the same time, older white residents of the city, their children having fled to the suburbs, were confronted with big, empty houses which they began to convert into apartments to rent out to newcomers. By the late 1970s, when many older property owners decided to sell, their homes were acquired by absentee landlords who in some cases did not have the time or interest to maintain the property as well as those who had actually lived there.

Today, many of the descendants of the first Latino immigrants have become established outside of Allentown, and a Spanish surname in Lower Macungie Township does not draw the reaction of surprise that it did thirty years ago.

Latinos are far from alone. Immigrants from Asia, Africa, the Indian Subcontinent, and the Middle East have made their homes in Lehigh County in recent decades, many of them coming to work in high-tech industries in western Lehigh County. They and their descendants represent the continually changing ethnic mix and religious diversity of county residents.

Home Rule

In the 1970s Lehigh County became the first county in the state to adopt a Home Rule Charter that allowed it to govern itself. The new charter totally altered the board of county commissioners, the principal administrative body in county government.

The office of county commissioner in Pennsylvania dates to the colonial era. It grew out of the Court of Quarter Sessions, the primary county governmental body of colonial Pennsylvania. Created by William Penn in his Frame of Government of 1682 for the first three counties of Chester, Bucks, and Philadelphia, it was based on a similar English institution that dated to 1388. The court met four times a year at the county seat to administer justice and perform non-judicial functions that included levying taxes, authorizing construction and maintenance of roads and bridges, and issuing tavern licenses. From its beginnings, and perhaps due to the vast distances and unsettled nature of the country it had to administer, the court found it difficult to efficiently perform its combined judicial and administrative responsibilities.

The office of county commissioner was originally created by statute in 1711 to help the court oversee tax collections. In 1722 and 1725, laws were passed making the office permanent, providing for three commissioners in each county, and giving them a term of three years. Although mentioned in Pennsylvania's Constitution of 1776, it was not until the Constitution of 1873 that the office of county commissioner achieved full constitutional status. The requirement that one of the three commissioners be of the minority party was, after much debate at the state constitutional convention of 1873, incorporated into the 1873 Constitution. But by the early 1900s, Progressive-era reformers were complaining that this attempt at checks and balances of power was largely circumvented by the majority party commissioners who used their influence to see to it that the minority party member was someone they could rely on to vote their way. The state's voters passed a constitutional amendment on November 2, 1909, to change the three-year term to four years.

Under the state's county code, the three county commissioners held both executive and legislative functions. They could draw up the budget and pass it themselves. A quorum of two commissioners was all that was needed to hold a meeting. A simple and uncomplicated process, it met the needs of the farmers and small-town residents of Lehigh County in the late nineteenth and early twentieth centuries.

By the 1970s, with more people than ever to legislate for, and more federal and state money to allocate and mandates to implement, concerns were expressed about so much power in so few hands. With the commissioners' ability to conduct business behind closed doors, the potential for abuse of power was clear.

On May 12, 1974, while the Watergate scandal that focused on abuse of governmental power in Washington D.C. was at its height, voters of Lehigh County approved the formation of a Government Study Commission to look into changes in county government. The eleven members elected to the study commission, six men and five women, were Barbara Benner, Allentown; Judith Ruhe Diehl, Lower Macungie Township; Austin Gavin, Upper Milford Township; Mary S. Jackson, Allentown; Bernadette Kuebler, Allentown; Emmaline K. Mohr,

Allentown; Gerald L Roth, Allentown; Morton Schneider, Allentown; Louis W. Wasser, Allentown; Wallace C. Worth, Upper Milford Township; and Robert K. Young, Upper Milford Township.

Gavin, a former executive with PPL and then on the administrative staff of Lehigh University, was chosen as chairman. The other commissioners had played prominent roles in the county's political and civic life. Some had held public office: Wasser had been Lehigh County Controller for thirty-six years, and Worth had served one and a half years as first assistant district attorney of Lehigh County. Young had been a solicitor for several municipalities and was then chairman of the Lehigh-Northampton Counties Joint Planning Commission. Benner and Mohr listed themselves as "active in the Republican Party," and Jackson and Roth called themselves "active in the Democratic Party." The others had served as volunteers in a variety of civic organizations.

In the process of creating the Home Rule Charter they were aided by local legal scholars such as attorney John Ashcraft III, who advised them throughout the process. Under a 1972 state law titled Act 62, the members of the study commission had three options. One was the Executive-Council Plan. This consisted of an elected county legislature and an elected executive. Another was the Council-Manager plan, an elected council that would hire a county manager. The third was adoption of a Home Rule Charter. This would allow the county, within certain restrictions defined by Act 62, to draw up its own plan. "By granting home rule the state is saying 'I have enough to do taking care of my business. You, the county, tend to your own business,' " was how the commission's pamphlet, *Report of the Lehigh County Government Study Commission*, described it for the average voter.

The study commission began by taking testimony of county officials. It also conducted ninety-two public meetings around the county to get input from citizens. "We estimate that the Study Commission expended approximately 5,000 man hours on the study," the report stated.

That the work on the Home Rule Charter was extremely important to the county's future could not be denied. Yet, in its edition of April 30, 1975, *The Morning Call* reported that just six people showed up for the commission's first public meeting the night before in West Bethlehem, at Nitschmann Junior High School. "The apathy demonstrated last night by West Bethlehem residents had many people wondering if it is an indication of the reception awaiting them at the rest of the public gatherings." Perhaps the public's reaction was less apathy than having something else on their mind. That evening, television was dominated by special reports showing the last helicopters leaving the roof of the U.S. Embassy in Saigon as South Vietnam fell to North Vietnam, ending a war that had deeply divided the nation for over a decade. Many subsequent meetings were well attended.

That summer, the study commission announced it had decided to ask Lehigh County voters to support a home rule charter plan. The crux of it would be the establishment of separate executive and legislative branches of county government. The chief reason for coming to this conclusion was the absence of checks and balances in the three-commissioner system. The study commission called it incompatible with the country's democratic traditions:

> Our federal constitution and all of our state constitutions are based on the principle of separation of powers and the system of checks and balances that go with it.
>
> Under the system of checks and balances each of the three branches of government—legislative, executive and judicial—serves as a check to the other. Each is looking over the shoulder and blowing the whistle when it appears that something is wrong in another branch.
>
> Our recent experience, at all levels of government, demonstrates the desirability of such a system. When legislative and the executive function is being exercised by the same people, as is the case in the present county government, there is likely to be less efficiency, less economy and less accountability than when the functions are separated.

The study commission noted that Lehigh County government was "now a $30 million operation and growing larger each year." Yet it was operating on a system devised when Pennsylvania was a colony ruled by the sons of William Penn. In conclusion, the study commission stated, the "three commissioner form of government is antiquated and not suited to modern times."

The Home Rule Charter drawn up by the study commission created a nine-member legislative body for the county. Five commissioners were to be elected from districts, the other four would be elected at large. All would be elected to four-year terms, staggered so that some were elected every two years. One county executive, elected to a four-year term, would have the executive duties, like proposing a budget, heretofore wielded by the three-member commission. The budget would then be sent on to the commission for hearings and a vote. "With one head, there is no question who is responsible," the study commissioners said.

One of the reasons the study commission gave for adopting the Home Rule Charter option was that it allocated to the county actions that previously were in the hands of the state legislature. Their report to the public outlined what they thought were the most important:

1.   There is a provision for initiative, under which the voters can compel the County legislature to adopt some proposed legislation. There is a provision for referendum under which voters can veto legislation adopted by the County legislature. The citizens of Lehigh County do not have either of these powers at present.

2.   The County legislators would not be able to increase their salary without voter approval.

3.   There is a provision in the Charter preventing the County government from taking any power being exercised by a township, borough or city without the consent of the township, borough or city. There is no such protection under the present government.

Although far from activists of the era in their thinking, the members of the study commission proposed changes that reflected the most popular slogan of radicals of the day, "power to the people." The purpose of adopting the Home Rule Charter was, the report said, "to move some of the power from the state legislature to the County legislature, that is, closer to the people of the county." The cure for the ills of democracy was to be more democracy.

The study commission preferred the flexibility of a Home Rule Charter because it allowed the retention of the elected row-office system, something that could not have been done if the county adopted one of the other forms of government offered in Act 62. Once again, the stated reason of the study commission was a belief in the democratic process: "The continued election of most of the row offices makes those officers directly accountable and answerable to the voters." Members of the commission believed that asking voters to eliminate the elected row officers may have been too much to ask. They all recognized that, with the exception of the District Attorney and the Coroner, all of the row offices were administrative jobs with no actual accountability to the general public. Row officers, however, had considerable political connections and the study commission members concluded that their opposition to a new form of government that removed them from elective office may have scuttled the entire Home Rule proposal.

The changes in the county row-office structure that the commissioners recommended were few. Their recommendation was to "eliminate the election of the Treasurer and Jury Commissioners since these offices are mainly routine and to combine the position of Prothonotary and the Clerk of Courts into one elective office." Both offices were among the oldest in the state. The title "Prothonotary" was rooted in a Greek word meaning "first scribe," a record-keeping official of the courts of the Greek-speaking Eastern Roman or Byzantine

Big Wheels Keep On Turning: Lehigh County's Velodrome Began As Bob Rodale's Dream

Fifty years ago most Americans were clear on at least one thing, bicycles were for kids. You got the one with training wheels when you were six. Somewhere around age sixteen or seventeen you got the permit, the license, and then the car. Adults who rode bicycles after that were considered a little weird, like people who didn't smoke or own a TV, wore socks with sandals, and ate granola. And wasn't bicycle racing as a sport something no real American had taken seriously since about 1916?

That was before 1967, when Bob Rodale took a trip to Winnipeg, Canada, to participate in the Pan-American Games as a skeet-shooter, was housed with a bunch of cyclists, and fell in love with their sport. "I noticed then what a beautiful sport bicycle racing is," he told *Evening Chronicle* sports writer Jack Lapos on his return. "Almost like a dance." A year later, he purchased thirty-three acres of land west of Trexlertown from Allentown's St John's Lutheran Church. Part of his reason was to give enough space to protect the nearby skeet range on which he often practiced, but there were other reasons. "Bob came to me one day and said, 'You know what we're going to do with the rest of that land? We're going to build a velodrome,' " recalled his wife Ardath in 1996. "I said, 'you must be kidding!' I didn't really know what a velodrome was."

Quietly, Rodale followed his dream. He went to Rome to look at what he had heard was the best velodrome in the world, and exchanged plans with his brother-in-law James Harter, an architect. For the next five years Rodale fought an uphill battle. Finally, on June 20, 1974, the Upper Macungie Township planners recommended approved of a velodrome.

The Rodales used $100,000 of their own money for excavation. Then Lehigh County stepped in and agreed to pay to complete the velodrome if Rodale staffed it. Twenty-four acres were donated to the county; the rest was retained by Rodale. When finished, it was the first velodrome in Pennsylvania, the third in the eastern United States, and the eleventh in the country.

The velodrome was proving to be a magnet even before opening day on October 12, 1975. Lehigh County Recreation Director John Honochick said, "A lot of people are coming in now and using it without authorization; and while it's practically completed, there is still work going on. If somebody gets hurt, he wouldn't be covered by insurance."

Clearly something had already changed in regard to bicycle racing. Primarily it was the new interest in health and fitness that the baby boom generation and publications produced by Rodale Press had spawned. If not quite mainstream, bicycle riding was emerging from its stigma of something only children did.

On opening day more than 100 bicyclists were on hand. There was nothing but praise for the new facility. Bill Lambert, chairman of the Board of Control of the U.S. Cycling Federation, said "it is one of, if not the best in the U.S."

Today the velodrome is part of the Bob Rodale Cycling and Fitness Park and is known as the Valley Preferred Cycling Center. It is as much a Lehigh County institution as Trexlertown resident and Olympic gold-medal winner cyclist Marty Nothstein, who trained there and is now its executive director—proof, if any more was needed, that bicycles are not just for kids.

(Rodale Press)

231

Empire. It is also used by clerics of the Roman Catholic Church who administer the church's governing statutes known as the Canon Law.

On hearing the word Prothonotary for the first time in Pittsburgh in 1948, President Harry Truman, who later called it the most impressive-sounding political title in the U.S., blurted out, "What the hell is a prothonotary?" The title appeared in Pennsylvania for the first time in 1707, applied to the chief record keeper of the county courts, the officer responsible for maintaining the records of the civil division of what is now the court of common pleas in each judicial district.

The roots of the office of Clerk of Courts go even further back in Pennsylvania history. The Pennsylvania Historical and Museum Commission (PHMC) notes on its website that "it is mentioned in the Duke of York's Book of Laws, under which the area later known as Pennsylvania was governed from 1664 to 1681, as the 'Clerk of the Court of Sessions.'" In those early days, the Clerk of Courts had administrative powers that included recording bonded servants, calling juries, and administering wills. When William Penn created the first counties under his 1682 Frame of Government, those functions were incorporated into the county court system. In time, the PHMC notes, the clerk's duties evolved to resemble more closely those of the modern-day clerk of courts.

The study commission also recommended that the clerk of the Orphans Court, who maintains the records of that judicial body, be appointed by the court instead of being a part of the Register of Wills office. The Register of Wills would continue to be elected and no changes would be made in the other row offices—District Attorney, Controller, Sheriff, Recorder of Deeds, and County Coroner. The only major modification of this system in Lehigh County occurred in 2008, when voters approved a charter amendment to subsume the duties of Clerk of Courts, Prothonotary, Recorder of Deeds, and Register of Wills into the new office of Clerk of Judicial Records.

On November 4, 1975, election day, Lehigh County voters had the following ballot question before them: "Shall the Home Rule Charter contained in the report dated August 26, 1975 of the Government Study Commission, prepared in accordance with the Home Rule Charter and Optional Plans Law, be adopted by the County of Lehigh."

By a greater than 2-1 margin, a vote of 31,201 to 12,499, the electorate chose to support the Home Rule Charter. *The Morning Call* the next day said the size of the victory margin "caught everyone by surprise." Lehigh County, traditionally considered archly conservative because of its Pennsylvania-German background, had become the first in the state to adopt Home Rule. Delaware County had changed its form of government, but opted for something other than home rule.

Expressing his pleasure and that of the whole study commission at the result, former

chairman Austin Gavin reminded the press that there still was a lot of work to do before the new form of government became reality on January 1, 1978. The three sitting commissioners, three members of the study group, and three voters selected by the study group would form a transition team. The team would draw up an administrative code, specify how the county departments would operate, and create a personnel code that would deal with ethics and conflict-of-interest questions.

In 1977 county voters would select six new commissioners who would replace the non-elected members of the transition team. When they took office in 1978 they would join the three existing commissioners, thus creating a board of nine as the Home Rule Charter required.

The three commissioners elected in 1975 would serve until the end of their four-year terms. Whereas the 1975 commissioners would continue to draw the $20,000-a-year salary they had received under the old plan, the newly elected commissioners that came in with home rule would receive part-time pay of $2,500 a year.

Not until January 1978, following the election in November 1977 of David K. Bausch as the first Lehigh County executive under the Home Rule Charter, did the new form of government begin to function as intended. Bausch, a Republican, was one of the three commissioners elected in 1975; the other two were Democrats Charles J. Kistler and J. Raymond Cramsey.

Bausch was the son of Dr. Elmer Bausch, a well-known local physician who had helped bring into the world many of Lehigh County's residents. Dave Bausch, as he was familiarly known, had long had a special interest in the health-care field. A former administrator of the Quakertown Hospital, in 1975 he was administrator of Cedarbrook Home and Hospital, the county's home for the elderly, whose roots went back to the County Home founded in the 1830s. The voters seemed to like Bausch. He was a popular figure who would serve as county executive for fourteen years, and in 2011 is still active in local politics.

Among the accomplishments during the first 100 days under Home Rule were the opening of Cedar View Apartments, a ten-story residential highrise for seniors and physically challenged adults near the county's Cedarbrook Nursing Home; progress on the county's new administrative and personnel code; and weekly press conferences.

A lot has happened since 1978 with Lehigh County's going to Home Rule. Bill Hansell began his involvement in local government as the first manager of the borough of Catasauqua in 1964, helped create the Home Rule Charter for Northampton County in 1976, and was involved on the national level with state and county management with the Pennsylvania League of Cities and as director of the International City/County Management Association. He recently finished a term as Lehigh County Commissioner and has observed the Home Rule process in action up close over the last thirty-plus years. Hansell made the following comments:

"Bausch, as the first county executive, really set the tone of a bipartisan working relationship between the commission and the county executive. It really seems like it depends on how they want to work together. Some of the executives have been very forthcoming in working with the commission. Others have held things close to the chest and refused to share. But what you have here are two co-equal branches of government and whenever you have that you are going to have to have tensions.

"Over the past few years, and particularly with the last election [November 2011], you have had a lot of hot rhetoric. I think the system is such that after a while that will die down and they will see that cooperation is the only way to make the system work as it was planned."

American Bicentennial

It was just by chance that these changes in Lehigh County's form of government were taking place at the same time as the nation was getting ready to celebrate its 200th birthday.

Lehigh County's Bicentennial Committee was established in 1971. Scott A. Trexler, who had long been active in Lehigh County historical circles, was its first chairman. His son, Scott A. Trexler II, who also had a passion for local history, had tragically died young in 1965. The LCHS research library was named for him.

In April 1973, Trexler became honorary chairman and William J. Albert of Catasauqua accepted the active role of chairman. A local businessman whose family roots in the Lehigh Valley went back to the eighteenth century and who had an ancestor in the American Revolution, Albert was then chairman of the Lehigh Valley Tourist Bureau.

In 1974, an executive committee was created to oversee the day-to-day running of the county's programs. Albert and co-chairman Eleanor Leh of Allentown, wife of John Henry Leh, whose family owned a longtime department store in the community, headed the executive committee. Mrs. Leh was very active in the Lehigh County Historical Society's Ladies Guild.

In March 1974, Lehigh County received approval from the Pennsylvania State Bicenten-

nial Commission for its programs. In August, the Lehigh County committee got word that they would receive $97,100 from the state commission for local events.

The Lehigh County committee encouraged and coordinated local events. To keep up the momentum, Albert's committee visited every community with a Bicentennial Road Show during 1975. By the end of 1976, over 200 Bicentennial-related programs and "happenings" had taken place. "Our goal was to have every one of the county's political subdivisions become a Bicentennial Community," Albert said. "By 1976, we had 100 percent participation in the county of Lehigh."

Several Lehigh County townships took the opportunity of the Bicentennial to write local histories. Among the most detailed were those done by North Whitehall and Lower Macungie. Under the title *The Early History of North Whitehall Township*, Joseph J. Hartman, Gladys Lutz, and Alice Lutz put together a detailed account of the period from the country's founding. It included family histories and a section on the township's historic homes. The Lower Macungie volume was researched and written by Craig and Ann Bartholomew, Tom Sipos, and Jim Stine. Their work, *A History of Lower Macungie Township*, focused on the life of the Pennsylvania-German farmers whose ancestors were the first European settlers of the township. In the thirty-six years since it was written, Lower Macungie's population has undergone explosive growth, with housing developments replacing farm fields. The 1976 history thus chronicles a way of life that is rapidly passing out of existence.

Other local histories published during the Bicentennial include *Upper Saucon: A Bicentennial Tribute 1743–1976*, published by the Upper Saucon Township Bicentennial Committee; South Whitehall's *South Whitehall Then and Now 1776–1976*,

Ticket for the Bicentennial multi-media show in Alburtis, produced by husband–wife team of Scott Stoneback and Francee Fuller. Using slides and a live cast of people, the show traced the history of the United States and Alburtis. The background is an actual ticket for the Catasauqua and Fogelsville Railroad.

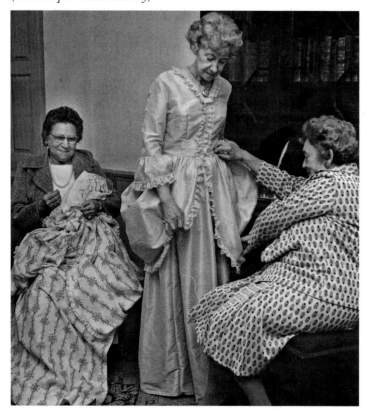

Volunteers working on colonial-style dresses for events at the George Taylor mansion, the Catasauqua home of a signer of the Declaration of Independence, during the Bicentennial. Dorothy Fullager is being fitted. (Catasauqua Public Library)

edited by noted folklorist and local historian Paul Wieand; *History of Weisenberg Township*, written by the Weisenberg Township Bicentennial Historical Committee; *Whitehall Commemorative Booklet 1730–1976*, compiled by the township's Commemorative Committee. The committees preparing these and other books and booklets published in 1976 have in common their efforts to speak with innumerable residents, and to record facts, photos, and memories before another generation died.

Events held throughout the county in the various boroughs and townships were historical tours, theatrical presentations, antique shows, old-fashioned picnics, parades, and fireworks. The biggest parade, by far, was the Lehigh County Bicentennial Committee's Grand Parade in Allentown on May 23, at which each bicentennial committee in Lehigh County was represented. A huge dinner dance was later held at Castle Garden, Dorney Park's popular dance hall, with many participants dressed in colonial costume. It was not at all uncommon during that Bicentennial summer to see local folks turn out for events dressed as close as they could to eighteenth-century attire.

Among the events in the planning stages in 1975 were a contest for designing a county logo, a contest for writing a county bicentennial theme song, and dedications of three industrial history museums. County Commissioner Donald Hoffman, an avid historian, was the force behind the museums, which commemorate forgotten but significant aspects of county history. At the Lock Ridge Furnace Museum in Alburtis, the county's leading role in the American industrial revolution through its extensive iron industry is interpreted. At Saylor Park in Coplay, early-generation cement kilns became the centerpiece of a museum marking the development of Portland cement at Coplay in the 1860s. Also under Hoffman's leadership, the county restored Haines Mill, a steam- and turbine-driven roller mill downstream from Dorney Park, and opened it as a museum during the Bicentennial celebrations.

The Northamptontowne Militia at the George Taylor house in Catasauqua during the 1976 Bicentennial. In the background is a former silk mill that later burned down. (Catasauqua Public Library)

Northamptontowne Militia

Parades, community celebrations, and numerous special events during the Bicentennial were enhanced by a group of re-enactors who called themselves the Northamptontowne Militia. They took their name from an eighteenth-century militia unit based in Allentown since, from its founding in 1762 until 1838, Allentown was known as Northampton town, or simply Northampton.

One of its founding members was A. James Shedlauskas, who became the first commander of the militia. Initially, the militia was formed to participate in the Liberty Bell Trek, a re-enactment of the 1777 journey by Continental troops and patriots who took Philadelphia's bells from the city to Zion Reformed UCC Church in Allentown to prevent their being melted and made into ammunition by the British.

In late April of 1974, George Longenbach, a member of the Liberty Bell Trek Committee (an offshoot of the Lehigh County Bicentennial Committee), talked to Shedlauskas about what kind of uniforms had been worn by Continental troops who accompanied the original wagon train. When Shedlauskas learned that the trek subcommittee had opted for a scaled-down uniform of a tri-corn hat, a hunting or rifle shirt, and a pair of trousers shortened to resemble colonial breeches, he proposed that he and his friends would outfit themselves as colonial troops as correctly as they could. Furthermore, they would assume the costs of uniforms and equipment themselves.

On November 18, the Northamptontowne Militia was formed. Shedlauskaus was elected commander. A very hectic year began in January 1975, when the militia held a recruiting event on Hamilton Street, complete with an officer in uniform and fife-and-drum music. During the year, recruits had to acquire authentic dress and practice eighteenth-century drills.

The Northamptontowne Militia's public debut was on Washington's Birthday, Saturday February 22, 1975. It featured a parade up Hamilton Street to Tenth and Linden, where

a wreath was laid at the old cemetery where many Revolutionary War veterans were buried. A recruiting table was set up at Hess's. "It caused quite a stir in downtown Allentown because in addition to the unique costumes and muskets, this group was marching against the flow of traffic," recalled Shedlauskaus. There would be a total of 108 events that required the Northamptontowne Militia's presence in 1976.

Leaser Trek

The Northamptontowne Militia was just one of the attractions in that year of 1976. In northwestern Lehigh County, Carl Snyder, businessman, Pennsylvania-German historian, and chairman of the Northwestern Lehigh Bicentennial Committee, had decided to honor Frederick Leaser of Lynn Township, one of the two farmers who had carried the Liberty Bell to Allentown in 1777.

In 1928 the Pennsylvania Historical Commission had placed a stone marker with a bronze tablet along Route 143 between Jacksonville and Wanamakers in upper Lehigh County to honor Leaser at the site of his original homestead. Since then, traffic on the road had increased to the point that it was difficult for drivers to even notice the plaque, much less read it. By the time of the Bicentennial, local groups decided that no greater honor could be done to the actual movers of the Liberty Bell than to move their monument to a safer location and rededicate it.

At exactly 9:30 a.m. on Saturday, September 11, under the watchful eye of trek master Carl Snyder, the wagons traveled toward the new site of Leaser's plaque. It had been moved by Lehigh County work crews on August 23 to a location closer to Leaser Lake so it could be seen.

A highlight of the hour-long program was the presentation of a flag and flagpole to Lehigh County by Bill Albert. County Commissioner Charles J. Kistler accepted them for the county. Among the honored guests were Maurice Leaser and his son Earl, fifth-

and sixth-generation descendants of Frederick Leaser. They had been present in 1928, when the plaque was dedicated the first time.

Liberty Bell Trek

The re-enactment of the Liberty Bell Trek, held the week of September 20–25, 1976, was undoubtedly the most ambitious of Lehigh County's many Bicentennial events.

The point person for the trek from the committee was Thomas Reilly. A fuel-oil marketer for the Gulf Oil Company in northeastern Pennsylvania, he was a member of a number of local civic organizations, among them the Allentown Exchange Club, the Lehigh County Historical Society, and the Liberty Bell Shrine, where he served as vice president. "It seemed like Tom was everywhere in those years," recalls Albert, who worked closely with Reilly and still remembers his shock and grief at his friend's tragically early death at the age of 55 on January 20, 1977.

The Trek began on Sunday, September 20, at 9 a.m. outside Independence Hall. A fiberglass replica of the Liberty Bell was then moved by members of the Northamptontowne Militia, groaning and straining as if the bell actually weighed a ton as they carried it on poles. It was placed aboard an open wagon driven by Melvin Bucks, a Mack Trucks worker, his wife Lillian, and eight-year-old daughter Kara.

At 8 a.m. the next morning the Trek embarked on the fifteen-mile trip to the Montgomeryville Mall. Many in the crowds lining the route were schoolchildren who had been let out of class to see the event. The trek set up near the mall, rain stopped, and local people turned out to see the encampment.

Early the next morning the Trek started for Quakertown, watched by large crowds. As it entered Bucks County, Reilly noticed that the crowds were bigger than ever. After a stop for lunch in Sellersville, the trek moved on to Quakertown. There the Northamptontowne Militia put on a military drill complete with musket practice.

Hellertown was the next scheduled stop, and the following day they moved on to Bethlehem. The Freedom High School Fife and Drum Corps led them into the historic part of Bethlehem. Robert Pharo, as Brother Ettwein, overseer of the community during the first Liberty Bell Trek, met them in front of the Single Brethren's House.

The Liberty Bell Trek moving through Hellertown on the way to Bethlehem.
(Reprinted with permission of The Morning Call. All Rights Reserved)

Members of the Northamptontowne Militia stand at attention when the
Liberty Bell arrives at Zion Church. (Reprinted with permission of
The Morning Call. All Rights Reserved)

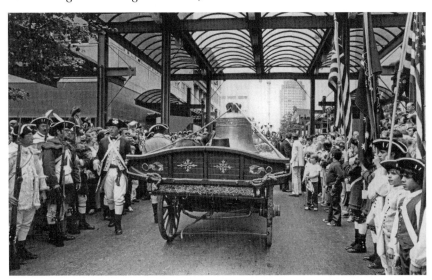

The contemporary Moravians' diary had recorded the breakdown in Bethlehem of the wagon carrying the Philadelphia bells, still the best-known event of the original trek. This may have been the time and place where Frederick Leaser of Lynn Township, whose wagon is said to have carried the bell from Philadelphia, turned it over to John Jacob Mickley of Whitehall Township, a member of Northampton County's General Committee of the Revolution. The incident was respectfully re-enacted.

Crowds started to line the route long before the scheduled arrival of the trek at Allentown's Zion Reformed UCC Church at noon on September 25. As the colorful cavalcade passed one woman shouted "thank you so much."

Despite all the planning and attention to detail that had characterized the trek, one little item was left out: the doorway to the shrine was too small. After a gallant effort, the Northamptontowne Militia carried the replica through the larger door of Zion Church.

With that, the official program was ended. Members of the trek still had one important duty to perform. Before disbanding at the Allentown Fairgrounds, they stopped at Allentown Hospital to pay tribute to the ailing Dr. Morgan Person, whose work in the late 1950s and early 1960s had led to the Liberty Bell Shrine's creation and the spirit behind the trek itself.

Epilogue

In the thirty-six years that have passed since the wagons of the Liberty Bell Trek rolled into the Allentown Fairgrounds for their final dispersal, the only constant in Lehigh County has been change.

From 1972 to 2002, an average of 1,280 acres of Lehigh County land a year has been converted to residential use from farms or open space. According to Jeff Zehr, Lehigh County's Farmland Preservation Officer, as of December 2011 the county had 245 farms, consisting of 20,397 acres of farmland, in preservation. Bob Stiffler, Director of Parks and Recreation for Lehigh County, states that the county currently has 4,543 acres of parkland under its jurisdiction. Statistics compiled by the Lehigh Valley Planning Commission show that, since 1970, 2,600 acres of land in the county have been converted from farm to warehouse and light industrial uses. Most is in the vicinity of the Route 22 and Route 100 interchange. The process began in 1972 with the completion of a large brewery by Schaefer Brewing Company.

Today, Lehigh County's total population stands at 349,497, with Allentown's at 118,032. The 2010 census shows that 18.8 percent of Lehigh County's population is Latino. This compares to a figure of 16.3 percent for the United States as a whole. Allentown has the largest concentration of Latinos, who make up 42.8 percent of its population. African Americans make up 4.9 percent of the county's population, and 2.9 percent are Asian.

According to the website USA.com in 2009, 30,945 of the Latinos in Lehigh County (59.65%) were of Puerto Rican ancestry and 3,353 (6.46%) called themselves South American. Those of Mexican background numbered 3,041 (5.86 %).

Of the Asian population, 3,789 (40.09 %) listed the nation of India as the source of their ancestry, 2,361 (24.98%) considered themselves of Chinese ethnicity, and 1,099 (11.63%) traced their roots to Vietnam. The statistic for India includes the entire subcontinent including Pakistan and Bangladesh.

Most of the white non-Latino population of Lehigh County (118,903; 35.27%) listed their ancestry as German. The next largest group (42,350; 12.56%) said they were of Irish ancestry and 34,268 (10.17%) were of Italian linage.

At each stage in its 200-year history, Lehigh County has faced challenges that to many at the time seemed insurmountable. The disappearance of wood as a cheap fuel in the 1820s seemed like a dead end until the use of anthracite coal as an industrial fuel, made

Lehigh County Courthouses: From 1812 To 2012

Lehigh County's first courthouse was in a tavern, innkeeper George Savitz's Compass Inn at Seventh and Hamilton streets to be exact. While Savitz was dispensing good cheer downstairs, justice was being served upstairs. The following year the judges moved to the upper room in the newly completed Lehigh County Prison at Fifth and Linden streets, near what is now the Allentown Art Museum.

By 1814 Lehigh County had acquired the plans for the Lycoming County courthouse and began building a similar structure on a lot at the northwest corner of Fifth and Hamilton, donated by Ann Penn Allen Greenleaf, the eldest daughter of James Allen. She lived across the street in a large home where Allentown's Post Office is today. When it was completed in August 1817, the handsome gray stone structure with a fine cupola cost $24,937.

It was 1864 before the county's growing population and judicial workload required something larger. Redesigned and enlarged by Allentown city engineer Gustavus Aschbach, with its spacious, elegant courtroom it served quite well until 1914. That year architect Henry Anderson presented the county commissioners with a plan for a totally new building in a formal, symmetrical style popular from 1890 to 1920 and known today as Second Renaissance Revival.

Only one wing was finished by 1917 when the U.S. entered World War I and most civilian construction was suspended. By war's end, building costs had risen. The completed wing had already cost $199,000, and opposition to higher taxes put the plans on the shelf. The new courthouse was never completed.

Not until 1954 were plans for a new county courthouse revived. County officials began the process by studying modern courthouse designs and setting aside funds. In July 1957, it was announced that the commissioners had asked Allentown architects Wolf & Hahn to draw up plans. In the primary election of 1961 the issue of the construction of a new courthouse was put to the voters. It passed 17,191 for, 10,276 against.

Work on the project on the northeast corner of Fifth and Hamilton began by tearing down the Acme Supermarket and the handsome Victorian mansions that lined that block of Hamilton Street. Once the land was cleared, the discovery that massive underground crevices honeycombed the site required the creation of a huge concrete pad, 3½ to 4 feet thick, over the entire area.

(Kurt Zwikl)

242

The official groundbreaking took place on May 28, 1962, on Lehigh County Day, as a part of Allentown's Bicentennial. In a unique ceremony suggested by William T. Hendrix, the Wolf & Hahn architect who designed the courthouse, earth taken from important historic places in the county's twenty-five political subdivisions was added to the site.

In late 1964, Lehigh County officials began moving from the old county courthouse into the new $8 million structure. The move was completed in February, 1965 and the commissioners formally took possession on March 15. On April 1, 1965, the "final session" of the Orphans Court was held in the old courthouse. President Judge Martin Coyne declared his final order was to "ring down the curtain" on the history of the county court system in the old building.

On June 2, 1965, the new Lehigh County Courthouse was officially dedicated in a ceremony that included the presence of Harold Barefoot Sanders of Texas, a U.S. Assistant Attorney General and close confidant of President Lyndon Johnson, to represent the federal government. Barefoot, as one participant in the ceremony noted, was his grandmother's maiden name. A number of local judges and former judges spoke of the beauty and modernity of the new building with its four fully air-conditioned courtrooms. *The Morning Call* speculated that now that there was no longer any use for it, the old courthouse could be torn down and used as a possible site for a Lehigh County Community College.

In ways no one could have foreseen in 1965, by the 1980s the county courthouse was no longer adequate. Growing county agencies were scattered at a number of downtown sites. Under the direction of county executive Jane Baker the county acquired the former Leh's department store, which had closed in 1994. It reopened, a totally transformed building, in 1998 as the Lehigh County Government Center, a $16.1 million conversion overseen by Allentown architect Benjamin Walbert. Baker felt it was important that the agencies remain in a single building in downtown Allentown.

Still more room was necessary. In 2010 the Lehigh County Courthouse of 1965 underwent a 208,000 square foot, $65 million renovation that included five new courtrooms and judges' chambers, jury deliberation rooms, and separate elevators for judges, prisoners, and the public. It also ended the 40-year-old problem of leaky windows on the building's upper stories that had first been noticed shortly after the courthouse opened in 1965.

(Lee Butz)

possible by the ingenuity of David Thomas, an immigrant from Wales, launched Lehigh County into an era of then-unknown growth and development.

In the 1870s the collapse of the iron-making boom, the core industry of the region, led many to say Lehigh County's best days were behind it. Growth slowed and population was stagnant. Then the introduction of silk and later other textile industries, many of which employed enterprising immigrants from eastern Europe and Italy, powered Lehigh County into the middle of the twentieth century.

The twentieth century was to attract a wealth of talent to the Lehigh Valley. The sturdy Pennsylvania-German General Harry C. Trexler set the example both in innovative industry like electrical power and creative philanthropy. Max Hess, father and son, brought their talents of marketing genius to what became a flourishing retail industry. Leonard Pool, a son of the Midwest, combined energy and drive to create a multi-billion-dollar industry, as the saying goes "out of thin air." There have been many others.

Now Lehigh County has crossed over into a new century with new challenges. Who knows what direction and what talented people will step forward and reshape the county's future? As those men and women did on March 6, 1812, cheering in the small towns and rural crossroads the birth of a place of their own, we can't know for certain. That future rests, as it always has, in the hands of its people. ✦

FROM WASHINGTON TO OBAMA LEHIGH COUNTY SINGS HAIL TO THE CHIEF

Many years ago it was common for small hotels across eastern Pennsylvania wanting to attract passing guests to put out signs that read "George Washington slept here." Presumably, if the beds there were good enough for the Father of his Country, how could you possibly turn it down?

As far as can be known, the first president never spent the night at any inn in what is now Lehigh County. But when Kurt Zwikl, a former state representative and lifelong student of presidential history, went looking, he discovered Washington was here, even if it was not to stay overnight, and at least one president did spend the night in Lehigh County while in office.

Washington rode into Allentown, then Northamptontown and in Northampton County, in July of 1782. He was on his way to Bethlehem to stop at the Sun Inn, where he did indeed spend the night. Although Washington never slept in Lehigh County he was friendly with members of Allentown's founding Allen family. James Allen, builder of Trout Hall, first met Washington during the popular horse races in Philadelphia before the Revolution. Both men apparently shared a strong interest in well-bred horses.

This relationship, despite politics, apparently persisted. During the British occupation of Philadelphia in 1777–78, Allen got a pass through American lines at Valley Forge from Washington so his wife, who was about to have a child, could do so in the city with her family, who were there, to aid her. Allen notes in his diary that on a previous visit to the general's headquarters he was received by Washington "with the utmost politeness."

Before Washington, John Adams had passed through Lehigh County at least twice and may have even stopped briefly at Trout Hall. When the British occupied Philadelphia, Adams, a member of Congress, fled first to Lancaster and then through Allentown to York, where the temporary capital was located.

In mid-November 1777, Adams passed through the region with his cousin Sam Adams on his way to Boston. James Allen noted in his dairy that "Mr. John Adams who passed thro' here a week ago spoke of it as a certain event and said the struggle was past and that

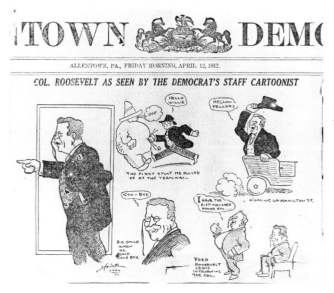

Independence was now unalterably settled." Whether Adams actually said these words directly to Allen, or Allen heard them secondhand, is still a subject of debate among local historians.

Zwikl admits that, as much as he admires Thomas Jefferson, he can find no proof that the primary author of the Declaration of Independence ever came through the Lehigh Valley. In fact, it was not till 1836 that a president or presidential candidate came this way again. It was retired General and Whig Party stalwart, William Henry Harrison.

Although beaten handily by Andrew Jackson's vice president Martin Van Buren that year, Harrison would run again and defeat Van Buren in 1840, when he passed through Lehigh County again after winning a smashing victory. After giving an especially long inaugural address outdoors, Harrison died three months later from pneumonia.

President Martin Van Buren, traveling between Washington and his home in New York, came into Lehigh County on June 16, 1839. He was approached by a large crowd at George Haberacker's Inn at the northeast corner of Seventh and Hamilton streets, where he spent the night. By doing so he made local history, being the first and so far the only president to stay overnight in Lehigh County while in office.

The next several years would witness the arrival of many presidential hopefuls, one of whom was elected president. Democrat James Buchanan, a native of Pennsylvania from Lancaster, came through at least once on a campaign swing in 1856, and probably many other times that have gone unrecorded.

Abraham Lincoln apparently never stopped in Lehigh County even to change trains. But the sixteenth president, whose family roots were in Berks County, knew quite clearly where Lehigh County was. On November 19, 1863, shortly before he gave the Gettysburg Address, Lincoln asked Constantine J. Erdman, a student attending Gettysburg College whose family home was in Center Valley, where he was from. Told "Lehigh County," Lincoln responded, "that's next to Berks County, isn't it?" Erdman acknowledged, somewhat startled, that it was. Lincoln nodded his head as his carriage rode off to the speaker's platform. Inspired by that day, Erdman entered politics and in the 1890s was elected Lehigh County's Congressman.

In April 1861, Lincoln had met members of the First Defenders from Lehigh County

who had come to the capitol's defense, including a young German immigrant named Ignatz Gresser who would later receive the Medal of Honor.

According to some sources, Lehigh County just missed a visit from President U.S. Grant. It is claimed that on January 20, 1872, Grant was scheduled to officiate at the dedication ceremonies of "The President," a huge pump designed to remove water from the Uebberoth Zinc Mine in Upper Saucon Township. The story is that he stopped to visit a friend on the way there, had a few drinks, and never made it.

Contemporary accounts of the event, however, make no mention of Grant having planned to be here and then having to cancel for being bibulous. It may be that the story became confused with the 1876 U.S. Centennial celebration in Philadelphia, where Grant started the giant Corliss engine.

Rutherford B. Hayes, a nineteenth-century president, made a campaign swing through Lehigh County as Governor of Ohio in 1875, looking for support and votes. He won the following year, and is sometimes best remembered for his wife, First Lady "Lemonade Lucy" Rutherford, who banned "booze" from the Executive Mansion.

Theodore Roosevelt visited the Lehigh Valley five times, at least three in Lehigh County. It would be many years before Gerald Ford would tie Roosevelt's record. One stop in 1905, when he was president, took place from the back of a train's observation car. Old photos show men and boys climbing to the top of telegraph poles to get a better view.

In April 1912, when he was hoping to win the Republican nomination from incumbent William Howard Taft, Roosevelt made a visit to Allentown two days before the Pennsylvania primary. His fifteen-minute speech at the Lyric Theater (today Symphony Hall) brought the house down. Two years later, in October of 1914, "Teddy" campaigned for Progressive Party candidates in Lehigh County. The crowds were not quite as big as they were in 1912, but Roosevelt could still draw them.

On May 1, 1911, Eugene V. Debs, Socialist candidate for president in 1912, spoke at the Lyric to a capacity crowd. In the 1912 election he received 901,255 votes nationally; 1,506 of them were from Lehigh County and 639 were from Northampton County, the

Eleanor Roosevelt toured Hanover Acres, a public housing project, on May 27, 1942, while in the Lehigh Valley to receive an honorary degree at Muhlenberg College. She spoke about winning the war and building a new world economy after it was over. (Kurt Zwikl)

Harry S. Truman was met by huge crowds at the railroad station when he stopped in Allentown in October 1948 during his whistlestop campaign tour of the country. On his right is U.S. Senator Francis Myers from Philadelphia. (Kurt Zwikl)

most votes both nationally and locally that a Socialist presidential candidate ever received.

Taft, who came in third in Lehigh County in the 1912 presidential election, was much more popular in Lehigh County after he left the presidency. He was in Lehigh County at least three times, once to help inaugurate a Masonic Lodge in 1913, another time to speak at the opening of the Allentown Hospital School of Nursing in 1915, and again during World War I in support the U.S. Army Ambulance Corps at Camp Crane, located at the Allentown Fair Grounds, in 1918. At that last visit, while staying at the Hotel Traylor, Taft was named the first honorary member of the Allentown Kiwanis Club.

Woodrow Wilson, the man who defeated both Taft and Roosevelt for the White House in 1912, had spoken at the Lyric Theater in February 1912, and again at a railroad stop several months later during the national election campaign.

Warren Harding, who followed Wilson to the White House, came to Allentown on December 13, 1917, to speak at the Odd Fellows Building on North Ninth Street. He was then a senator from Ohio. General Harry C. Trexler introduced him at the meeting as "the next president of the U.S." at a time when he was largely a "dark horse" and Wilson and the Democrats were at the height of their popularity. A blizzard struck that night, forcing Harding to spend the night at the Livingston Club, a private men's club on Seventh Street

that maintained rooms for its more-favored members like Trexler and Bethlehem Steel CEO Charlie Schwab. In 1920, Harding's name emerged from the "famous smoke-filled room" of Republican Party bosses at the Chicago Convention and he beat Democrat James M. Cox and his running mate, young Franklin Delano Roosevelt, for the White House.

It was 1936 before another president came through Lehigh County. On August 15 that year, President Franklin Roosevelt traveled through the area while on his way to examine flood damage in Wilkes-Barre and Scranton. "Crowds gathered all along the Lehigh Valley Railroad from Mauch Chunk (now Jim Thorpe) to Slatington, Northampton, Cementon, Catasauqua and Easton," Zwikl wrote in the October 1996 issue of Lehigh Valley Magazine.

In Allentown threatening storm clouds did not deter the nearly 2,000 people who had gathered at various vantage points to catch a glimpse of the Chief Executive. According to The Morning Call, Roosevelt "sat on the right side of the observation car facing the rear of the train, his hand waving in friendly greeting. The train had barely pulled out of sight on its way to Bethlehem when it rained, rained in torrents, but no one seemed to care—they had just seen the president.

President Harry S. Truman came chugging through the Lehigh Valley during his famous whistle-stop campaign in October 1948. From the back of the train he was greeted in Allentown, Bethlehem, and Easton. His successor in the White House, then still General Dwight David Eisenhower, was photographed in 1948 at the Allentown Howard Johnson's on Union Boulevard. With him were his wife Mamie and her mother. They were on their way to Washington from West Point after seeing their new grandson David for the first time.

An even more obscure visit of a future president came in 1957, when a Hollywood actor named Ronald Reagan, then a spokesperson for General Electric, toured the company's south-side Allentown facility and spoke to the Allentown Chamber of Commerce as a luncheon guest.

The 1960 presidential election that brought three presidents-to-be to Lehigh County

Senator John F. Kennedy speaking at Center Square, Allentown, in October 1960, during his campaign for the presidency. (Kurt Zwikl)

is Zwikl's favorite. That October, John F. Kennedy, Richard M. Nixon, and Lyndon B. Johnson all were here. Nixon's running mate, Henry Cabot Lodge, also passed through. Johnson, JFK'S running mate, arrived first on October 18. He spoke briefly at Cedar Crest College and that evening addressed a rally at the Frolics Ballroom in east Allentown.

Nixon was next, arriving four days later. He was seen by an estimated over 100,000 people during the visit, including a capacity crowd at Muhlenberg College's Memorial Hall. This was his second campaign trip to the county, having come in 1952 as Eisenhower's running mate. He would return in 1968 when he was running again for his successful presidential campaign.

John F. Kennedy arrived in the early morning of October 28, 1960. A crowd of 15,000 was on hand, despite the early hour of 1:00 a.m., to greet him at ABE airport. Kennedy was driven to the Hotel Bethlehem, where later that morning he addressed a crowd of 400 at breakfast. From there it was on to a large rally at Moravian College and an even larger one at Center Square in Allentown. Crowds were so dense that Kennedy's car was surrounded and barely able to make it through.

Gerald Ford, who became president in 1974 following Nixon's resignation, was to visit Lehigh County at least five times, four as a member of Congress and a fifth time as a former president. Jimmy Carter spoke at Hess's Department Store in 1976 when he was campaigning in the Pennsylvania Primary.

George Herbert Walker Bush was in Allentown as president in 1992; he had also campaigned here in 1980 when seeking the Republican presidential nomination. In 1998 he returned to speak at Kutztown University.

William Jefferson "Bill" Clinton came to Lehigh County in 1995 after a speech at Kutztown University. He stopped briefly at a local diner where for a time his coffee cup was

enshrined on the wall. In 2008
he spoke at a campaign rally for
his wife Hillary. In August 2010,
Clinton spoke in support of the
congressional campaign of Bethlehem mayor John Callahan at the
Allentown home of Gregg and
Cindy Feinberg.

President George W. Bush
made a campaign stop at Lehigh
Parkway on October 1, 2004,
as a part of his re-election campaign. He had campaigned here
in September 2000 when he was
running for his first term.

President Barrack Obama
campaigned in Lehigh County in
2008, speaking to an overflow
crowd at Muhlenberg College.
He also appeared at nearby
Bethlehem on April 20, 2008.
He returned again on December
4, 2009, to speak at Allentown
Metal Works, the Hamilton Family
Diner, and Lehigh Carbon Community College.

"The Lehigh Valley's population, diversity and geographic location along with the presence of
local television stations are likely
to continue to attract future presidents to the region," says Zwikl. "And of course there is
that other significant ingredient: Votes."

Crowds gathered at A-B-E Airport to welcome Richard Nixon in October, 1960. (Lehigh County Historical Society)

Hess's models on the sidewalk in front of the store in 1968, when the main presidential candidates were Richard Nixon, Hubert H. Humphrey, and Eugene McCarthy. (William Zwikl photo)

SPECIAL SECTION

PROFILES OF BUSINESSES AND ORGANIZATIONS OF LEHIGH COUNTY

(Lee Butz)

Coca-Cola Bottling Company
Of The Lehigh Valley

Coca-Cola Bottling Company of the Lehigh Valley began as a franchise located on Tenth Avenue in Bethlehem. For 70 years, it was known as Quaker State Coca-Cola Bottling before adopting its current name in 1981. Coca-Cola Bottling Company of the Lehigh Valley is part of the 5th largest bottling franchise in the United States and sells over 5 million cases of Coca-Cola products each year.

Now located in a state-of-the art facility on Industrial Drive in Bethlehem, Coca-Cola Bottling Company of the Lehigh Valley is one of only two plants nationwide that produces its products with real sugar made from cane or beet sugar. In addition, it is one of only three U.S. plants that qualify for an alternative water process, which eliminates water chemicals and increases production capacity.

Coca-Cola Bottling Company of the Lehigh Valley is committed to improving the communities in which it does business. The company's Vice President & General Manager, Joe Brake, has been honored with the "Greater Lehigh Valley Chamber Foundation Award," the "LifePath & Lehigh Valley Chapter of PICPA, Community Service Award," the "Bert Daday Community Service Award" by

the Hispanic American Organization, and the "Distinguished Citizen's Award of the Boy Scouts of America, Minsi Trails Council." Mr. Brake serves as President of the Minsi Trails Council as well as President of the Pennsylvania Beverage Association.

The company made an impact in local and national news during March 2007 when it announced it would be the naming sponsor for a new minor league baseball stadium in the region, a park that is now the home of the Lehigh Valley IronPigs. Lehigh County's Coca-Cola Park is the first professional sports venue in the U.S. to bear the Coca-Cola name.

LEHIGH VALLEY HEALTH NETWORK

In 1899, a group of 13 auxiliary members raised money for a good cause. The result—the birth of The Allentown Hospital at 17th and Chew streets in Allentown.

Nearly 70 years later, Leonard Parker Pool had a vision. The founder of Air Products and Chemicals, Inc., was fortunate to have the resources to afford the cancer care his wife, Dorothy, needed in New York City. After her death in 1967, Leonard wanted to help others in the Lehigh Valley who couldn't afford to travel out of the area for high-quality care. His vision led to the creation of what today is Lehigh Valley Hospital–Cedar Crest.

The superior, regional hospital Pool envisioned is now Lehigh Valley Health Network. It includes more than 10,000 colleagues driven by A Passion for Better Medicine. They are guided by the health network's mission—to heal, comfort and care for the people of our community.

The health network includes:

• Two full-service hospitals: Lehigh Valley Hospital with clinical campuses on Cedar Crest Boulevard in Salisbury Township and on 17th Street in Allentown; and Lehigh Valley Hospital-Muhlenberg in Bethlehem.

• Community health centers located in Bath, Bethlehem Township, Emmaus, Hamburg, Kutztown, Moselem Springs, Saucon Valley, Trexlertown, and Upper Bucks (in partnership with Grand View Hospital).

• Primary care and specialty physicians, more

than 1,200, including more than 500 who are employed by the health network.

• Pharmacy services at all three hospital campuses.

• Imaging services with the latest high-tech diagnostic equipment.

• CareWorks retail health clinics (in partnership with Geisinger Health System) in Allentown and Schnecksville.

• Community clinics, including 40 primary and specialty clinics.

• Health Network Laboratories, providing medical laboratory tests from critical medical applications to drug screenings.

• Valley Preferred, linking employers and individuals with quality health coverage.

AIR PRODUCTS

Leonard Parker Pool founded Air Products in 1940 in Detroit, Michigan, on a simple, but revolutionary idea: the "on-site" concept of producing and selling industrial gases. Although his idea to combine existing technology with a novel marketing concept was ingenious, immediate orders were not forthcoming. Frustrated, but undaunted, Pool seized opportunity and, instead, sold mobile generators to produce oxygen for use by the military in high-altitude flights during World War II.

Air Products quickly outgrew Detroit and moved its operations to Chattanooga, Tennessee, where it produced 240 oxygen generators for the armed forces and for "lend-lease" to foreign allies. After the war, the company refocused its sights on commercial markets by setting up operations in Pennsylvania's Lehigh Valley.

Air Products moved from Chattanooga to Pennsylvania in 1946 to be closer to the industrial markets of the Northeast and benefit from the area's high quality workforce. Initially, the company set up operations in the former Donaldson Iron Works building in Emmaus, which it purchased for $75,000. The company then moved to its present site in Trexlertown in 1958.

When Air Products moved to the Lehigh Valley in 1946, it employed 80 people and had annual sales of approximately $1.4 million. Today, Air Products has operations in over 40 countries, 18,900 employees around the globe, and fiscal 2011 revenues of $10.1 billion.

Air Products serves customers in industrial, energy, technology, and healthcare markets worldwide with a unique portfolio of atmo-spheric gases, process and specialty gases, performance materials, and equipment and services. The company has built leading positions in key growth markets such as semiconductor materials, refinery hydrogen, home healthcare services, natural gas liquefaction, and advanced coatings and adhesives. The company is recognized for its innovative culture, operational excellence, and commitment to safety and the environment.

PPL Corporation

Tracing its roots to Thomas Edison himself and headquartered in Allentown since its incorporation, PPL Corporation has been empowering economic vitality and quality of life for the communities it serves for nearly a century.

The people of PPL Corporation provide reliable, safe, competitively priced energy to their customers and competitive returns to their shareowners.

PPL has grown from a company with customers and facilities in eastern and central Pennsylvania to one of the largest companies in the U.S. utility sector. The company now provides electricity delivery service to 10 million customers and owns and operates about 19,000 megawatts of generating capacity from the East Coast to the Pacific Northwest.

The family of PPL companies – from Pennsylvania, to Kentucky, to Montana, to England and Wales – has built an enduring reputation for safety, the highest quality customer service, environmental stewardship and exemplary corporate citizenship.

The company's solid mix of high-performing businesses creates an attractive investment for shareowners, producing consistently solid earnings and payment of dividends for more than 250 consecutive quarters.

PPL Corporation is built on a solid foundation of three essential building blocks: exceptional people; extraordinary assets; and a proven understanding of the utility sector.

PPL is proud to call Lehigh County home and the company is absolutely committed to being a positive force in all the communities in which they do business. PPL supports economic development efforts, donates to agencies that work to improve communities and, encourages its 17,000 employees around the world to give generously of their time and money to improve the quality of life in their communities.

HIGHMARK BLUE SHIELD

For more than 70 years, Highmark Blue Shield's commitment to the community has consistently been among the company's highest priorities. This commitment is very much aligned with the company's mission of ensuring access to affordable health-care coverage for the widest possible cross section of the community, and helping people live longer and healthier lives.

An independent licensee of the Blue Cross and Blue Shield Association, Highmark serves 4.8 million members through the company's health-care benefits business. With corporate offices in Pittsburgh, Highmark is one of the largest Blue Shield plans in the nation and has had an office in the Lehigh Valley since 2001. It serves about 1 million members in the Central Pennsylvania and Lehigh Valley region.

Highmark's history of helping families and companies with their health insurance needs dates to the 1930s, when its predecessor companies were established to help Pennsylvania residents pay for health care.

Highmark was created in 1996 by the consolidation of two Pennsylvania licensees of the Blue Cross and Blue Shield Association – Pennsylvania Blue Shield (now Highmark Blue

Shield) and Blue Cross of Western Pennsylvania (now Highmark Blue Cross Blue Shield).

The company has nearly 20,000 employees nationally, with more than 4,000 in Central Pennsylvania and the Lehigh Valley.

Highmark Blue Shield supports initiatives aligned with fulfilling the company's mission and building strong relationships within the communities where customers and employees live and work. Since 2001, Highmark Blue Shield has awarded more than $1.3 million in grants and sponsorships to local organizations in the Lehigh Valley.

BOYLE CONSTRUCTION, INC.

Serving the greater Lehigh Valley since 1977, Boyle is one of the most respected names in the construction industry and one of the region's leading firms in public construction management.

Boyle fosters long-term client relationships. Many of its clients are returning customers or are obtained through referrals.

Boyle Construction (originally Boyle & Moore, Inc.) was founded by Anthony J. Boyle, who serves today as chairman, working with his son, Sean, who is president of the company. Tony's philosophy—that service and quality should drive the business—is the cornerstone of the company.

Boyle contracts a limited number of projects, allowing it to focus resources and maintain a hands-on approach. Its principals are directly involved in every project, assuring the best quality results.

The company performs a broad range of construction services, including construction management, design-build, and general construction. Most Boyle projects benefit from some form of construction management and

many include a combination of these three services.

Boyle has been recognized for its community participation through honors such as the Bethlehem Chamber of Commerce Small Business of the Year award.

The people of Boyle believe that pride in their work and superior customer service result in successful projects. Eighty-five percent of its business is repeat clients.

With headquarters in Bethlehem, Boyle has 25 full-time employees and was ranked among the best places to work in Pennsylvania in 2008.

The firm's most significant recent local projects include Melt Restaurant, the Levitt Pavilion, and the Lehigh County Detoxification and Treatment Center.

THE MORNING CALL

The Morning Call traces its Lehigh County lineage back to Samuel S. Woolever, who founded a Saturday evening weekly called *The Critic* in 1883. In 1895, the publication was renamed *The Morning Call*. David Miller, a reporter for The Critic, and his brother Sam bought the paper in 1904.

The Miller family continued to run the newspaper for the next four decades. Following David Miller's death in 1958, his sons, Donald P. and Samuel W., succeeded him as publishers. Samuel died in 1967, and soon afterward Donald's son, Edward D. Miller, joined him in running the paper. The newspaper was sold in 1984 to the Times Mirror Company, one of the country's top five newspaper companies. In 2000, the Tribune Company acquired Times Mirror and with it *The Morning Call*.

The company launched its news website, themorningcall.com, in September 1996.

Today, *The Morning Call* employs 460 people and reaches more than 400,000 Lehigh Valley area adults in one week. Seven out of 10 adults turn to the newspaper and its website for news and information.

The Morning Call has received numerous national newspaper design awards over the years, including:

2011 Gold ADDY® for Life. Read all about it. Mixed, Multi-Media, Consumer Branding Campaign. The ADDY® Awards represent the true spirit of creative excellence by recognizing all forms of advertising from media of all types, creative by all sizes and entrants of all levels from anywhere in the world.

G. Richard Dew Award for Outstanding Journalism (2011), highest recognition by the Pennsylvania Newspaper Association, for breaking-news coverage and follow-up investigations of a gas explosion in Allentown that killed five and leveled a city block.

John V.R. Bull Freedom of Information Award, Pennsylvania Newspaper Association (2010), for an investigation into how the Bethlehem Area School District's investment in risky derivatives cost taxpayers millions of dollars.

Dew Award (2007), for an investigation that revealed lax enforcement and flaws in the state's dog-kennel inspection system and led the state to put its inspection records online.

ALVIN H. BUTZ, INC.

Alvin H. Butz, Inc., was founded in 1920 and has been continuously operated as a family-owned and -operated company since then. Butz provides exceptional, comprehensive construction-management services, led by strong values and complete customer satisfaction.

The firm possesses significant experience in the construction of healthcare facilities, colleges/universities, corporate office buildings, hi-tech manufacturing facilities, sports and entertainment venues, government buildings, K-12 schools, and retail buildings.

Alvin H. Butz, Inc., is a wholly owned subsidiary of Butz Enterprises, and along with our sister companies, Alexander Building Construction Co. and Shoemaker Construction Co., has been consistently ranked among the nation's Top 400 Construction Management Firms since 1981 by ENR, McGraw-Hill's construction-industry magazine. Butz Enterprises provides construction management and contracting services in Eastern Pennsylvania, Northern Delaware, New Jersey, New York, and Maryland.

In December 2006, the company moved their South Whitehall Township headquarters into a new, 85,000 square foot, Class A office building (pictured here) demonstrating their commitment to the long-term growth and success of the City of Allentown. And the firm has announced plans to have a 50,000 square foot expansion to their Ninth and Hamilton streets location available for lease in early 2013.

Butz's notable Lehigh County projects include: Allentown Parking Authority – Government Area Parking Deck; B. Braun Medical, Inc. – Molding & OEM Expansion; Coca-Cola Park; Lutron Electronics, Inc. – CB-5 Office Building; Muhlenberg College – Performing Arts Center; Olympus Corporation of the Americas – Corporate Headquarters ; Parkland School District – High School; Lehigh Valley Hospital – John and Dorothy Morgan Cancer Center; Allentown School District renovations and additions at Allen High School, Dieruff High School, Roosevelt Elementary School, Ramos Elementary School, and South Mountain and Trexler Middle Schools.

DeSales University

Shortly after being appointed as the first bishop of the Diocese of Allentown by Pope John XXIII, the Most Reverend Joseph McShea announced a drive to expand the education system in the five-county diocese. Part of this initiative was a request to the Oblates of St. Frances de Sales to establish a Catholic liberal arts college in the diocese.

Planning began in the spring of 1962, and the charter for Allentown College of St. Francis de Sales, located in Center Valley, was granted two years later. Classes began for freshmen in September 1965 and the college was fully accredited by the Middle States Association during the 1969–70 academic year. The college became co-educational in 1970 and it established ACCESS, its very popular continuing-education program, in 1977.

The college continued to grow its programs and in 1998 became the first Catholic college in the country to offer a major in marriage and family studies.

The institution achieved university status in 2000 and officially changed its name to DeSales University on January 1, 2001.

Recently, the university announced its first doctoral program, a doctor of nursing practice, that began in January 2012.

Today, DeSales has 1,579 traditional undergraduate students and 1,620 adult evening undergraduate and graduate students. The university employs about 450 full-time faculty and staff.

The university is especially well known for its theater program: More than 60,000 people have attended performances at the Labuda Center for the Performing Arts through the undergraduate "Act 1" theater program and through DeSales' Pennsylvania Shakespeare Festival professional theatre company.

LEHIGH VALLEY IRON PIGS

Co-owners Joe Finley and Craig Stein brought major-league-affiliate baseball back to the Lehigh Valley in a big way in 2008.

Playing in the beautiful, new Coca-Cola Park, which was built in cooperation with Lehigh County, the Iron Pigs have become one of the most successful franchises in minor league baseball. The International League Triple A affiliate of the Philadelphia Phillies has drawn more than 2.5 million people to Coca-Cola Park in its first four years. In 2011, the Iron Pigs drew more fans than any other minor league team in the country.

The Iron Pigs have received numerous honors since 2008, including Ballpark Digest's "Ballpark of the Year" award and "Best Game Operations and Presentation" award as chosen by gameops.com. In 2009, Kurt Landes, the Iron Pigs' general manager, was named the International League's "Executive of the Year."

In recognition of the team's early success, the Iron Pigs were awarded the International League All-Star Game in 2010, an event that

brought significant attention to the Lehigh Valley as a tourist and business destination.

The Iron Pigs organization also is very active in the community. The Iron Pigs Charities foundation was established even before the first pitch was thrown at Coca-Cola Park. In just four years, the foundation has contributed more than $xxx,000 to organizations that are improving the quality of life in the Lehigh Valley.

LUTRON ELECTRONICS, CO., INC.

In 1961, Joel Spira developed the first commercially successful electronic solid-state light dimmer for incandescent lamps. He and his wife Ruth founded Lutron Electronics to market the innovation, and the patent they received was the very first issued to the tiny, high-tech start-up.

The incandescent-light dimmer was just the first in a steady stream of innovations that continues to this day. Spira and Lutron would go on to invent the first high-frequency dimming ballast, linear slide dimmer, electronic ballast for compact fluorescent lamps, infrared remote-controlled dimmer, architectural lighting control system, and the first successful two-way radio frequency lighting control system. These and thousands of other innovations have resulted in an intellectual property portfolio that includes over 2,000 global patents.

Acknowledging these important advancements, the Smithsonian Institution requested that Lutron donate many of its early products, technical papers, and marketing ma-

terials to the Electricity Collection of the National Museum of American History in Washington, D.C.

Meanwhile, Lutron continues to write its own history with ultra-sophisticated, highly aesthetic energy-saving products and solutions. The most recent ones control HVAC systems, small appliances, and window shades (in addition to lights), thus opening a whole new chapter in the story of this high-tech powerhouse.

Now celebrating 50 years in the Lehigh Valley, Lutron offers over 45,000 products to a global customer base, and still maintains local production and distribution facilities in addition to its world headquarters in Coopersburg.

From the Statue of Liberty to the Bank of China … from Windsor Castle to millions of homes, Lutron dimmers and systems combine energy savings with elegance, and bring a little bit of the Lehigh Valley wherever Lutron products are installed.

EXPRESS-TIMES (LEHIGH VALLEY MEDIA GROUP)

Years ago, John Strohmeyer, the Pulitzer Prize-winning editor of *The Bethlehem Globe-Times*, said if there was red dust on the cars in the morning, all was well with Bethlehem. What he meant was if Bethlehem Steel was living up to its name, the city and its citizens could be secure in a brighter future.

Bethlehem is one of the nation's few cities divided by two counties and a stream. The Lehigh County borough of West Bethlehem joined its Monocacy Creek and Northampton County neighbor Bethlehem in 1904. When, a few years later, Steel icon Charles Schwab created a Christmas city by manufacturing a union between South Bethlehem and the other former boroughs, it cemented a divided identity—one city, two counties.

The Times had been on the job for 50 years by the time Archibald Johnston took office as the city's first mayor, and *The Globe* was about to mark a quarter century.

Times and businesses change. Steel is long gone, replaced by glistening hubs of entertainment and manufacturing that draw visitors and businesses from around the globe.

And *The Globe*, too, has evolved, bequeathing its *Times* to *The Express* in 1991,

to form a new media company with deep roots in Lehigh County and a bright future serving county residents.

Lehigh Valley Media Group—*The Express-Times* and lehighvalleylive.com—is driven by the same fire that made *The Globe-Times'* Lehigh County edition a must-read for generations. Get the news first and best. And get it to the readers.

PENN STATE LEHIGH VALLEY

Through the efforts of a local citizens' committee in cooperation with Penn State's School of Engineering, one of the University's first permanent technical centers opened in 1912 as the Allentown Engineering Extension in the attic of the Stevens School.

Women first enrolled at the campus in 1917, with many training for positions in local steel and cement companies to replace men serving in WWI. During WWII, the campus again trained women to assist the war effort, in partnership with the Consolidated Vultee Aircraft Corporation.

As industry in the Lehigh Valley grew, so did demand for programs to train its citizens to fill those positions. In 1951, the center moved to Ridge Avenue in Allentown, where, in 1955, it graduated one of the first associate degree classes in the nation. As baby boomers entered college in the late 1960s, enrollment grew both in Allentown and at University Park. Across the state, Penn State centers and campuses began offering the first two years of a baccalaureate degree to ensure students access to a Penn State education.

In 1977, Penn State Allentown moved to a newly built campus in Fogelsville located on forty acres of land donated by the Mohr family. Here, the campus saw exponential growth with the addition of four-year degree programs and the expansion of continuing education opportunities.

In 2009, spurred by continued growth, Penn State Lehigh Valley began writing a new chapter in its history by relocating to a facility in Center Valley.

Celebrating its centennial in 2012, Penn State Lehigh Valley has the distinction of be-

ing the oldest continuously running campus outside of University Park. While the campus' name and location have changed over the years, its mission has not—still emphasizing Penn State's original land-grant institution mission of offering lifelong learning opportunities to the community.

EASTERN INDUSTRIES

Eastern Industries, Inc., began in 1941 as Eastern Lime Corporation, with its principal operation and office in Kutztown. The company was primarily engaged in the business of producing chemical-grade limestone for cement companies, crushed stone for ready-mix concrete, and highway construction and agricultural limestone.

In 1965, the name was changed to the present Eastern Industries, Inc. Over the course of the next ten years, there were many acquisitions to increase its product base for customers.

In 1976, Eastern Industries, Inc., was bought by the Stabler Companies and it continued to grow over the next three decades before New Enterprise Lime & Stone Company acquired the Stabler Companies, including Eastern Industries, Inc.

Today, with more than sixty years in the construction-materials and construction-services business, Eastern Industries, Inc., is a well-established, well-recognized, and highly respected company that provides a wide array of construction products and services. Through the many acquisitions and new product lines, the company has experienced continued growth, becoming a recognized leader, and stable, one-stop supplier for our customers.

Eastern Industries, Inc., takes enormous pride in our more than 700 employees, who have had a considerable impact on the economic, educational, social, and cultural development of the communities in which they live and work. They recognize and support the company's commitment to maintaining a cleaner, safer environment, demonstrating their support through community volunteer efforts.

LEHIGH CARBON COMMUNITY COLLEGE

Since its founding in 1966, Lehigh Carbon Community College had been responding to the need of area communities by providing affordable, accessible, and high quality education.

With 110 associate degree and certified programs, LCCC has benefitted tens of thousands of students through face-to-face instruction, hybrid programs, and online education. Through the dual-credit enrollment program, more than 1,200 high school students have earned college credits while attending high school.

In pursuing its vision to achieve national prominence and academic excellence as a comprehensive community college, LCCC also has contributed more than 3 million non-credit and credit workforce training hours throughout its service area, training more than 15,000 employees.

The college has more than 1,100 employees, 265 of whom are full-time. At present, there are nearly 7,700 hundred students enrolled in credit programs and more than 12,000 noncredit students.

LCCC was officially formed in 1966 through the combined efforts of all nine Lehigh County school districts in conjunction with two school districts in Carbon County. The college's first classes were held in the Old Lehigh County Courthouse on Hamilton Street. The college moved to its current home in Schnecksville three years later.

The college recently opened its second Business Enterprise Center, which offers assistance to those students who are interested in forming a business. This resource center

provides help at all points in the business formation process, from developing the business plan to identifying potential funding to providing physical space as a business incubator.

Many of LCCC's programs are recognized nationally, including its "English as a Second Language" program, its "Paralegal Studies" degree and its "Kitchen and Bath Design" degree. LCCC has more than 40 articulation agreements with four-year colleges and universities, allowing an easy transfer into most bachelor's degree programs.

JAINDL COMPANIES

The Jaindl family has raised premium holiday turkeys at its farms in Orefield for more than 70 years, earning a reputation for breeding superior tasting, healthful turkeys and maintaining the tradition of quality established by the company's founders.

The company was founded in the early 1930s, when John L. Jaindl and his son Fred bought five turkey poults (young turkeys) from a local farmer.

Fred and his father John continued as partners until 1965, when Fred purchased his father's interest in the farm. By that time, they were raising and marketing 200,000 birds and farming 500 acres annually. John L. Jaindl continued to work as general manager until his passing in 1980. David Jaindl, Fred's son, then took over as general manager and continued in that position until purchasing the family farm in 2005.

Today the company is operated by the third and fourth generation of Jaindls. David Jaindl – with the management assistance of

his siblings John, Alice, and Cathy and his nephew John Jr. – oversees the operation that currently produces more than 750,000 turkeys and farms over 10,000 acres annually.

Jaindl's specially bred, broad-breasted turkeys are world-renowned, having up to 50 percent more white meat than any other turkeys.

Jaindl Farms prides itself on its dedication to and from its employees. The average employee has been with Jaindl for more than 15 years. Many, including general manager Richard Gildner, have been with the company for more than 40 years.

WFMZ CHANNEL 69

When residents in Pennsylvania's Lehigh Valley area want to know what is happening, they turn to 69 WFMZ-TV, which is owned and operated by Maranatha Broadcasting Company. From its location on South Mountain in Allentown, WFMZ-TV reaches over 2.6 million households throughout eastern Pennsylvania and western New Jersey via cable, satellite, and over the air via high definition television.

News is a major commitment at WFMZ-TV. With 74 live half-hour newscasts each week, the station has grown dramatically since broadcasting its first signal on Thanksgiving Day 1976. Today, the station employs more than 140 people. The 69 Newscast and Election Central results programming are perennial winners and nominees for Mid-Atlantic Emmy Awards, and Associated Press and Pennsylvania Association of Broadcasters awards. A true innovator, the station launched a Spanish-language newscast, Edicion en Espanol, in 2003 to serve the growing Hispanic population in the region.

69 WFMZ-TV's technical operation is constantly being upgraded. This allows the staff to use the latest technology to more efficiently gather information and deliver news on multiple platforms to its loyal viewers. The station operates four channels available via antenna and most cable systems. The main channel, 69.1, presents many first-run television shows and live 69News broadcasts. The popular AccuWeather Chan-

nel at 69.2 provides up-to-the-minute weather forecasts, with traffic and weather cameras. The Memorable Entertainment Channel (MeTV) is at 69.3, and the Retro Television Channel at 69.4.

WFMZ-TV provides an exceptional level of local sports programming, covering all high school, college, and professional sports in the region. With four full-time meteorologists, the 69 News AccuWeather Department is second to none, providing complete weather information on newscasts, on the 24/7 AccuWeather Channel, and via its wfmz.com website and smartphone apps. A highlight of each year is WFMZ-TV's Emmy Award-winning live coverage of the Freddy Awards, which recognize excellence in musical theatre performances at local high schools. Whatever is happening in the community, WFMZ-TV is there. With its significant reach in the region, WFMZ-TV also provides support to dozens of community fundraising events for civic and non-profit organizations.

VIA Media

Viamedia was originally formed in December 1991 as Target Select Cable Advertising. Owned by several local private investors, they operated from a small building in West Allentown with a staff of six representing Service Electric, Twin County Cable (now RCN), and Blue Ridge Cable (now Blue Ridge Communications).

In January 1996 Target Select launched its own local television channel, LVTV, which aired cable classified programming. A similar format aired on Blue Ridge Communications' TV-13.

Target Select was sold to *The Morning Call* (a Tribune Company) in March of 2000.

In September 2001, several of the original partners of Target Select along with several new business partners founded Viamedia, Inc., operating from Lexington, KY. They represented WOW Internet Cable in Chicago, Detroit, Columbus and Cleveland (totaling over 310,000 subscribers).

Target Select continued to operate under The Tribune until August 2003 when the principals of Target Select and Viamedia, Inc., purchased the company.

In early 2006, Target Select moved from their West Allentown location to a much larger facility on Adler Place in Bethlehem (where it operates from today).

Recognizing the need to improve video production, Target Select expanded their small production capabilities to a larger, full-service video production company, Vertical Creative Group (formerly known as Icarus Communications).

In April 2007, Target Select changed their name to Viamedia LLC, for consistency with its then-sister company, Viamedia Inc.

With the addition of an outside investment company in January 2010, Viamedia LLC and Viamedia Inc. began operating as one company — Viamedia. Viamedia has continued to grow throughout the years, and now represents over 20 video providers in more than 50 markets in the United States totaling 4.2M+ subscribers, with 500,000+ in Pennsylvania alone. There are over 400 employees with 67 based in Pennsylvania offices.

AMERICAN BANK

In early 1996 a group of local entrepreneurs, led by real estate developer and turkey farmer Frederick Jaindl, had an idea of establishing a "nationwide" community bank focused on serving both the Lehigh Valley community with a local branch and customers across the United States through online banking. On July 1, 1996, the Board of Directors filed an application with the Pennsylvania Department of Banking and on June 6, 1997, American Bank opened its headquarters at 4029 West Tilghman Street in Allentown.

American Bank flourished through the turn of the century and it surpassed $500 million in assets in April 2004. Since then, American Bank has been recognized as one of the most cost-efficient banks in the country. Through the hard work and diligence of its team members, American Bank ended 2011 with zero non-performing loans, an accomplishment for any bank navigating through one of the worst economic environments since the Great Depression.

Much of American Bank's success can be attributed to its fifty team members and the leadership set forth by its Board of Directors. Today, Mark Jaindl, Chairman, President and CEO, is surrounded by directors whose strong business acumen and commitment to excellence serve American Bank well. In addition to Mr. Jaindl, the current Board of Directors includes Martin Spiro, Phillip Schwartz, John W. Galuchie,

John Eureyecko, Michael Molewski and Donald Whiting.

American Bank has been recognized as a 5-Star rated Superior Bank, the highest rating available by BauerFinancial, Inc., the nation's leading bank rating firm. American Bank continues to focus on building safe and sound long-term relationships, based on superior service and high ethical standards, while meeting the needs of its customers in a responsive and proactive manner.

BIBLIOGRAPHY

BOOKS

Adams, Anna. *Hidden From History: The Latino Community of Allentown, Pennsylvania*. Allentown: Lehigh County Historical Society, 2000.

Allen, Frederick Lewis. *Only Yesterday*. New York: Harper & Row, 1931.

Archer, Robert F. *A History of the Lehigh Valley Railroad: The Route of the Black Diamond*. Forest Park, IL: Heimburger House Publishing, 1977.

Barba, Preston A. *They Came to Emmaus: A History*. Second edition. Emmaus Heritage Committee [1985].

Bartholomew, Ann, Craig L. Bartholomew, and James G. Stine. *A History of Lower Macungie Township*. Second edition, Lower Macungie Township Historical Society, 1996.

Bartholomew, Craig L., and Lance E. Metz. *The Anthracite Iron Industry of the Lehigh Valley*. Easton, PA: Center for Canal History and Technology, 1988.

Bartholomew, Ann, and Carol M. Front. *Images of America: Allentown*. Charleston, SC: Arcadia Publishing, 2002.

Beck, Bill. *PP&L: 75 Years of Powering the Future*. Eden Prairie, MI: Viking Press, 1995.

Bloom, Ken, and Marian Wolbers. *Allentown, A Pictorial History*. The Donning Company, 1984.

Callow, Alexander B. Jr. *American Urban History: An Interpretive Reader with Commentaries*. New York: Oxford University Press, 1973.

Fogleman, Aaron Spencer. *Hopeful Journeys: German Immigration, Settlement, and Political Culture in Colonial America 1717–1775*. Philadelphia: University of Pennsylvania Press, 1996.

Fox, Martha Capwell. I*mages of America: Catasauqua and North Catasauqua*. Charleston, SC: Arcadia Publishing, 2002.

———. "Seams of Coal, Beams of Steel, Skeins of Silk: The Silk Industry in the Delaware-Lehigh Heritage Corridor." *Canal History and Technology Proceedings*. Vol XXI. Easton, PA. 2002.

———. "The Iron Borough: An Industrial History of Catasauqua, Pennsylvania." *Canal History and Technology Proceedings*. Vol XXX. Easton, PA. 2011.

Front, Carol M., Joan M. Christopher, and Martha Capwell Fox. I*mages of America: The Lehigh Valley Cement Industry*. Charleston, SC: Arcadia Publishing, 2005.

Gensey, Karen L. *Whitehall Pennsylvania: The Golden Strip of the Lehigh Valley*. Self-published, 2004.

Halma, Robert, and Carl S. Oplinger. *The Lehigh Valley: A Natural and Environmental History*. University Park, PA: The Pennsylvania State University Press. 2001.

Hellerich, Mahlon H., ed. *Allentown 1762–1987: A 225-Year History*. Vol One, 1762–1920, and Vol Two, 1921–1987. Lehigh County Historical Society, 1987.

Klein, Philip S., and Ari Hoogenboom. *A History of Pennsylvania*. University Park, PA: The Pennsylvania State University Press, 1980.

Lord, Walter. *The Good Years 1900–1914*. New York: Harper & Row, 1960.

Mathews, Alfred, and Austin N. Hungerford. *History of the Counties of Lehigh and Carbon in the Commonwealth of Pennsylvania*. Philadelphia: Everts & Richards, 1884.

Matthews, Richard E. *Lehigh County Pennsylvania In the Civil War: An Account*. Lehighton, PA: Times News Printing, 1989.

Miller, Benjamin LeRoy. *Lehigh County Pennsylvania Geology and Geography*. Pennsylvania Geological Survey, Fourth Series. 1941.

Montville, John B. *Mack: A Living Legend of the Highway*. Tucson, AZ: AZTEX Corporation, 1981.

Nevins, Allen, and Henry Steele Commager. *A Short History of the United States*. New York: Random House, Inc., 1945.

Newman, Paul Douglas. *Fries's Rebellion: The Enduring Struggle for the American Revolution*. Philadelphia: University of Pennsylvania Press, 2004.

Roberts, Charles Rhoads, John Baer Stoudt, Thomas H. Krick, and William J. Dietrich. *Anniversary History of Lehigh County, Pennsylvania*. 3 vols. Lehigh County Historical Society, 1914.

Swaine, Robert T. *The Cravath Firm and Its Predecessors 1819–1948*. 3 vols. New York: Ad-Lit Press, 1948.

Walton, Izaak Charles Cotton. *The Compleat Angler* (1653). London: Bracken Books edition, 1985.

Whelan, Frank A. *Harry C. Trexler: His Life and Legacy*. Allentown;, PA: Lehigh County Historical Society, 2004.

———. "That Oily Herrenhutter: John Rice, The Jacksonian Era, and the Collapse of the Northampton Bank 1820–1861." *Canal History and Technology Proceedings*. Vol. IX, 1990.

———. *The Life and Inspiration of Obadiah Becker: Founder of the Allentown Rescue Mission*. Allentown, PA, 2010.

Whelan, Frank A., and Kurt D Zwikl. *Images of America: Hess's Department Store*. Charleston, SC: Arcadia Press. 2008.

Yates, Ross W. *History of the Lehigh Valley Region*. LVPC, 2006. First published 1963.

PROCEEDINGS of the Lehigh County Historical Society

Roberts, Charles R. "The Jennings or Geisinger Farm and its Owners." 1930.

Williams, David G. "The Lower Jordan Valley Pennsylvania German Settlement." Vol. 18, 1950.

Kistler, Ruth Moser, and John K. Heyl. "William Allen: Founder of Allentown: James Allen: Builder of Trout Hall." Vol. 24. 1962.

Hellerich, Mahlon H., ed. *Lehigh County Historical Society Proceedings*. Vol. 32, 1978.

Cowen, Richard W., ed. *Lehigh County Historical Society Proceedings*. Vol. 43. 2002.

Wittman, Robert H. "Those Were the Days." Columns by John Y. Kohl. Vol. 44, 2004.

NEWSPAPERS

The Morning Call. Allentown, PA.

The Evening Chronicle. Allentown, PA.

The Chronicle and News. Allentown PA.

The Daily News. Allentown PA.

Der Unabhaengiger Republikaner. Allentown PA.

The Macungie Progress. Macungie PA.

The Lancaster Journal. Lancaster PA.

The Lancaster Herald. Lancaster PA.

The New York Times. New York.

OFFICIAL DOCUMENTS

"Journals of the Twenty-Second House of Representatives of the Commonwealth of Pennsylvania; Commenced at Lancaster, on Tuesday, the third of December, in the year of our Lord one thousand eight hundred and eleven and of The Commonwealth of Pennsylvania the Thirty Sixth." Lancaster, PA, 1811.

"Journal of the Senate of the Commonwealth of Pennsylvania which commenced the third day of December in the Year of Our Lord, One Thousand Eight Hundred and Eleven, And of the Independence Of America the Thirty Sixth." Vol. XXII. Lancaster, PA, 1811.

"Minutes of the Meetings of Lehigh County Commissioners." Vol. I, 1913–1920.

INDEX